GLORIOUS WRESTLING ALLIANCE
ULTIMATE CHAMPIONSHIP EDITION

ABOUT THE AUTHOR

Josh Hicks is a cartoonist from South Wales. He was born there in 1991 and has no plans to leave. He currently lives in Cardiff with his partner and their cat. He has yet to wrestle professionally.

ACKNOWLEDGMENTS

Dedicated to Rachel. Special thanks to Ioan Morris, my family, and anyone who helped support or make this book in any way.

Story and art by Josh Hicks

First American edition published in 2021 by Graphic Universe™

Copyright © 2019 by Josh Hicks

Graphic Universe™ is a trademark of Lerner Publishing Group, Inc.

Graphic Universe™
An imprint of Lerner Publishing Group, Inc.
241 First Avenue North
Minneapolis, MN 55401 USA

For reading levels and more information, look up this title at www.lernerbooks.com.

Library of Congress Cataloging-in-Publication Data

Names: Hicks, Josh, author, artist.
Title: Glorious Wrestling Alliance : ultimate championship edition / Josh Hicks.
Description: First American edition. | Minneapolis : Graphic Universe, 2021. | Audience: Ages 14–18 | Audience: Grades 10–12 | Summary: "Step into the ring at Glorious Wrestling Alliance, the universe's least-professional wrestling company. Collected in colossal full color for the first time, this hilarious love letter to pro wrestling covers identity, anxiety, and leg drops" —Provided by publisher.
Identifiers: LCCN 2021004427 (print) | LCCN 2021004428 (ebook) | ISBN 9781541589797 (library binding) | ISBN 9781728431086 (paperback) | ISBN 9781728438795 (ebook)
Subjects: LCSH: Graphic novels. | CYAC: Graphic novels. | Wrestling—Fiction. | Identity—Fiction.
Classification: LCC PZ7.7.H5325 Glo 2021 (print) | LCC PZ7.7.H5325 (ebook) | DDC 741.5/9429—dc23

LC record available at https://lccn.loc.gov/2021004427
LC ebook record available at https://lccn.loc.gov/2021004428

Manufactured in the United States of America
1-47489-48033-3/15/2021

GLORIOUS WRESTLING ALLIANCE
ULTIMATE CHAMPIONSHIP EDITION

JOSH HICKS

GRAPHIC UNIVERSE™ • MINNEAPOLIS

CHAPTER ONE
ONE NIGHT ONLY

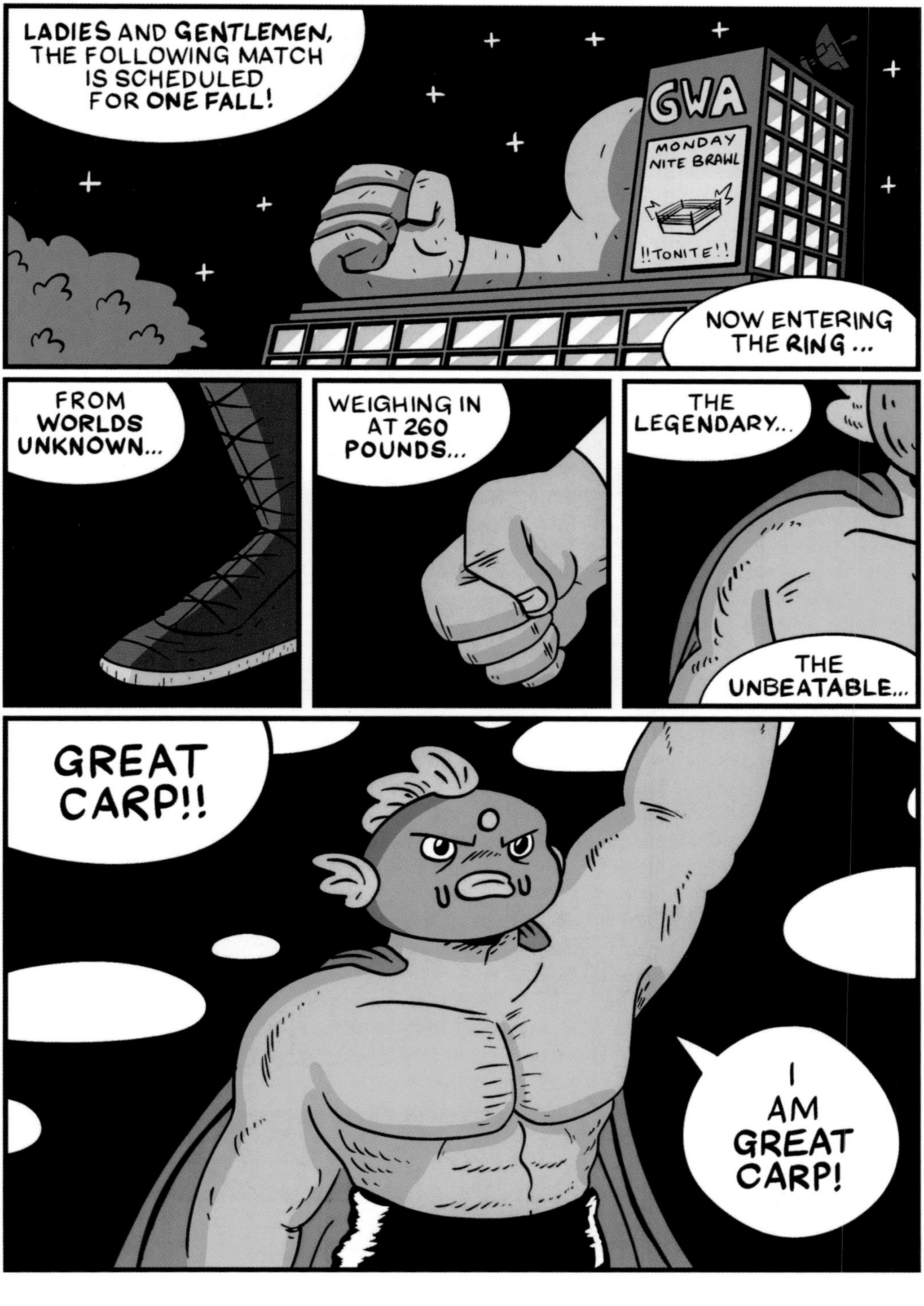
LADIES AND GENTLEMEN, THE FOLLOWING MATCH IS SCHEDULED FOR ONE FALL!
GWA
MONDAY NITE BRAWL
!!TONITE!!
NOW ENTERING THE RING...
FROM WORLDS UNKNOWN...
WEIGHING IN AT 260 POUNDS...
THE LEGENDARY...
THE UNBEATABLE...
GREAT CARP!!
I AM GREAT CARP!

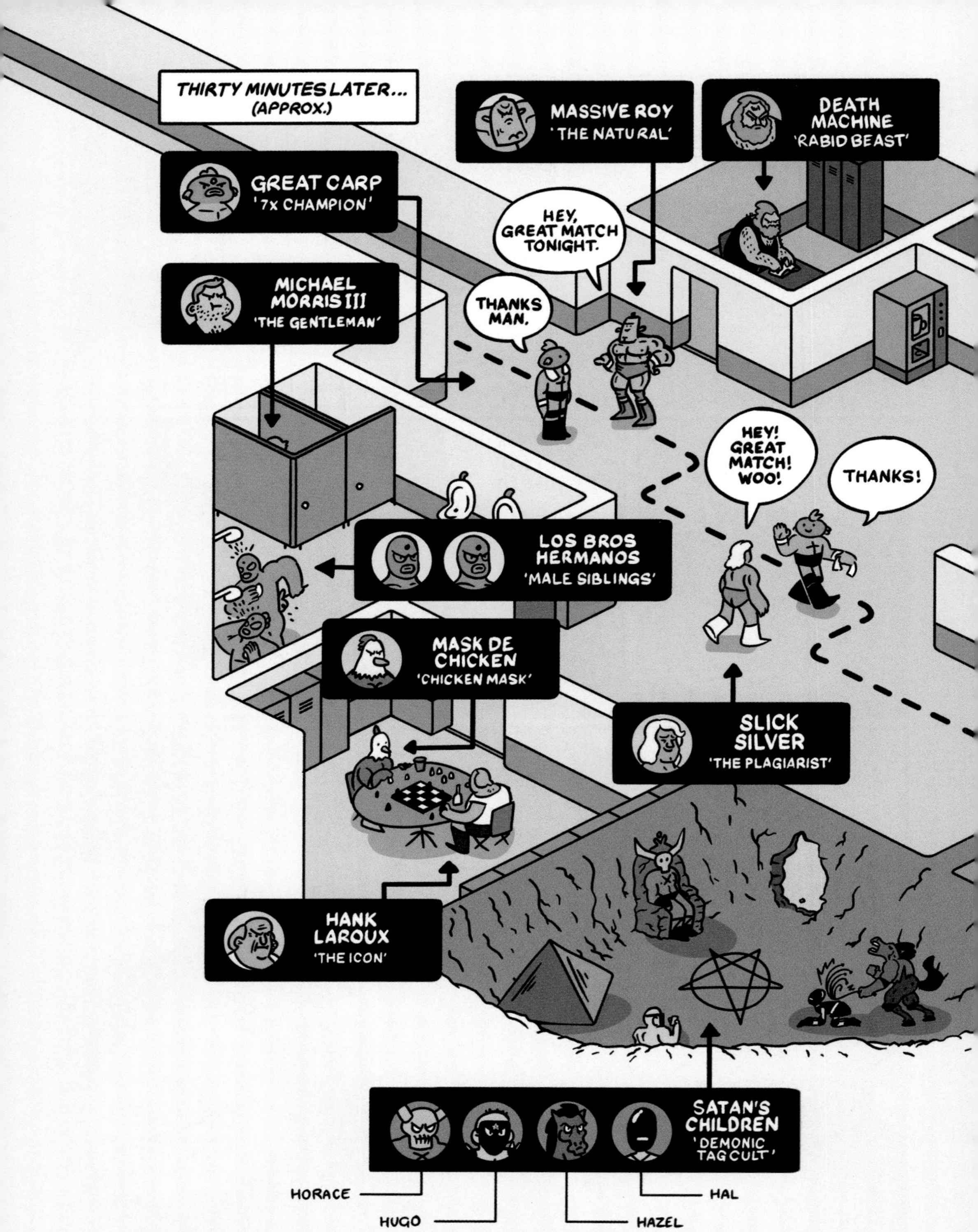
THIRTY MINUTES LATER... (APPROX.)
MASSIVE ROY 'THE NATURAL'
DEATH MACHINE 'RABID BEAST'
GREAT CARP '7x CHAMPION'
HEY, GREAT MATCH TONIGHT.
THANKS MAN.
MICHAEL MORRIS III 'THE GENTLEMAN'
HEY! GREAT MATCH! WOO!
THANKS!
LOS BROS HERMANOS 'MALE SIBLINGS'
MASK DE CHICKEN 'CHICKEN MASK'
SLICK SILVER 'THE PLAGIARIST'
HANK LAROUX 'THE ICON'
SATAN'S CHILDREN 'DEMONIC TAG CULT'
HORACE
HUGO
HAZEL
HAL

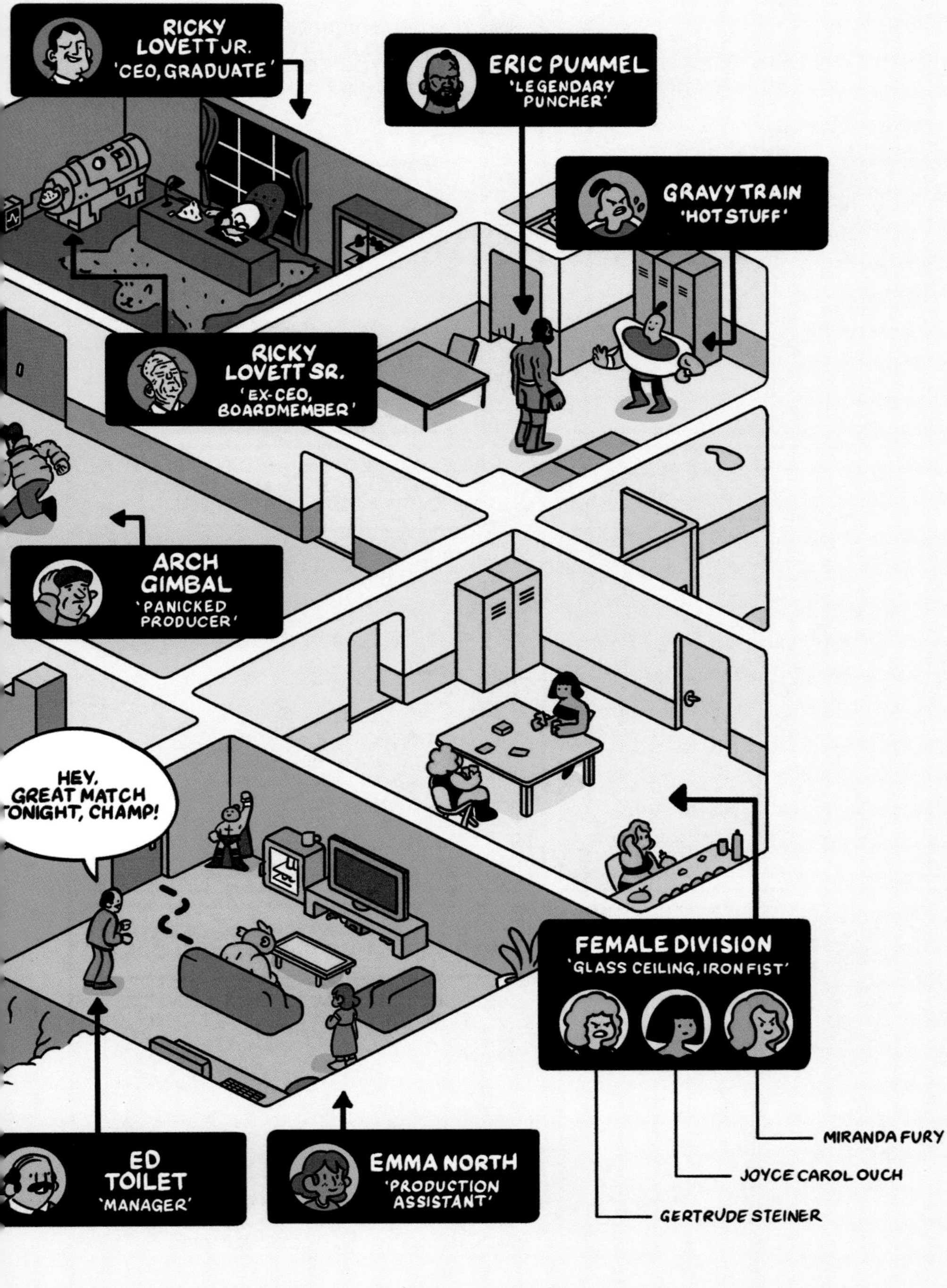
RICKY LOVETT JR.
'CEO, GRADUATE'
ERIC PUMMEL
'LEGENDARY PUNCHER'
GRAVY TRAIN
'HOT STUFF'
RICKY LOVETT SR.
'EX-CEO, BOARDMEMBER'
ARCH GIMBAL
'PANICKED PRODUCER'
HEY, GREAT MATCH TONIGHT, CHAMP!
FEMALE DIVISION
'GLASS CEILING, IRON FIST'
MIRANDA FURY
JOYCE CAROL OUCH
GERTRUDE STEINER
ED TOILET
'MANAGER'
EMMA NORTH
'PRODUCTION ASSISTANT'

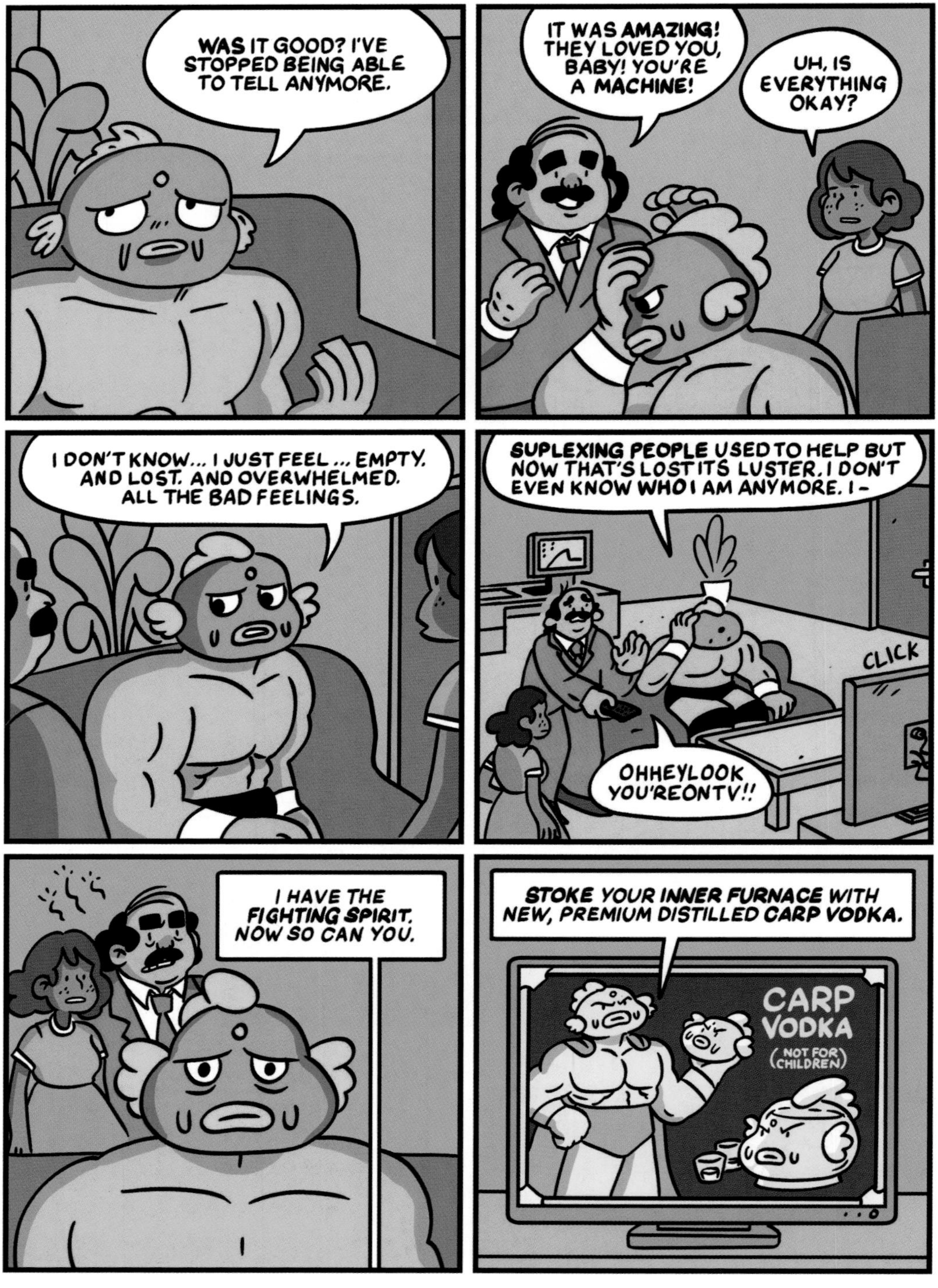
WAS IT GOOD? I'VE STOPPED BEING ABLE TO TELL ANYMORE.
IT WAS AMAZING! THEY LOVED YOU, BABY! YOU'RE A MACHINE!
UH, IS EVERYTHING OKAY?
I DON'T KNOW... I JUST FEEL ... EMPTY. AND LOST. AND OVERWHELMED. ALL THE BAD FEELINGS.
SUPLEXING PEOPLE USED TO HELP BUT NOW THAT'S LOST ITS LUSTER. I DON'T EVEN KNOW WHO I AM ANYMORE. I-
CLICK
OHHEYLOOK YOU'REONTV!!
I HAVE THE FIGHTING SPIRIT. NOW SO CAN YOU.
STOKE YOUR INNER FURNACE WITH NEW, PREMIUM DISTILLED CARP VODKA.
CARP VODKA
(NOT FOR CHILDREN)

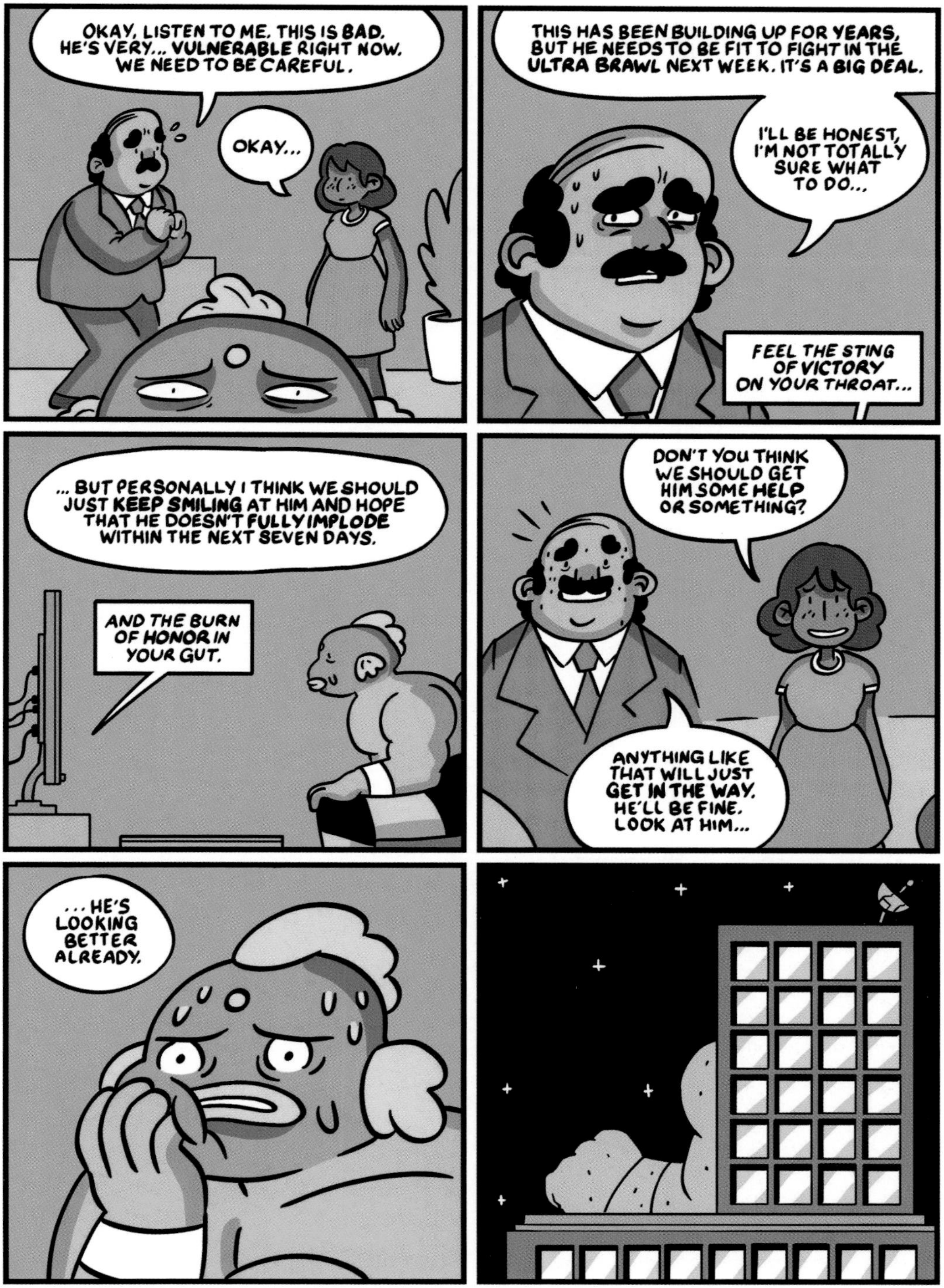

OKAY, LISTEN TO ME. THIS IS BAD. HE'S VERY... VULNERABLE RIGHT NOW. WE NEED TO BE CAREFUL.
OKAY...
THIS HAS BEEN BUILDING UP FOR YEARS, BUT HE NEEDS TO BE FIT TO FIGHT IN THE ULTRA BRAWL NEXT WEEK. IT'S A BIG DEAL.
I'LL BE HONEST, I'M NOT TOTALLY SURE WHAT TO DO...
FEEL THE STING OF VICTORY ON YOUR THROAT...
... BUT PERSONALLY I THINK WE SHOULD JUST KEEP SMILING AT HIM AND HOPE THAT HE DOESN'T FULLY IMPLODE WITHIN THE NEXT SEVEN DAYS.
AND THE BURN OF HONOR IN YOUR GUT.
DON'T YOU THINK WE SHOULD GET HIM SOME HELP OR SOMETHING?
ANYTHING LIKE THAT WILL JUST GET IN THE WAY. HE'LL BE FINE. LOOK AT HIM...
... HE'S LOOKING BETTER ALREADY.

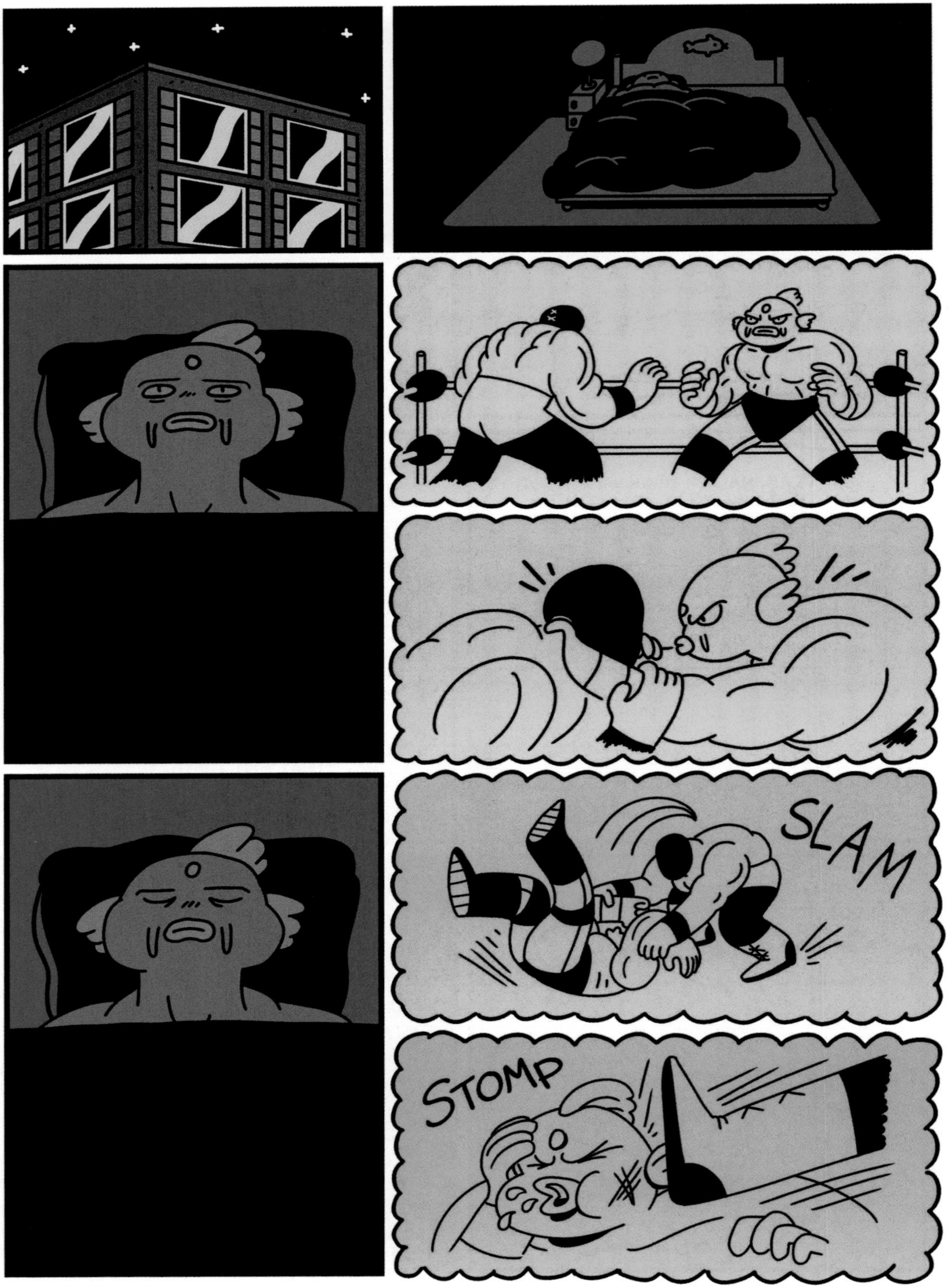
SLAM
STOMP

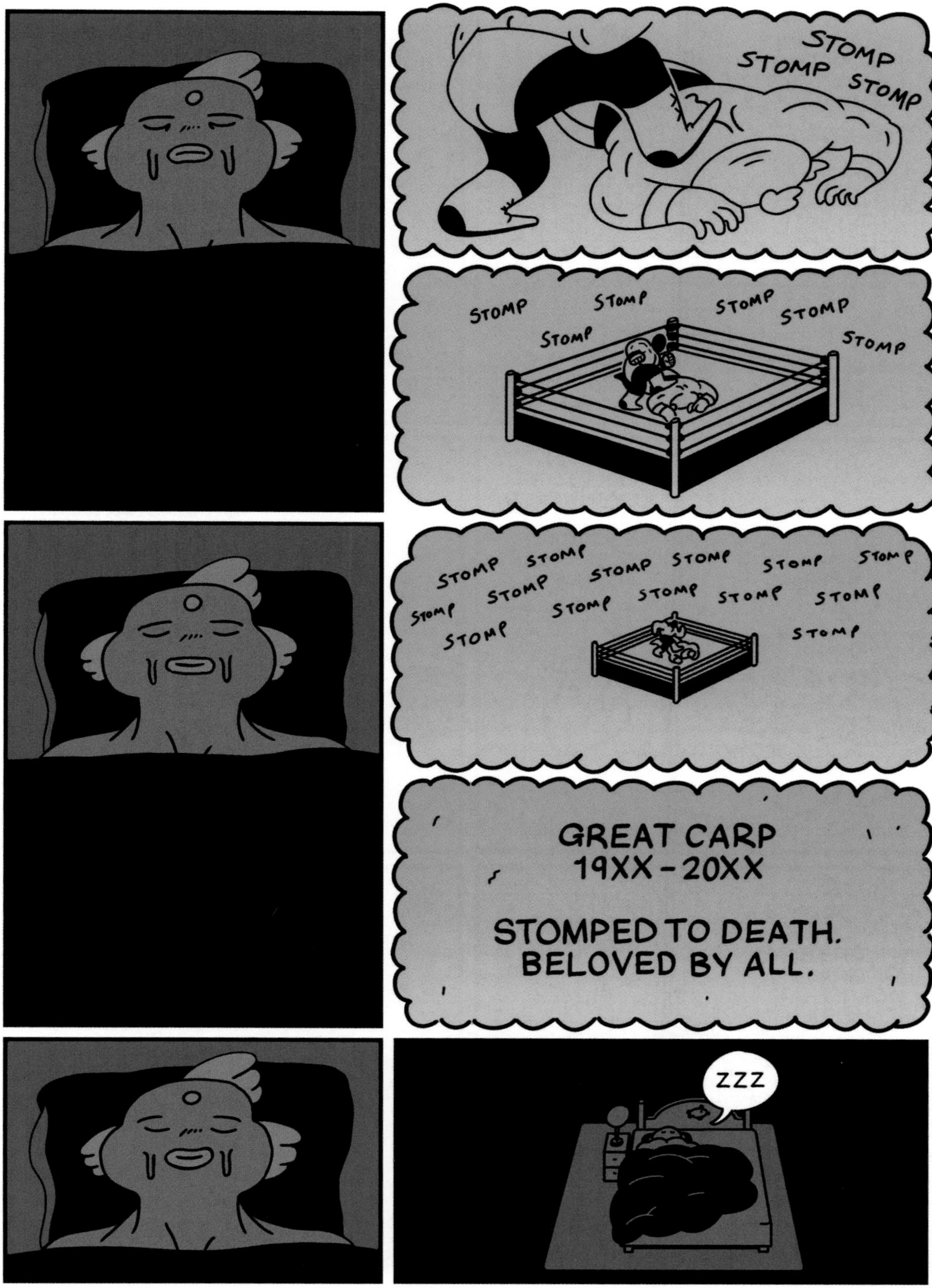
STOMP
STOMP
STOMP
STOMP
STOMP
STOMP
STOMP
STOMP
STOMP
STOMP STOMP
STOMP STOMP
STOMP STOMP STOMP
STOMP STOMP STOMP STOMP
STOMP STOMP STOMP
STOMP
STOMP
GREAT CARP
19XX - 20XX
STOMPED TO DEATH.
BELOVED BY ALL.
ZZZ

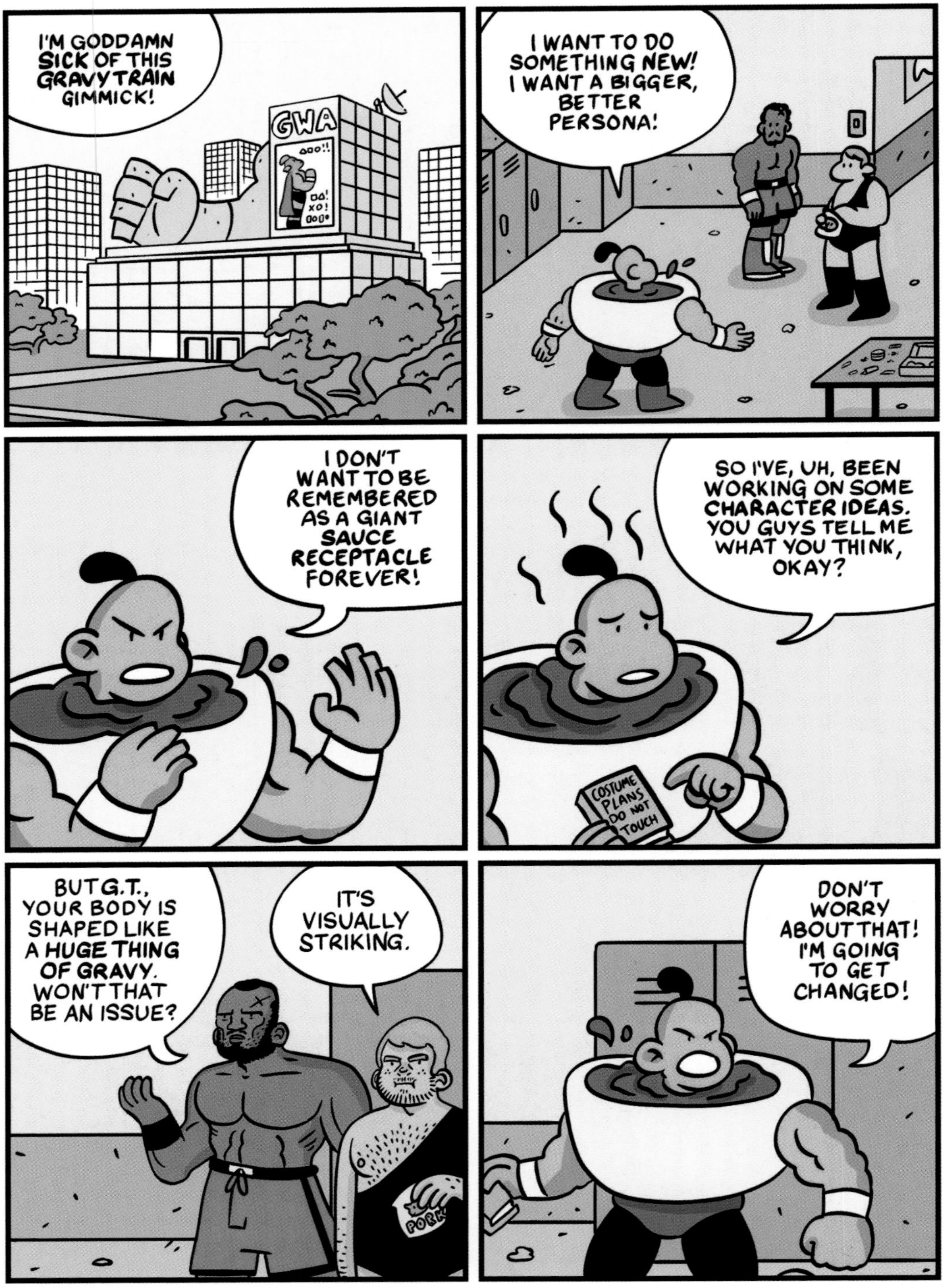
I'M GODDAMN SICK OF THIS GRAVY TRAIN GIMMICK!
GWA
I WANT TO DO SOMETHING NEW! I WANT A BIGGER, BETTER PERSONA!
I DON'T WANT TO BE REMEMBERED AS A GIANT SAUCE RECEPTACLE FOREVER!
SO I'VE, UH, BEEN WORKING ON SOME CHARACTER IDEAS. YOU GUYS TELL ME WHAT YOU THINK, OKAY?
COSTUME PLANS DO NOT TOUCH
BUT G.T., YOUR BODY IS SHAPED LIKE A HUGE THING OF GRAVY. WON'T THAT BE AN ISSUE?
IT'S VISUALLY STRIKING.
DON'T WORRY ABOUT THAT! I'M GOING TO GET CHANGED!

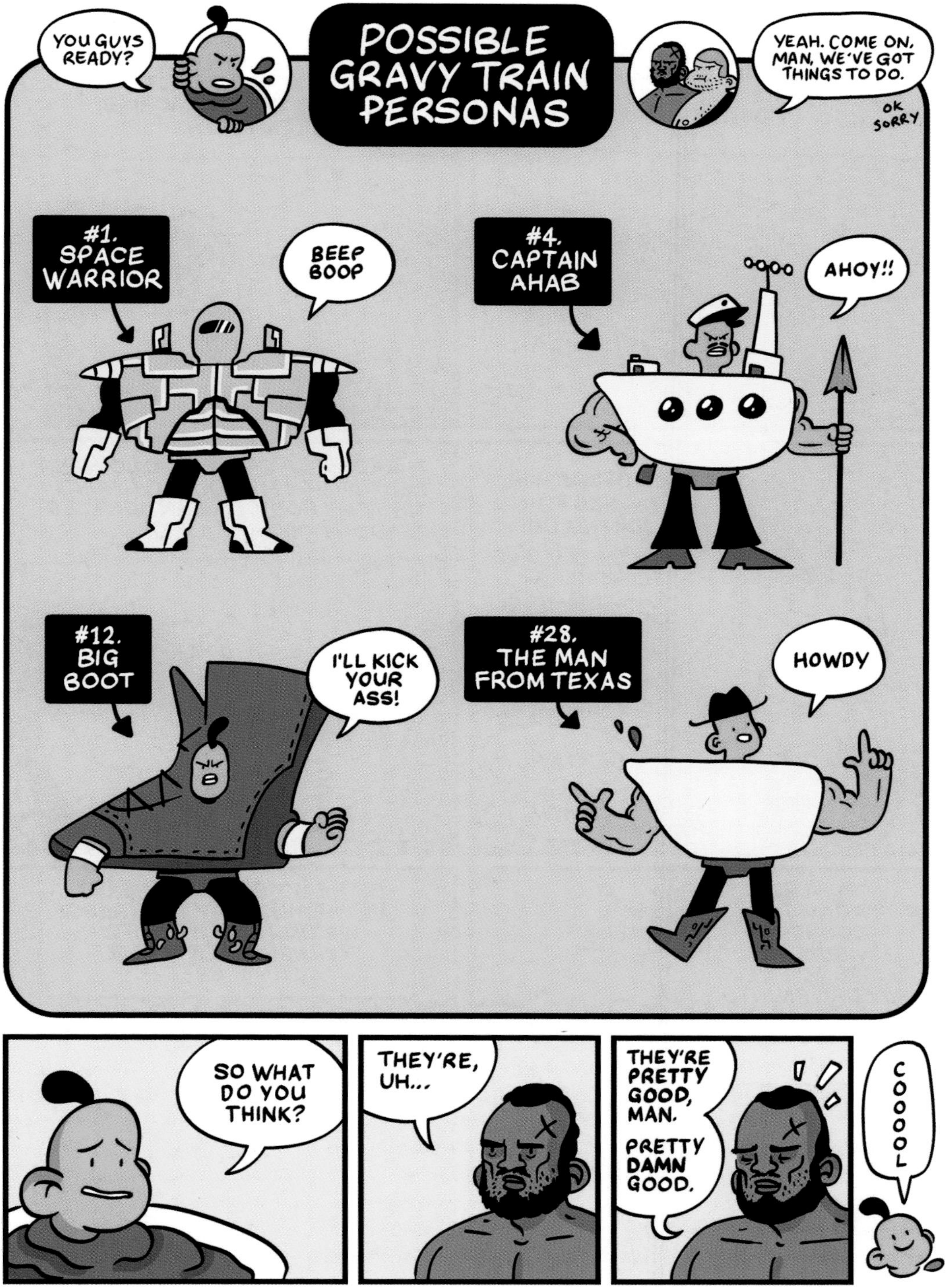
YOU GUYS READY?
POSSIBLE GRAVY TRAIN PERSONAS
YEAH. COME ON, MAN, WE'VE GOT THINGS TO DO.
OK SORRY
#1. SPACE WARRIOR
BEEP BOOP
#4. CAPTAIN AHAB
AHOY!!
#12. BIG BOOT
I'LL KICK YOUR ASS!
#28. THE MAN FROM TEXAS
HOWDY
SO WHAT DO YOU THINK?
THEY'RE, UH...
THEY'RE PRETTY GOOD, MAN.
PRETTY DAMN GOOD.
COOOOL

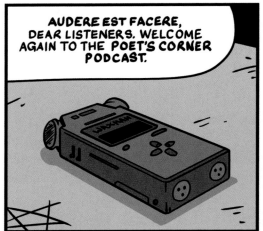

AUDERE EST FACERE, DEAR LISTENERS. WELCOME AGAIN TO THE *POET'S CORNER* PODCAST.

WITH ME TODAY IS PROFESSIONAL WRESTLER DEATH MACHINE, WHOSE NEW COLLECTION, *POEMS BY DEATH MACHINE,* IS OUT NOW.

HELLO.

KILL

DEATH MACHINE, THANKS FOR JOINING US.

WOULD YOU CARE TO START BY READING ONE OF YOUR NEW PIECES?

CERTAINLY.

AHEM.

THERE LIES A CEASELESS LONGING, DEEP WITHIN MY SOUL / GRIPPING TIGHT MY BODY, LIKE AN ACHILLES TENDON HOLD.

KILL

FRUITLESS I ROAM THE COUNTRY WHERE WE USED TO LIVE / PILEDRIVEN INTO MEMORY, WITH NOTHING LEFT TO GIVE.

SO HEAVY BEATS MY HEART, AND HEAVY SWAY THE TREES / WILTING LIKE WEIGHT'D TURNBUCKLES, IN THE AUTUMN BREEZE.

WOW.

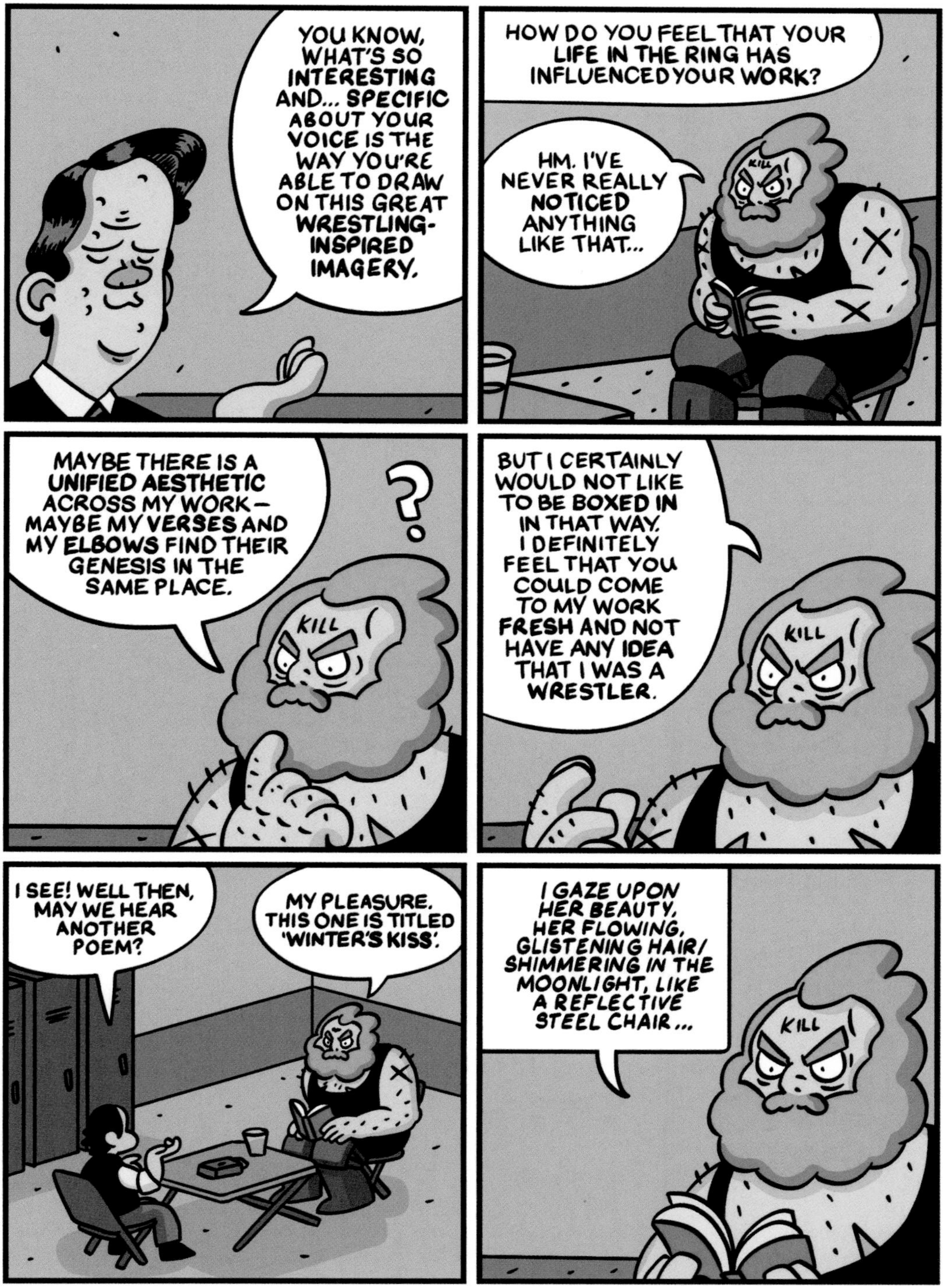
YOU KNOW, WHAT'S SO INTERESTING AND... SPECIFIC ABOUT YOUR VOICE IS THE WAY YOU'RE ABLE TO DRAW ON THIS GREAT WRESTLING-INSPIRED IMAGERY.
HOW DO YOU FEEL THAT YOUR LIFE IN THE RING HAS INFLUENCED YOUR WORK?
HM. I'VE NEVER REALLY NOTICED ANYTHING LIKE THAT...
KILL
MAYBE THERE IS A UNIFIED AESTHETIC ACROSS MY WORK—MAYBE MY VERSES AND MY ELBOWS FIND THEIR GENESIS IN THE SAME PLACE.
?
KILL
BUT I CERTAINLY WOULD NOT LIKE TO BE BOXED IN IN THAT WAY. I DEFINITELY FEEL THAT YOU COULD COME TO MY WORK FRESH AND NOT HAVE ANY IDEA THAT I WAS A WRESTLER.
KILL
I SEE! WELL THEN, MAY WE HEAR ANOTHER POEM?
MY PLEASURE. THIS ONE IS TITLED 'WINTER'S KISS'.
I GAZE UPON HER BEAUTY, HER FLOWING, GLISTENING HAIR/ SHIMMERING IN THE MOONLIGHT, LIKE A REFLECTIVE STEEL CHAIR...
KILL

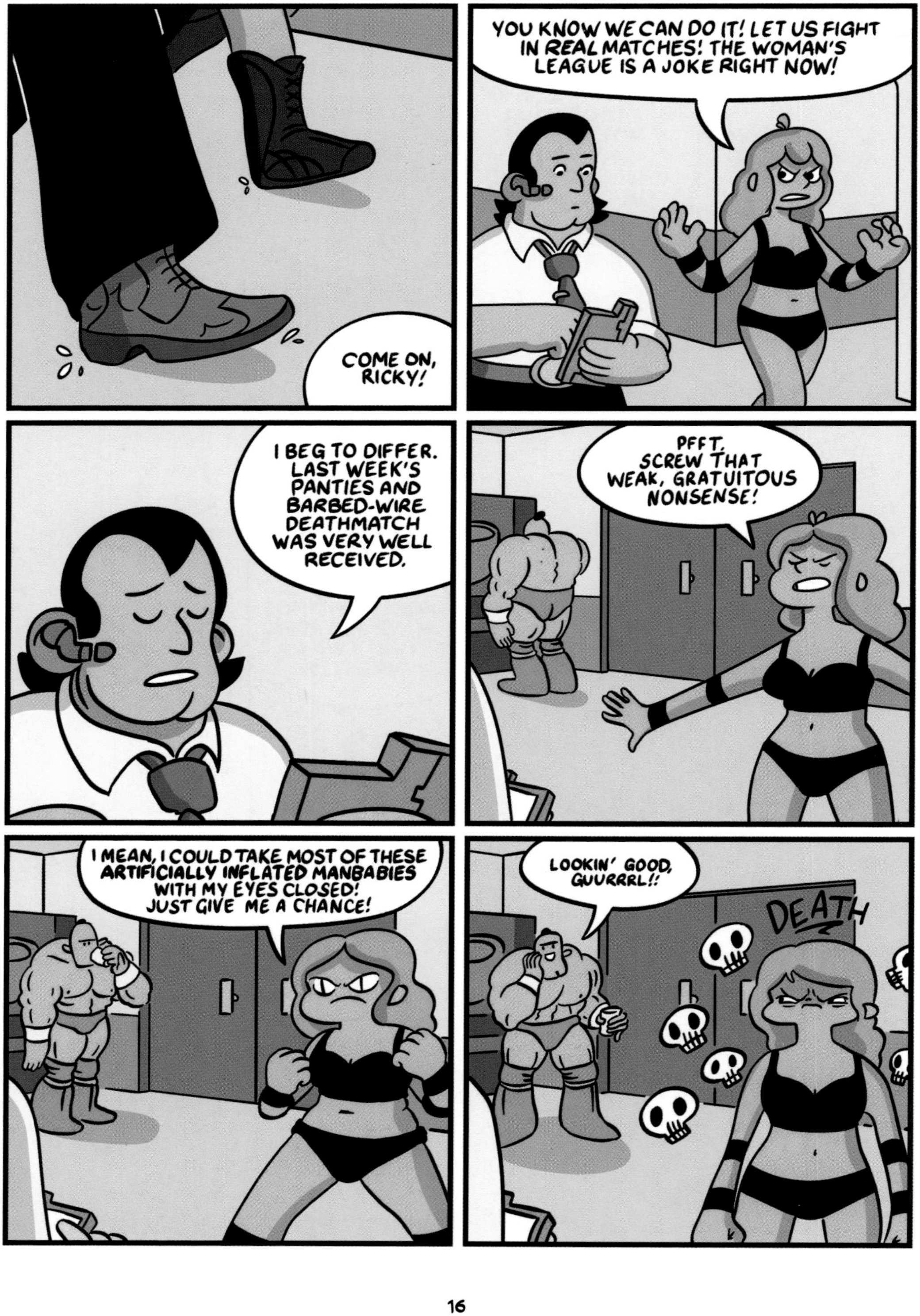
COME ON, RICKY!
YOU KNOW WE CAN DO IT! LET US FIGHT IN REAL MATCHES! THE WOMAN'S LEAGUE IS A JOKE RIGHT NOW!
I BEG TO DIFFER. LAST WEEK'S PANTIES AND BARBED-WIRE DEATHMATCH WAS VERY WELL RECEIVED.
PFFT. SCREW THAT WEAK, GRATUITOUS NONSENSE!
I MEAN, I COULD TAKE MOST OF THESE ARTIFICIALLY INFLATED MANBABIES WITH MY EYES CLOSED! JUST GIVE ME A CHANCE!
LOOKIN' GOOD, GUURRRL!!
DEATH

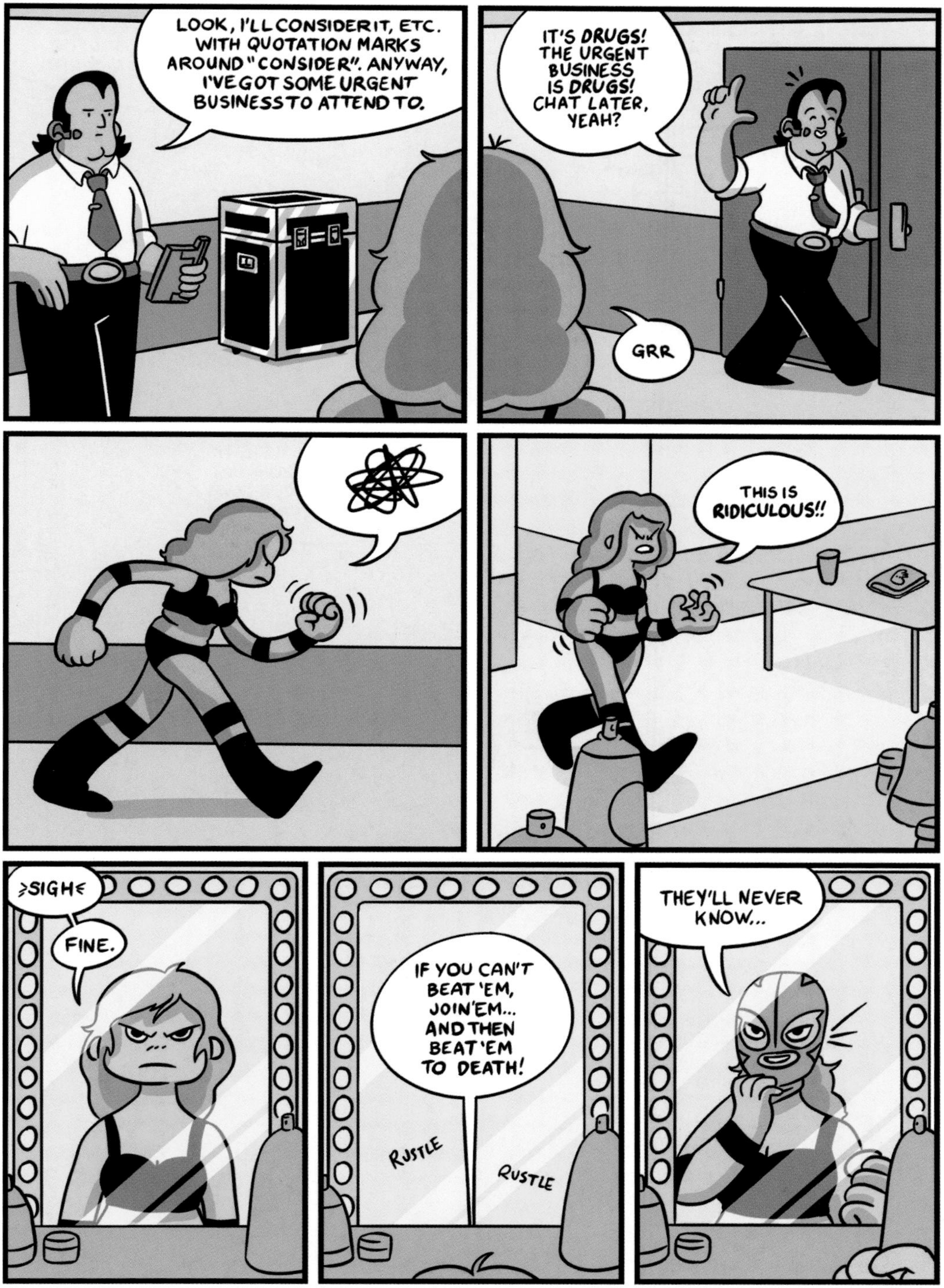
LOOK, I'LL CONSIDER IT, ETC. WITH QUOTATION MARKS AROUND "CONSIDER". ANYWAY, I'VE GOT SOME URGENT BUSINESS TO ATTEND TO.
IT'S DRUGS! THE URGENT BUSINESS IS DRUGS! CHAT LATER, YEAH?
GRR
THIS IS RIDICULOUS!!
>SIGH<
FINE.
IF YOU CAN'T BEAT 'EM, JOIN 'EM... AND THEN BEAT 'EM TO DEATH!
RUSTLE
RUSTLE
THEY'LL NEVER KNOW...

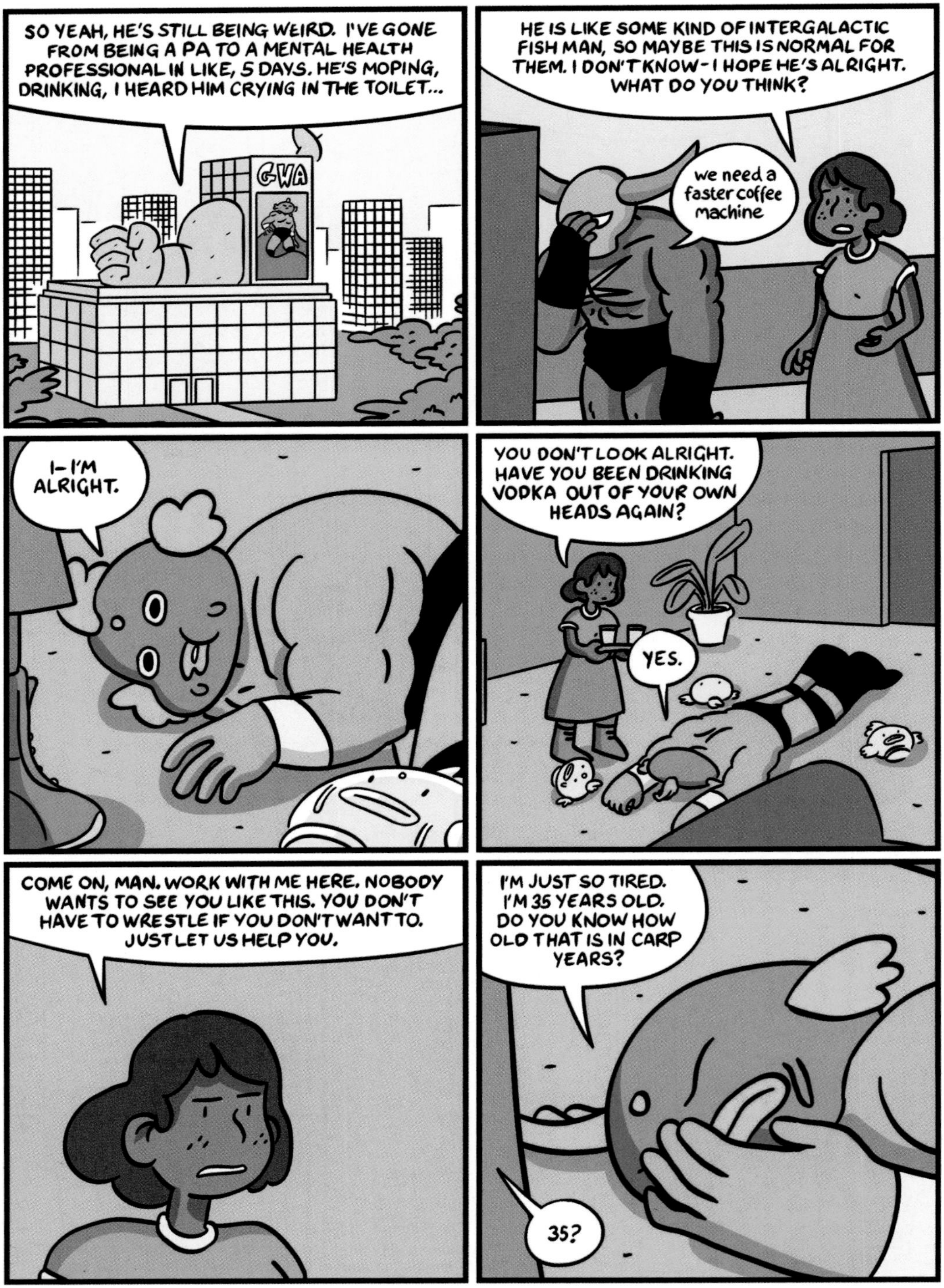
SO YEAH, HE'S STILL BEING WEIRD. I'VE GONE FROM BEING A PA TO A MENTAL HEALTH PROFESSIONAL IN LIKE, 5 DAYS. HE'S MOPING, DRINKING, I HEARD HIM CRYING IN THE TOILET...
GWA
HE IS LIKE SOME KIND OF INTERGALACTIC FISH MAN, SO MAYBE THIS IS NORMAL FOR THEM. I DON'T KNOW - I HOPE HE'S ALRIGHT. WHAT DO YOU THINK?
we need a faster coffee machine
I- I'M ALRIGHT.
YOU DON'T LOOK ALRIGHT. HAVE YOU BEEN DRINKING VODKA OUT OF YOUR OWN HEADS AGAIN?
YES.
COME ON, MAN. WORK WITH ME HERE. NOBODY WANTS TO SEE YOU LIKE THIS. YOU DON'T HAVE TO WRESTLE IF YOU DON'T WANT TO. JUST LET US HELP YOU.
I'M JUST SO TIRED. I'M 35 YEARS OLD. DO YOU KNOW HOW OLD THAT IS IN CARP YEARS?
35?

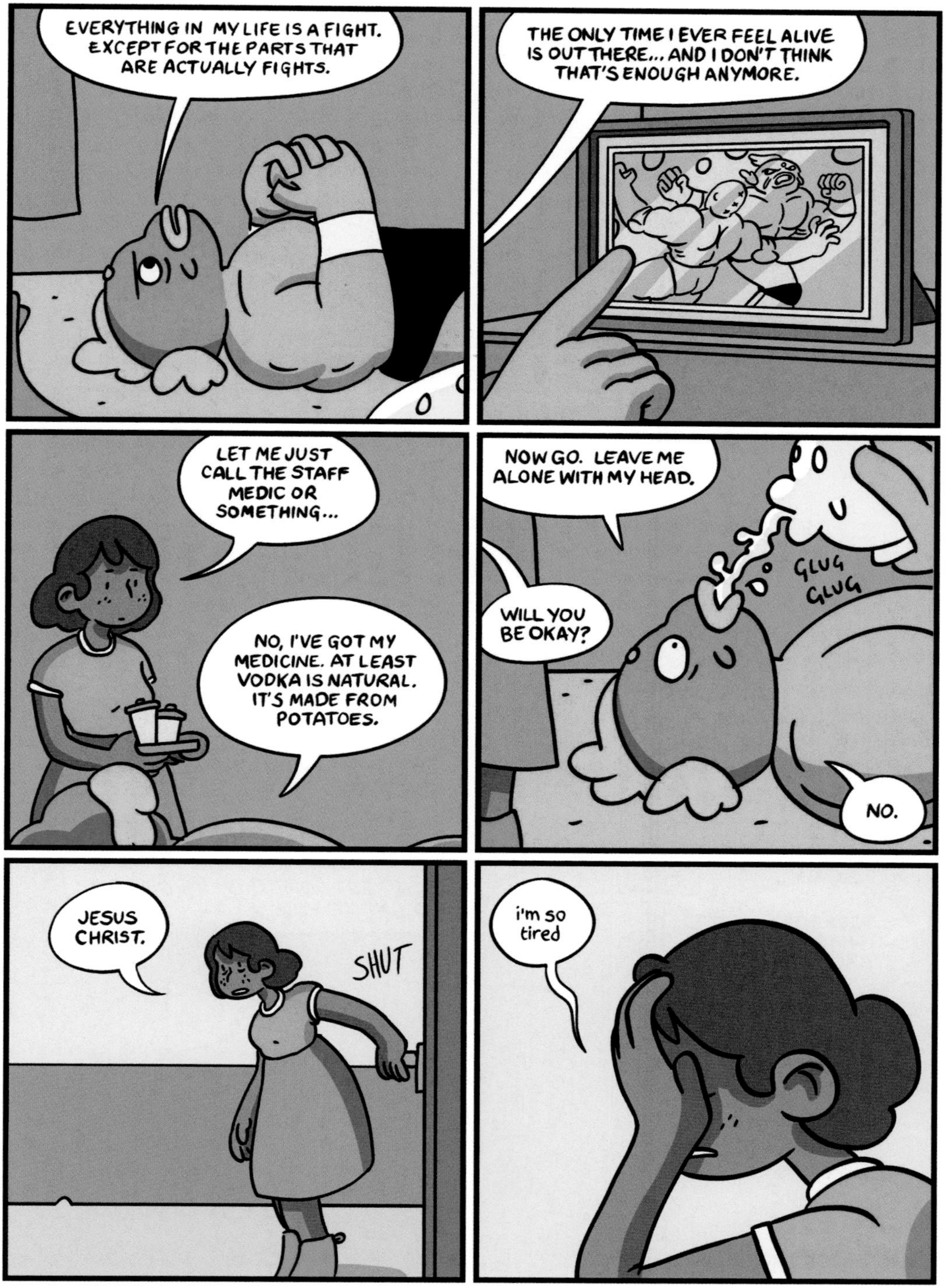
EVERYTHING IN MY LIFE IS A FIGHT. EXCEPT FOR THE PARTS THAT ARE ACTUALLY FIGHTS.
THE ONLY TIME I EVER FEEL ALIVE IS OUT THERE... AND I DON'T THINK THAT'S ENOUGH ANYMORE.
LET ME JUST CALL THE STAFF MEDIC OR SOMETHING...
NO, I'VE GOT MY MEDICINE. AT LEAST VODKA IS NATURAL. IT'S MADE FROM POTATOES.
NOW GO. LEAVE ME ALONE WITH MY HEAD.
GLUG GLUG
WILL YOU BE OKAY?
NO.
JESUS CHRIST.
SHUT
i'm so tired

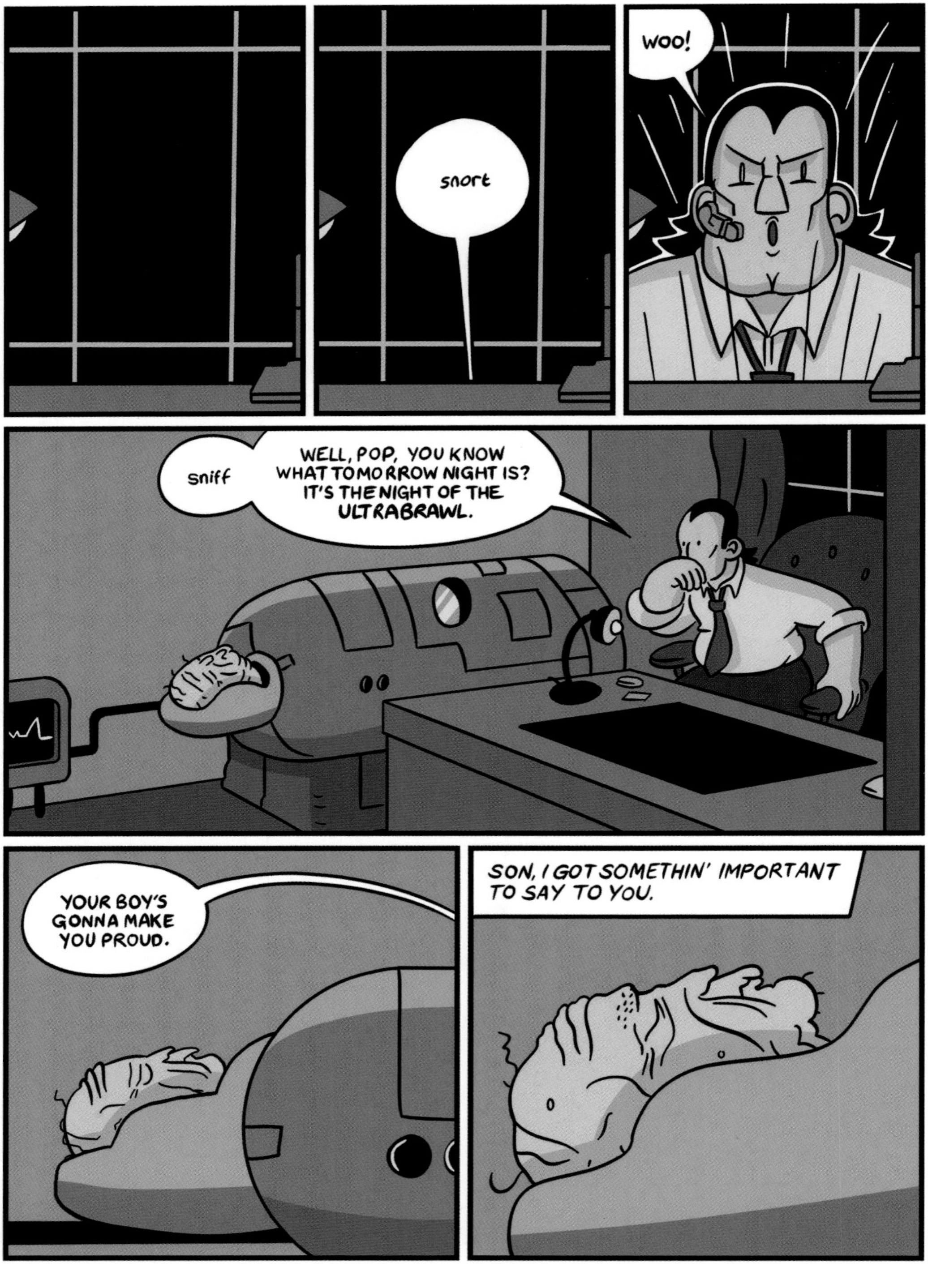
snort
WOO!
sniff
WELL, POP, YOU KNOW WHAT TOMORROW NIGHT IS? IT'S THE NIGHT OF THE ULTRABRAWL.
YOUR BOY'S GONNA MAKE YOU PROUD.
SON, I GOT SOMETHIN' IMPORTANT TO SAY TO YOU.

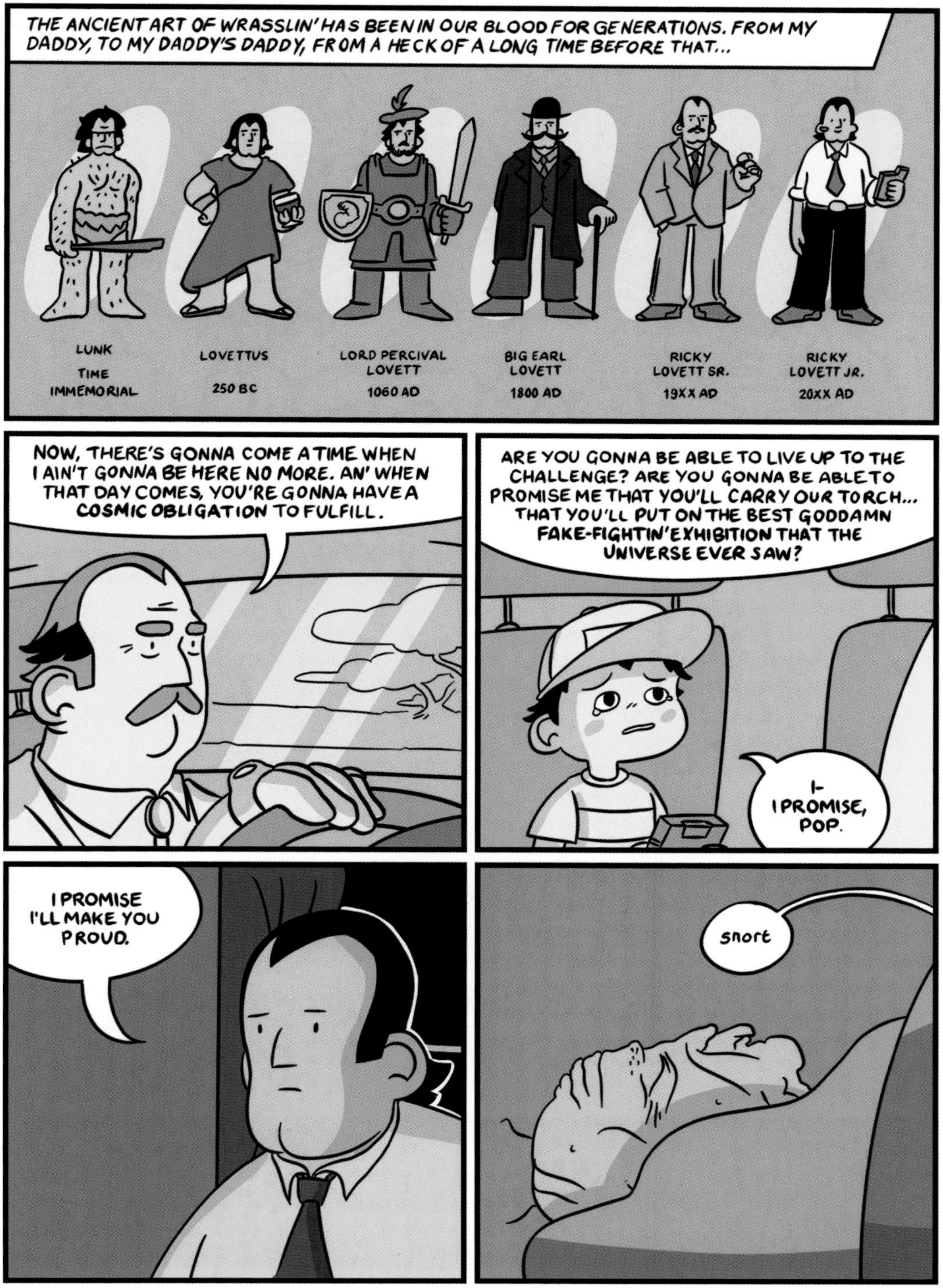
THE ANCIENT ART OF WRASSLIN' HAS BEEN IN OUR BLOOD FOR GENERATIONS. FROM MY DADDY, TO MY DADDY'S DADDY, FROM A HECK OF A LONG TIME BEFORE THAT...
LUNK TIME IMMEMORIAL
LOVETTUS 250 BC
LORD PERCIVAL LOVETT 1060 AD
BIG EARL LOVETT 1800 AD
RICKY LOVETT SR. 19XX AD
RICKY LOVETT JR. 20XX AD
NOW, THERE'S GONNA COME A TIME WHEN I AIN'T GONNA BE HERE NO MORE. AN' WHEN THAT DAY COMES, YOU'RE GONNA HAVE A COSMIC OBLIGATION TO FULFILL.
ARE YOU GONNA BE ABLE TO LIVE UP TO THE CHALLENGE? ARE YOU GONNA BE ABLE TO PROMISE ME THAT YOU'LL CARRY OUR TORCH... THAT YOU'LL PUT ON THE BEST GODDAMN FAKE-FIGHTIN' EXHIBITION THAT THE UNIVERSE EVER SAW?
I- I PROMISE, POP.
I PROMISE I'LL MAKE YOU PROUD.
snort

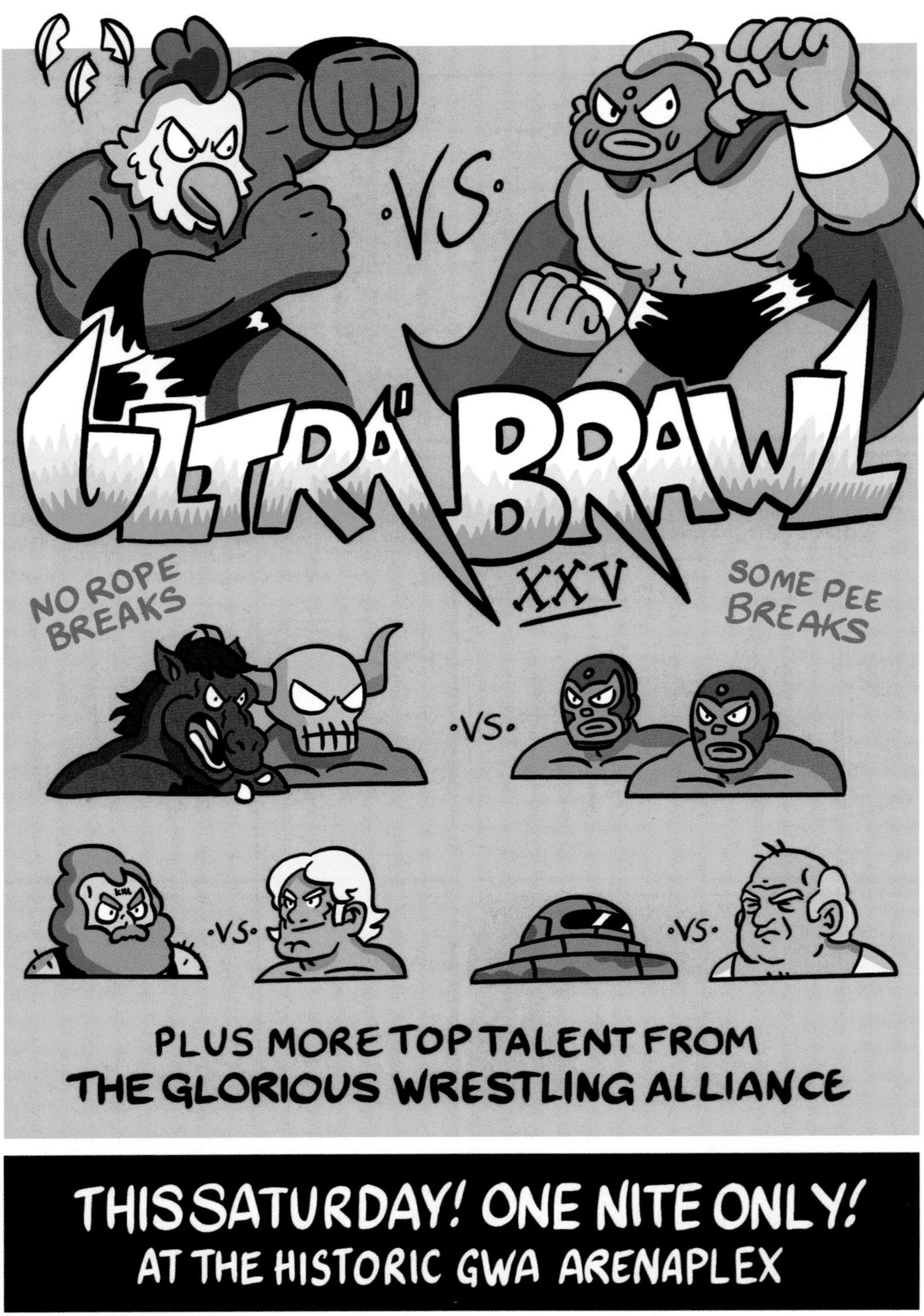
VS
ULTRA BRAWL
XXV
NO ROPE BREAKS
SOME PEE BREAKS
VS
VS
VS
PLUS MORE TOP TALENT FROM
THE GLORIOUS WRESTLING ALLIANCE
THIS SATURDAY! ONE NITE ONLY!
AT THE HISTORIC GWA ARENAPLEX

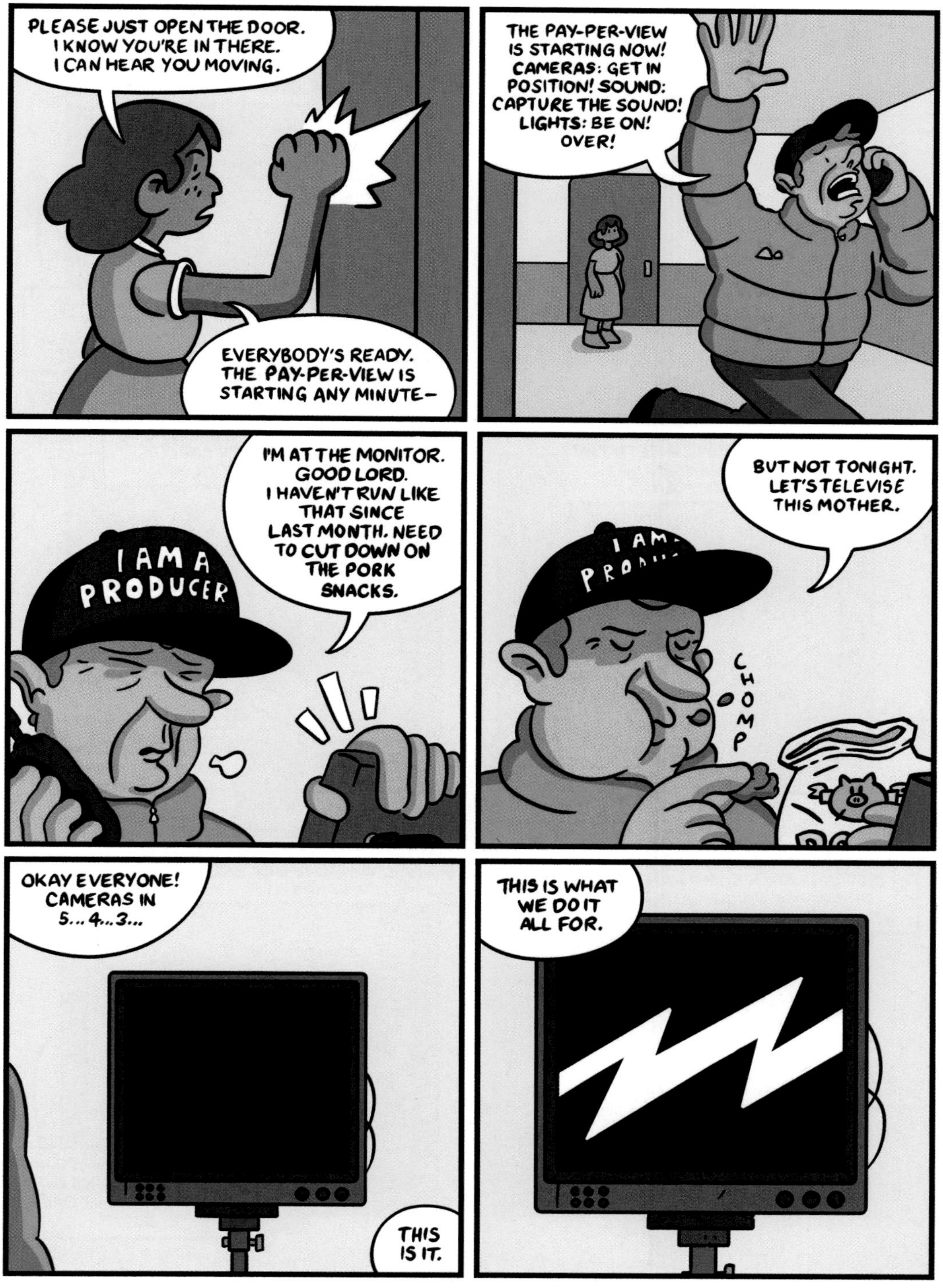
PLEASE JUST OPEN THE DOOR. I KNOW YOU'RE IN THERE. I CAN HEAR YOU MOVING.
EVERYBODY'S READY. THE PAY-PER-VIEW IS STARTING ANY MINUTE—
THE PAY-PER-VIEW IS STARTING NOW! CAMERAS: GET IN POSITION! SOUND: CAPTURE THE SOUND! LIGHTS: BE ON! OVER!
I'M AT THE MONITOR. GOOD LORD. I HAVEN'T RUN LIKE THAT SINCE LAST MONTH. NEED TO CUT DOWN ON THE PORK SNACKS.
I AM A PRODUCER
BUT NOT TONIGHT. LET'S TELEVISE THIS MOTHER.
CHOMP
OKAY EVERYONE! CAMERAS IN 5... 4... 3...
THIS IS IT.
THIS IS WHAT WE DO IT ALL FOR.

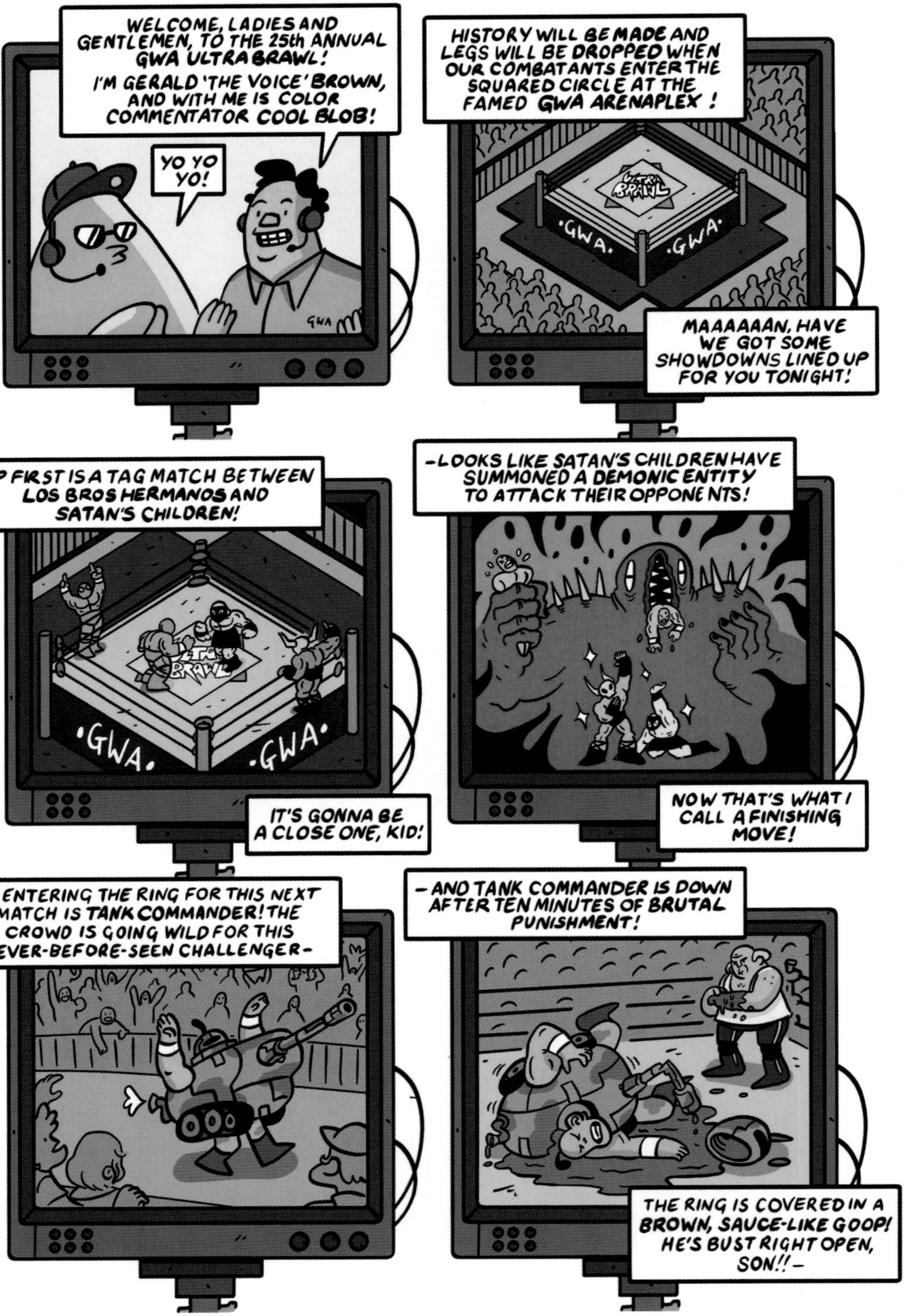
WELCOME, LADIES AND GENTLEMEN, TO THE 25th ANNUAL GWA ULTRA BRAWL!
I'M GERALD 'THE VOICE' BROWN, AND WITH ME IS COLOR COMMENTATOR COOL BLOB!
YO YO YO!
GWA
HISTORY WILL BE MADE AND LEGS WILL BE DROPPED WHEN OUR COMBATANTS ENTER THE SQUARED CIRCLE AT THE FAMED GWA ARENAPLEX!
ULTRA BRAWL
GWA
GWA
MAAAAAAN, HAVE WE GOT SOME SHOWDOWNS LINED UP FOR YOU TONIGHT!
UP FIRST IS A TAG MATCH BETWEEN LOS BROS HERMANOS AND SATAN'S CHILDREN!
GWA
GWA
IT'S GONNA BE A CLOSE ONE, KID!
-LOOKS LIKE SATAN'S CHILDREN HAVE SUMMONED A DEMONIC ENTITY TO ATTACK THEIR OPPONENTS!
NOW THAT'S WHAT I CALL A FINISHING MOVE!
-ENTERING THE RING FOR THIS NEXT MATCH IS TANK COMMANDER! THE CROWD IS GOING WILD FOR THIS NEVER-BEFORE-SEEN CHALLENGER-
-AND TANK COMMANDER IS DOWN AFTER TEN MINUTES OF BRUTAL PUNISHMENT!
THE RING IS COVERED IN A BROWN, SAUCE-LIKE GOOP! HE'S BUST RIGHT OPEN, SON!!-

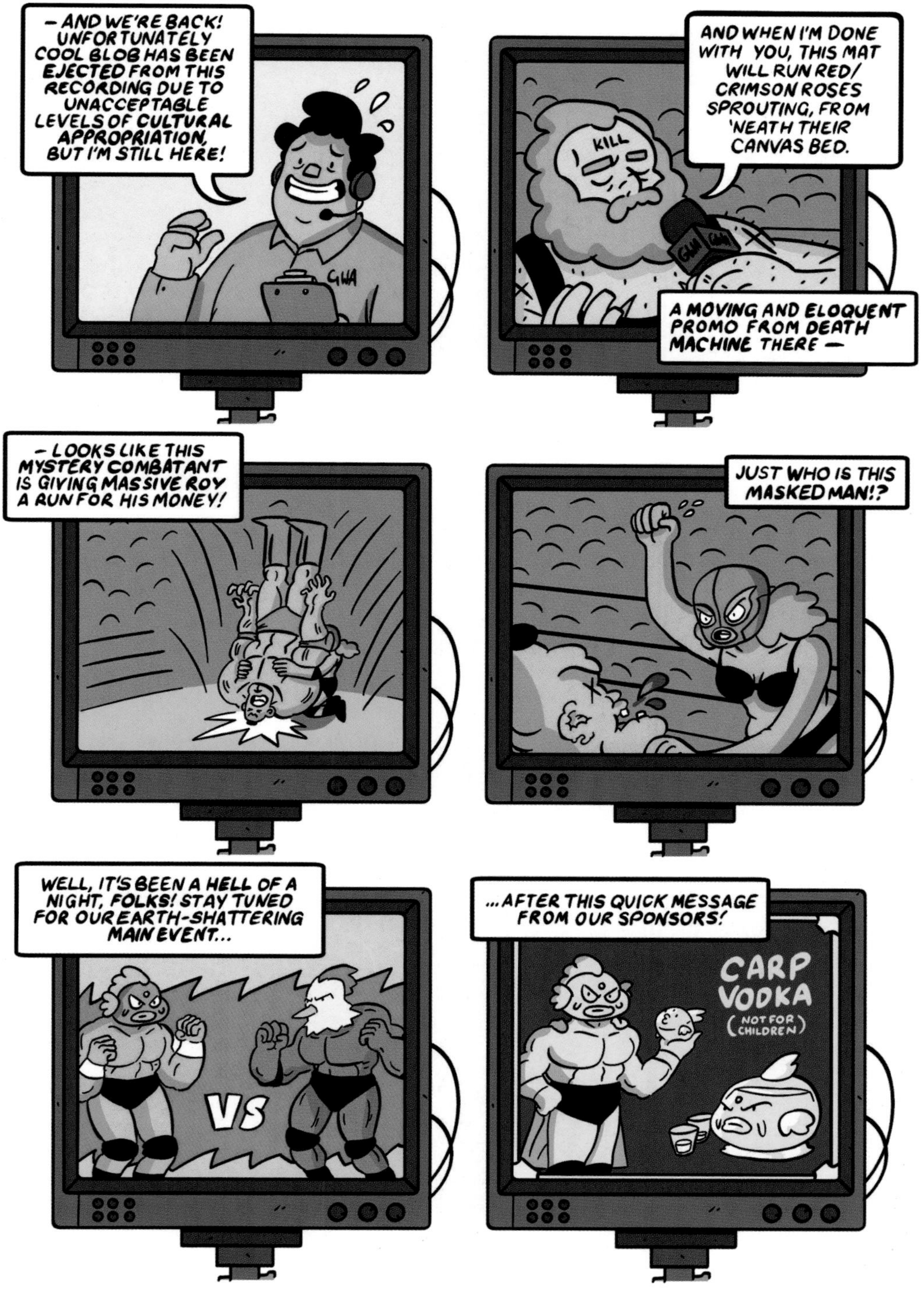
– AND WE'RE BACK! UNFORTUNATELY COOL BLOB HAS BEEN EJECTED FROM THIS RECORDING DUE TO UNACCEPTABLE LEVELS OF CULTURAL APPROPRIATION, BUT I'M STILL HERE!
GWA
AND WHEN I'M DONE WITH YOU, THIS MAT WILL RUN RED/ CRIMSON ROSES SPROUTING, FROM 'NEATH THEIR CANVAS BED.
KILL
GWA
A MOVING AND ELOQUENT PROMO FROM DEATH MACHINE THERE –
– LOOKS LIKE THIS MYSTERY COMBATANT IS GIVING MASSIVE ROY A RUN FOR HIS MONEY!
JUST WHO IS THIS MASKED MAN!?
WELL, IT'S BEEN A HELL OF A NIGHT, FOLKS! STAY TUNED FOR OUR EARTH-SHATTERING MAIN EVENT...
VS
...AFTER THIS QUICK MESSAGE FROM OUR SPONSORS!
CARP VODKA
(NOT FOR CHILDREN)

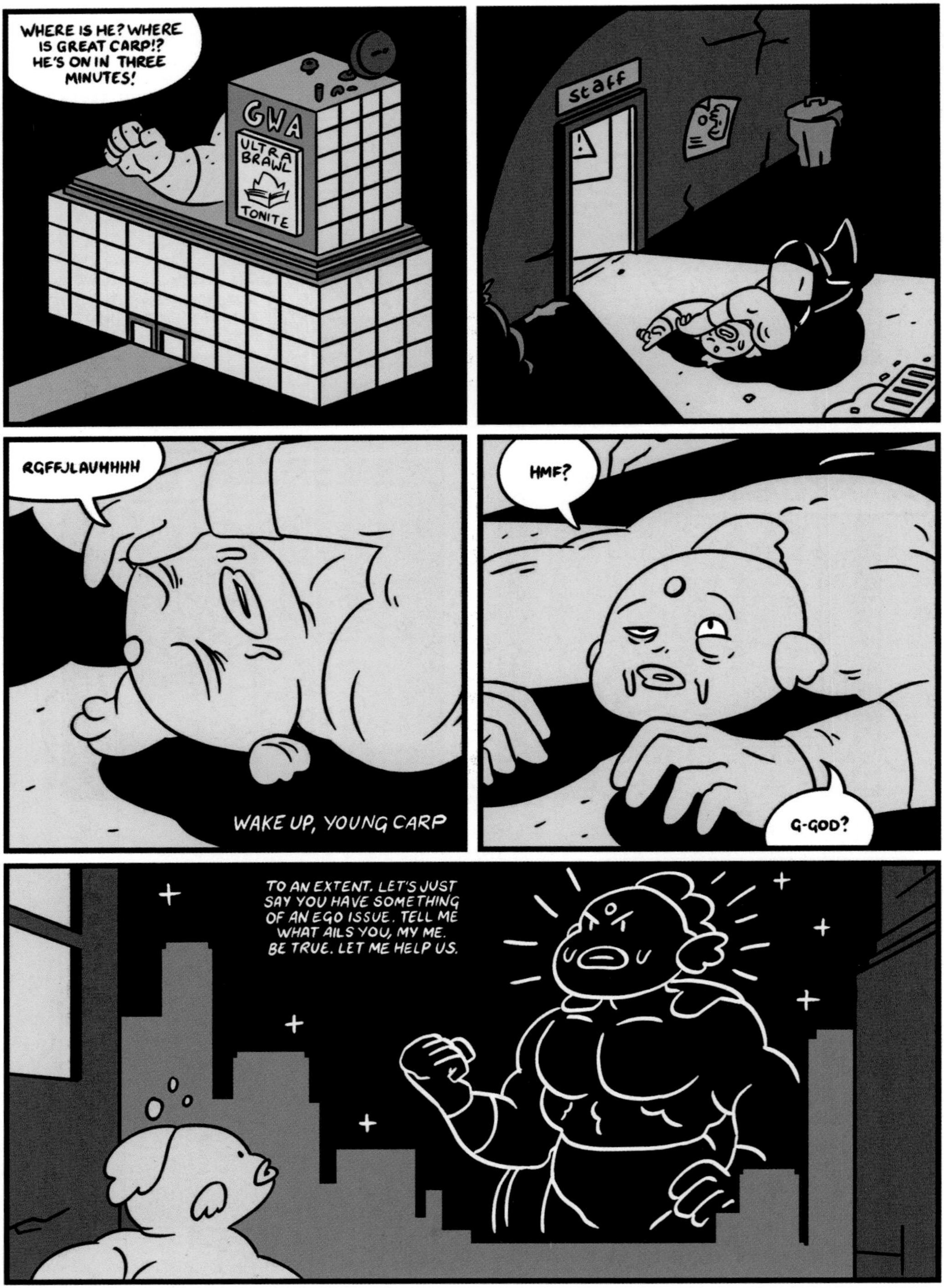
WHERE IS HE? WHERE IS GREAT CARP!? HE'S ON IN THREE MINUTES!
GWA
ULTRA BRAWL
TONITE
staff
RGFFJLAUHHHH
WAKE UP, YOUNG CARP
HMF?
G-GOD?
TO AN EXTENT. LET'S JUST SAY YOU HAVE SOMETHING OF AN EGO ISSUE. TELL ME WHAT AILS YOU, MY ME. BE TRUE. LET ME HELP US.

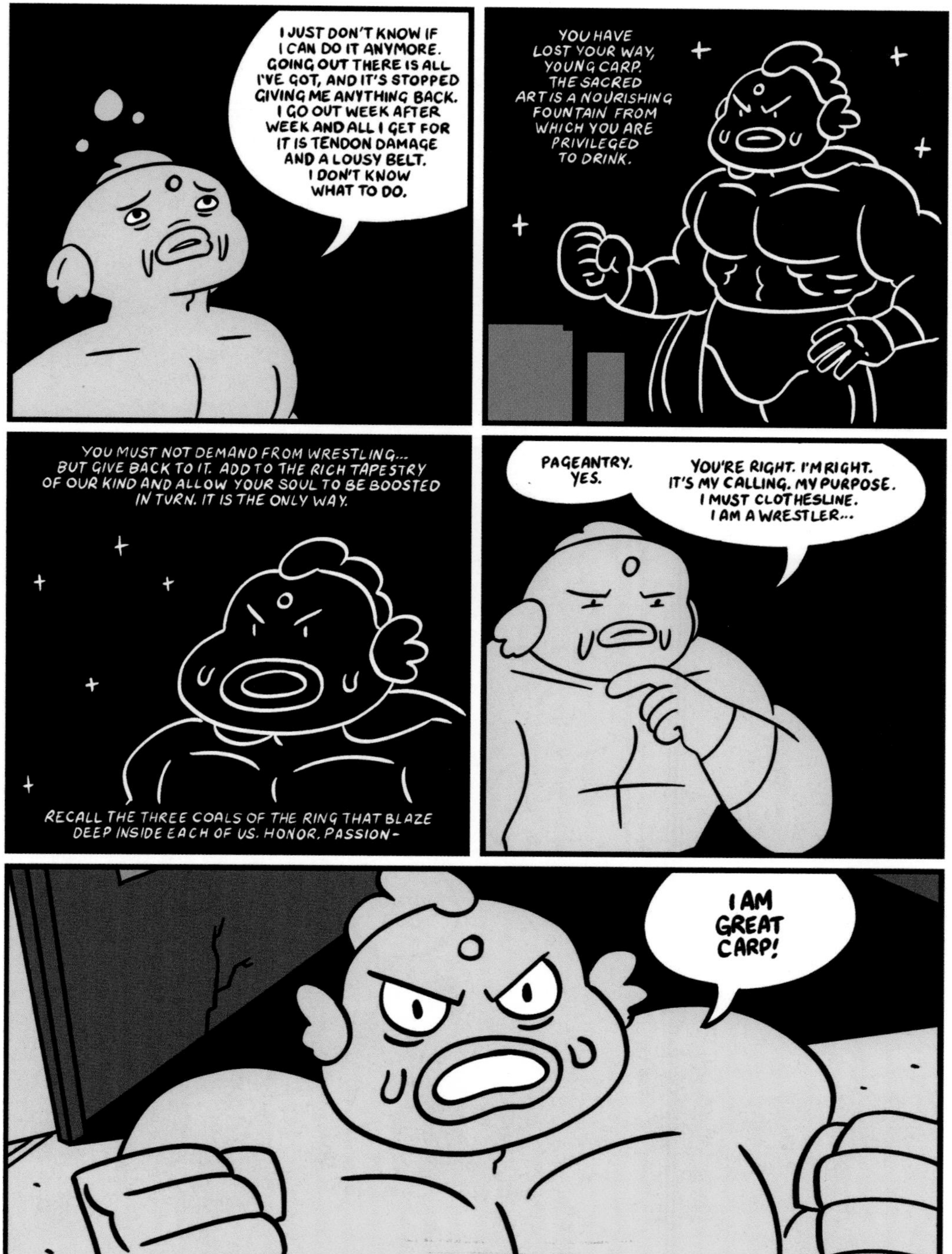
I JUST DON'T KNOW IF I CAN DO IT ANYMORE. GOING OUT THERE IS ALL I'VE GOT, AND IT'S STOPPED GIVING ME ANYTHING BACK. I GO OUT WEEK AFTER WEEK AND ALL I GET FOR IT IS TENDON DAMAGE AND A LOUSY BELT. I DON'T KNOW WHAT TO DO.
YOU HAVE LOST YOUR WAY, YOUNG CARP. THE SACRED ART IS A NOURISHING FOUNTAIN FROM WHICH YOU ARE PRIVILEGED TO DRINK.
YOU MUST NOT DEMAND FROM WRESTLING... BUT GIVE BACK TO IT. ADD TO THE RICH TAPESTRY OF OUR KIND AND ALLOW YOUR SOUL TO BE BOOSTED IN TURN. IT IS THE ONLY WAY.
RECALL THE THREE COALS OF THE RING THAT BLAZE DEEP INSIDE EACH OF US. HONOR, PASSION-
PAGEANTRY. YES.
YOU'RE RIGHT. I'M RIGHT. IT'S MY CALLING. MY PURPOSE. I MUST CLOTHESLINE. I AM A WRESTLER...
I AM GREAT CARP!

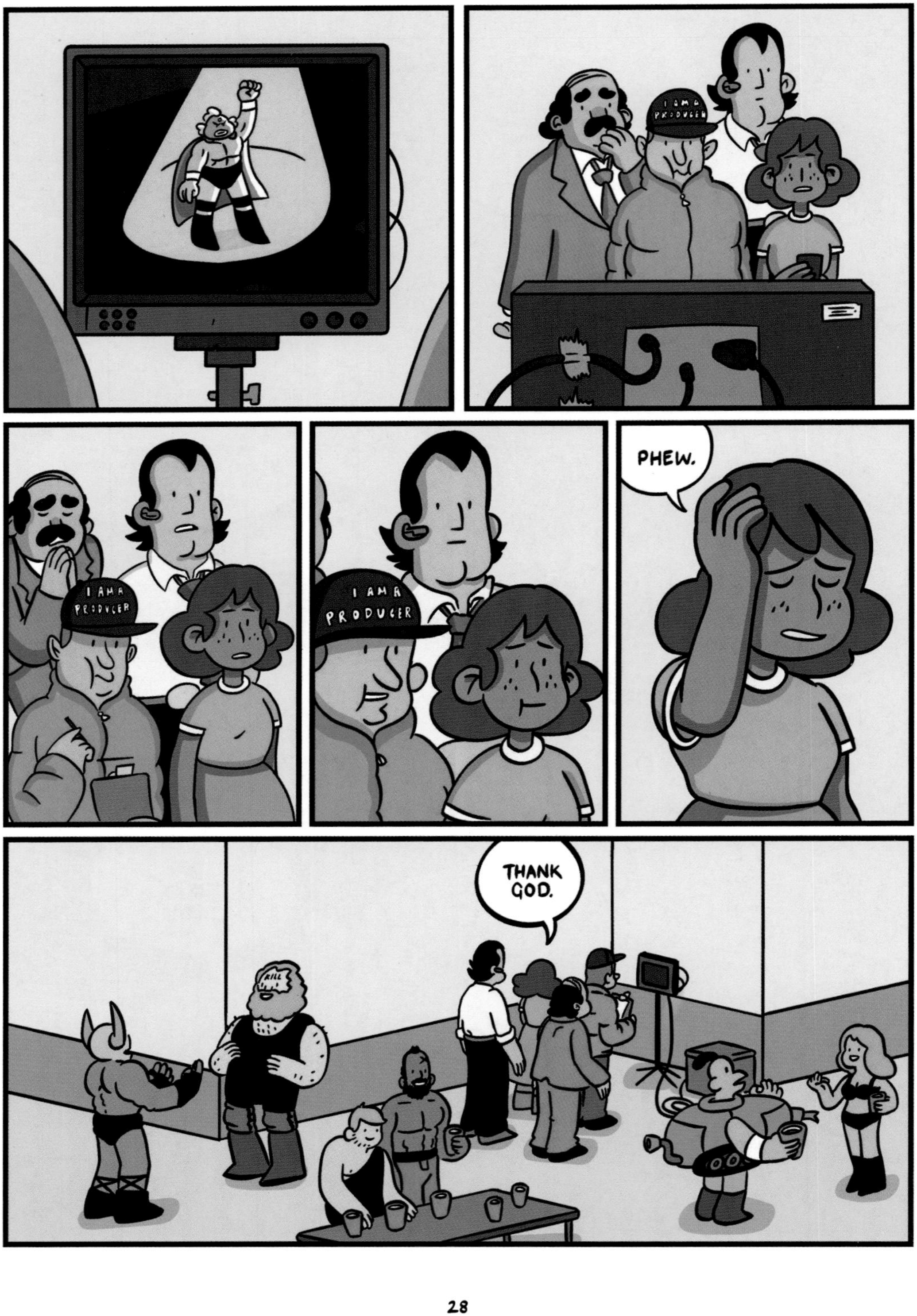
I AM A PRODUCER
I AM A PRODUCER
I AM A PRODUCER
PHEW.
THANK GOD.

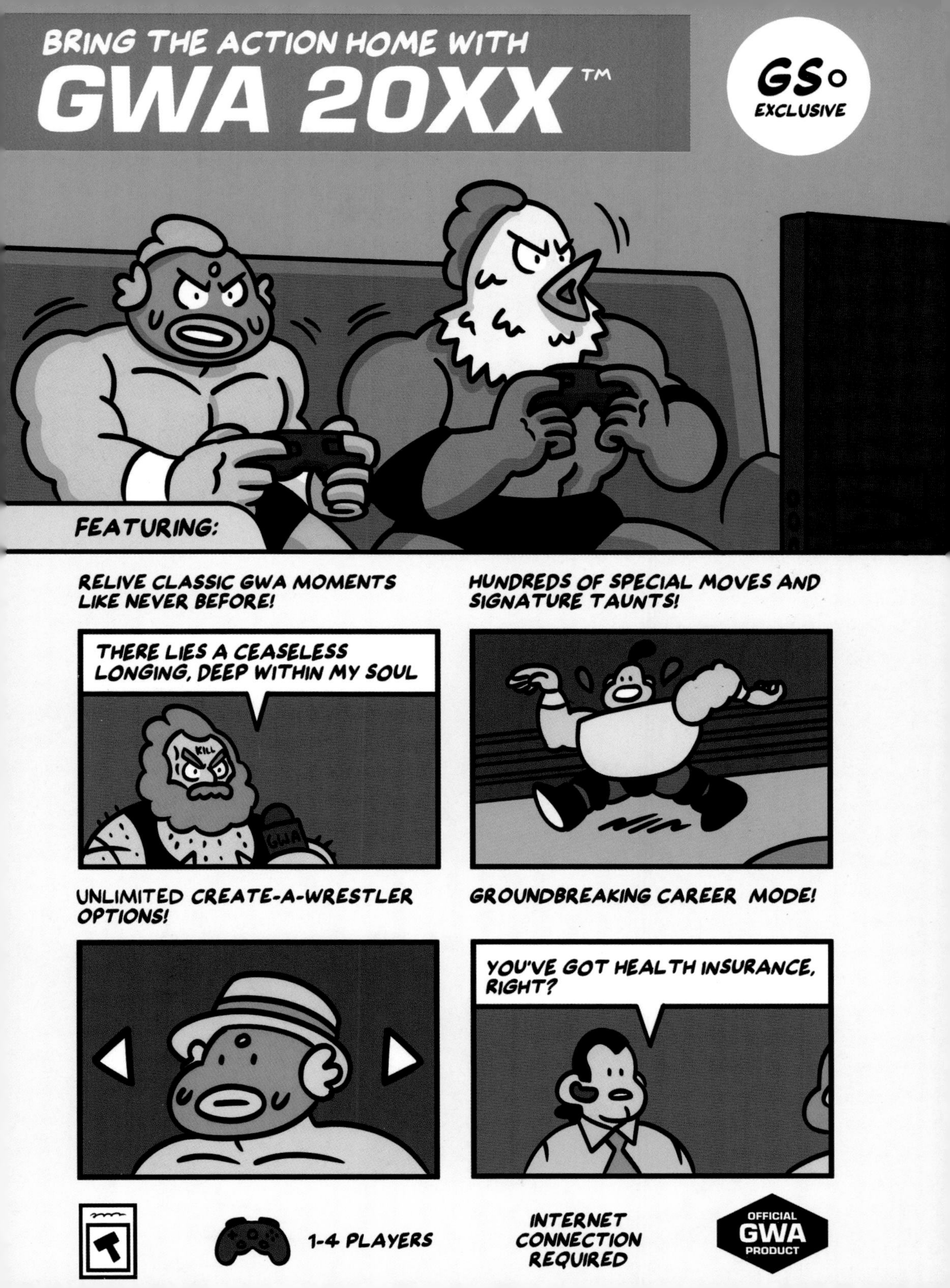
BRING THE ACTION HOME WITH
GWA 20XX™
GS EXCLUSIVE
FEATURING:
RELIVE CLASSIC GWA MOMENTS LIKE NEVER BEFORE!
THERE LIES A CEASELESS LONGING, DEEP WITHIN MY SOUL
KILL
GWA
HUNDREDS OF SPECIAL MOVES AND SIGNATURE TAUNTS!
UNLIMITED CREATE-A-WRESTLER OPTIONS!
GROUNDBREAKING CAREER MODE!
YOU'VE GOT HEALTH INSURANCE, RIGHT?
1-4 PLAYERS
INTERNET CONNECTION REQUIRED
OFFICIAL GWA PRODUCT

CHAPTER TWO

GRAPPLING ROAD

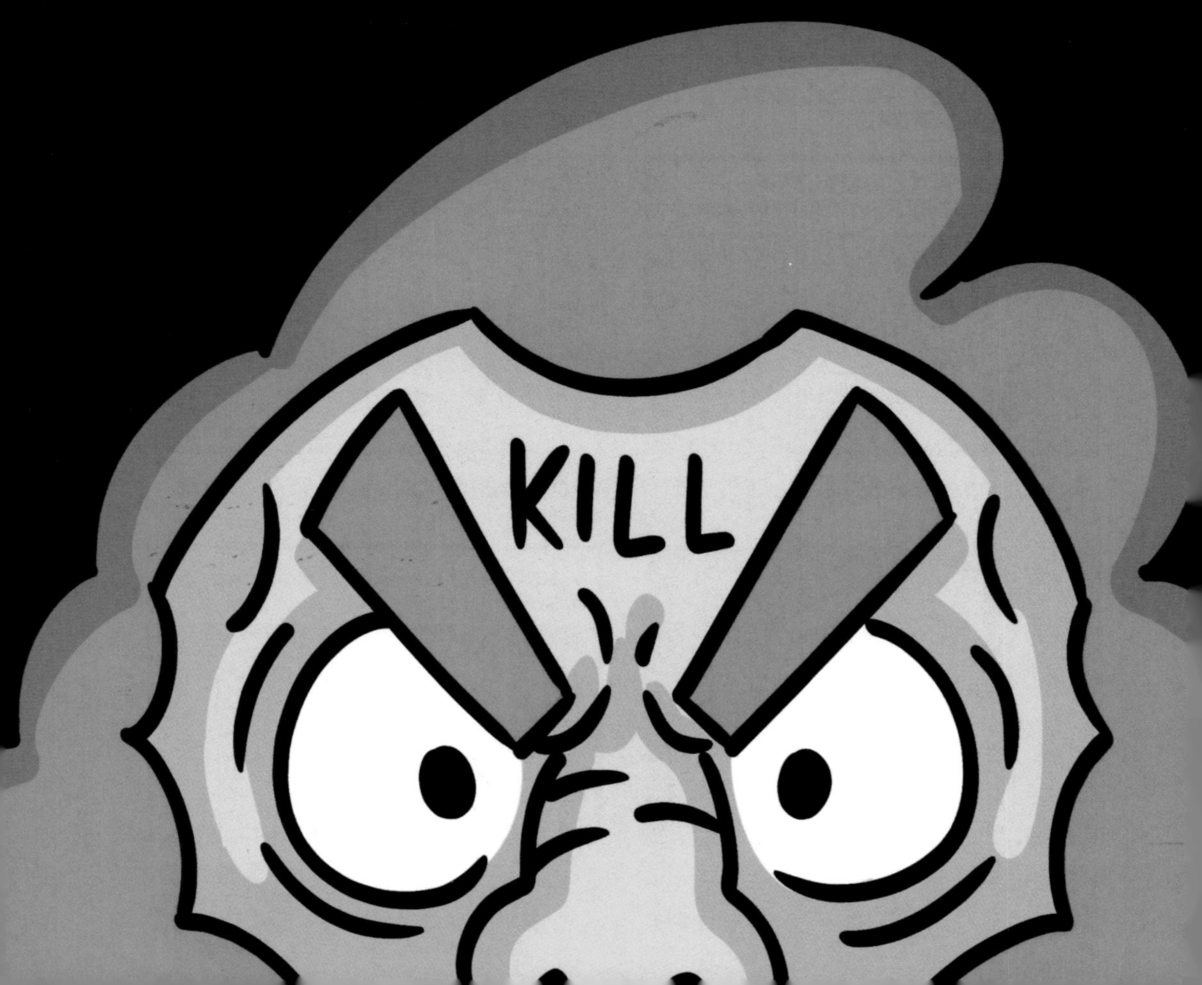
KILL

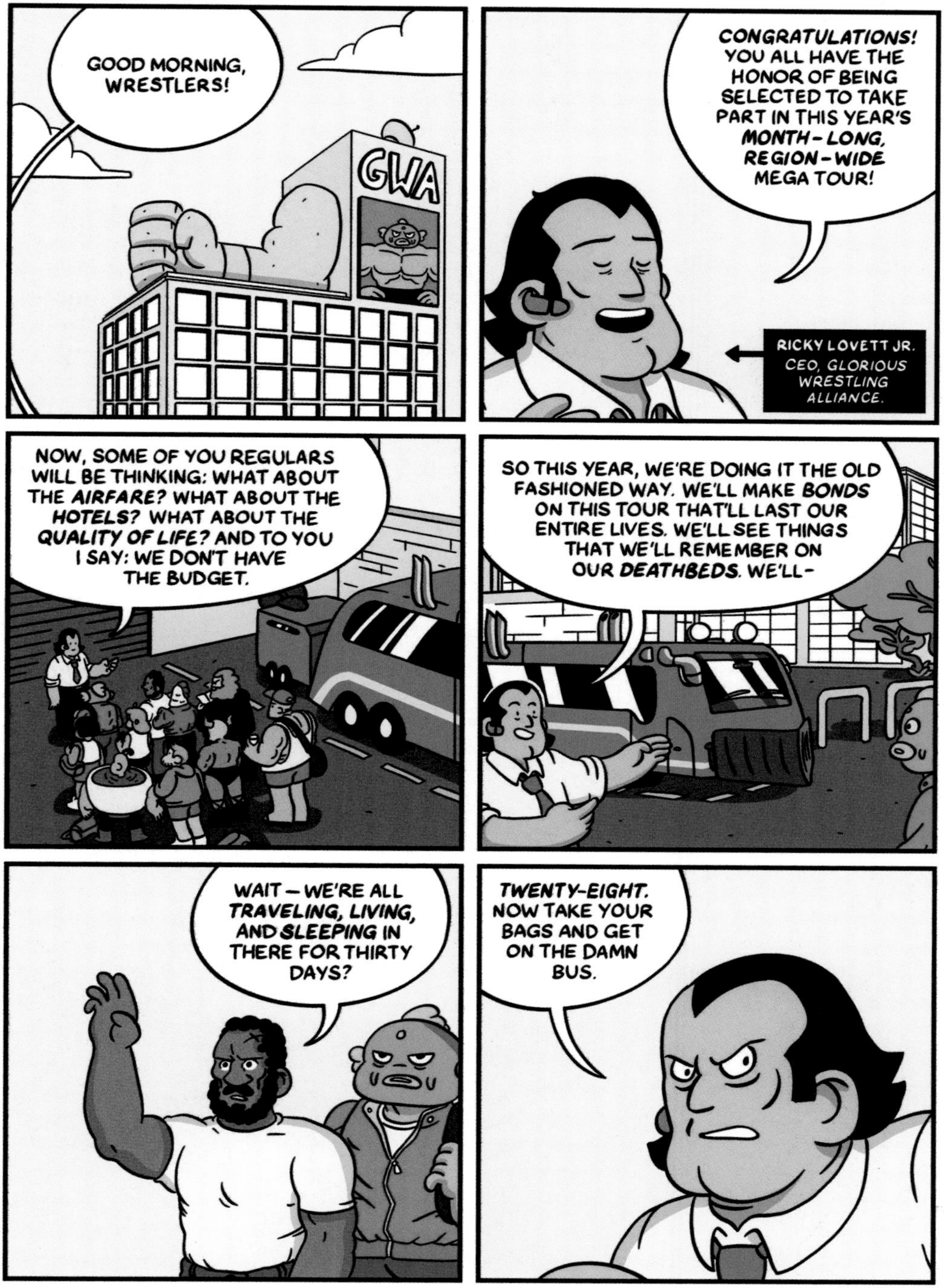
GOOD MORNING, WRESTLERS!
GWA
CONGRATULATIONS! YOU ALL HAVE THE HONOR OF BEING SELECTED TO TAKE PART IN THIS YEAR'S MONTH-LONG, REGION-WIDE MEGA TOUR!
RICKY LOVETT JR. CEO, GLORIOUS WRESTLING ALLIANCE.
NOW, SOME OF YOU REGULARS WILL BE THINKING: WHAT ABOUT THE AIRFARE? WHAT ABOUT THE HOTELS? WHAT ABOUT THE QUALITY OF LIFE? AND TO YOU I SAY: WE DON'T HAVE THE BUDGET.
SO THIS YEAR, WE'RE DOING IT THE OLD FASHIONED WAY. WE'LL MAKE BONDS ON THIS TOUR THAT'LL LAST OUR ENTIRE LIVES. WE'LL SEE THINGS THAT WE'LL REMEMBER ON OUR DEATHBEDS. WE'LL-
WAIT — WE'RE ALL TRAVELING, LIVING, AND SLEEPING IN THERE FOR THIRTY DAYS?
TWENTY-EIGHT. NOW TAKE YOUR BAGS AND GET ON THE DAMN BUS.

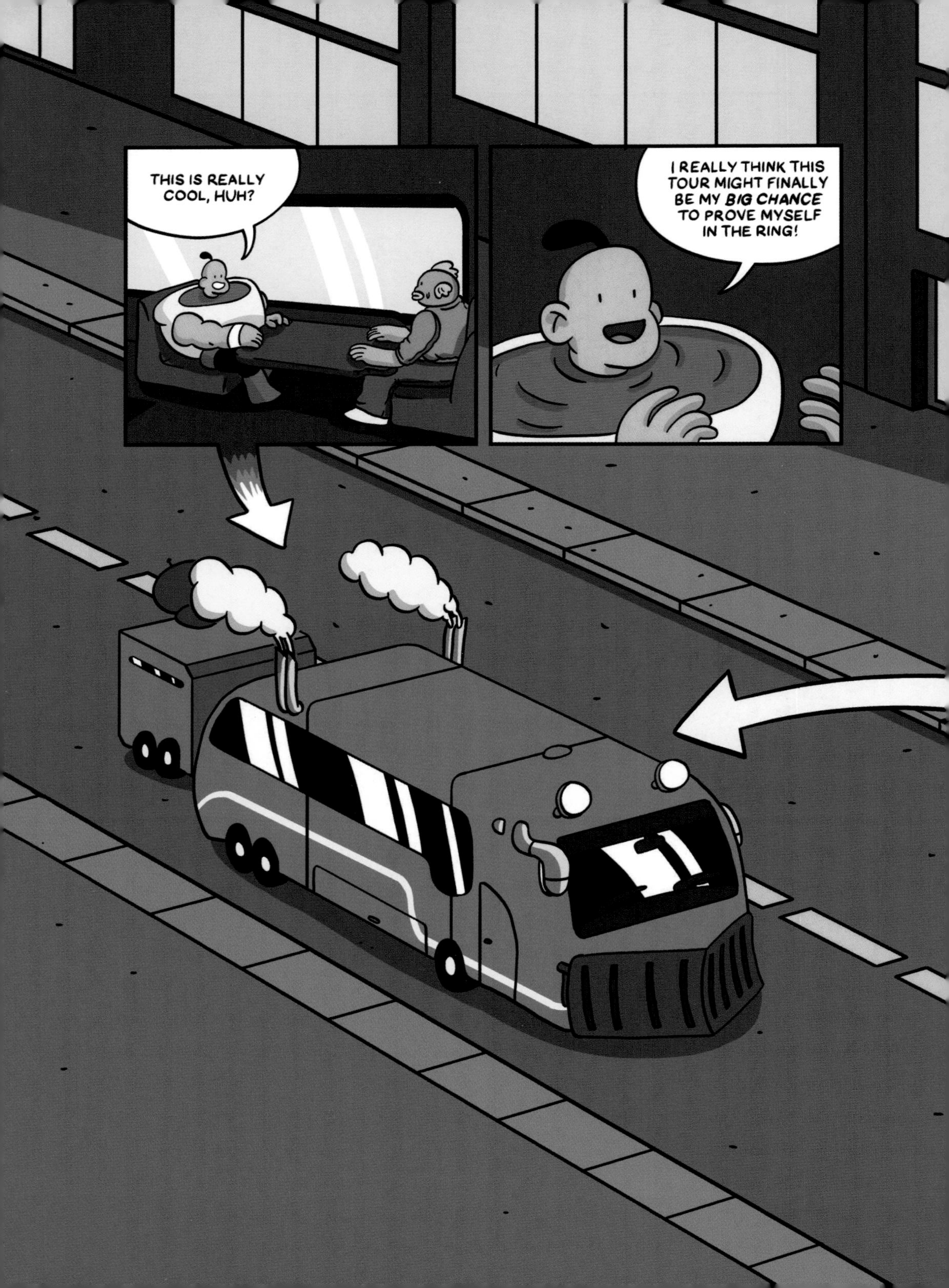
THIS IS REALLY COOL, HUH?
I REALLY THINK THIS TOUR MIGHT FINALLY BE MY *BIG CHANCE* TO PROVE MYSELF IN THE RING!

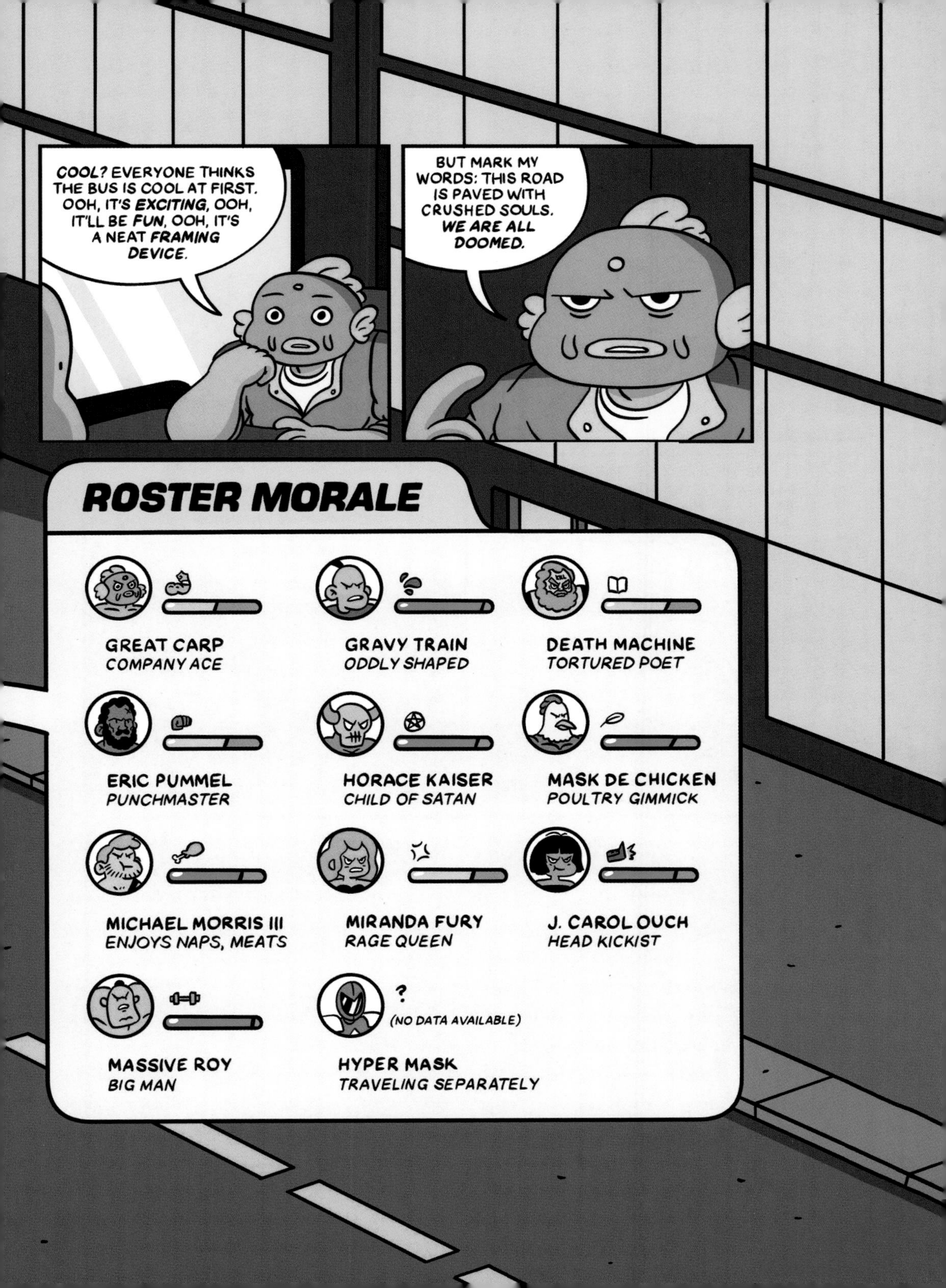
COOL? EVERYONE THINKS THE BUS IS COOL AT FIRST. OOH, IT'S EXCITING, OOH, IT'LL BE FUN, OOH, IT'S A NEAT FRAMING DEVICE.
BUT MARK MY WORDS: THIS ROAD IS PAVED WITH CRUSHED SOULS. WE ARE ALL DOOMED.
ROSTER MORALE
GREAT CARP
COMPANY ACE
GRAVY TRAIN
ODDLY SHAPED
DEATH MACHINE
TORTURED POET
ERIC PUMMEL
PUNCHMASTER
HORACE KAISER
CHILD OF SATAN
MASK DE CHICKEN
POULTRY GIMMICK
MICHAEL MORRIS III
ENJOYS NAPS, MEATS
MIRANDA FURY
RAGE QUEEN
J. CAROL OUCH
HEAD KICKIST
MASSIVE ROY
BIG MAN
?
(NO DATA AVAILABLE)
HYPER MASK
TRAVELING SEPARATELY

DAY 6 131 HOURS OF ROAD DUGGAN PLAZA HALL

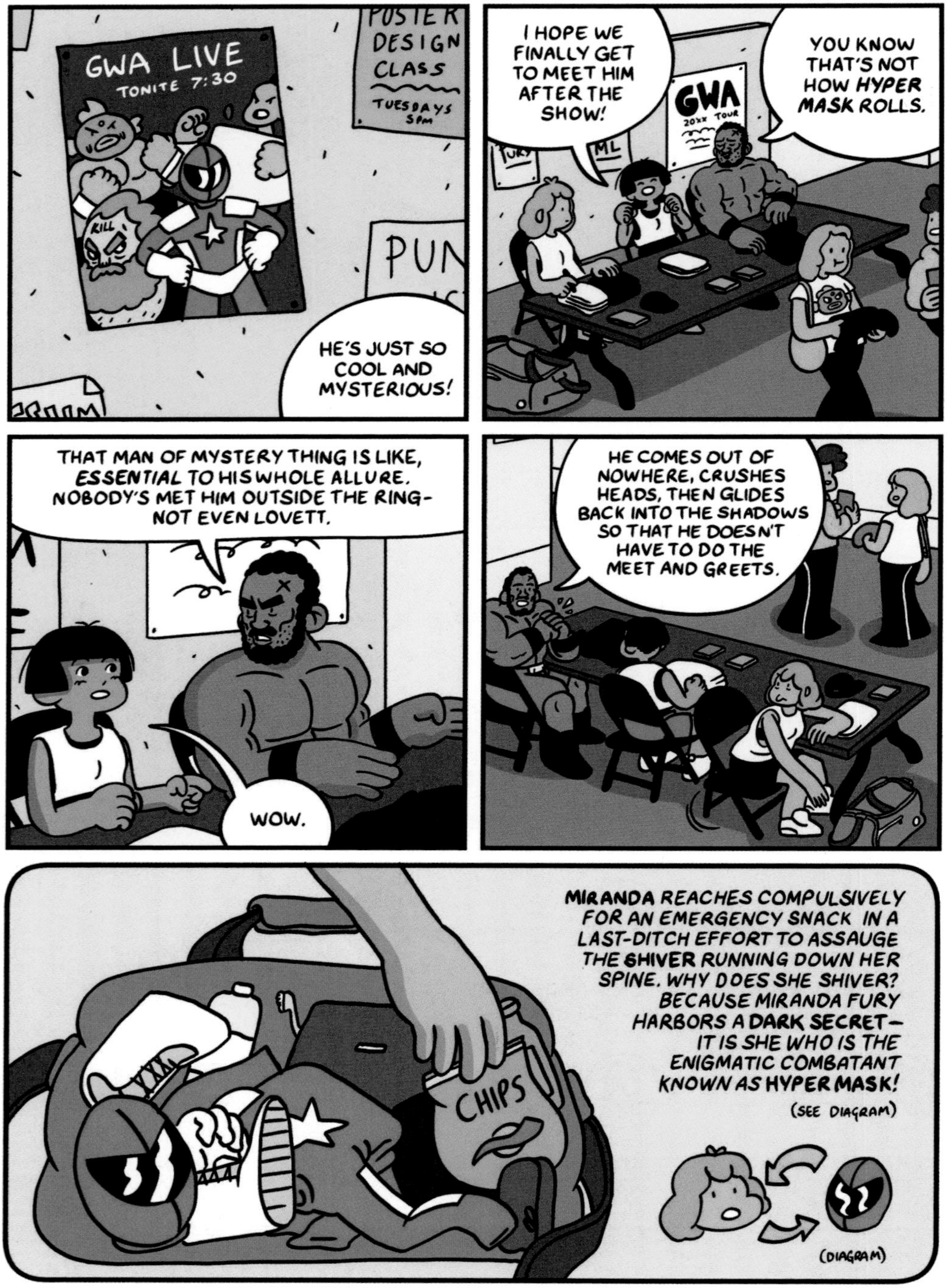
GWA LIVE
TONITE 7:30
POSTER DESIGN CLASS
TUESDAYS 5PM
HE'S JUST SO COOL AND MYSTERIOUS!
I HOPE WE FINALLY GET TO MEET HIM AFTER THE SHOW!
GWA
20XX TOUR
YOU KNOW THAT'S NOT HOW HYPER MASK ROLLS.
THAT MAN OF MYSTERY THING IS LIKE, ESSENTIAL TO HIS WHOLE ALLURE. NOBODY'S MET HIM OUTSIDE THE RING- NOT EVEN LOVETT.
WOW.
HE COMES OUT OF NOWHERE, CRUSHES HEADS, THEN GLIDES BACK INTO THE SHADOWS SO THAT HE DOESN'T HAVE TO DO THE MEET AND GREETS.
MIRANDA REACHES COMPULSIVELY FOR AN EMERGENCY SNACK IN A LAST-DITCH EFFORT TO ASSAUGE THE SHIVER RUNNING DOWN HER SPINE. WHY DOES SHE SHIVER? BECAUSE MIRANDA FURY HARBORS A DARK SECRET— IT IS SHE WHO IS THE ENIGMATIC COMBATANT KNOWN AS HYPER MASK!
(SEE DIAGRAM)
CHIPS
(DIAGRAM)

I LOVE HIM! I EVEN MADE THIS *CUSTOM ACTION FIGURE* IN HIS IMAGE!

IT'S GOT HIS NEW OUTFIT AND EVERYTHING!

COOL.

INITIALLY COMPELLED TO DON HER MASKED GUISE BY THE COMPANY'S *ARCHAIC GENDER-BASED BOOKING POLICIES,* MIRANDA NOW FINDS HERSELF CONFLICTED IN REGARDS TO HER CREATION.

DOES SHE FEEL *PRIDE* IN HER ACCOMPLISHMENTS? *SHAME* IN HER SECRECY? *JEALOUSY* OF HER OWN ALTER-EGO'S SUCCESSES? MIRANDA CAN'T TELL.

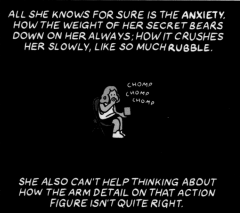

ALL SHE KNOWS FOR SURE IS THE *ANXIETY.* HOW THE WEIGHT OF HER SECRET BEARS DOWN ON HER ALWAYS; HOW IT CRUSHES HER SLOWLY, LIKE SO MUCH *RUBBLE.*

CHOMP CHOMP CHOMP

SHE ALSO CAN'T HELP THINKING ABOUT HOW THE ARM DETAIL ON THAT ACTION FIGURE ISN'T QUITE RIGHT.

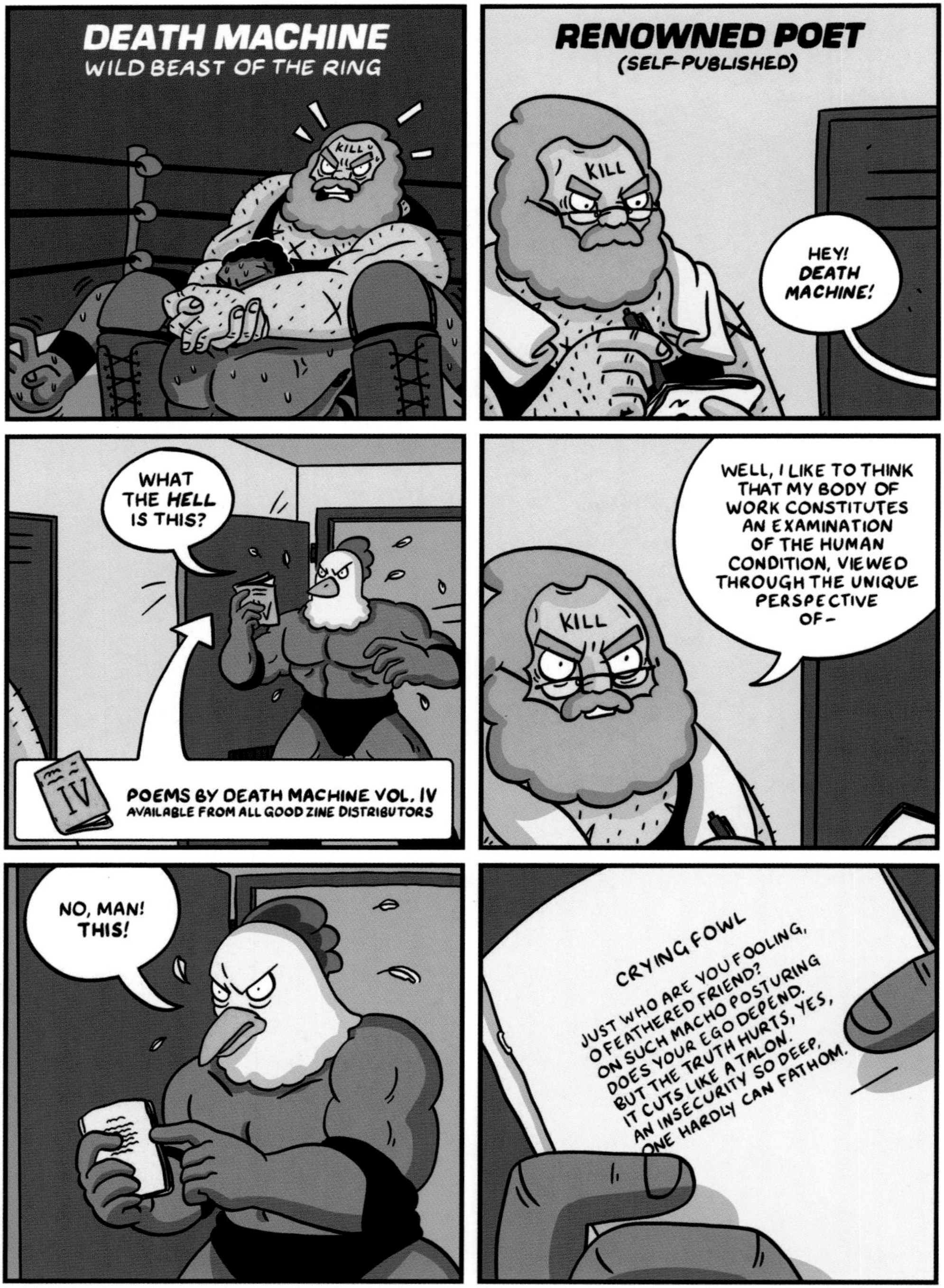
DEATH MACHINE
WILD BEAST OF THE RING
KILL
RENOWNED POET
(SELF-PUBLISHED)
KILL
HEY! DEATH MACHINE!
WHAT THE HELL IS THIS?
IV
POEMS BY DEATH MACHINE VOL. IV
AVAILABLE FROM ALL GOOD ZINE DISTRIBUTORS
WELL, I LIKE TO THINK THAT MY BODY OF WORK CONSTITUTES AN EXAMINATION OF THE HUMAN CONDITION, VIEWED THROUGH THE UNIQUE PERSPECTIVE OF-
KILL
NO, MAN! THIS!
CRYING FOWL
JUST WHO ARE YOU FOOLING,
O FEATHERED FRIEND?
ON SUCH MACHO POSTURING
DOES YOUR EGO DEPEND.
BUT THE TRUTH HURTS, YES,
IT CUTS LIKE A TALON.
AN INSECURITY SO DEEP,
ONE HARDLY CAN FATHOM.

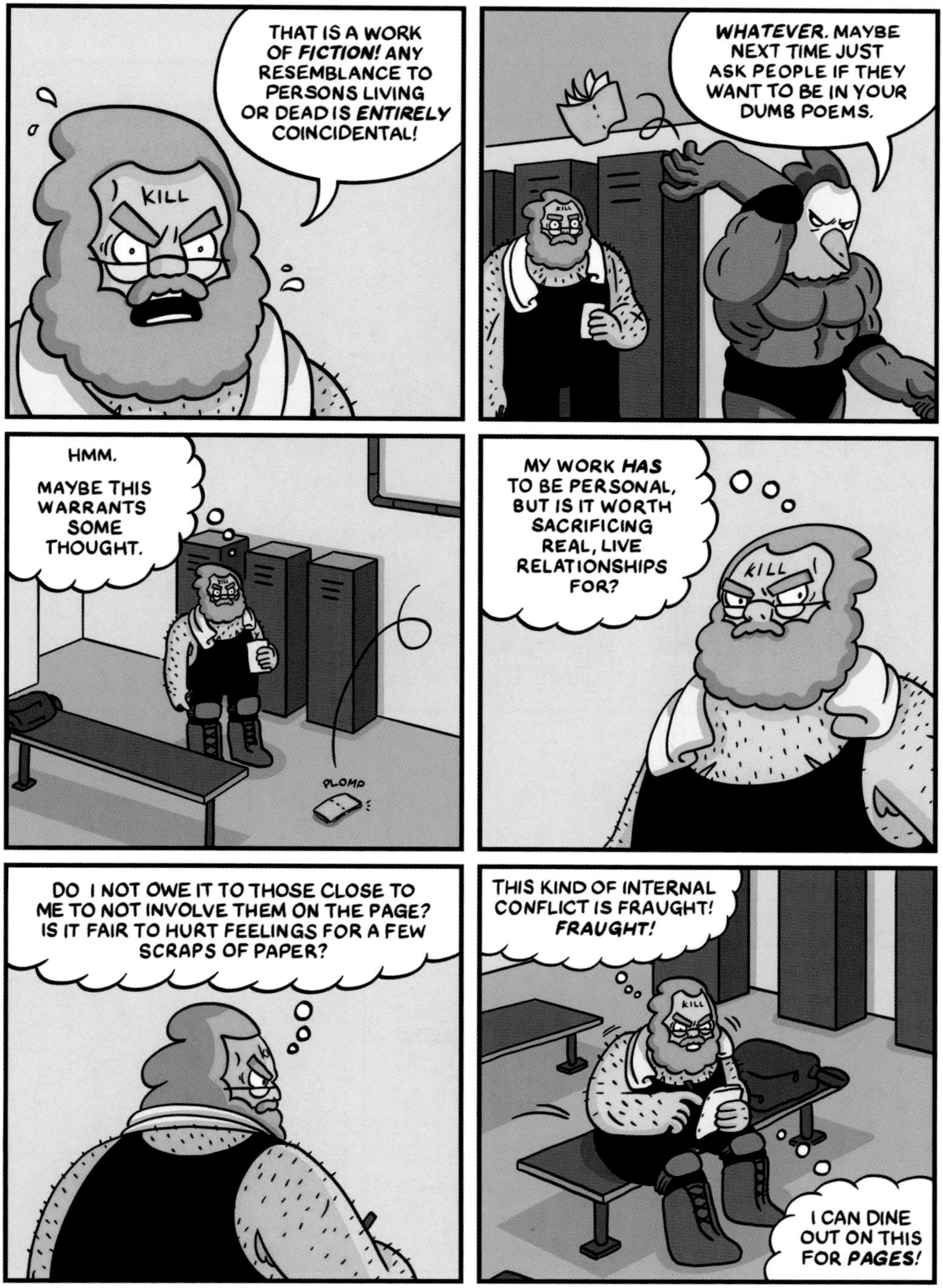
THAT IS A WORK OF FICTION! ANY RESEMBLANCE TO PERSONS LIVING OR DEAD IS ENTIRELY COINCIDENTAL!
KILL
WHATEVER. MAYBE NEXT TIME JUST ASK PEOPLE IF THEY WANT TO BE IN YOUR DUMB POEMS.
HMM.
MAYBE THIS WARRANTS SOME THOUGHT.
PLOMP
MY WORK HAS TO BE PERSONAL, BUT IS IT WORTH SACRIFICING REAL, LIVE RELATIONSHIPS FOR?
KILL
DO I NOT OWE IT TO THOSE CLOSE TO ME TO NOT INVOLVE THEM ON THE PAGE? IS IT FAIR TO HURT FEELINGS FOR A FEW SCRAPS OF PAPER?
THIS KIND OF INTERNAL CONFLICT IS FRAUGHT! FRAUGHT!
KILL
I CAN DINE OUT ON THIS FOR PAGES!

PROGRESS REPORT

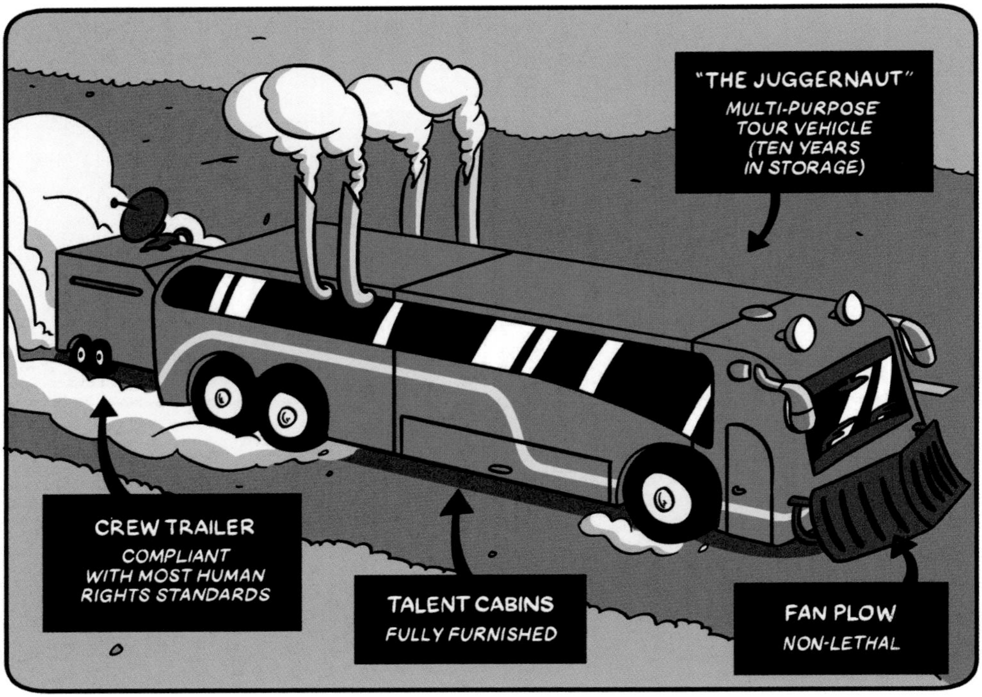
"THE JUGGERNAUT"
MULTI-PURPOSE TOUR VEHICLE (TEN YEARS IN STORAGE)
CREW TRAILER
COMPLIANT WITH MOST HUMAN RIGHTS STANDARDS
TALENT CABINS
FULLY FURNISHED
FAN PLOW
NON-LETHAL

DAY 19

438 HOURS OF ROAD

ROSTER MORALE

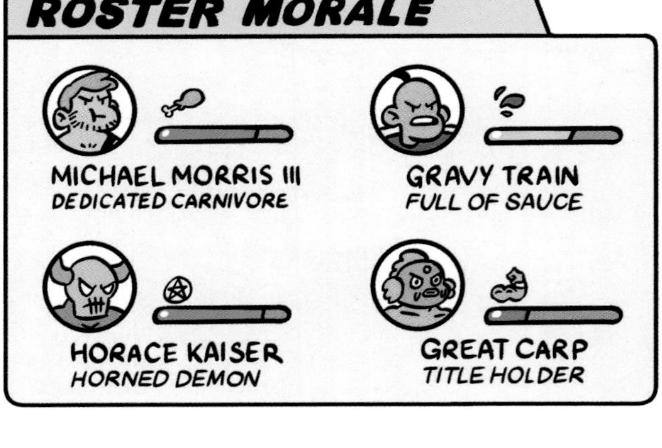
MICHAEL MORRIS III
DEDICATED CARNIVORE
GRAVY TRAIN
FULL OF SAUCE
HORACE KAISER
HORNED DEMON
GREAT CARP
TITLE HOLDER

ROUTE

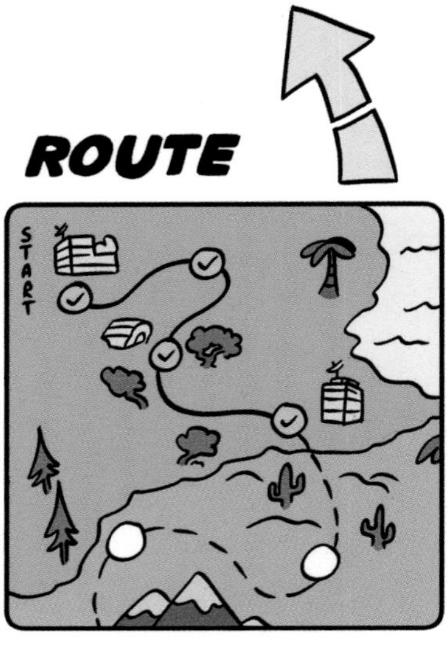
START

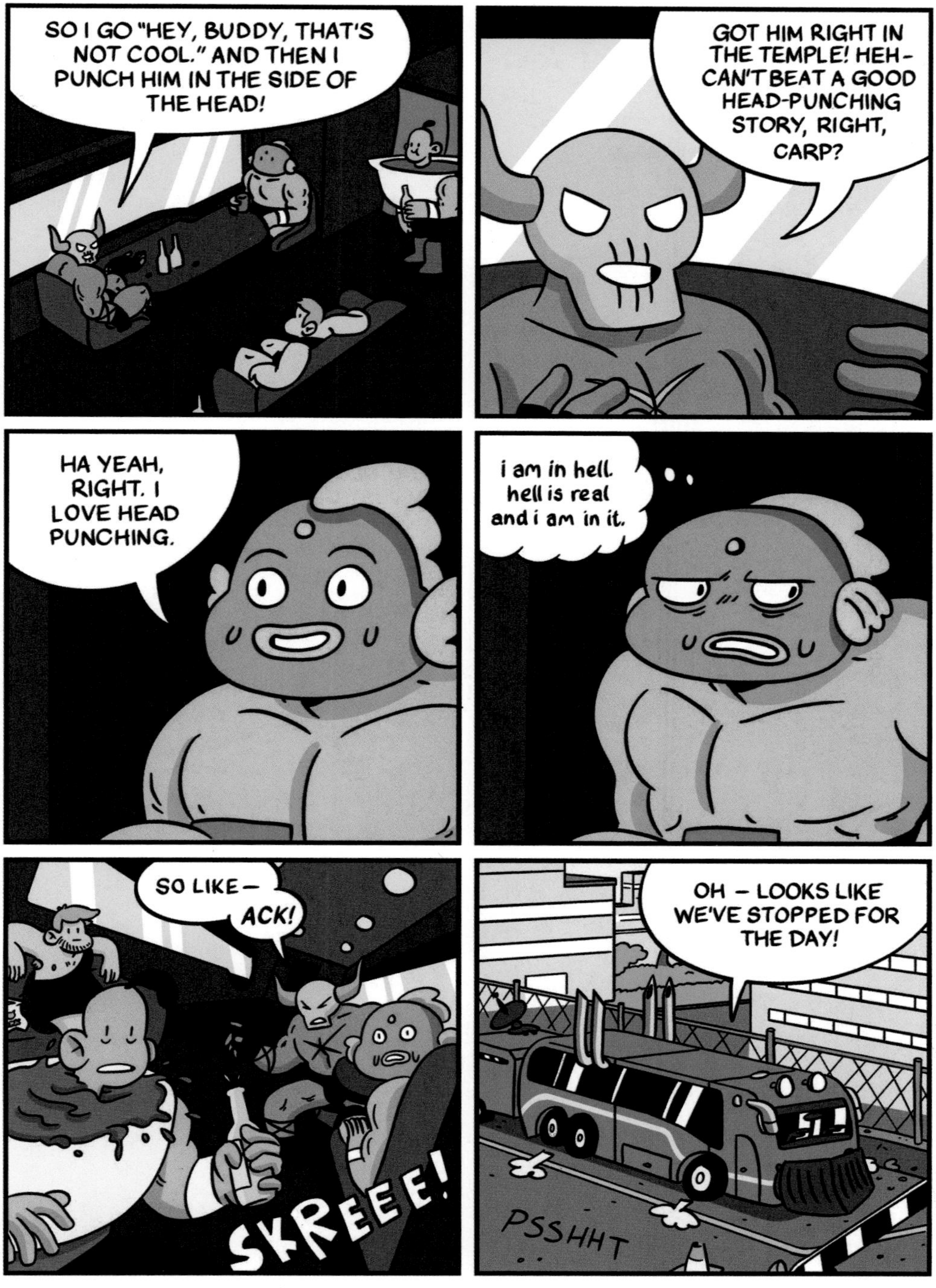
SO I GO "HEY, BUDDY, THAT'S NOT COOL." AND THEN I PUNCH HIM IN THE SIDE OF THE HEAD!
GOT HIM RIGHT IN THE TEMPLE! HEH - CAN'T BEAT A GOOD HEAD-PUNCHING STORY, RIGHT, CARP?
HA YEAH, RIGHT. I LOVE HEAD PUNCHING.
i am in hell. hell is real and i am in it.
SO LIKE—
ACK!
SKREEEE!
OH – LOOKS LIKE WE'VE STOPPED FOR THE DAY!
PSSHHT

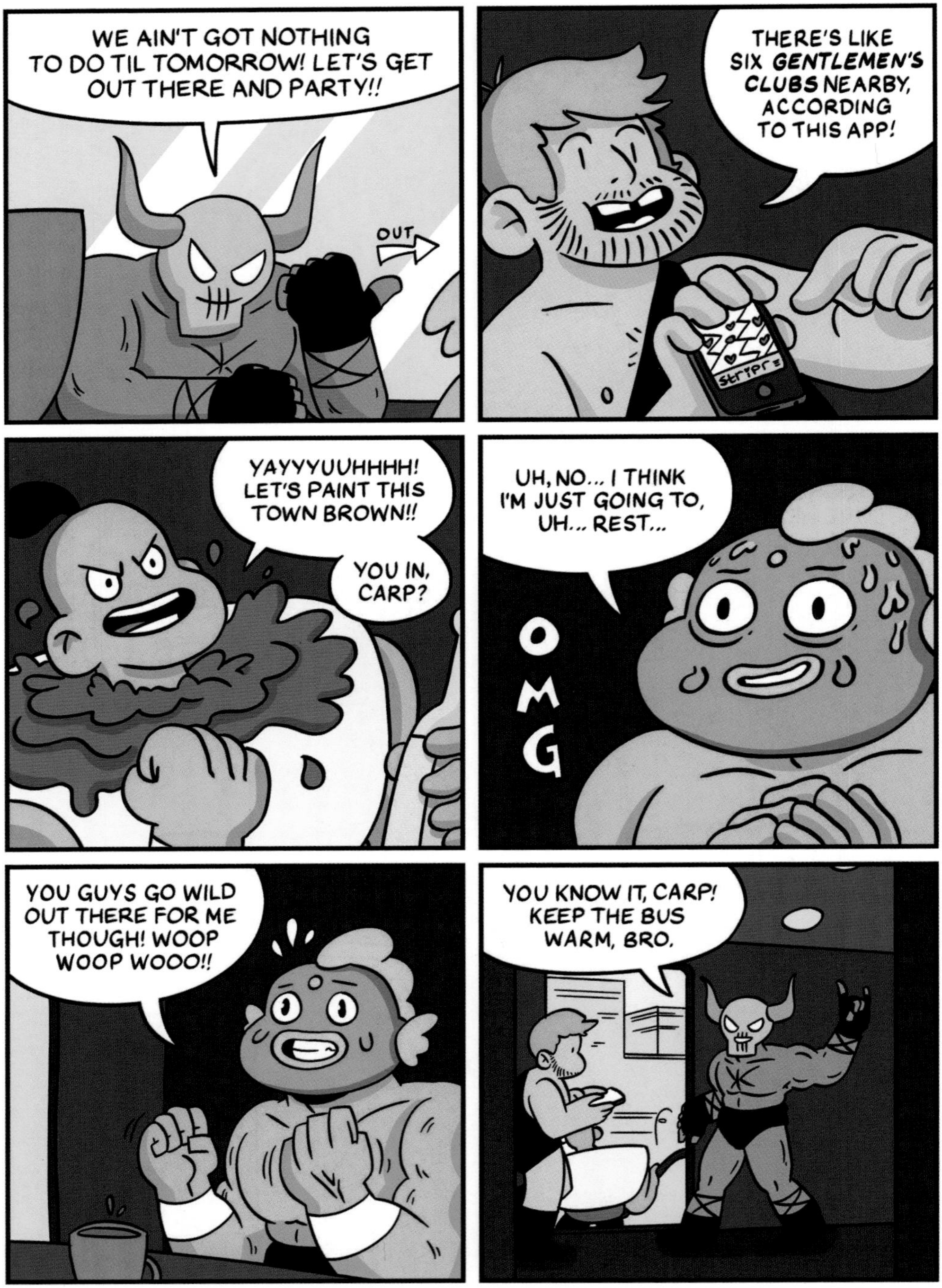
WE AIN'T GOT NOTHING TO DO TIL TOMORROW! LET'S GET OUT THERE AND PARTY!!
OUT
THERE'S LIKE SIX GENTLEMEN'S CLUBS NEARBY, ACCORDING TO THIS APP!
strypr
YAYYYUUHHHH! LET'S PAINT THIS TOWN BROWN!!
YOU IN, CARP?
UH, NO... I THINK I'M JUST GOING TO, UH... REST...
OMG
YOU GUYS GO WILD OUT THERE FOR ME THOUGH! WOOP WOOP WOOO!!
YOU KNOW IT, CARP! KEEP THE BUS WARM, BRO.

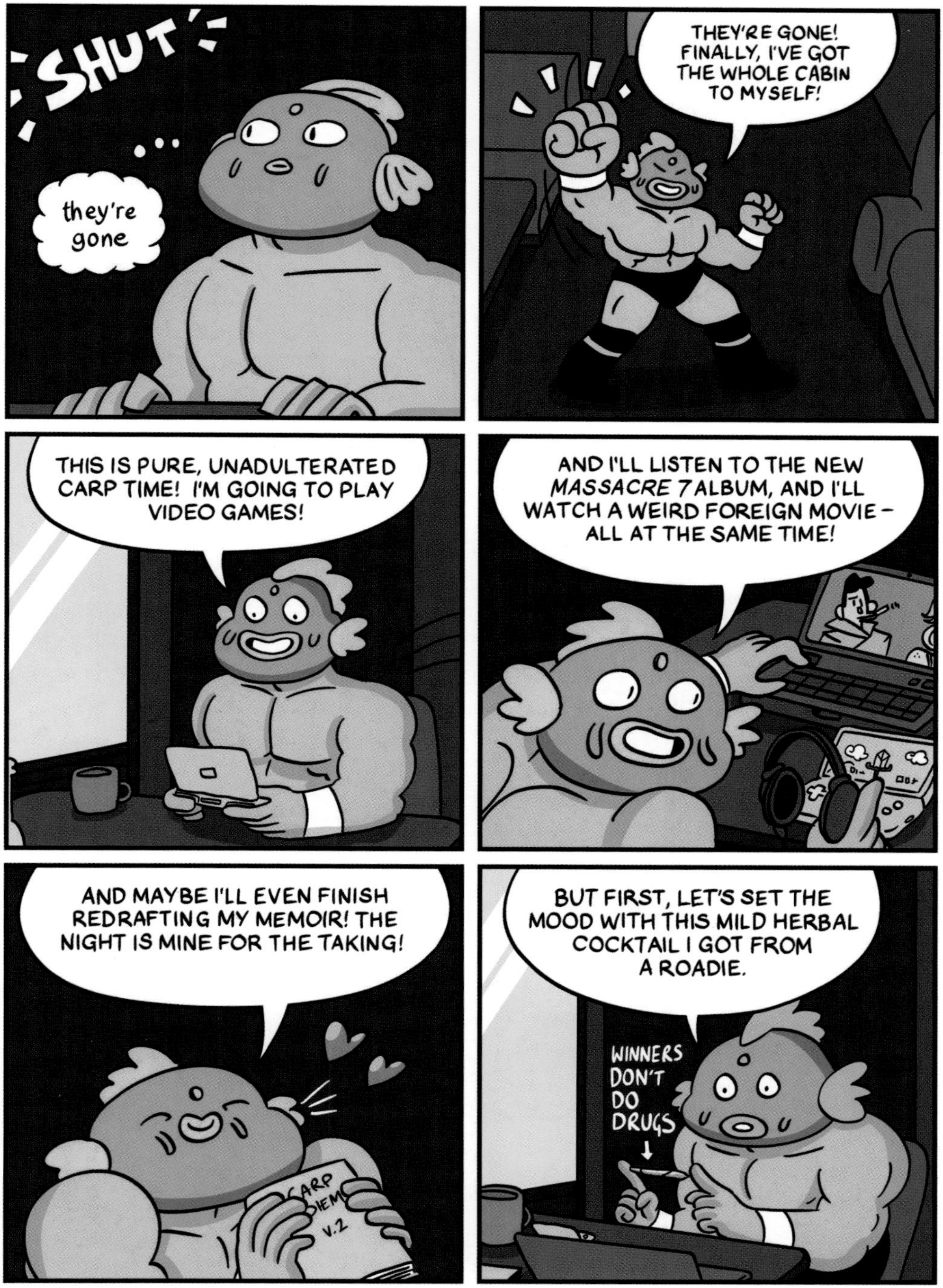
SHUT
...
they're gone
THEY'RE GONE! FINALLY, I'VE GOT THE WHOLE CABIN TO MYSELF!
THIS IS PURE, UNADULTERATED CARP TIME! I'M GOING TO PLAY VIDEO GAMES!
AND I'LL LISTEN TO THE NEW *MASSACRE 7* ALBUM, AND I'LL WATCH A WEIRD FOREIGN MOVIE – ALL AT THE SAME TIME!
AND MAYBE I'LL EVEN FINISH REDRAFTING MY MEMOIR! THE NIGHT IS MINE FOR THE TAKING!
CARP DIEM V.2
BUT FIRST, LET'S SET THE MOOD WITH THIS MILD HERBAL COCKTAIL I GOT FROM A ROADIE.
WINNERS DON'T DO DRUGS

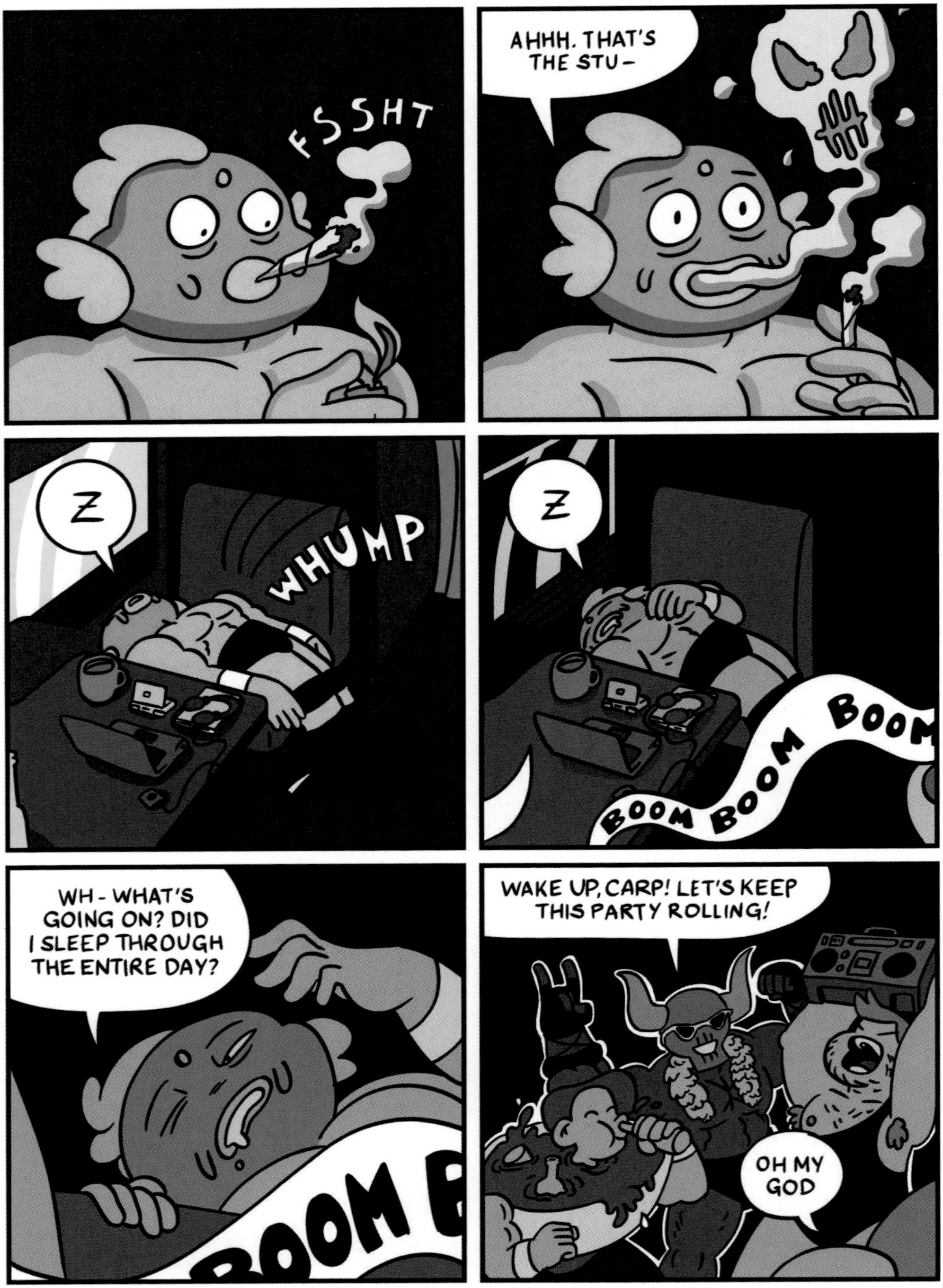
FSSHT
AHHH. THAT'S THE STU-
Z
WHUMP
Z
BOOM BOOM BOOM
WH-WHAT'S GOING ON? DID I SLEEP THROUGH THE ENTIRE DAY?
WAKE UP, CARP! LET'S KEEP THIS PARTY ROLLING!
OH MY GOD

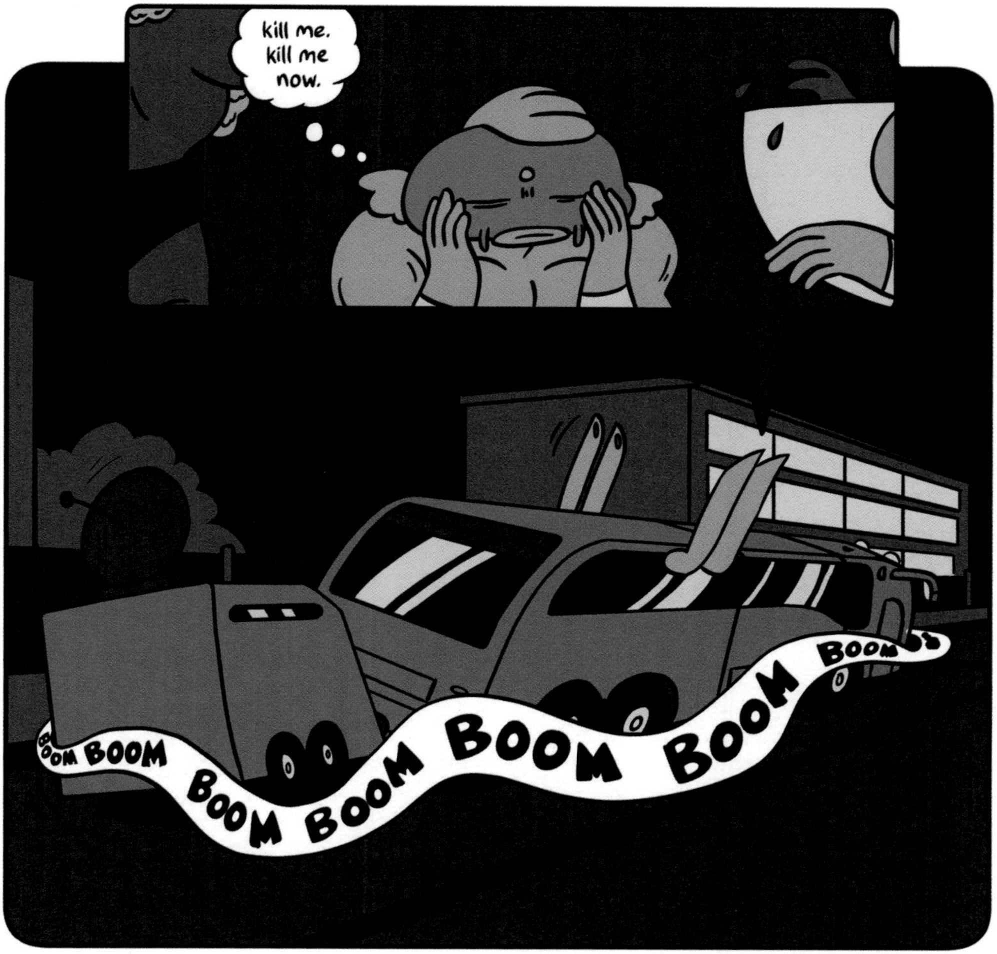
kill me.
kill me
now.
BOOM BOOM
BOOM BOOM
BOOM
BOOM
BOOM

DAY 20

453 HOURS OF ROAD

ROSTER MORALE

MICHAEL MORRIS III
HAVING A PLEASANT TIME

GRAVY TRAIN
75% ALCOHOL

HORACE KAISER
SLAVE TO THE RHYTHM

GREAT CARP
GENTLY SOBBING

CARPRADIO ♫

MASSACRE 7

TOP SECRET EPISODE

GENRE: STAB ROCK

1 ALL-OUT ASSAULT
2 36-HOUR SLUGFEST
3 ROOFTOP FRENZY B
4 EVERYTHING GOES WRONG
5 INFERNAL BLEEDING
6 FINAL ASSIGNMENT
7 SEX & FURY
8 MY HEART IS YOURS (COVER)

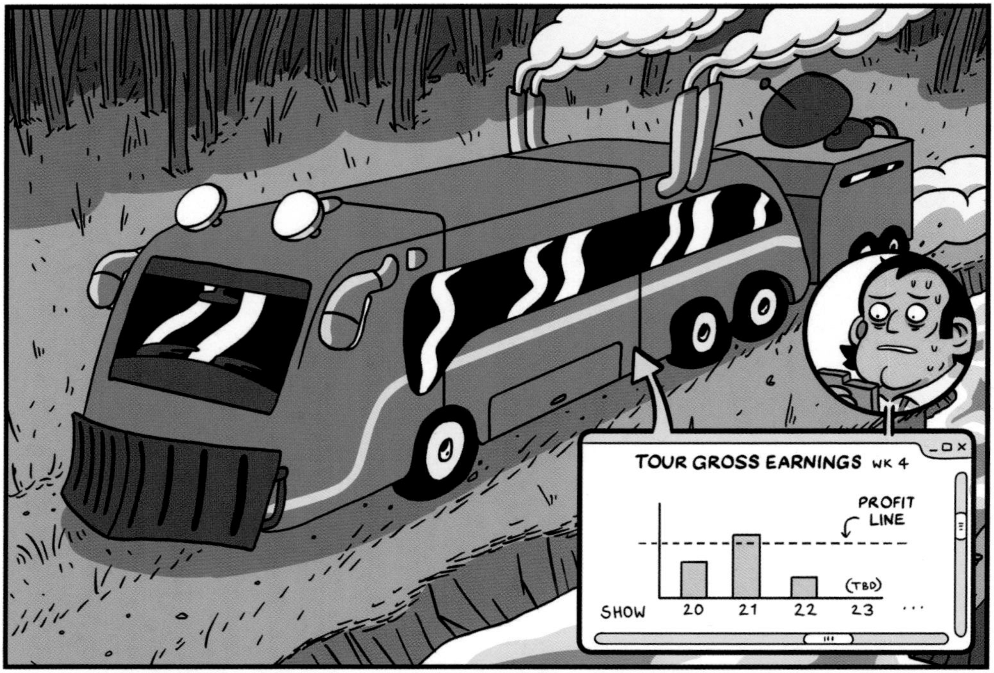
TOUR GROSS EARNINGS WK 4
PROFIT LINE
(TBD)
SHOW 20 21 22 23 ...

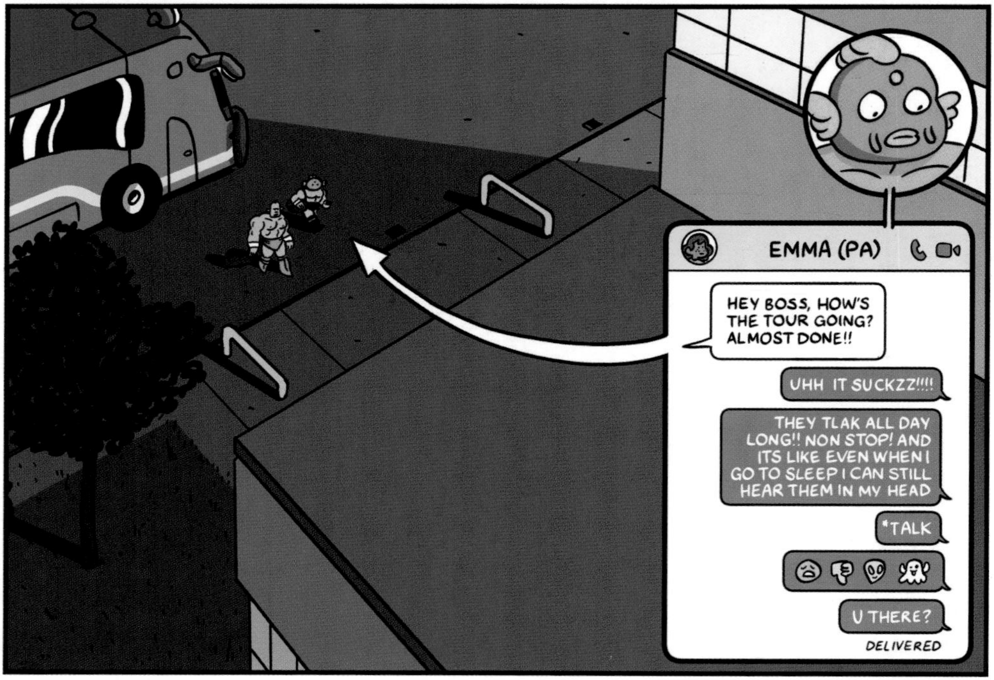
EMMA (PA)
HEY BOSS, HOW'S THE TOUR GOING? ALMOST DONE!!
UHH IT SUCKZZ!!!!
THEY TLAK ALL DAY LONG!! NON STOP! AND ITS LIKE EVEN WHEN I GO TO SLEEP I CAN STILL HEAR THEM IN MY HEAD
*TALK
U THERE?
DELIVERED

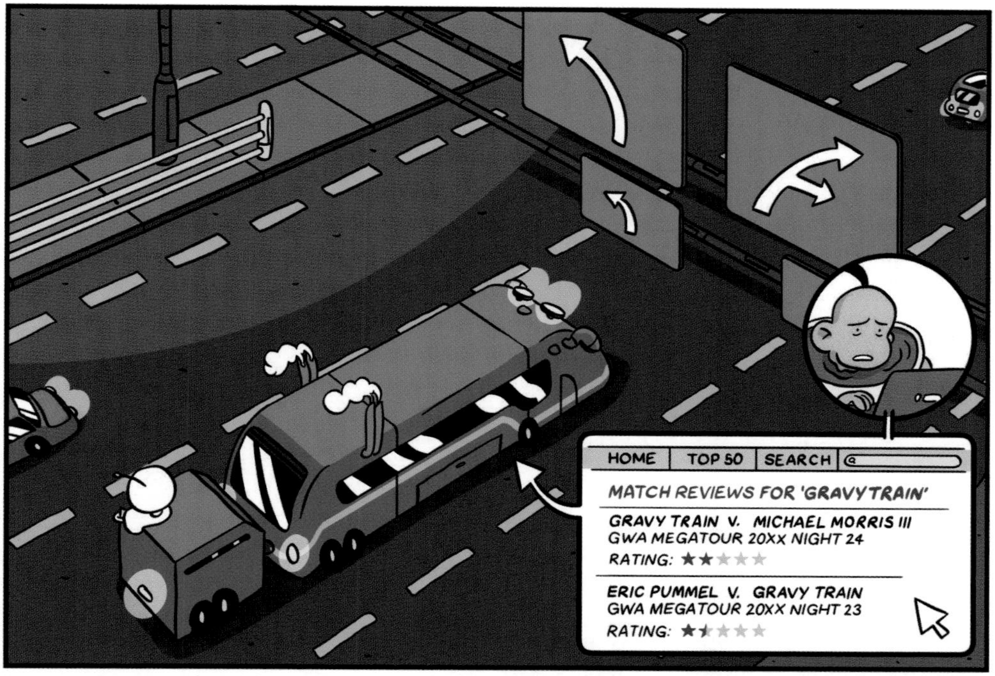
HOME
TOP 50
SEARCH
MATCH REVIEWS FOR 'GRAVY TRAIN'
GRAVY TRAIN V. MICHAEL MORRIS III
GWA MEGATOUR 20XX NIGHT 24
RATING:
ERIC PUMMEL V. GRAVY TRAIN
GWA MEGATOUR 20XX NIGHT 23
RATING:

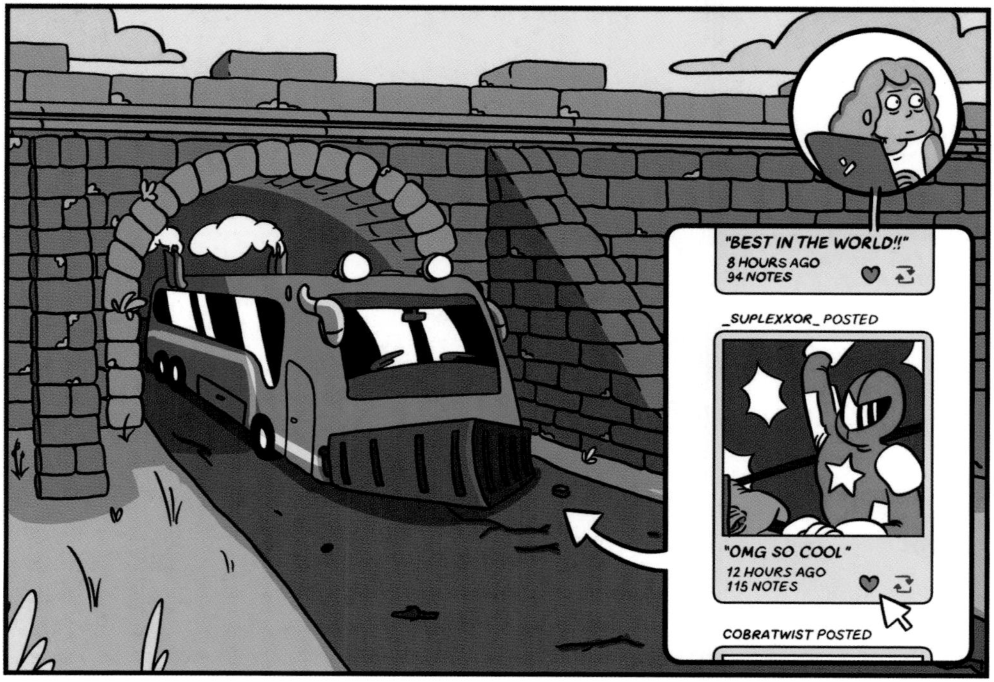
"BEST IN THE WORLD!!"
8 HOURS AGO
94 NOTES
SUPLEXXOR POSTED
"OMG SO COOL"
12 HOURS AGO
115 NOTES
COBRATWIST POSTED

DAY 27 *628 HOURS OF ROAD* *ROADSLOP SERVICE STOP*

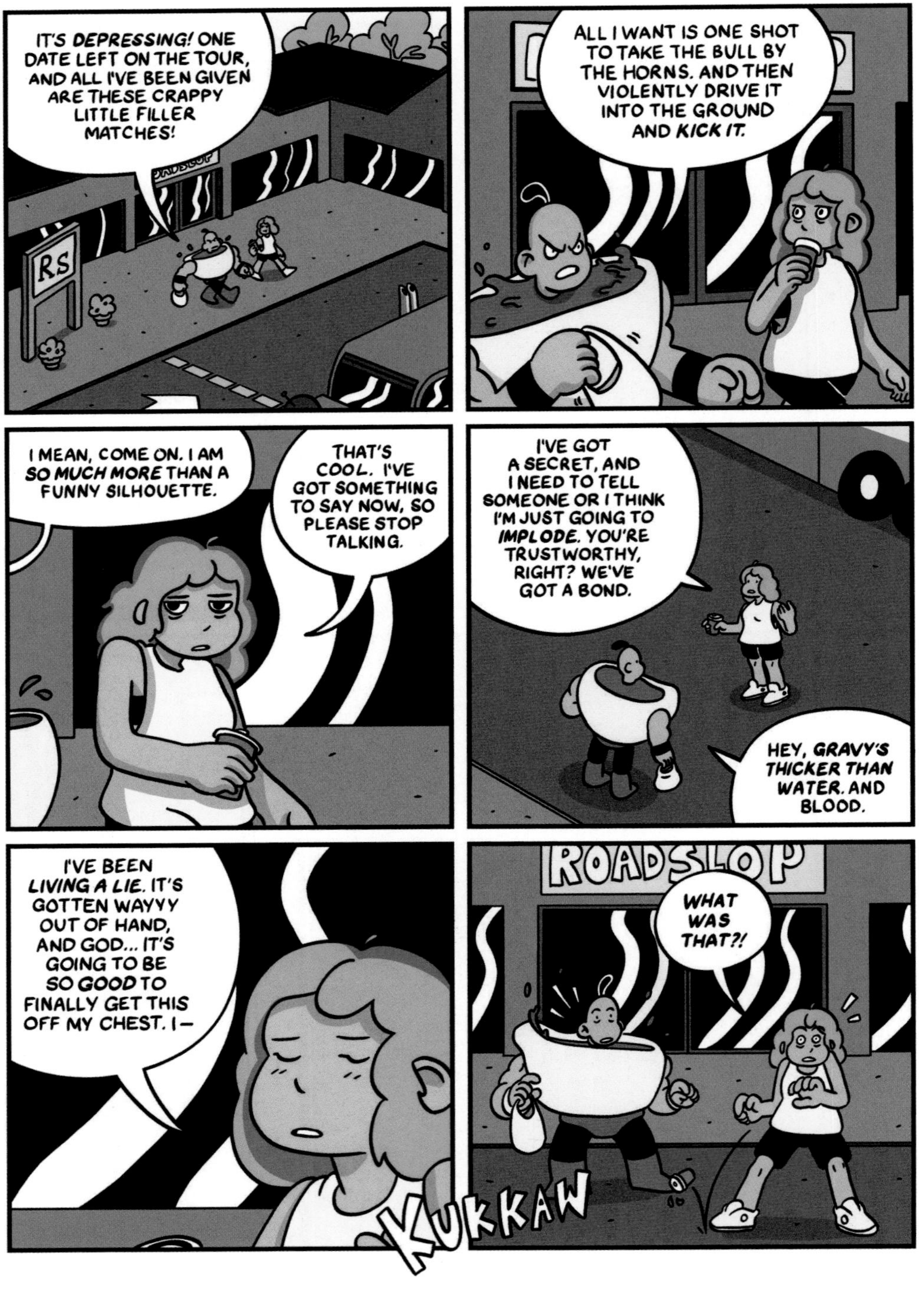

IT'S *DEPRESSING!* ONE DATE LEFT ON THE TOUR, AND ALL I'VE BEEN GIVEN ARE THESE CRAPPY LITTLE FILLER MATCHES!
ROADSLOP
RS
ALL I WANT IS ONE SHOT TO TAKE THE BULL BY THE HORNS. AND THEN VIOLENTLY DRIVE IT INTO THE GROUND AND *KICK IT.*
I MEAN, COME ON. I AM *SO MUCH MORE* THAN A FUNNY SILHOUETTE.
THAT'S *COOL.* I'VE GOT SOMETHING TO SAY NOW, SO PLEASE STOP TALKING.
I'VE GOT A SECRET, AND I NEED TO TELL SOMEONE OR I THINK I'M JUST GOING TO *IMPLODE.* YOU'RE TRUSTWORTHY, RIGHT? WE'VE GOT A BOND.
HEY, *GRAVY'S THICKER THAN WATER.* AND BLOOD.
I'VE BEEN *LIVING A LIE.* IT'S GOTTEN WAYYY OUT OF HAND, AND GOD... IT'S GOING TO BE SO *GOOD* TO FINALLY GET THIS OFF MY CHEST. I—
KUKKAW
ROADSLOP
WHAT WAS THAT?!

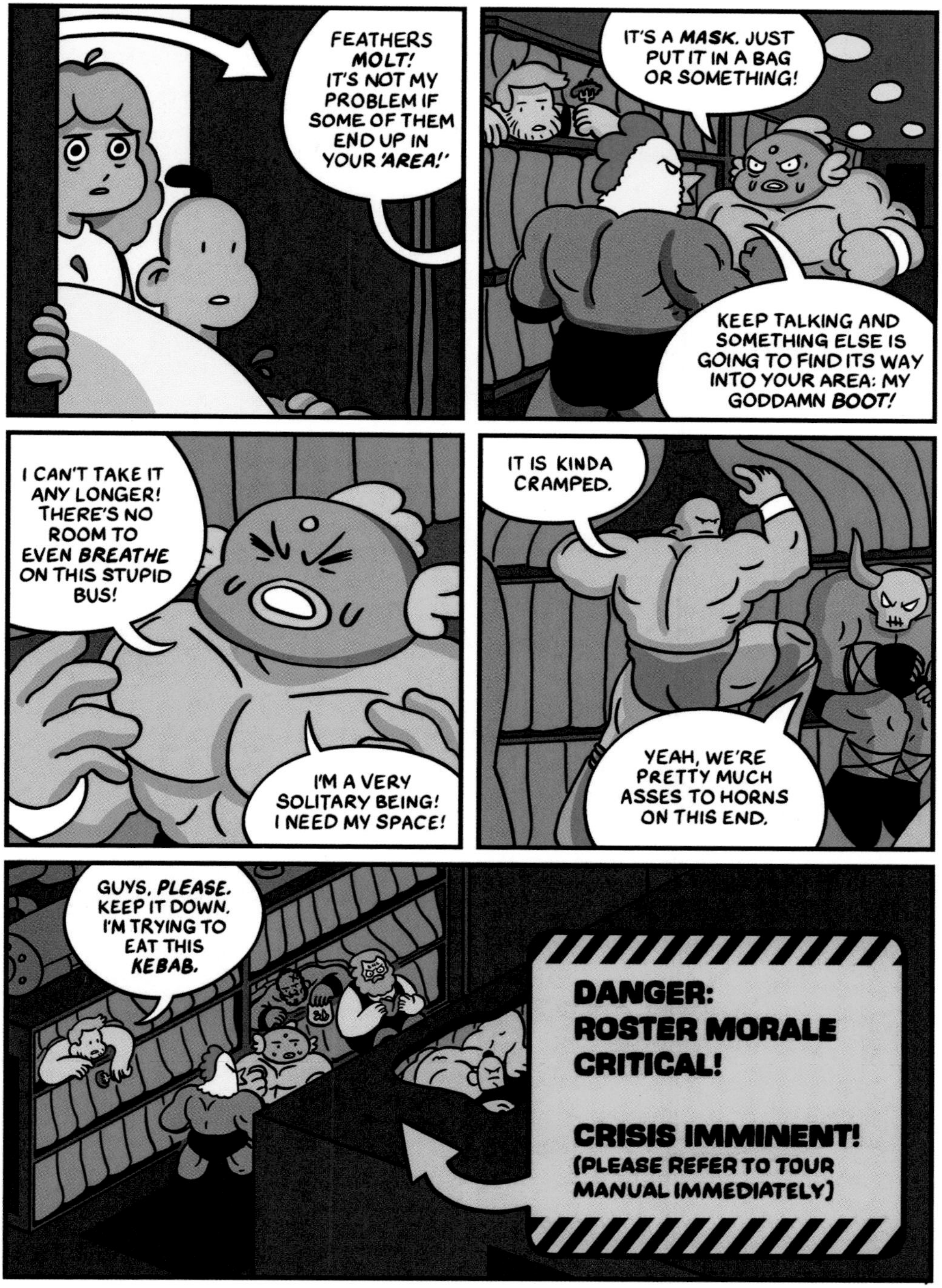
FEATHERS MOLT! IT'S NOT MY PROBLEM IF SOME OF THEM END UP IN YOUR 'AREA!'
IT'S A MASK. JUST PUT IT IN A BAG OR SOMETHING!
KEEP TALKING AND SOMETHING ELSE IS GOING TO FIND ITS WAY INTO YOUR AREA: MY GODDAMN BOOT!
I CAN'T TAKE IT ANY LONGER! THERE'S NO ROOM TO EVEN BREATHE ON THIS STUPID BUS!
I'M A VERY SOLITARY BEING! I NEED MY SPACE!
IT IS KINDA CRAMPED.
YEAH, WE'RE PRETTY MUCH ASSES TO HORNS ON THIS END.
GUYS, PLEASE. KEEP IT DOWN. I'M TRYING TO EAT THIS KEBAB.
DANGER: ROSTER MORALE CRITICAL!
CRISIS IMMINENT!
(PLEASE REFER TO TOUR MANUAL IMMEDIATELY)

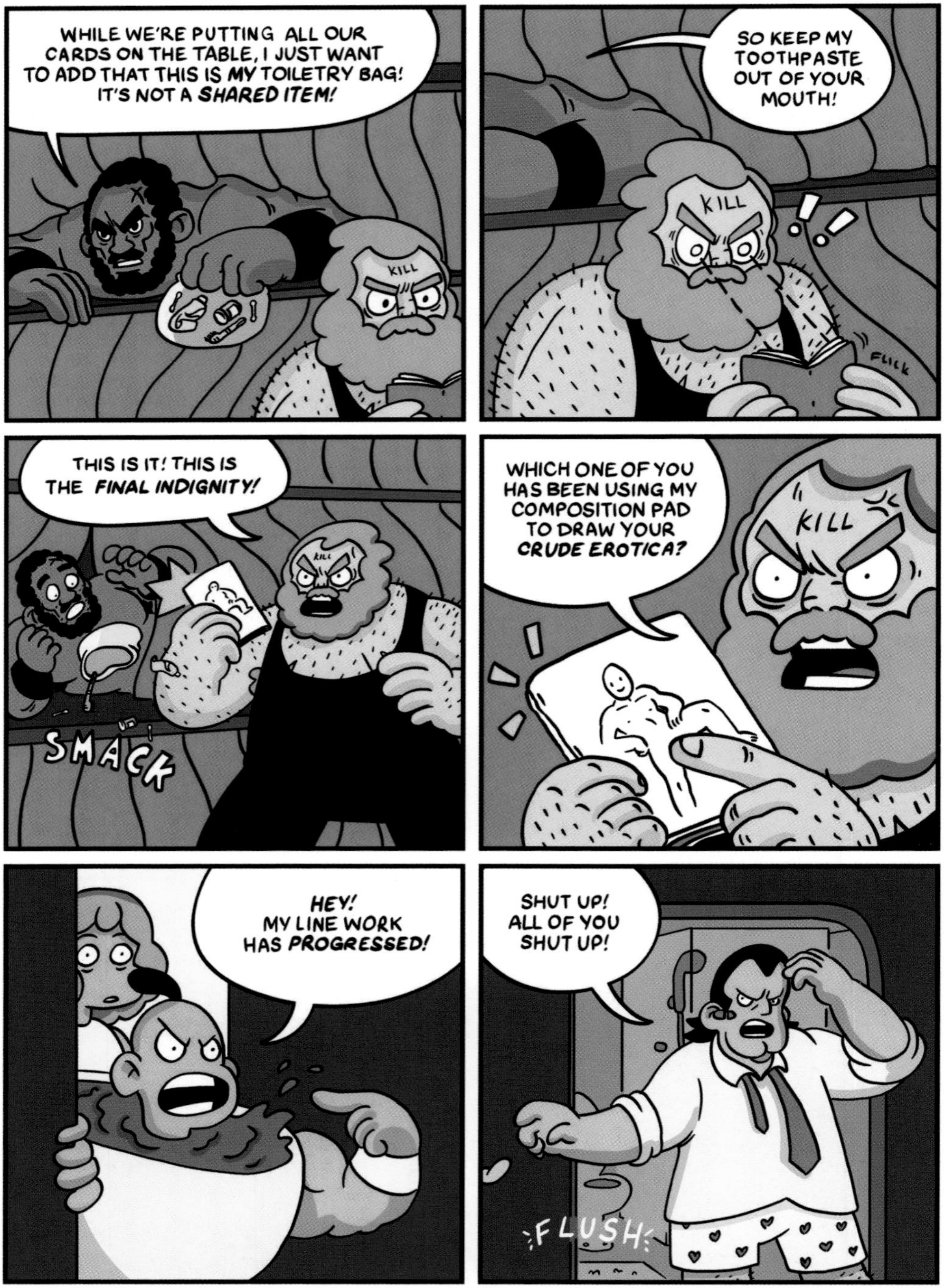
WHILE WE'RE PUTTING ALL OUR CARDS ON THE TABLE, I JUST WANT TO ADD THAT THIS IS MY TOILETRY BAG! IT'S NOT A SHARED ITEM!
SO KEEP MY TOOTHPASTE OUT OF YOUR MOUTH!
FLICK
THIS IS IT! THIS IS THE FINAL INDIGNITY!
SMACK
WHICH ONE OF YOU HAS BEEN USING MY COMPOSITION PAD TO DRAW YOUR CRUDE EROTICA?
HEY! MY LINE WORK HAS PROGRESSED!
SHUT UP! ALL OF YOU SHUT UP!
FLUSH

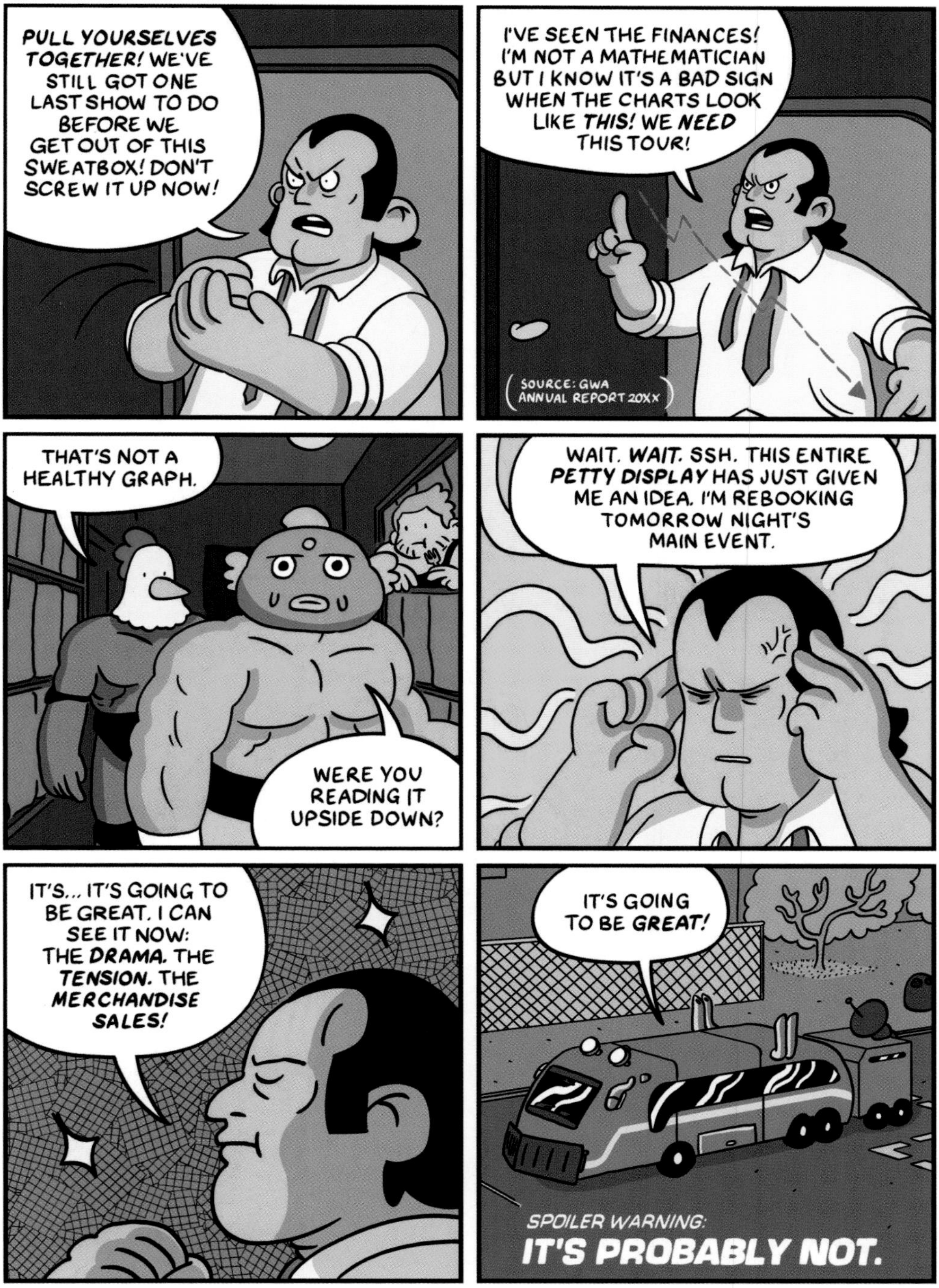
PULL YOURSELVES TOGETHER! WE'VE STILL GOT ONE LAST SHOW TO DO BEFORE WE GET OUT OF THIS SWEATBOX! DON'T SCREW IT UP NOW!
I'VE SEEN THE FINANCES! I'M NOT A MATHEMATICIAN BUT I KNOW IT'S A BAD SIGN WHEN THE CHARTS LOOK LIKE THIS! WE NEED THIS TOUR!
(SOURCE: GWA ANNUAL REPORT 20XX)
THAT'S NOT A HEALTHY GRAPH.
WERE YOU READING IT UPSIDE DOWN?
WAIT. WAIT. SSH. THIS ENTIRE PETTY DISPLAY HAS JUST GIVEN ME AN IDEA. I'M REBOOKING TOMORROW NIGHT'S MAIN EVENT.
IT'S... IT'S GOING TO BE GREAT. I CAN SEE IT NOW: THE DRAMA. THE TENSION. THE MERCHANDISE SALES!
IT'S GOING TO BE GREAT!
SPOILER WARNING:
IT'S PROBABLY NOT.

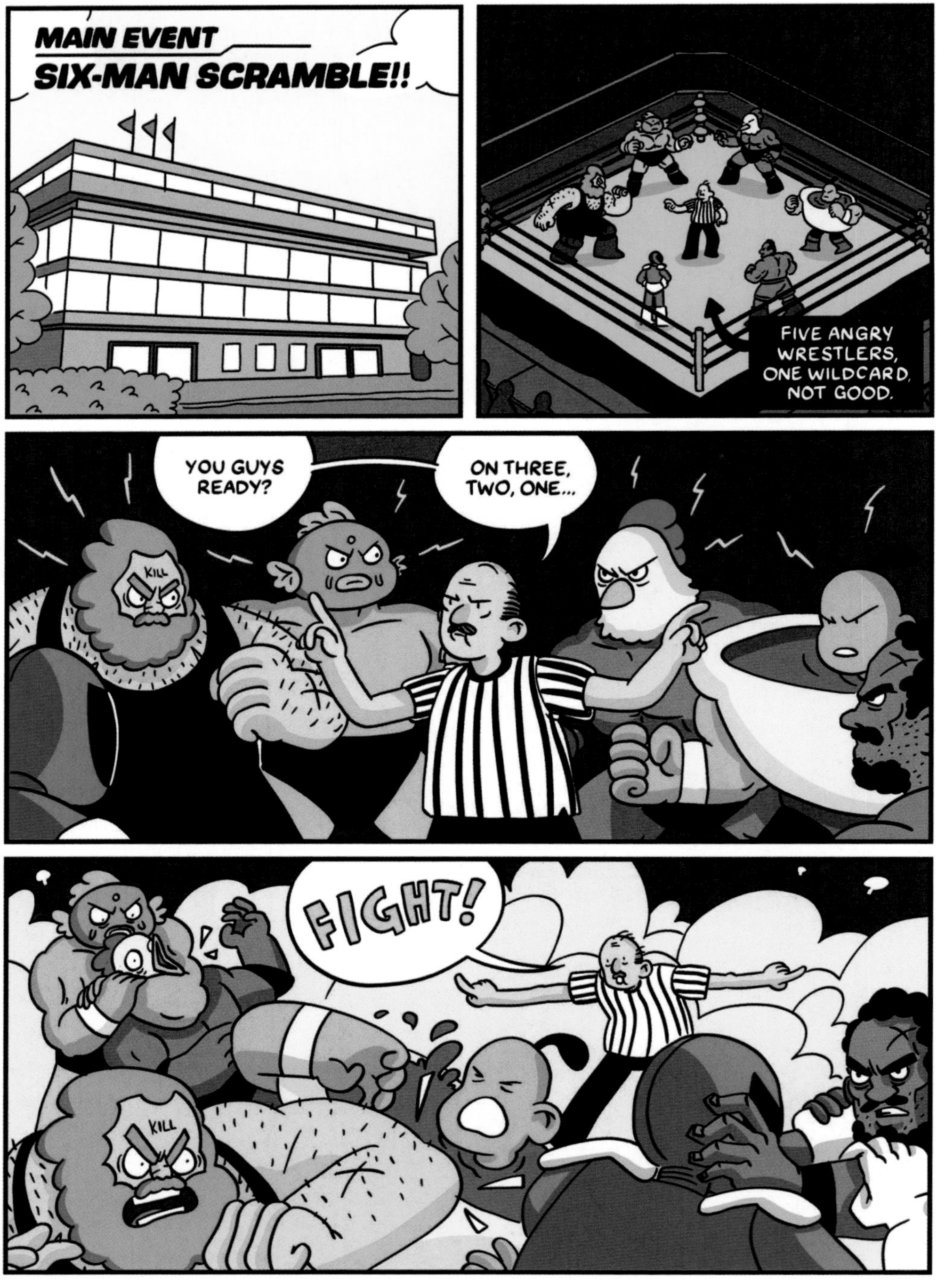
MAIN EVENT
SIX-MAN SCRAMBLE!!
FIVE ANGRY WRESTLERS, ONE WILDCARD. NOT GOOD.
YOU GUYS READY?
ON THREE, TWO, ONE...
KILL
FIGHT!
KILL

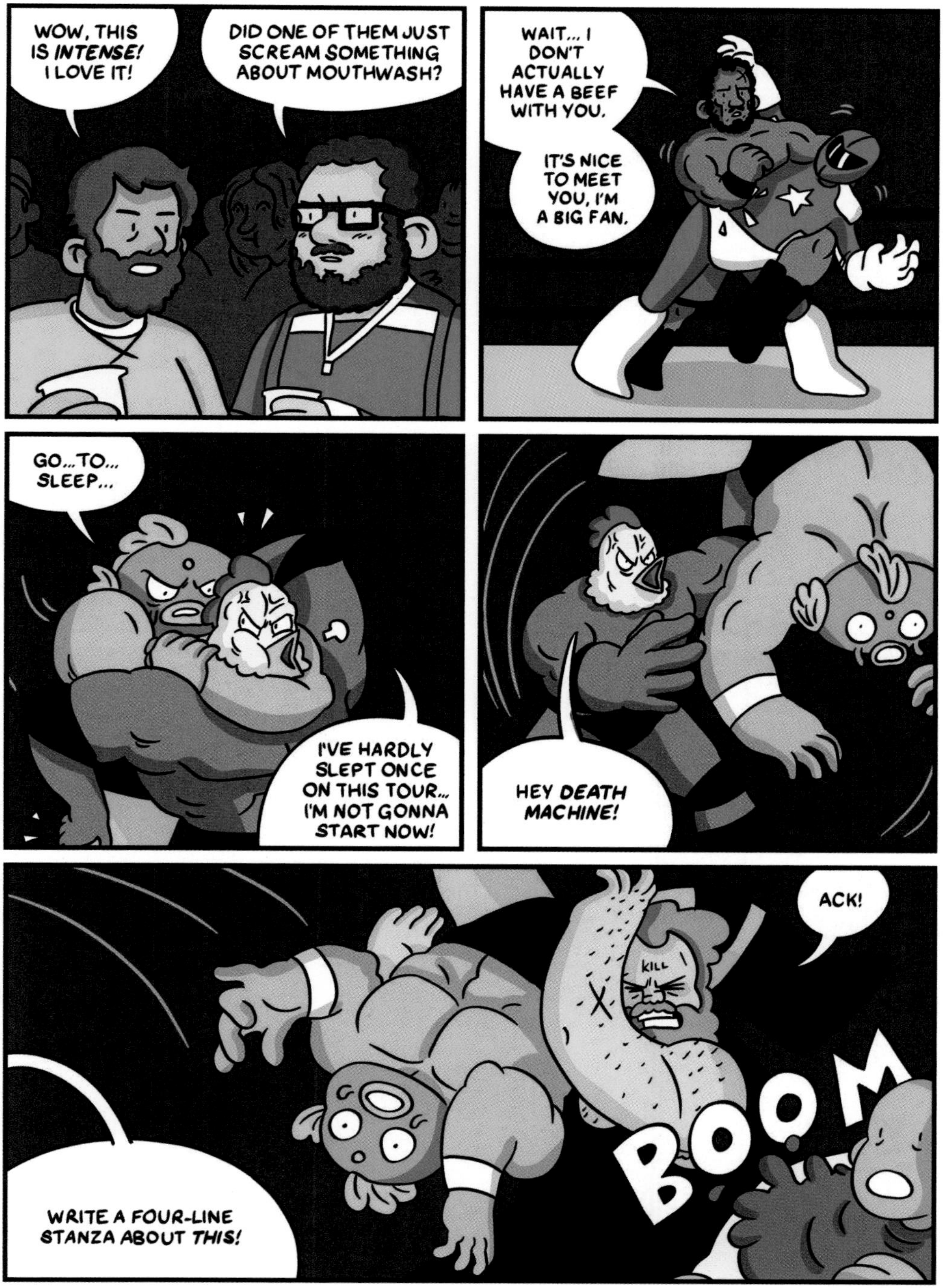
WOW, THIS IS *INTENSE!* I LOVE IT!
DID ONE OF THEM JUST SCREAM SOMETHING ABOUT MOUTHWASH?
WAIT... I DON'T ACTUALLY HAVE A BEEF WITH YOU.
IT'S NICE TO MEET YOU, I'M A BIG FAN.
GO...TO... SLEEP...
I'VE HARDLY SLEPT ONCE ON THIS TOUR... I'M NOT GONNA START NOW!
HEY *DEATH MACHINE!*
ACK!
KILL
BOOM
WRITE A FOUR-LINE STANZA ABOUT *THIS!*

DID YOU HEAR THAT? *GET A SHARPIE!* I WANT IT ON SHIRTS, HATS, BADGES — ANYTHING THAT CAN BE SOLD! *NOW!*

SQUUAAWK!

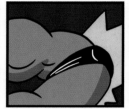

PANT
PANT
PANT

WHUMF

I THINK... WE LET THINGS GET A LITTLE OUT OF HAND.

I CAN'T EVEN REMEMBER ALL THE REASONS WHY I'M MAD.

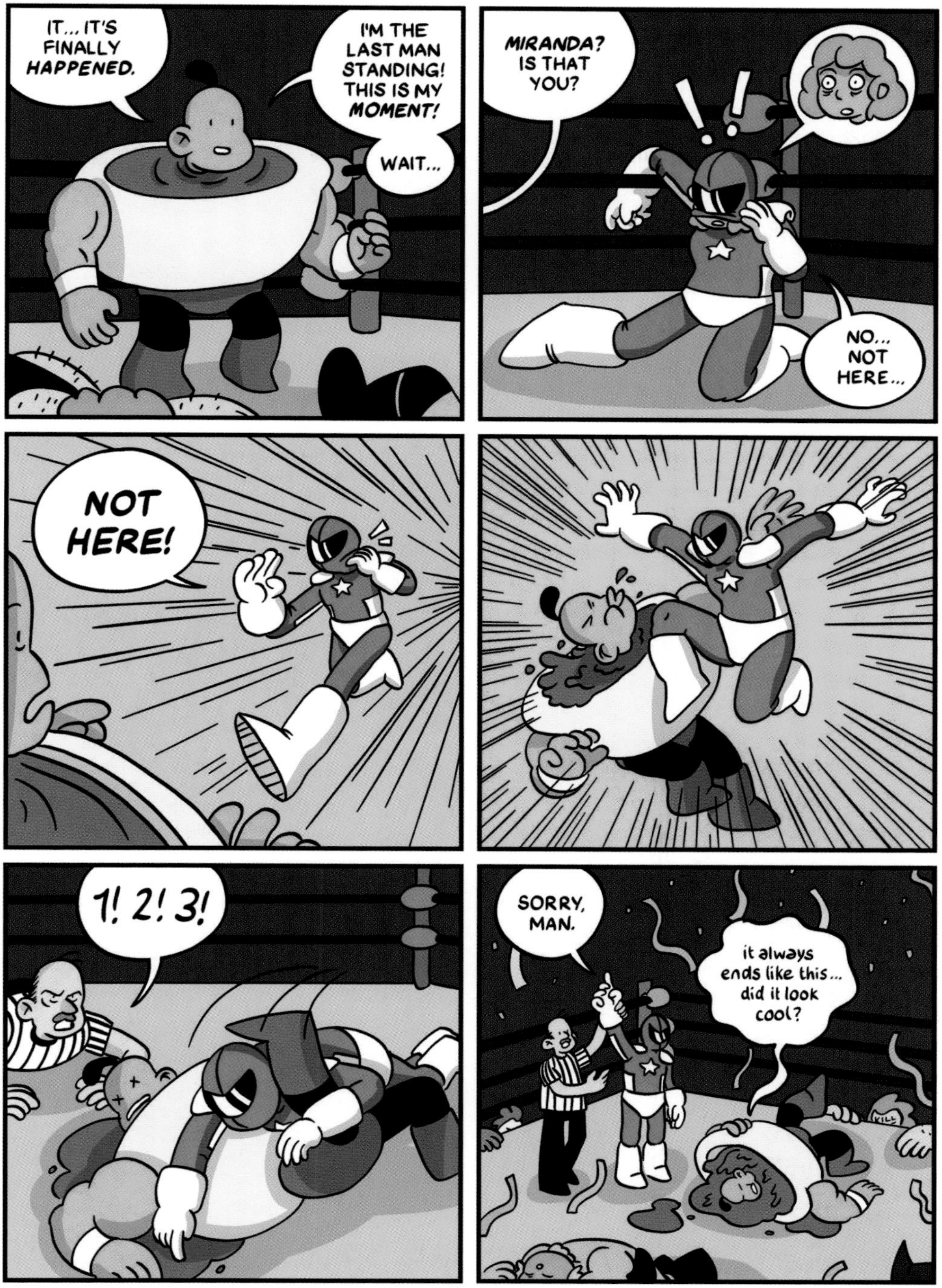
IT... IT'S FINALLY HAPPENED.
I'M THE LAST MAN STANDING! THIS IS MY MOMENT!
WAIT...
MIRANDA? IS THAT YOU?
!!
NO... NOT HERE...
NOT HERE!
1! 2! 3!
SORRY, MAN.
it always ends like this... did it look cool?

DAY 28 665 HOURS OF ROAD AZTECA PREMIUM MOTEL

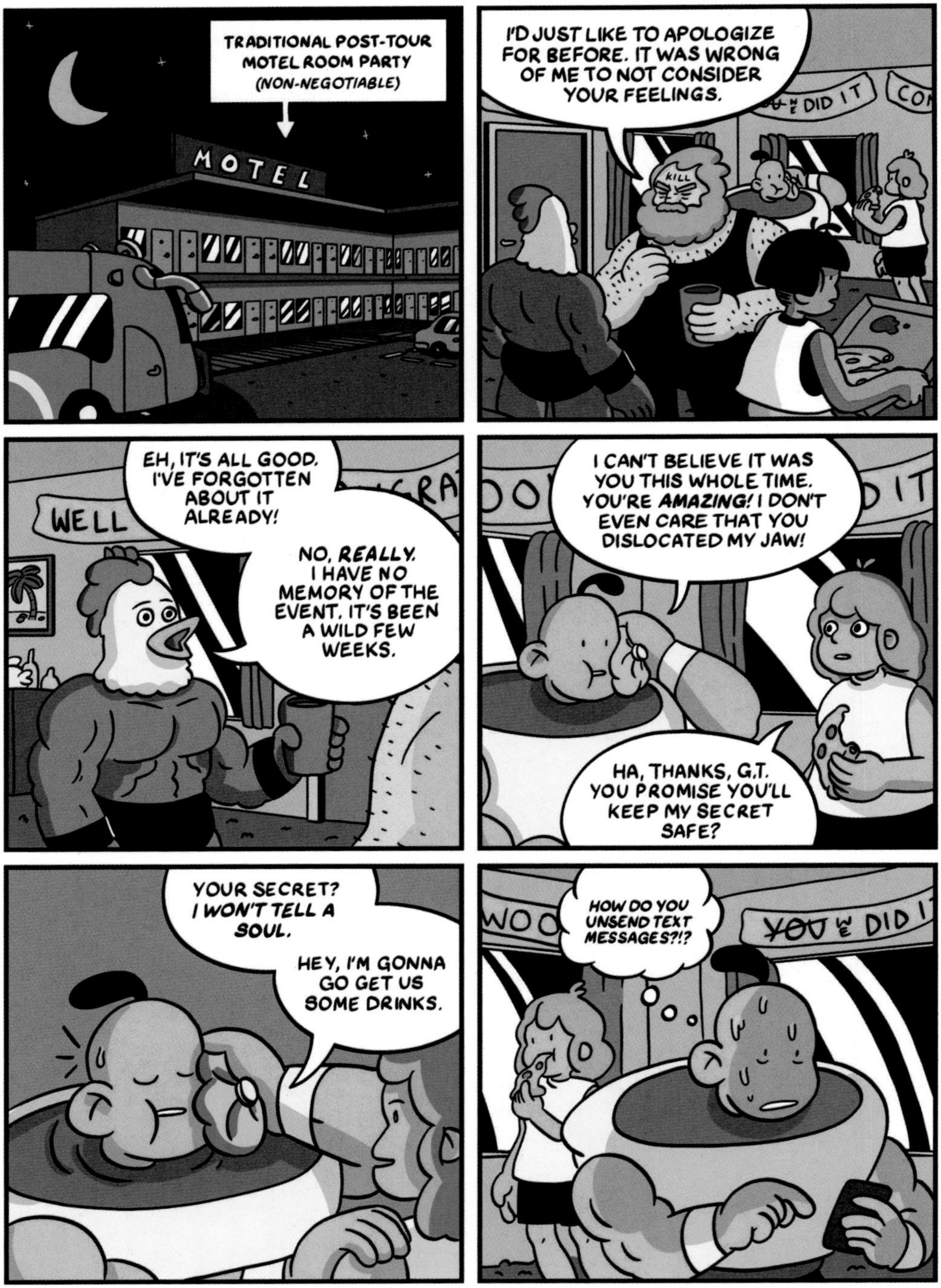
TRADITIONAL POST-TOUR MOTEL ROOM PARTY (NON-NEGOTIABLE)
MOTEL
I'D JUST LIKE TO APOLOGIZE FOR BEFORE. IT WAS WRONG OF ME TO NOT CONSIDER YOUR FEELINGS.
EH, IT'S ALL GOOD. I'VE FORGOTTEN ABOUT IT ALREADY!
NO, REALLY. I HAVE NO MEMORY OF THE EVENT. IT'S BEEN A WILD FEW WEEKS.
I CAN'T BELIEVE IT WAS YOU THIS WHOLE TIME. YOU'RE AMAZING! I DON'T EVEN CARE THAT YOU DISLOCATED MY JAW!
HA, THANKS, G.T. YOU PROMISE YOU'LL KEEP MY SECRET SAFE?
YOUR SECRET? I WON'T TELL A SOUL.
HEY, I'M GONNA GO GET US SOME DRINKS.
HOW DO YOU UNSEND TEXT MESSAGES?!?

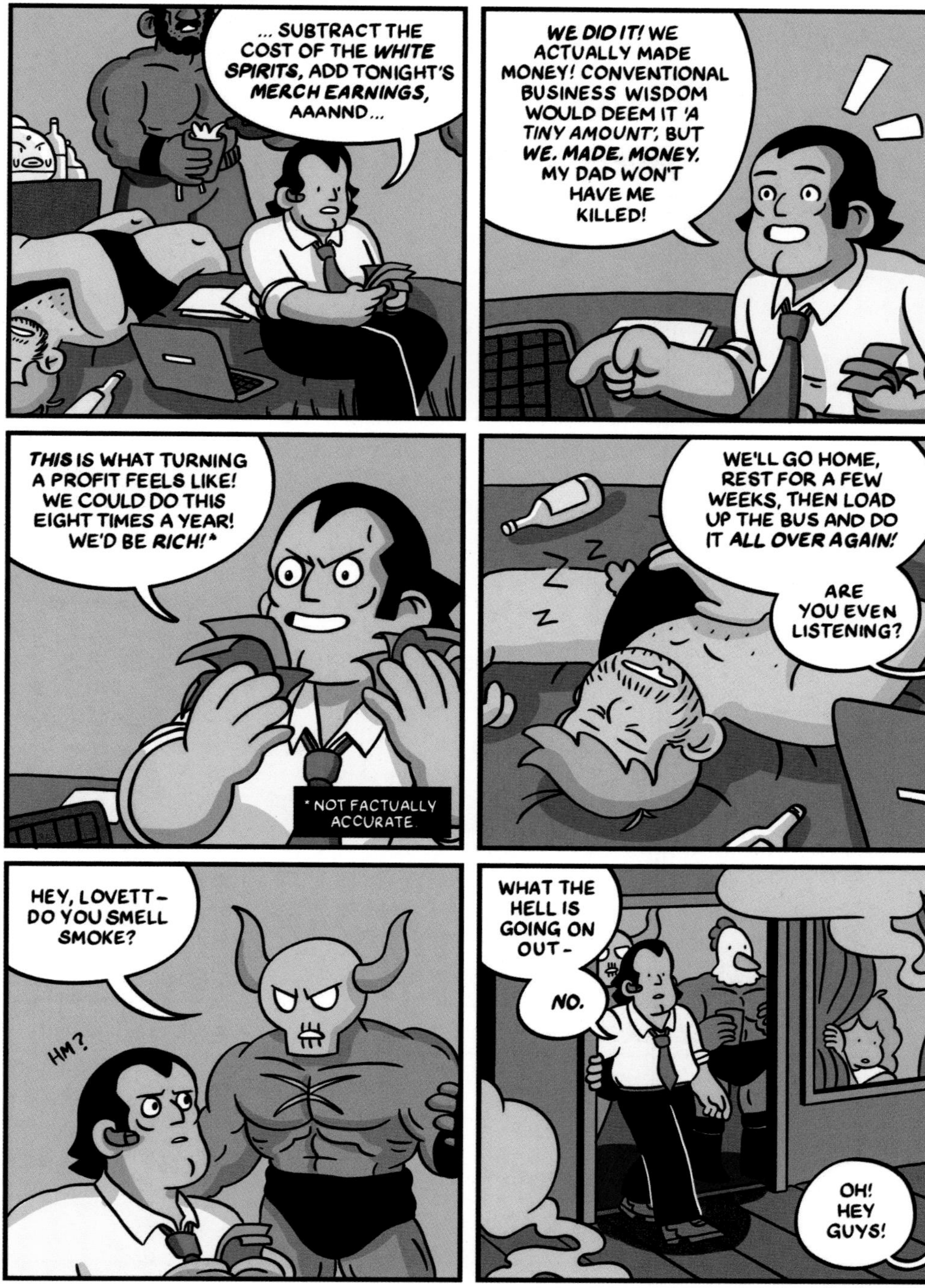
... SUBTRACT THE COST OF THE WHITE SPIRITS, ADD TONIGHT'S MERCH EARNINGS, AAANND...
WE DID IT! WE ACTUALLY MADE MONEY! CONVENTIONAL BUSINESS WISDOM WOULD DEEM IT 'A TINY AMOUNT', BUT WE. MADE. MONEY. MY DAD WON'T HAVE ME KILLED!
THIS IS WHAT TURNING A PROFIT FEELS LIKE! WE COULD DO THIS EIGHT TIMES A YEAR! WE'D BE RICH!*
* NOT FACTUALLY ACCURATE.
WE'LL GO HOME, REST FOR A FEW WEEKS, THEN LOAD UP THE BUS AND DO IT ALL OVER AGAIN!
Z Z Z Z
ARE YOU EVEN LISTENING?
HEY, LOVETT - DO YOU SMELL SMOKE?
HM?
WHAT THE HELL IS GOING ON OUT -
NO.
OH! HEY GUYS!

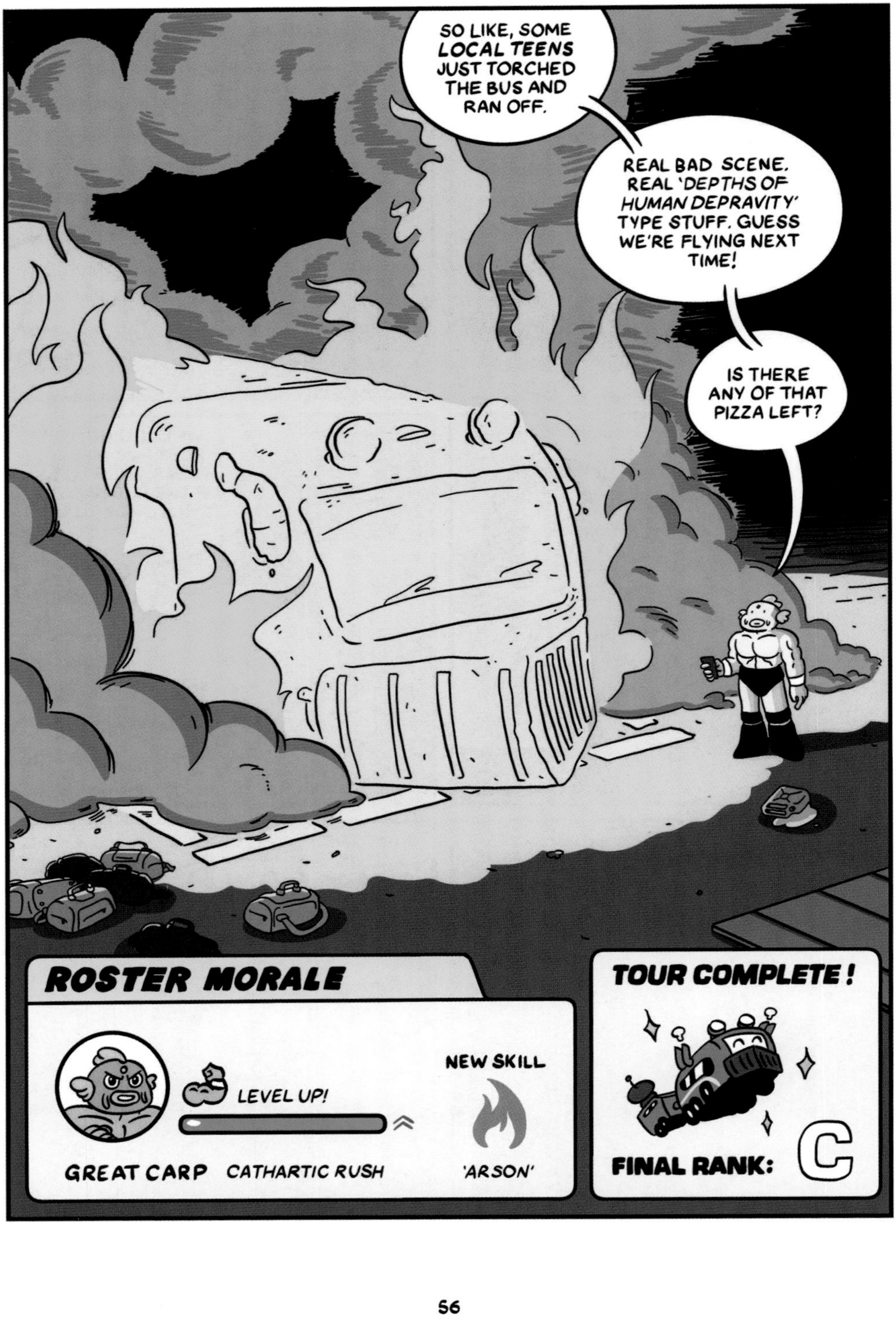
SO LIKE, SOME LOCAL TEENS JUST TORCHED THE BUS AND RAN OFF.
REAL BAD SCENE. REAL 'DEPTHS OF HUMAN DEPRAVITY' TYPE STUFF. GUESS WE'RE FLYING NEXT TIME!
IS THERE ANY OF THAT PIZZA LEFT?
ROSTER MORALE
LEVEL UP!
GREAT CARP
CATHARTIC RUSH
NEW SKILL
'ARSON'
TOUR COMPLETE!
FINAL RANK: C

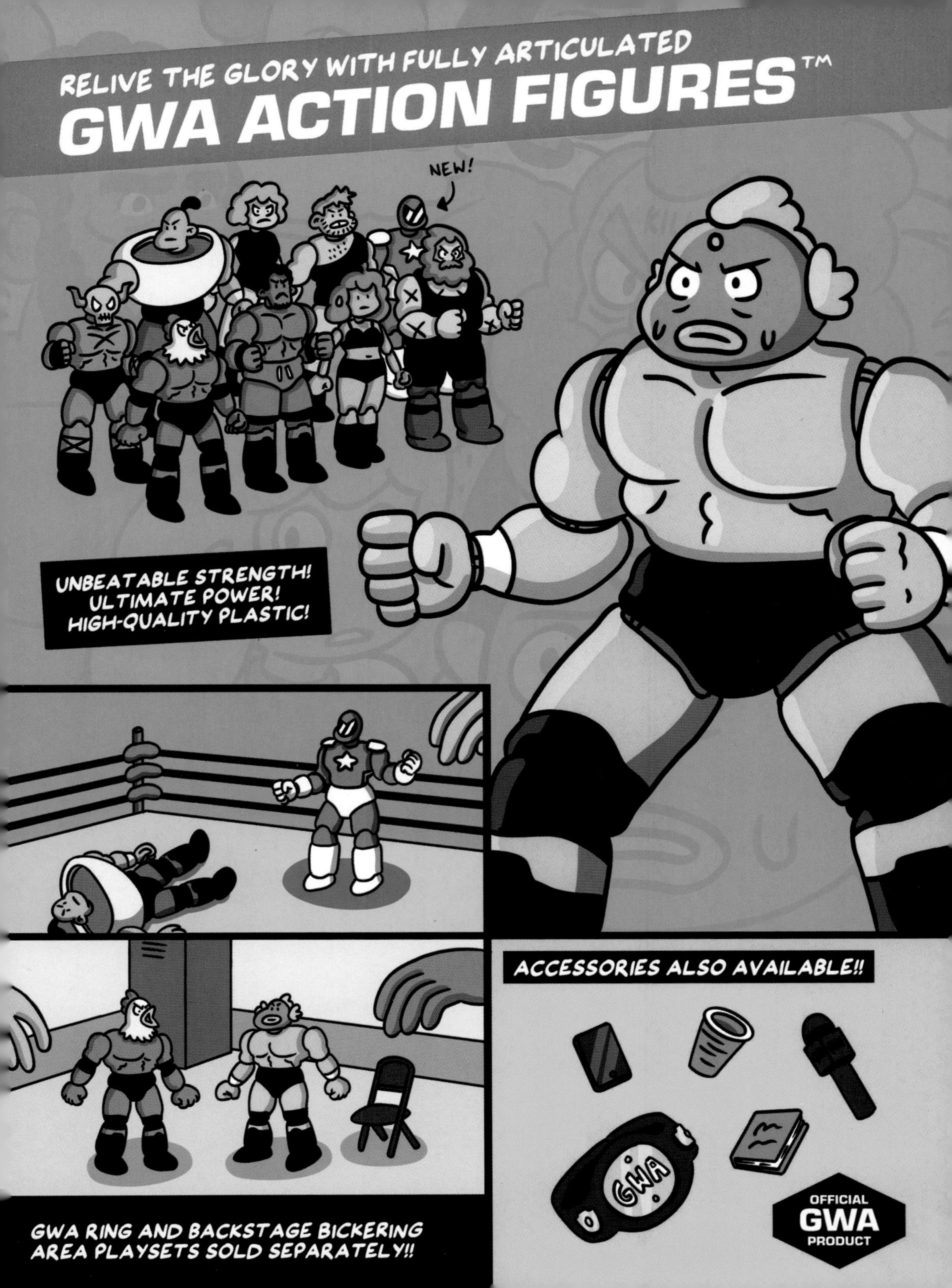

RELIVE THE GLORY WITH FULLY ARTICULATED
GWA ACTION FIGURES™
NEW!
UNBEATABLE STRENGTH!
ULTIMATE POWER!
HIGH-QUALITY PLASTIC!
ACCESSORIES ALSO AVAILABLE!!
GWA
OFFICIAL GWA PRODUCT
GWA RING AND BACKSTAGE BICKERING
AREA PLAYSETS SOLD SEPARATELY!!

CHAPTER THREE

GLORIOUS WRESTLING APOCALYPSE

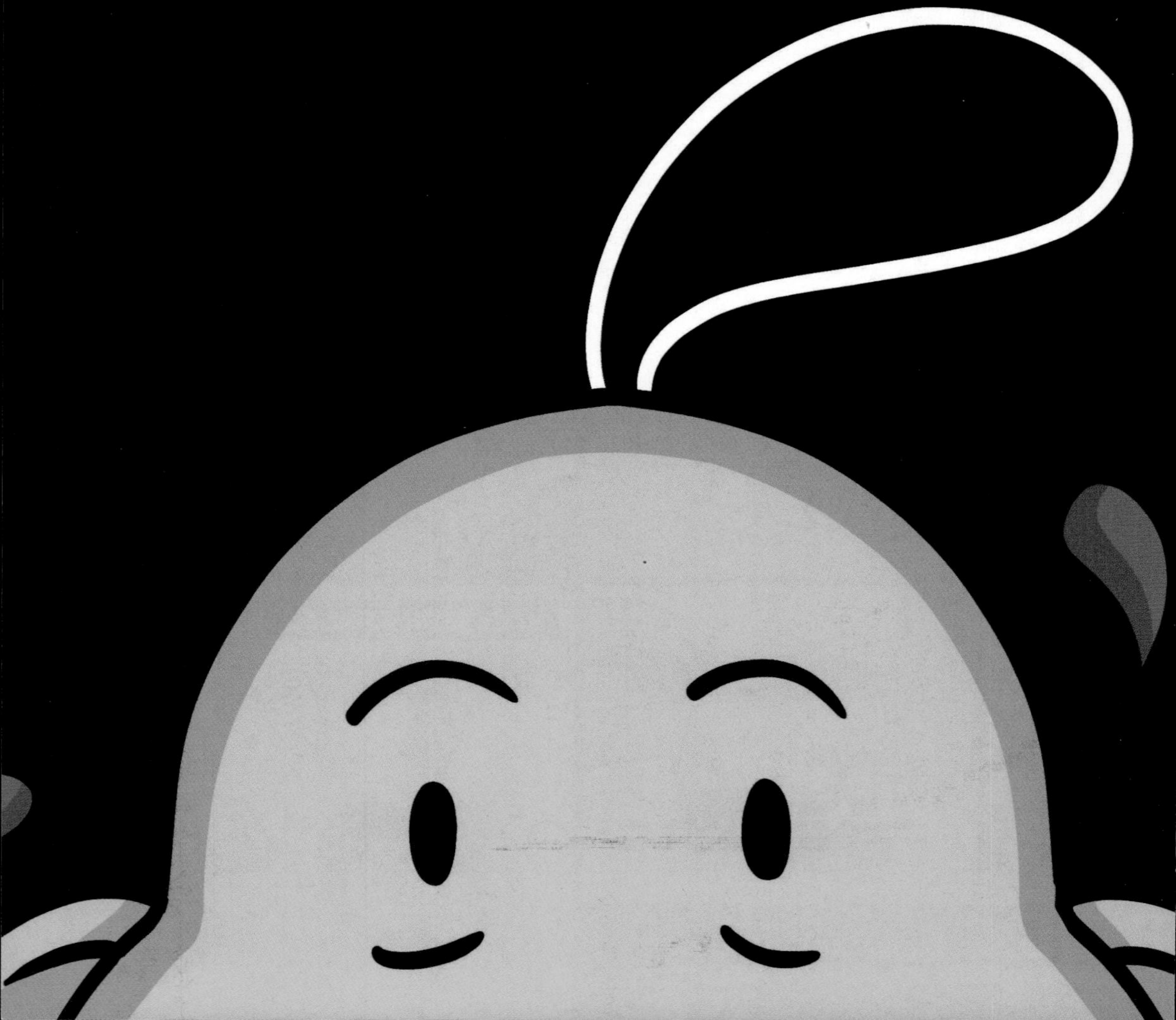

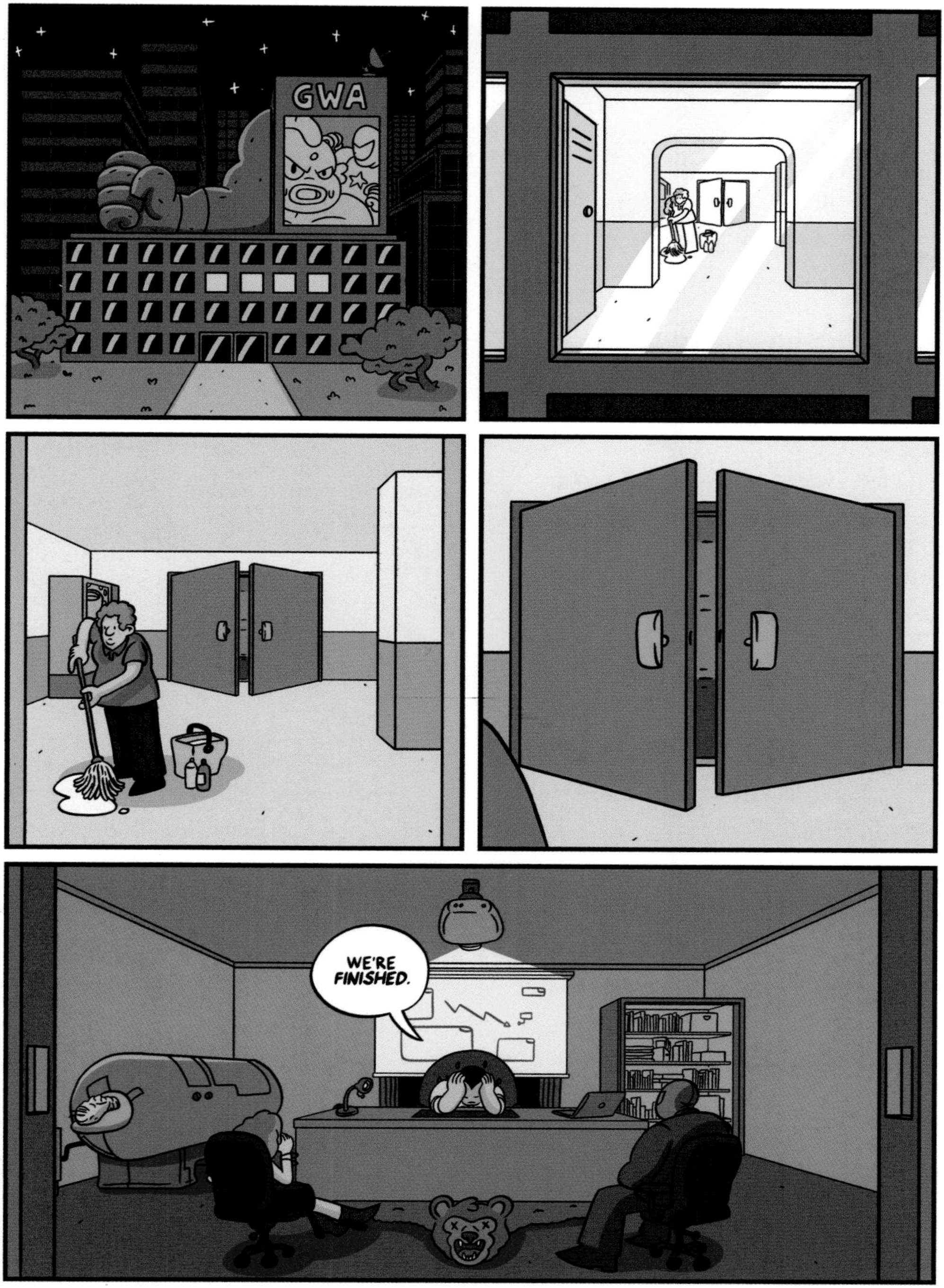
GWA
WE'RE FINISHED.

I'M DONE. I'M OUT OF OPTIONS. NOTHING WE DO IS GOING TO PULL US OUT OF THIS HOLE.

RICKY LOVETT JR., ACTING CEO

-204.607

CAN'T WE JUST DELETE THIS GODDAMN *INFOSHEET?* KNOWING HOW SCREWED I AM DOWN TO ONE DECIMAL PLACE IS BAD ENOUGH – I DON'T NEED *THREE.*

YOU CANNOT SIMPLY SEND YOUR FAILURES TO THE *RECYCLE BIN,* LOVETT.

I JUST WANNA SAY: YOU'RE LIKE, LITERALLY *KILLING* DAD.

EL FINANCIERO ÁNGEL INVESTOR

VICKY LOVETT CHIEF OF PUBLIC RELATIONS

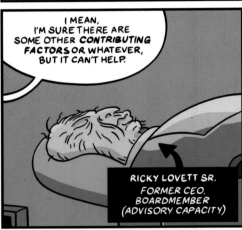

I MEAN, I'M SURE THERE ARE SOME OTHER *CONTRIBUTING FACTORS* OR WHATEVER, BUT IT CAN'T HELP.

RICKY LOVETT SR., FORMER CEO, BOARDMEMBER (ADVISORY CAPACITY)

THERE HAS TO BE SOMETHING ON THERE WE CAN CUT DOWN ON. WHAT ABOUT 'DRUGS & MISC.'?

TRUST ME, I'VE GOTTEN THAT AS LOW AS IT'LL GO.

DON'T EVEN TALK TO ME ABOUT THE 'MISC.'

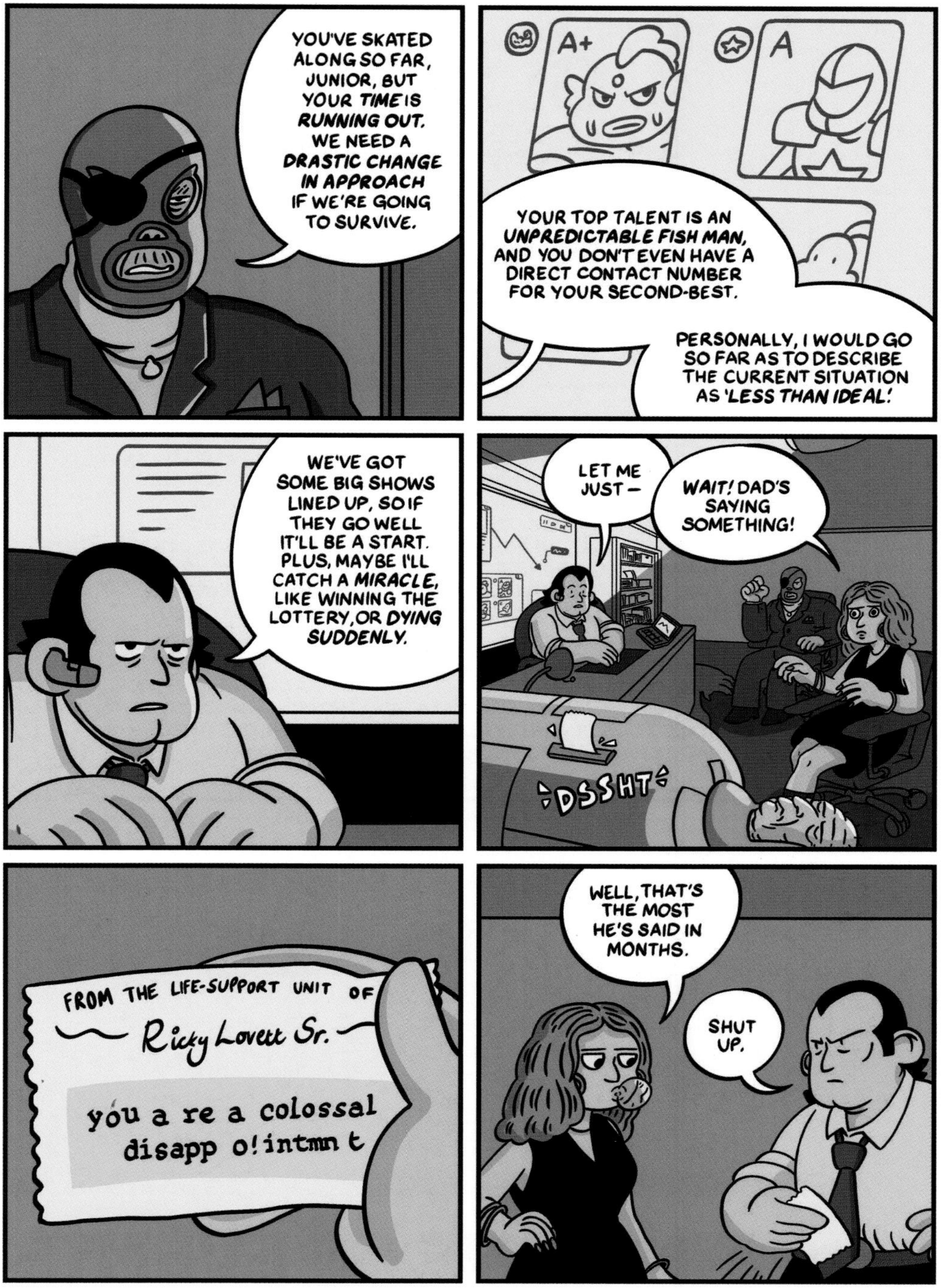
YOU'VE SKATED ALONG SO FAR, JUNIOR, BUT YOUR *TIME* IS *RUNNING OUT.* WE NEED A *DRASTIC CHANGE IN APPROACH* IF WE'RE GOING TO SURVIVE.
A+
A
YOUR TOP TALENT IS AN *UNPREDICTABLE FISH MAN,* AND YOU DON'T EVEN HAVE A DIRECT CONTACT NUMBER FOR YOUR SECOND-BEST.
PERSONALLY, I WOULD GO SO FAR AS TO DESCRIBE THE CURRENT SITUATION AS '*LESS THAN IDEAL!*'
WE'VE GOT SOME BIG SHOWS LINED UP, SO IF THEY GO WELL IT'LL BE A START. PLUS, MAYBE I'LL CATCH A *MIRACLE,* LIKE WINNING THE LOTTERY, OR *DYING SUDDENLY.*
LET ME JUST —
WAIT! DAD'S SAYING SOMETHING!
DSSHT
FROM THE LIFE-SUPPORT UNIT OF
Ricky Lovett Sr.
you a re a colossal disapp o!intmn t
WELL, THAT'S THE MOST HE'S SAID IN MONTHS.
SHUT UP.

GLORIOUS WRESTLING  APOCALYPSE

THIS DOCUMENT CHARTS A MOMENT IN TIME THAT IS POPULARLY DUBBED THE MOST TURBULENT IN GWA HISTORY. THOUGH THIS STANDPOINT IS SOMEWHAT VALID, IT IS THE OPINION OF THIS AUTHOR THAT THOSE THAT HOLD THIS VIEW WOULD DO WELL TO REMEMBER THE ARMED UPRISING THAT TOOK PLACE ONLY THREE DECADES PRIOR, AS WELL AS THE EVENTS OF 'BLACK TUESDAY' — A FREAK INCIDENT SO COMPLEX AND BAFFLING THAT NO MERE GRAPH OR DIAGRAM WOULD BEGIN TO DO IT JUSTICE.

REGARDLESS, THIS PERIOD SERVED AS A CATALYST FOR GREAT CHANGE WITHIN THE ORGANIZATION, AND IS NOT WITHOUT NOTE. IT ALSO CONVENIENTLY LENDS ITSELF TO BOTH THE TIMELINE AND 24-PAGE COMIC MEDIUMS, SO: HAPPY READING!!

 1

 2

 3

▶▶ TIMELINE OF EVENTS

OR THE FALL OF THE
GLORIOUS WRESTLING ALLIANCE
(AN HISTORICAL ACCOUNT IN COMICS FORM)

KEY PLAYERS  IN NO PARTICULAR ORDER

GREAT CARP	HYPER MASK	MIRANDA FURY
COMPANY ACE, REIGNING CHAMPION, FISH HEAD.	MYSTERIOUS MASKED SUPERSTAR.	STAR OF WOMEN'S DIVISION. SECRETLY HYPER MASK!
DEATH MACHINE	GRAVY TRAIN	RICKY LOVETT JR.
WILD BEAST, FRUSTRATED POET.	LITERALLY MADE OF GRAVY.	UNDER-QUALIFIED CEO. PANICKED.

1- BUSINESS AS USUAL; 2 - OPPORTUNITIES IN MERCHANDISING; 3 - THE ART LIFE;

4 - NEW GIMMICK, SAME GRAVY TRAIN; 5 - MASKED NO MORE;

6 - A FUTILE GAMBIT; 7 - APOCALYPSE

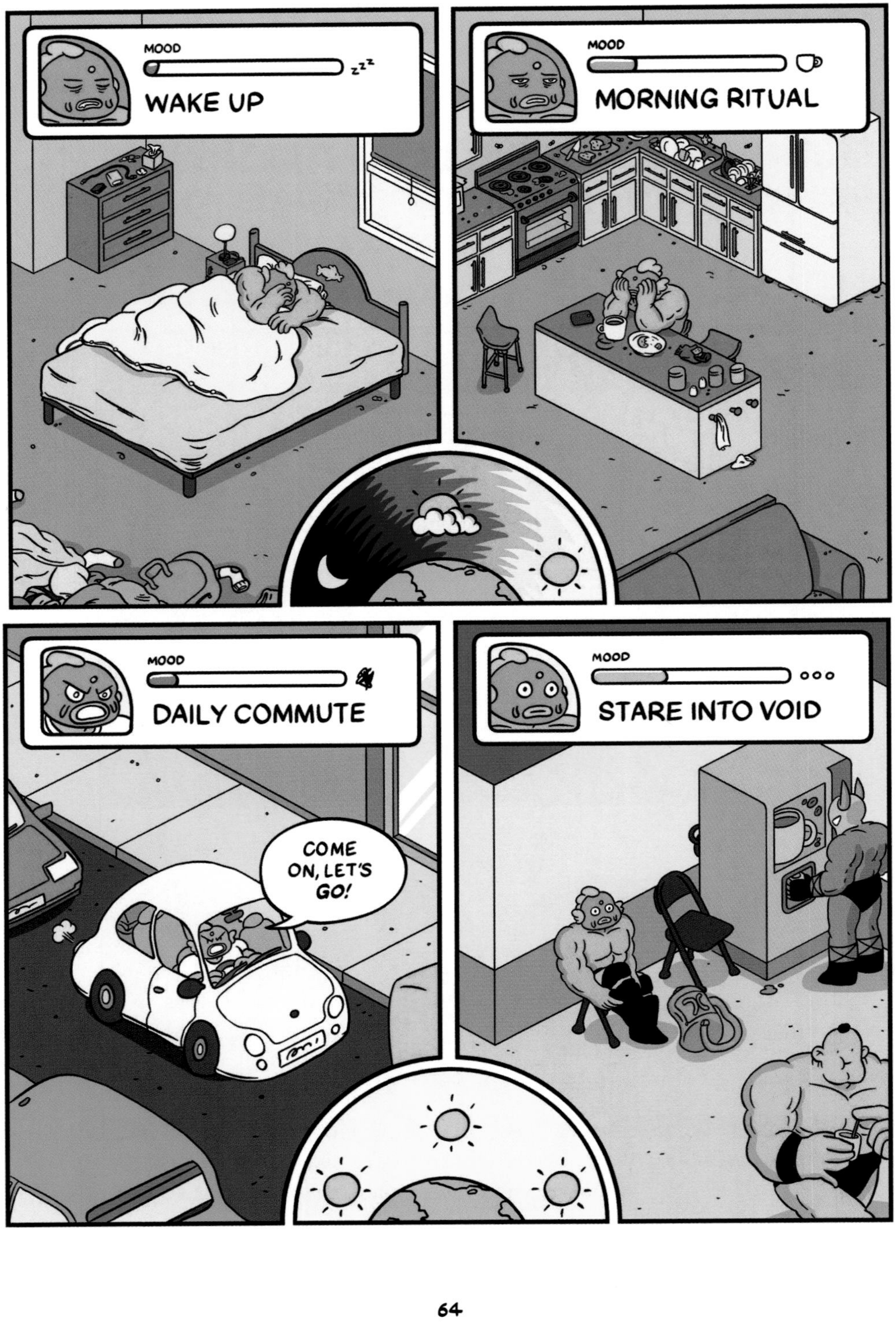
MOOD
WAKE UP
MOOD
MORNING RITUAL
MOOD
DAILY COMMUTE
COME ON, LET'S GO!
MOOD
STARE INTO VOID

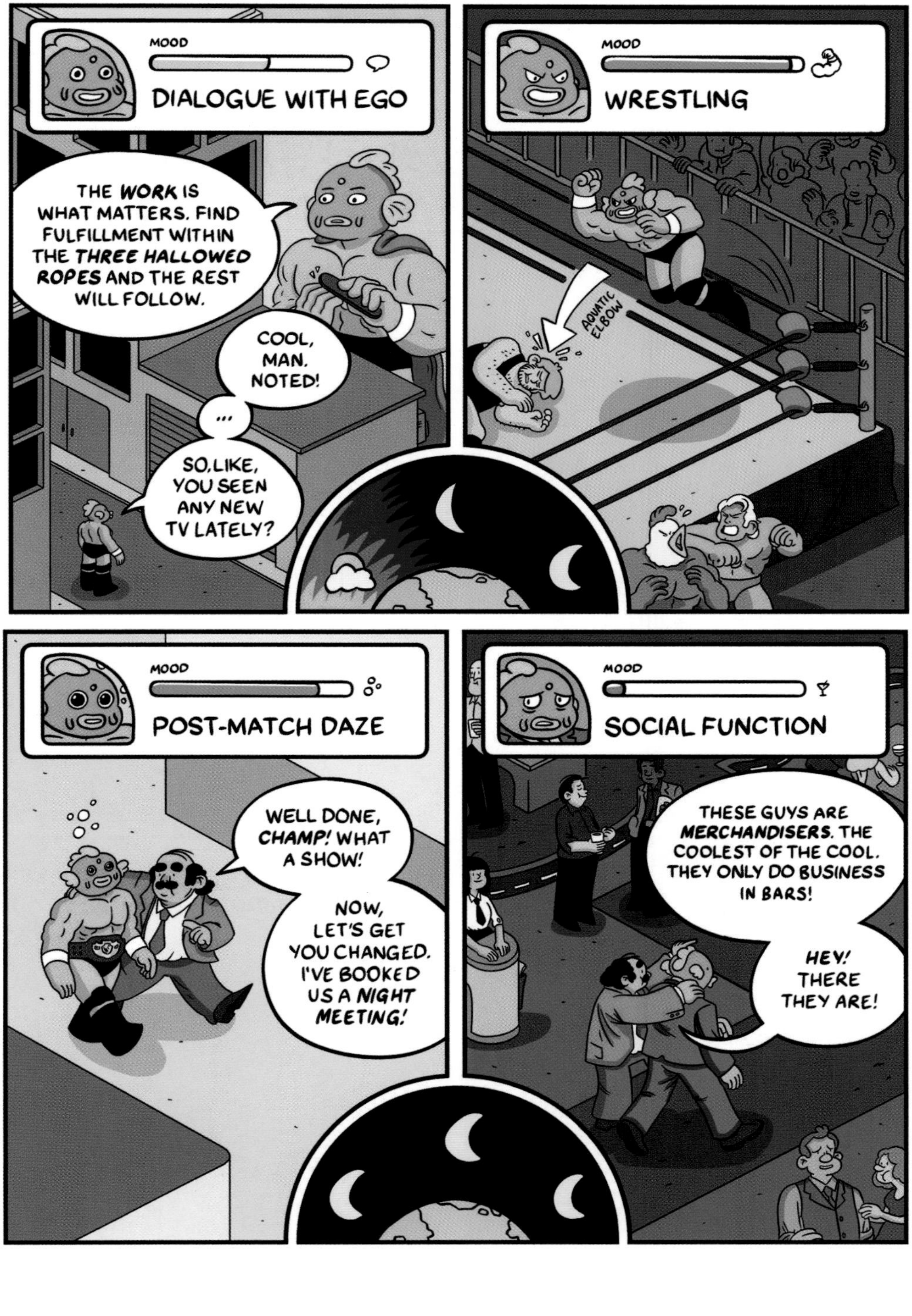
MOOD
DIALOGUE WITH EGO
THE WORK IS WHAT MATTERS. FIND FULFILLMENT WITHIN THE THREE HALLOWED ROPES AND THE REST WILL FOLLOW.
COOL, MAN. NOTED!
...
SO, LIKE, YOU SEEN ANY NEW TV LATELY?
MOOD
WRESTLING
AQUATIC ELBOW
MOOD
POST-MATCH DAZE
WELL DONE, CHAMP! WHAT A SHOW!
NOW, LET'S GET YOU CHANGED. I'VE BOOKED US A NIGHT MEETING!
MOOD
SOCIAL FUNCTION
THESE GUYS ARE MERCHANDISERS. THE COOLEST OF THE COOL. THEY ONLY DO BUSINESS IN BARS!
HEY! THERE THEY ARE!

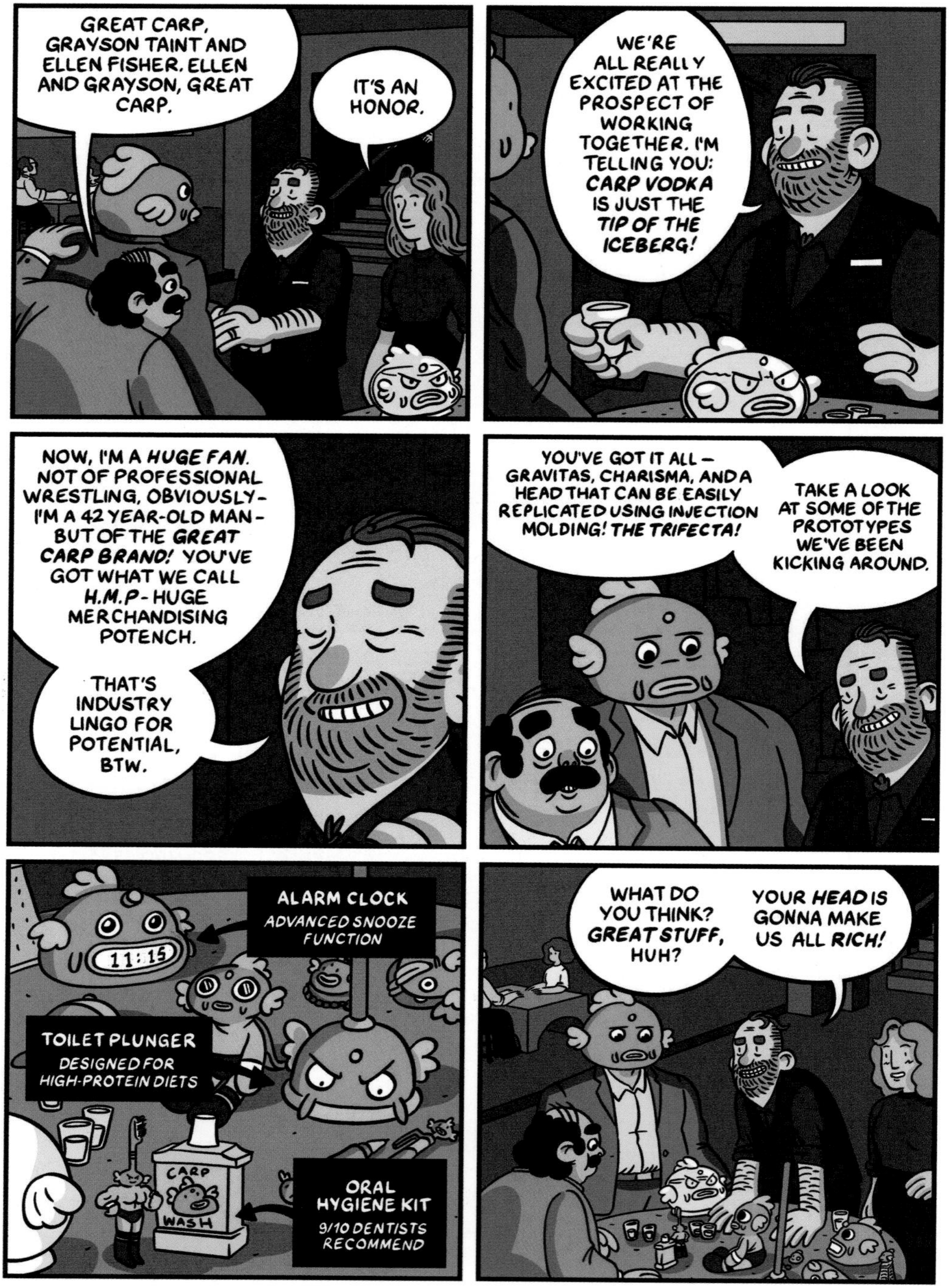
GREAT CARP, GRAYSON TAINT AND ELLEN FISHER. ELLEN AND GRAYSON, GREAT CARP.
IT'S AN HONOR.
WE'RE ALL REALLY EXCITED AT THE PROSPECT OF WORKING TOGETHER. I'M TELLING YOU: CARP VODKA IS JUST THE TIP OF THE ICEBERG!
NOW, I'M A HUGE FAN. NOT OF PROFESSIONAL WRESTLING, OBVIOUSLY- I'M A 42 YEAR-OLD MAN- BUT OF THE GREAT CARP BRAND! YOU'VE GOT WHAT WE CALL H.M.P- HUGE MERCHANDISING POTENCH.
THAT'S INDUSTRY LINGO FOR POTENTIAL, BTW.
YOU'VE GOT IT ALL- GRAVITAS, CHARISMA, AND A HEAD THAT CAN BE EASILY REPLICATED USING INJECTION MOLDING! THE TRIFECTA!
TAKE A LOOK AT SOME OF THE PROTOTYPES WE'VE BEEN KICKING AROUND.
ALARM CLOCK
ADVANCED SNOOZE FUNCTION
11:15
TOILET PLUNGER
DESIGNED FOR HIGH-PROTEIN DIETS
CARP WASH
ORAL HYGIENE KIT
9/10 DENTISTS RECOMMEND
WHAT DO YOU THINK? GREAT STUFF, HUH?
YOUR HEAD IS GONNA MAKE US ALL RICH!

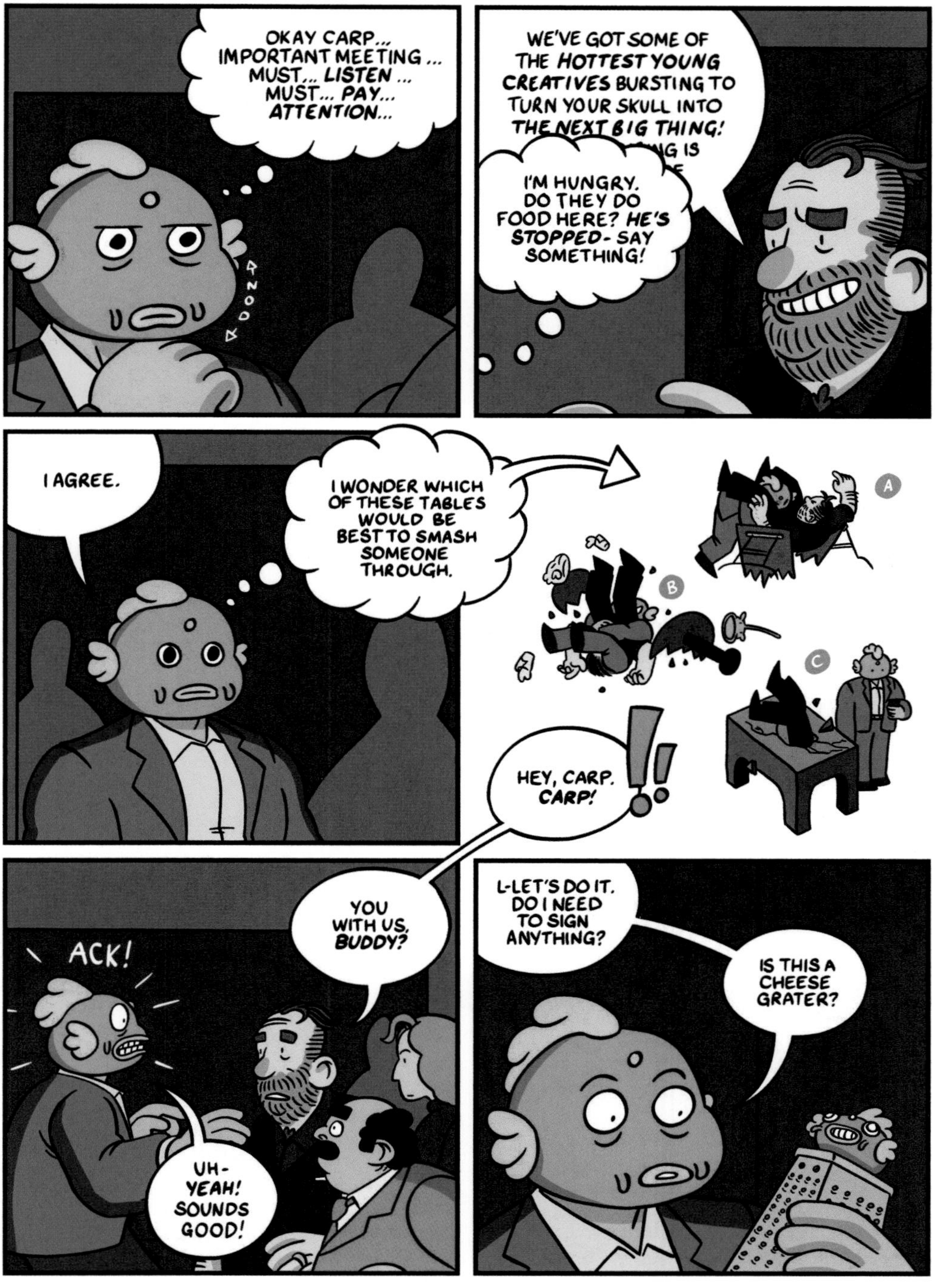

OKAY CARP... IMPORTANT MEETING... MUST... LISTEN... MUST... PAY... ATTENTION...
WE'VE GOT SOME OF THE HOTTEST YOUNG CREATIVES BURSTING TO TURN YOUR SKULL INTO THE NEXT BIG THING!
I'M HUNGRY. DO THEY DO FOOD HERE? HE'S STOPPED- SAY SOMETHING!
I AGREE.
I WONDER WHICH OF THESE TABLES WOULD BE BEST TO SMASH SOMEONE THROUGH.
A
B
C
HEY, CARP. CARP!
ACK!
YOU WITH US, BUDDY?
UH- YEAH! SOUNDS GOOD!
L-LET'S DO IT. DO I NEED TO SIGN ANYTHING?
IS THIS A CHEESE GRATER?

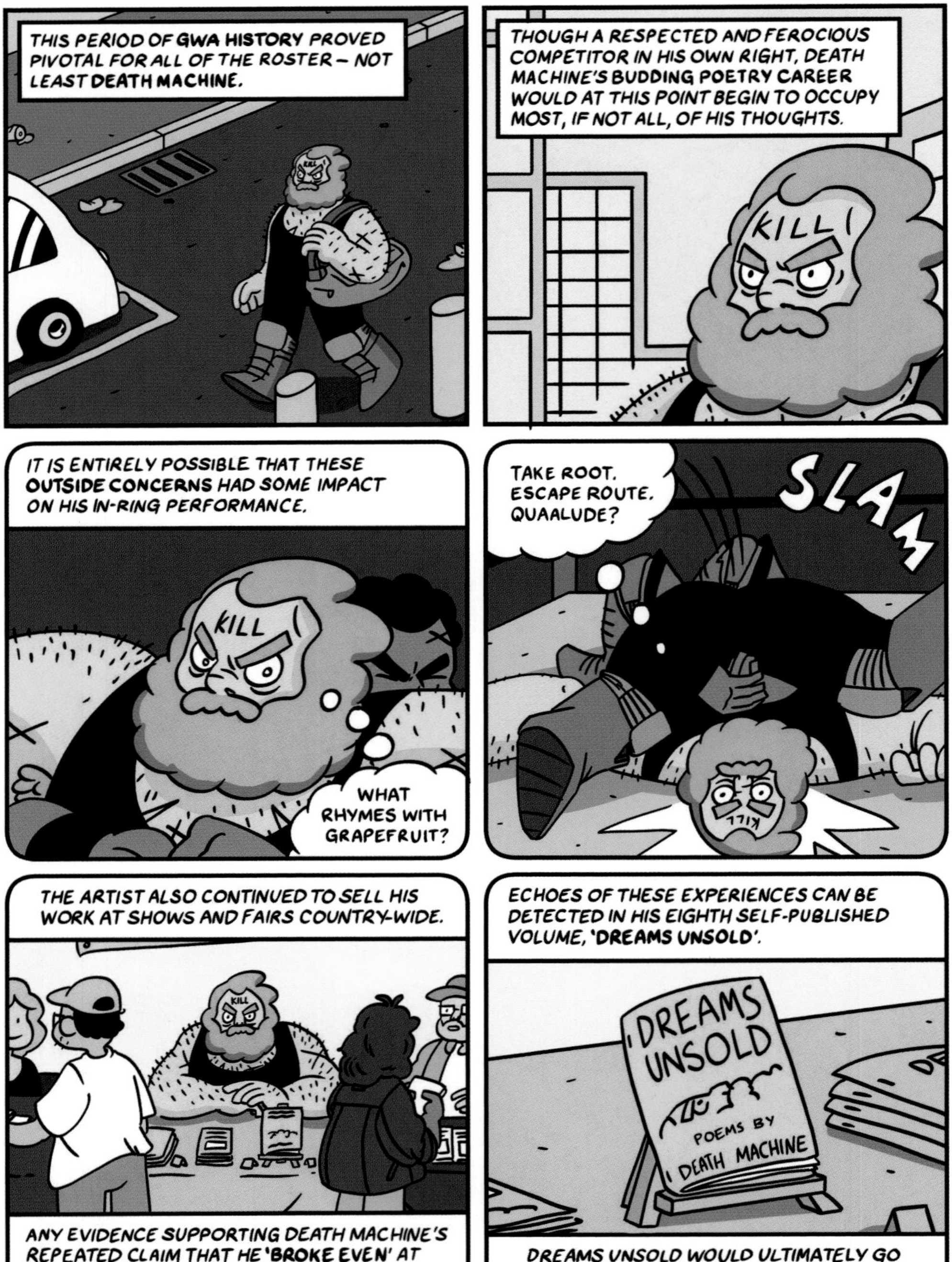
THIS PERIOD OF GWA HISTORY PROVED PIVOTAL FOR ALL OF THE ROSTER – NOT LEAST DEATH MACHINE.
KILL
THOUGH A RESPECTED AND FEROCIOUS COMPETITOR IN HIS OWN RIGHT, DEATH MACHINE'S BUDDING POETRY CAREER WOULD AT THIS POINT BEGIN TO OCCUPY MOST, IF NOT ALL, OF HIS THOUGHTS.
KILL
IT IS ENTIRELY POSSIBLE THAT THESE OUTSIDE CONCERNS HAD SOME IMPACT ON HIS IN-RING PERFORMANCE.
KILL
WHAT RHYMES WITH GRAPEFRUIT?
TAKE ROOT. ESCAPE ROUTE. QUAALUDE?
SLAM
KILL
THE ARTIST ALSO CONTINUED TO SELL HIS WORK AT SHOWS AND FAIRS COUNTRY-WIDE.
KILL
ANY EVIDENCE SUPPORTING DEATH MACHINE'S REPEATED CLAIM THAT HE 'BROKE EVEN' AT SUCH EVENTS HAS YET TO SURFACE.
ECHOES OF THESE EXPERIENCES CAN BE DETECTED IN HIS EIGHTH SELF-PUBLISHED VOLUME, 'DREAMS UNSOLD'.
DREAMS UNSOLD
POEMS BY
DEATH MACHINE
DREAMS UNSOLD WOULD ULTIMATELY GO ON TO SELL 16 COPIES (PRINT RUN: 250).

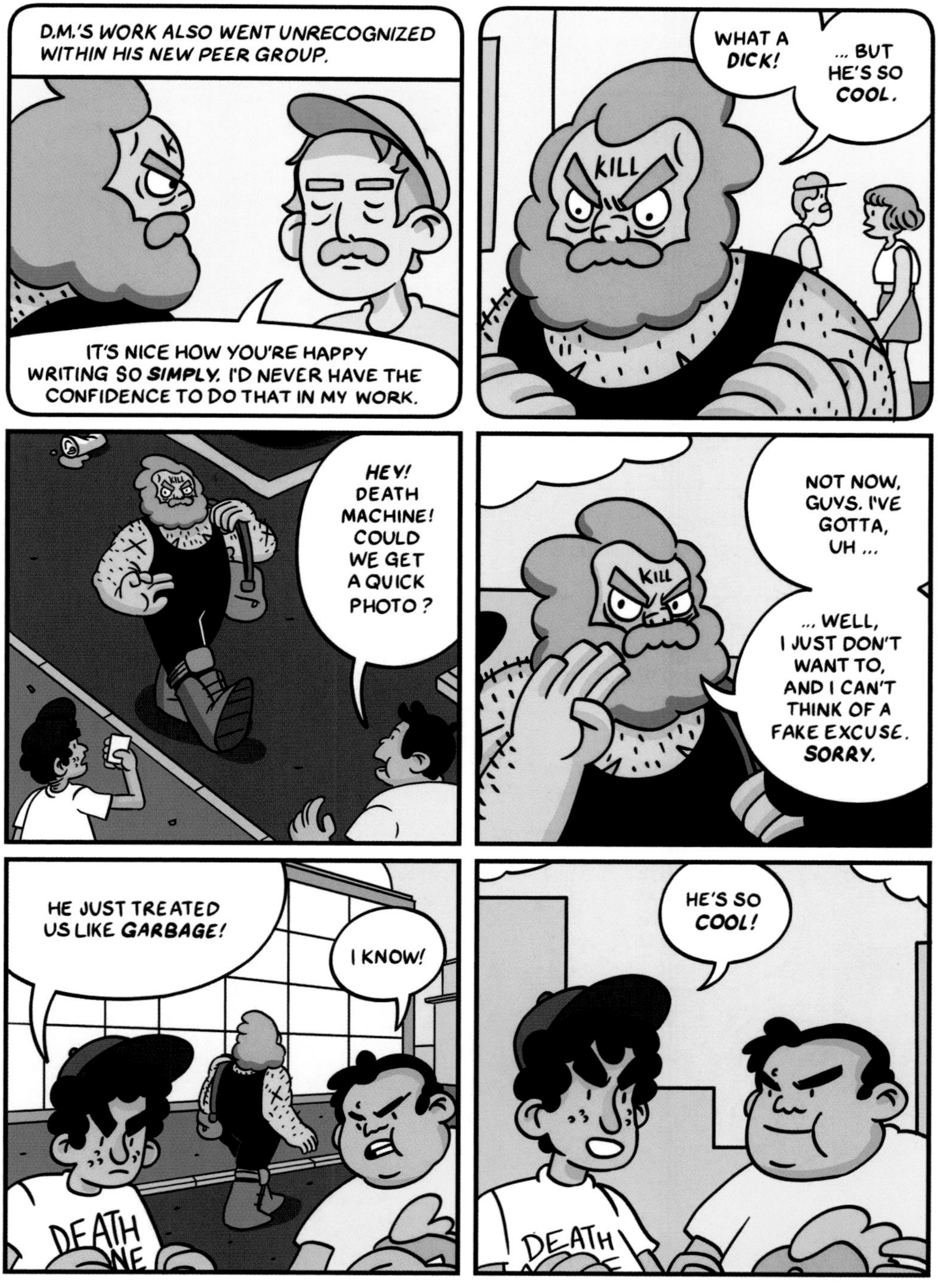
D.M.'S WORK ALSO WENT UNRECOGNIZED WITHIN HIS NEW PEER GROUP.
IT'S NICE HOW YOU'RE HAPPY WRITING SO **SIMPLY.** I'D NEVER HAVE THE CONFIDENCE TO DO THAT IN MY WORK.
KILL
WHAT A **DICK!**
... BUT HE'S SO **COOL.**
KILL
HEY! DEATH MACHINE! COULD WE GET A QUICK PHOTO?
KILL
NOT NOW, GUYS. I'VE GOTTA, UH ...
... WELL, I JUST DON'T WANT TO, AND I CAN'T THINK OF A FAKE EXCUSE. **SORRY.**
HE JUST TREATED US LIKE **GARBAGE!**
I KNOW!
HE'S SO **COOL!**

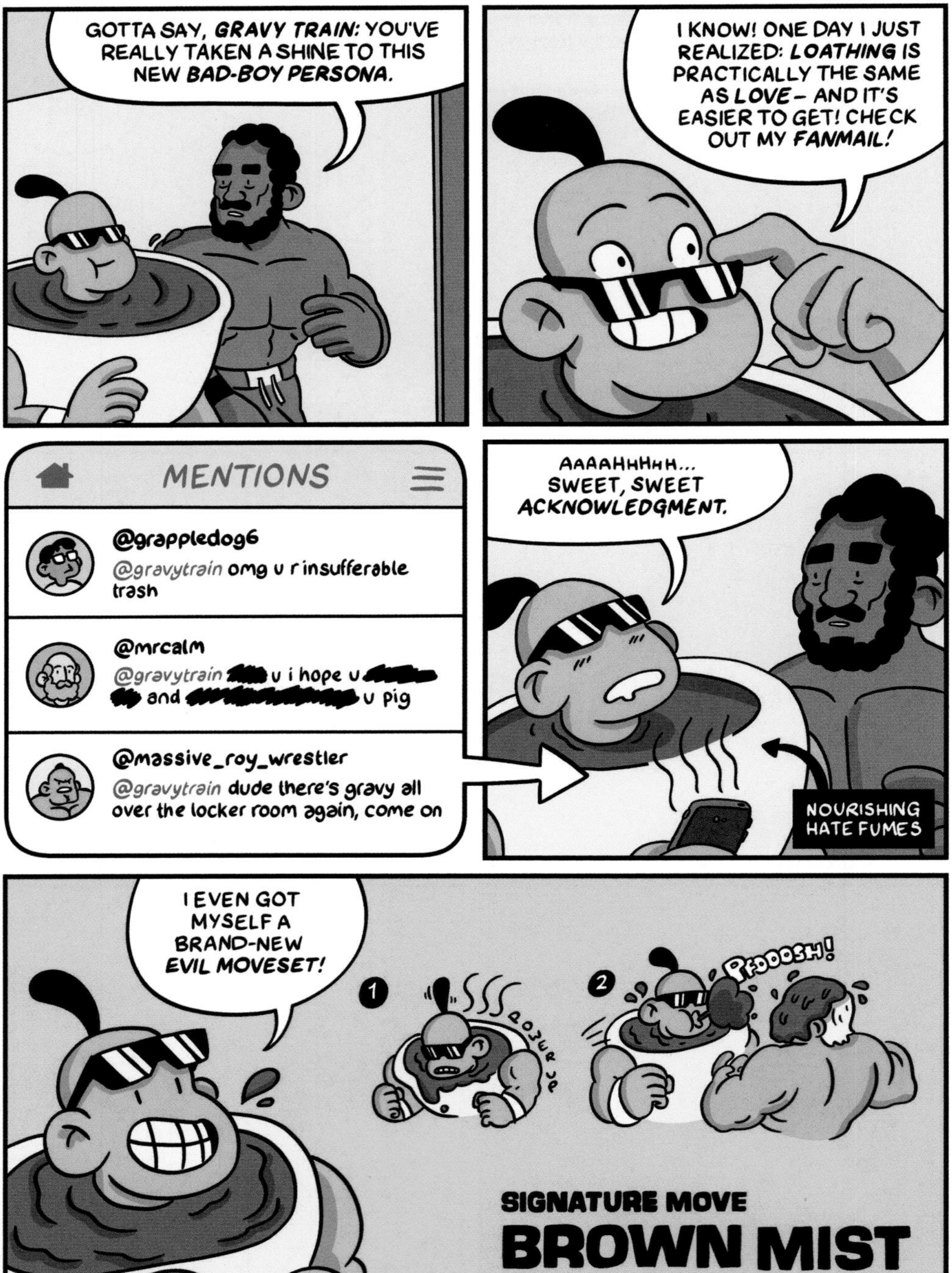
GOTTA SAY, GRAVY TRAIN: YOU'VE REALLY TAKEN A SHINE TO THIS NEW BAD-BOY PERSONA.
I KNOW! ONE DAY I JUST REALIZED: LOATHING IS PRACTICALLY THE SAME AS LOVE– AND IT'S EASIER TO GET! CHECK OUT MY FANMAIL!
MENTIONS
@grappledog6
@gravytrain omg u r insufferable trash
@mrcalm
@gravytrain [redacted] u i hope u [redacted] and [redacted] u pig
@massive_roy_wrestler
@gravytrain dude there's gravy all over the locker room again, come on
AAAAHHHHH... SWEET, SWEET ACKNOWLEDGMENT.
NOURISHING HATE FUMES
I EVEN GOT MYSELF A BRAND-NEW EVIL MOVESET!
1
POWER UP
2
PFOOOSH!
SIGNATURE MOVE
BROWN MIST

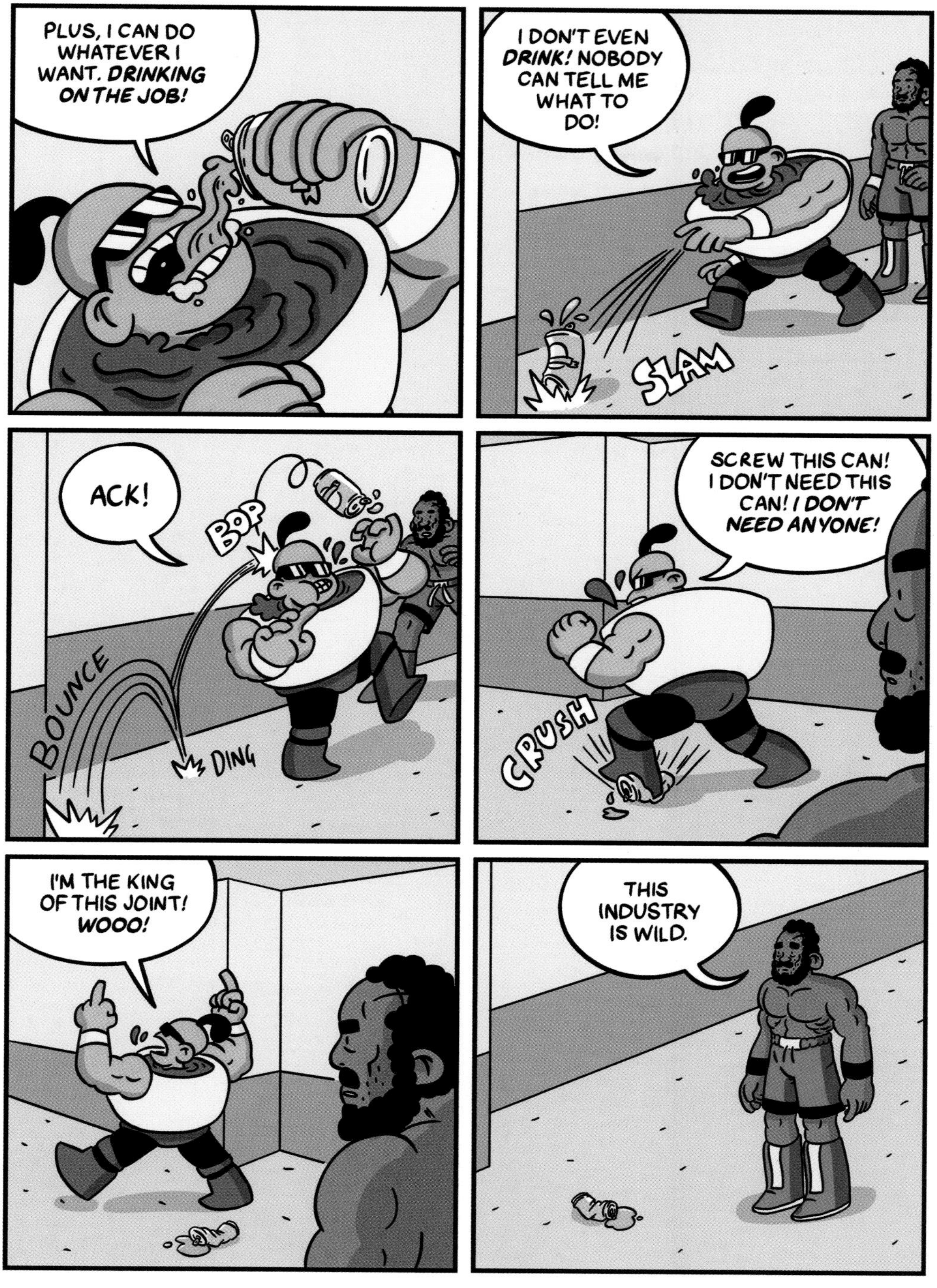

PLUS, I CAN DO WHATEVER I WANT. DRINKING ON THE JOB!
I DON'T EVEN DRINK! NOBODY CAN TELL ME WHAT TO DO!
SLAM
ACK!
BOP
BOUNCE
DING
SCREW THIS CAN! I DON'T NEED THIS CAN! I DON'T NEED ANYONE!
CRUSH
I'M THE KING OF THIS JOINT! WOOO!
THIS INDUSTRY IS WILD.

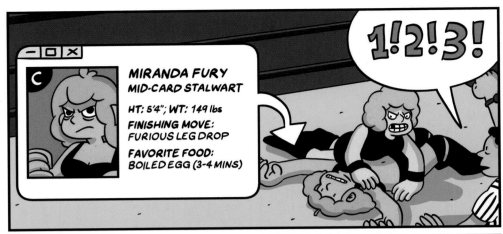

MIRANDA FURY
MID-CARD STALWART

HT: 5'4"; WT: 149 lbs

FINISHING MOVE:
FURIOUS LEG DROP

FAVORITE FOOD:
BOILED EGG (3-4 MINS)

1!2!3!

I WAS ON FIRE TONIGHT! THAT CROWD WAS AT MY FEET. EATIN' OUTTA THE PALM OF MY SWEATY HAND!

AND HEY, YOU WERE OKAY TOO!

GUYS! HYPER MASK IS ON NEXT! WE'RE ALL GONNA HANG OUT AND WATCH FROM THE BACK! YOU IN?

ER, I'M GOOD. I'M GONNA SHOWER. FOR LIKE THE ENTIRE MATCH, PROBABLY.

PFT, SHOWER. I'D BE SHOWERING IN YOUR TEARS IF YOU KNEW HYPER MASK'S TRUE IDENTITY, LOSERS.

"OOH, I'M THE BEST. HERE – HAVE SOME UNSOLICITED FEEDBACK. HERE'S A CLUMSY MIXED METAPHOR TO GO WITH IT."

SICK OF IT!

MASSACRE 7

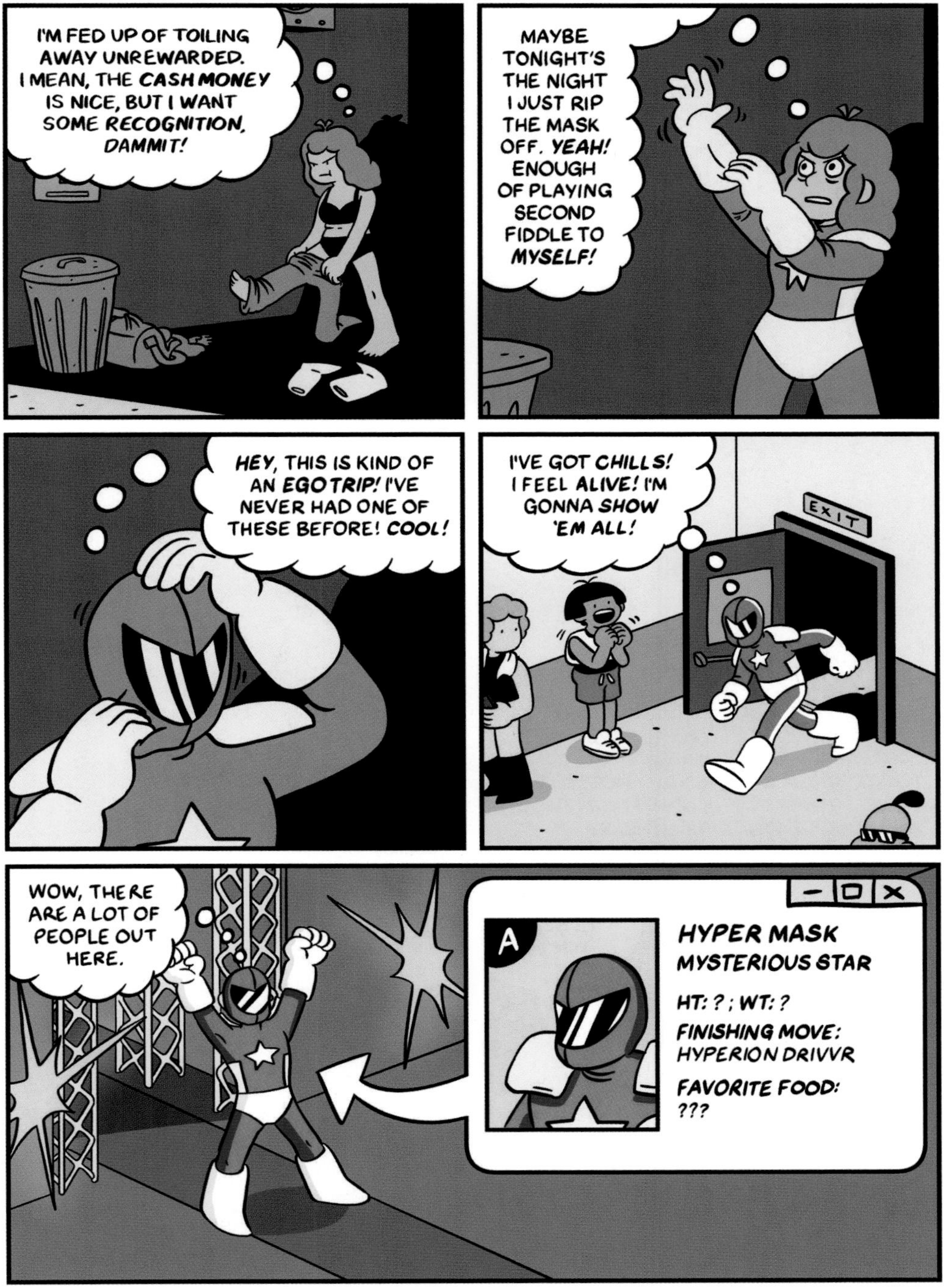
I'M FED UP OF TOILING AWAY UNREWARDED. I MEAN, THE CASH MONEY IS NICE, BUT I WANT SOME RECOGNITION, DAMMIT!
MAYBE TONIGHT'S THE NIGHT I JUST RIP THE MASK OFF. YEAH! ENOUGH OF PLAYING SECOND FIDDLE TO MYSELF!
HEY, THIS IS KIND OF AN EGO TRIP! I'VE NEVER HAD ONE OF THESE BEFORE! COOL!
I'VE GOT CHILLS! I FEEL ALIVE! I'M GONNA SHOW 'EM ALL!
EXIT
WOW, THERE ARE A LOT OF PEOPLE OUT HERE.
A
HYPER MASK
MYSTERIOUS STAR
HT: ? ; WT: ?
FINISHING MOVE:
HYPERION DRIVVR
FAVORITE FOOD:
???

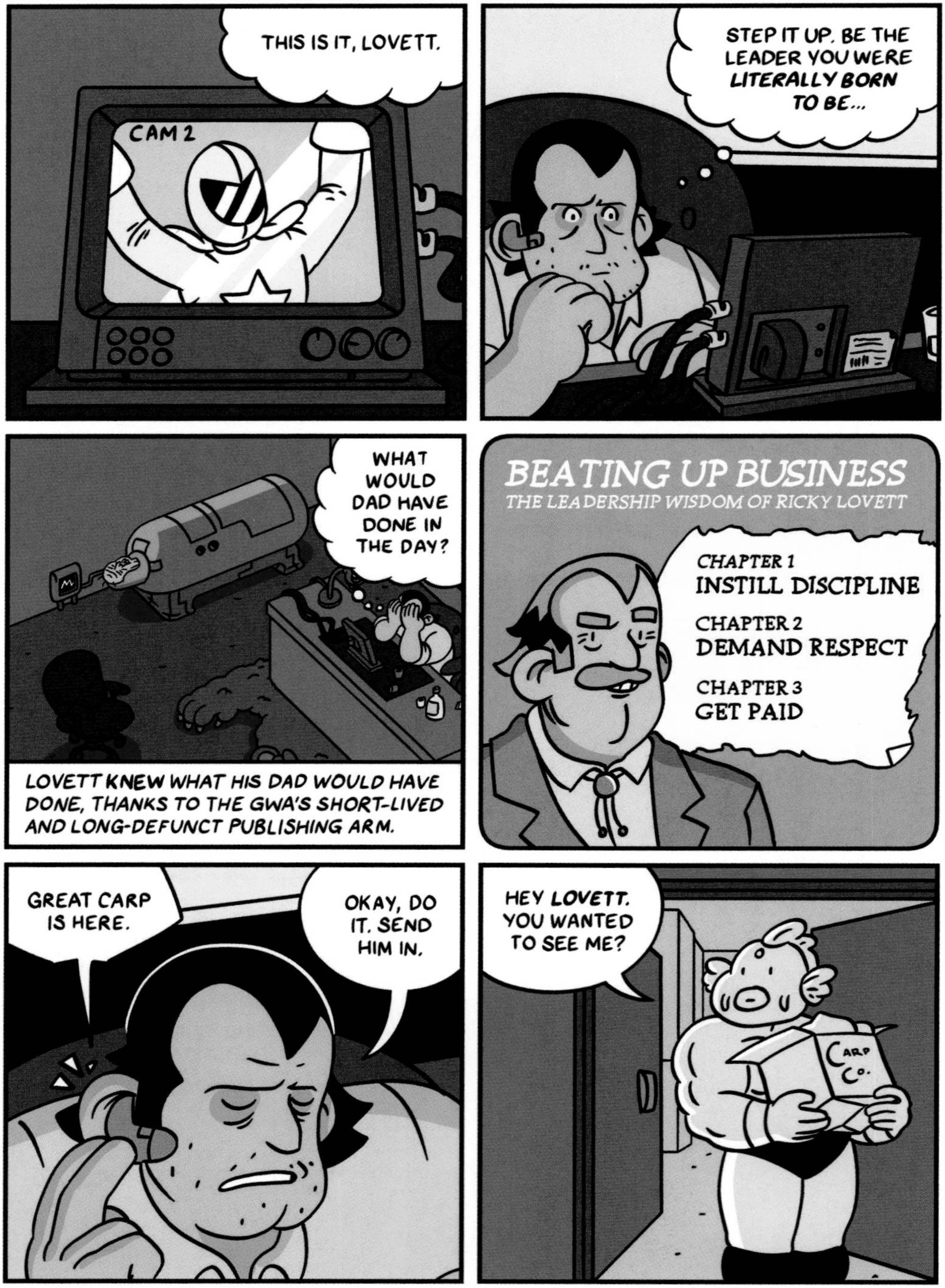
THIS IS IT, LOVETT.
CAM 2
STEP IT UP. BE THE LEADER YOU WERE LITERALLY BORN TO BE...
WHAT WOULD DAD HAVE DONE IN THE DAY?
LOVETT KNEW WHAT HIS DAD WOULD HAVE DONE, THANKS TO THE GWA'S SHORT-LIVED AND LONG-DEFUNCT PUBLISHING ARM.
BEATING UP BUSINESS
THE LEADERSHIP WISDOM OF RICKY LOVETT
CHAPTER 1
INSTILL DISCIPLINE
CHAPTER 2
DEMAND RESPECT
CHAPTER 3
GET PAID
GREAT CARP IS HERE.
OKAY, DO IT. SEND HIM IN.
HEY LOVETT. YOU WANTED TO SEE ME?
CARP CO.

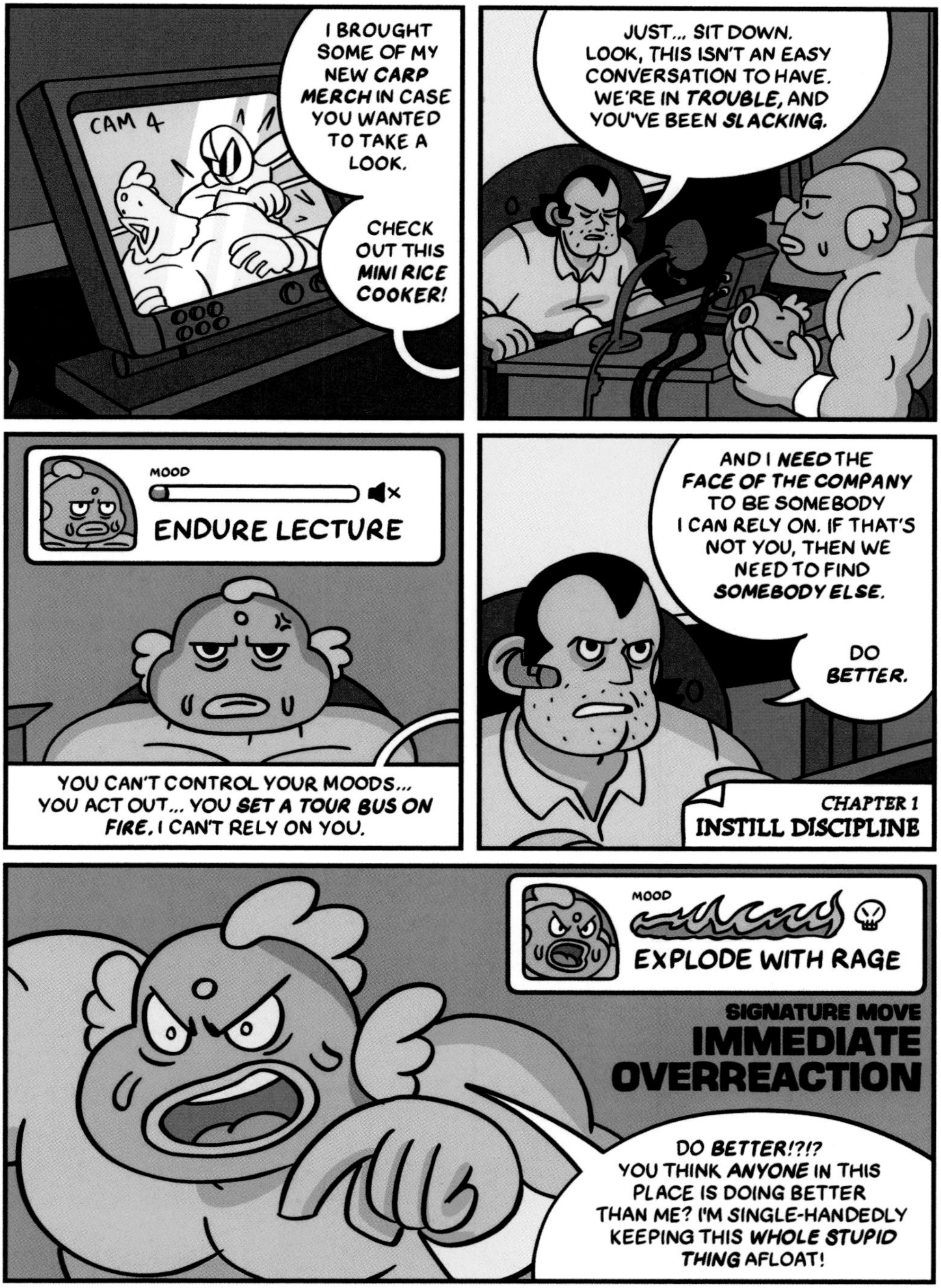

CAM 4
I BROUGHT SOME OF MY NEW CARP MERCH IN CASE YOU WANTED TO TAKE A LOOK.
CHECK OUT THIS MINI RICE COOKER!
JUST... SIT DOWN. LOOK, THIS ISN'T AN EASY CONVERSATION TO HAVE. WE'RE IN TROUBLE, AND YOU'VE BEEN SLACKING.
MOOD
ENDURE LECTURE
YOU CAN'T CONTROL YOUR MOODS... YOU ACT OUT... YOU SET A TOUR BUS ON FIRE. I CAN'T RELY ON YOU.
AND I NEED THE FACE OF THE COMPANY TO BE SOMEBODY I CAN RELY ON. IF THAT'S NOT YOU, THEN WE NEED TO FIND SOMEBODY ELSE.
DO BETTER.
CHAPTER 1
INSTILL DISCIPLINE
MOOD
EXPLODE WITH RAGE
SIGNATURE MOVE
IMMEDIATE OVERREACTION
DO BETTER!?!? YOU THINK ANYONE IN THIS PLACE IS DOING BETTER THAN ME? I'M SINGLE-HANDEDLY KEEPING THIS WHOLE STUPID THING AFLOAT!

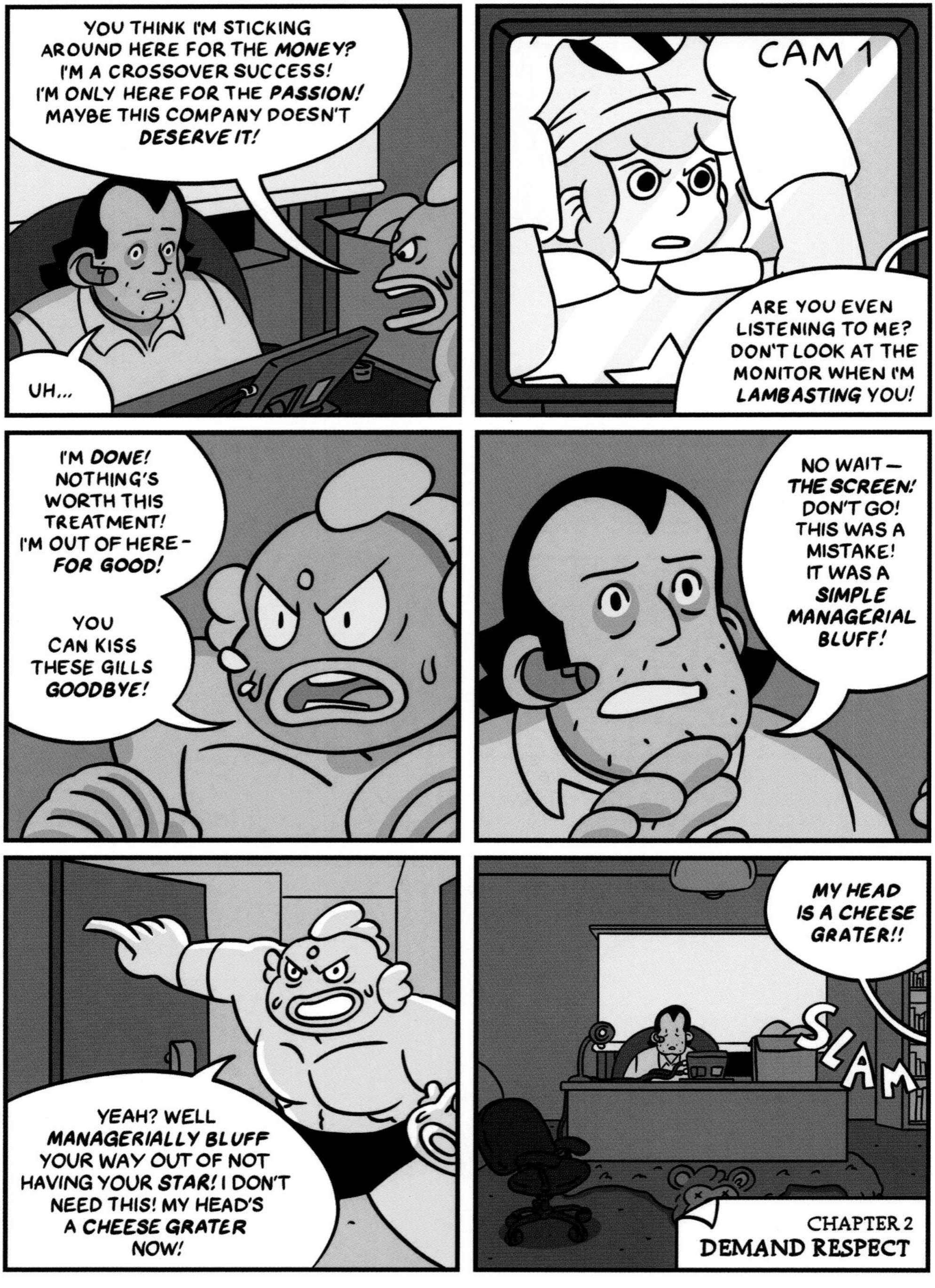
YOU THINK I'M STICKING AROUND HERE FOR THE MONEY? I'M A CROSSOVER SUCCESS! I'M ONLY HERE FOR THE PASSION! MAYBE THIS COMPANY DOESN'T DESERVE IT!
UH...
CAM 1
ARE YOU EVEN LISTENING TO ME? DON'T LOOK AT THE MONITOR WHEN I'M LAMBASTING YOU!
I'M DONE! NOTHING'S WORTH THIS TREATMENT! I'M OUT OF HERE - FOR GOOD!
YOU CAN KISS THESE GILLS GOODBYE!
NO WAIT— THE SCREEN! DON'T GO! THIS WAS A MISTAKE! IT WAS A SIMPLE MANAGERIAL BLUFF!
YEAH? WELL MANAGERIALLY BLUFF YOUR WAY OUT OF NOT HAVING YOUR STAR! I DON'T NEED THIS! MY HEAD'S A CHEESE GRATER NOW!
MY HEAD IS A CHEESE GRATER!!
SLAM
CHAPTER 2
DEMAND RESPECT

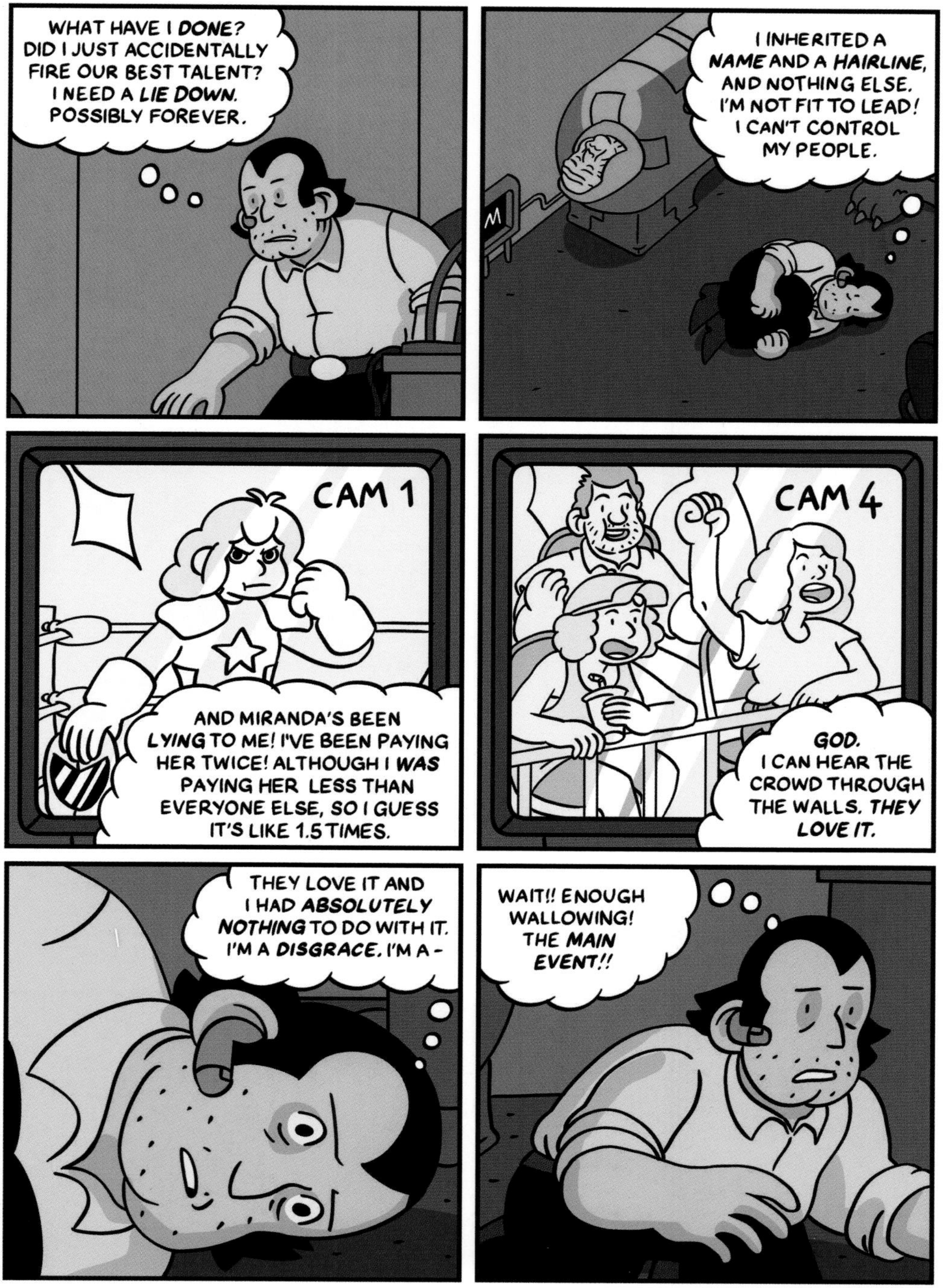
WHAT HAVE I DONE? DID I JUST ACCIDENTALLY FIRE OUR BEST TALENT? I NEED A LIE DOWN. POSSIBLY FOREVER.
I INHERITED A NAME AND A HAIRLINE, AND NOTHING ELSE. I'M NOT FIT TO LEAD! I CAN'T CONTROL MY PEOPLE.
CAM 1
AND MIRANDA'S BEEN LYING TO ME! I'VE BEEN PAYING HER TWICE! ALTHOUGH I WAS PAYING HER LESS THAN EVERYONE ELSE, SO I GUESS IT'S LIKE 1.5 TIMES.
CAM 4
GOD. I CAN HEAR THE CROWD THROUGH THE WALLS. THEY LOVE IT.
THEY LOVE IT AND I HAD ABSOLUTELY NOTHING TO DO WITH IT. I'M A DISGRACE. I'M A -
WAIT!! ENOUGH WALLOWING! THE MAIN EVENT!!

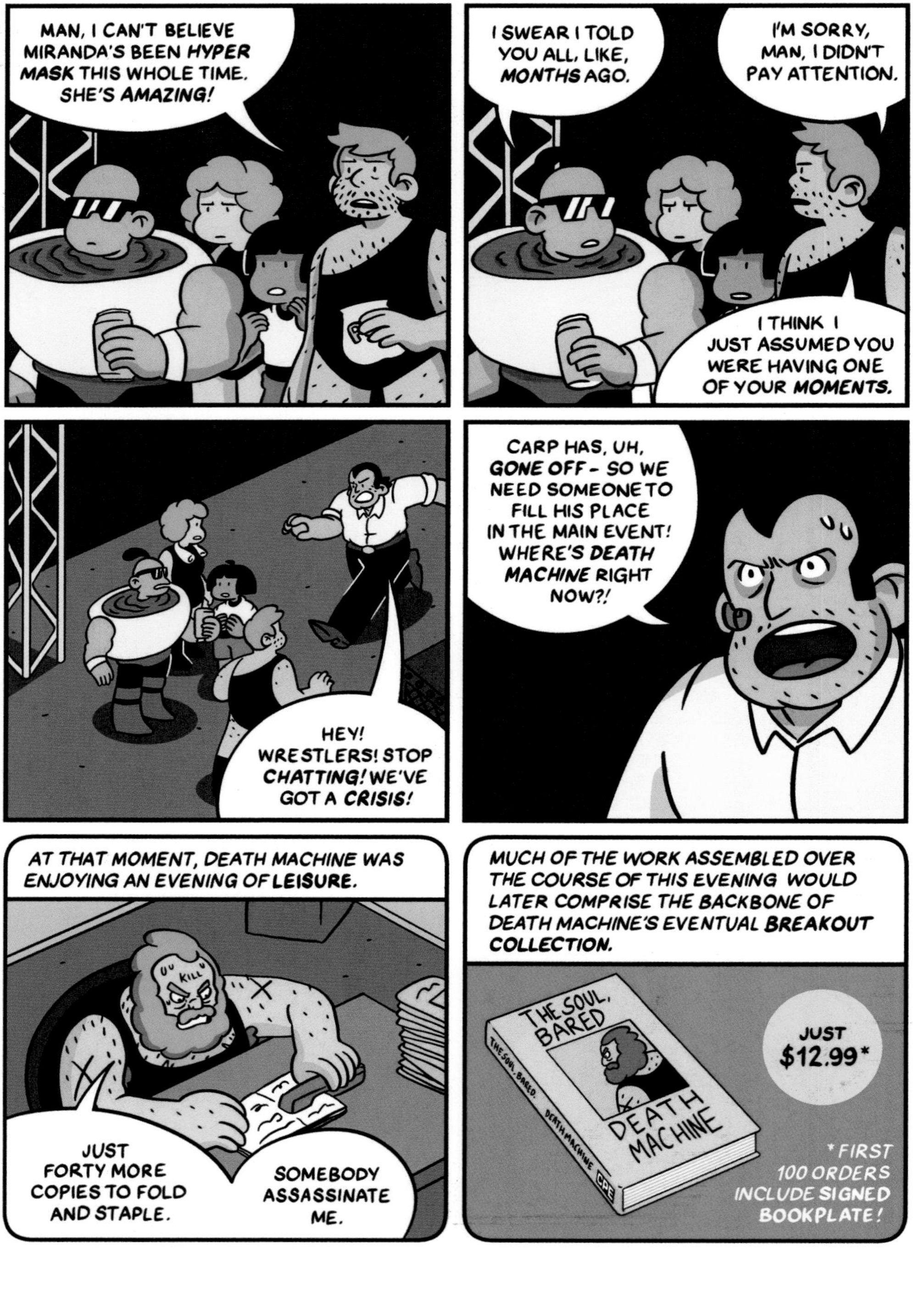
MAN, I CAN'T BELIEVE MIRANDA'S BEEN HYPER MASK THIS WHOLE TIME. SHE'S AMAZING!
I SWEAR I TOLD YOU ALL, LIKE, MONTHS AGO.
I'M SORRY, MAN, I DIDN'T PAY ATTENTION.
I THINK I JUST ASSUMED YOU WERE HAVING ONE OF YOUR MOMENTS.
HEY! WRESTLERS! STOP CHATTING! WE'VE GOT A CRISIS!
CARP HAS, UH, GONE OFF - SO WE NEED SOMEONE TO FILL HIS PLACE IN THE MAIN EVENT! WHERE'S DEATH MACHINE RIGHT NOW?!
AT THAT MOMENT, DEATH MACHINE WAS ENJOYING AN EVENING OF LEISURE.
KILL
JUST FORTY MORE COPIES TO FOLD AND STAPLE.
SOMEBODY ASSASSINATE ME.
MUCH OF THE WORK ASSEMBLED OVER THE COURSE OF THIS EVENING WOULD LATER COMPRISE THE BACKBONE OF DEATH MACHINE'S EVENTUAL BREAKOUT COLLECTION.
THE SOUL, BARED
DEATH MACHINE
THE SOUL, BARED. DEATH MACHINE
JUST $12.99*
* FIRST 100 ORDERS INCLUDE SIGNED BOOKPLATE!

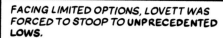
FACING LIMITED OPTIONS, LOVETT WAS FORCED TO STOOP TO UNPRECEDENTED LOWS.

GRAVY TRAIN HEADLINING A MAIN EVENT... DAD MUST BE SPINNING IN HIS *12ft* METAL LIFE-SUPPORT UNIT.

IS THAT MIRANDA?

MY OFFICE, *NOW.*

LEAVE IT, LOVETT. I JUST MADE YOU MORE POTENTIAL CASH IN ONE NIGHT THAN YOU'VE MADE IN YEARS.

CHAPTER 3
GET PAID

I'LL SEE YOU ON *MONDAY.*

NOBODY KNOWS WHEN *EXACTLY* LOVETT KNEW THAT HIS DAYS AT THE HEAD OF THE GWA WERE NUMBERED. MANY HAVE CITED THIS EXCHANGE AS THE TURNING POINT...

... WHILE OTHERS HAVE SUGGESTED THAT IT WAS THE RECEIPT OF A HEFTY MEDICAL BILL FOR IN-RING GRAVY BURNS.

TSSST

ARGGHH! I CAN SMELL MY OWN *SKIN!*

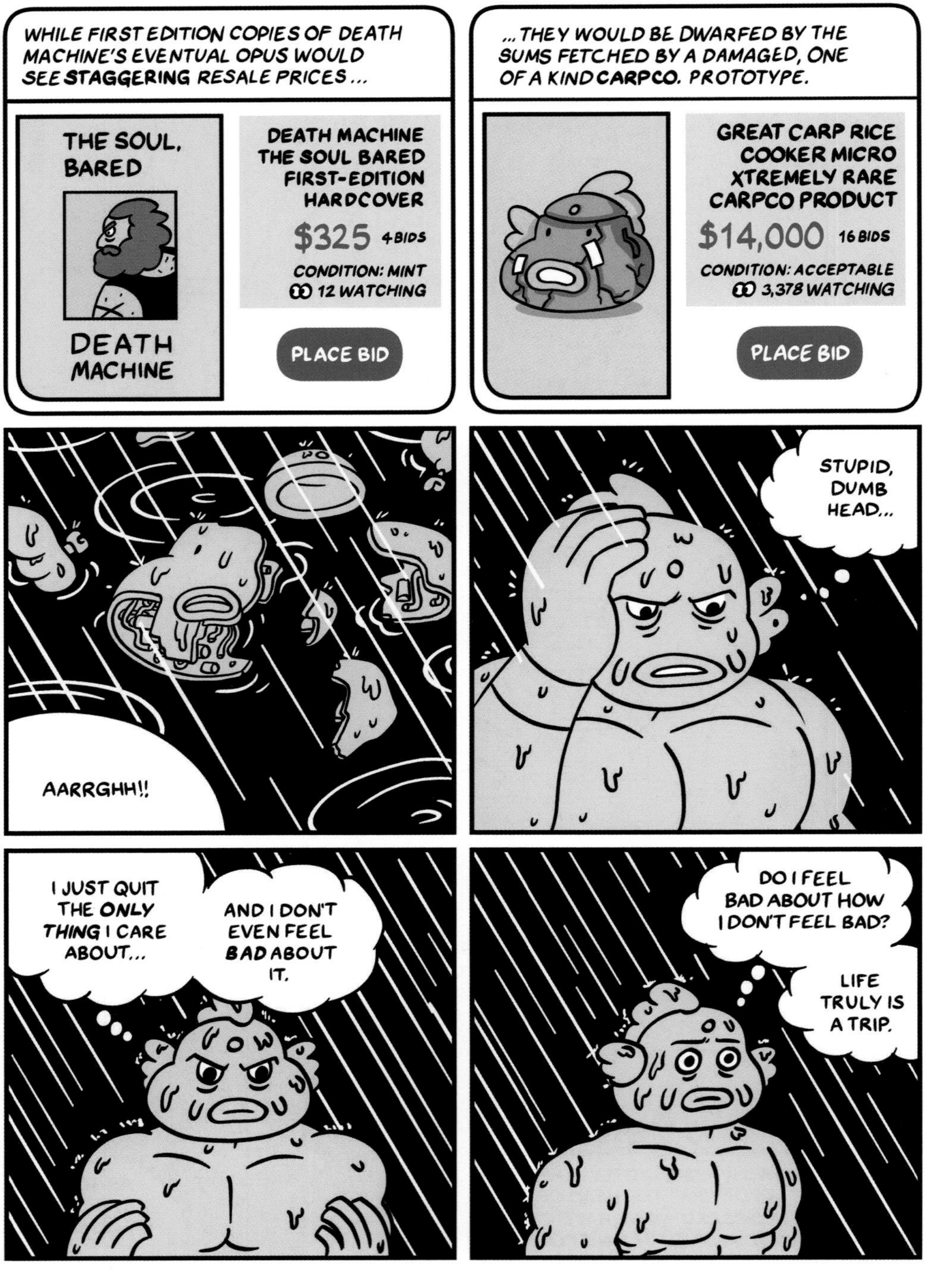
WHILE FIRST EDITION COPIES OF DEATH MACHINE'S EVENTUAL OPUS WOULD SEE STAGGERING RESALE PRICES...
THE SOUL, BARED
DEATH MACHINE
DEATH MACHINE THE SOUL BARED FIRST-EDITION HARDCOVER
$325 4 BIDS
CONDITION: MINT
12 WATCHING
PLACE BID
...THEY WOULD BE DWARFED BY THE SUMS FETCHED BY A DAMAGED, ONE OF A KIND CARPCO. PROTOTYPE.
GREAT CARP RICE COOKER MICRO XTREMELY RARE CARPCO PRODUCT
$14,000 16 BIDS
CONDITION: ACCEPTABLE
3,378 WATCHING
PLACE BID
AARRGHH!!
STUPID, DUMB HEAD...
I JUST QUIT THE ONLY THING I CARE ABOUT...
AND I DON'T EVEN FEEL BAD ABOUT IT.
DO I FEEL BAD ABOUT HOW I DON'T FEEL BAD?
LIFE TRULY IS A TRIP.

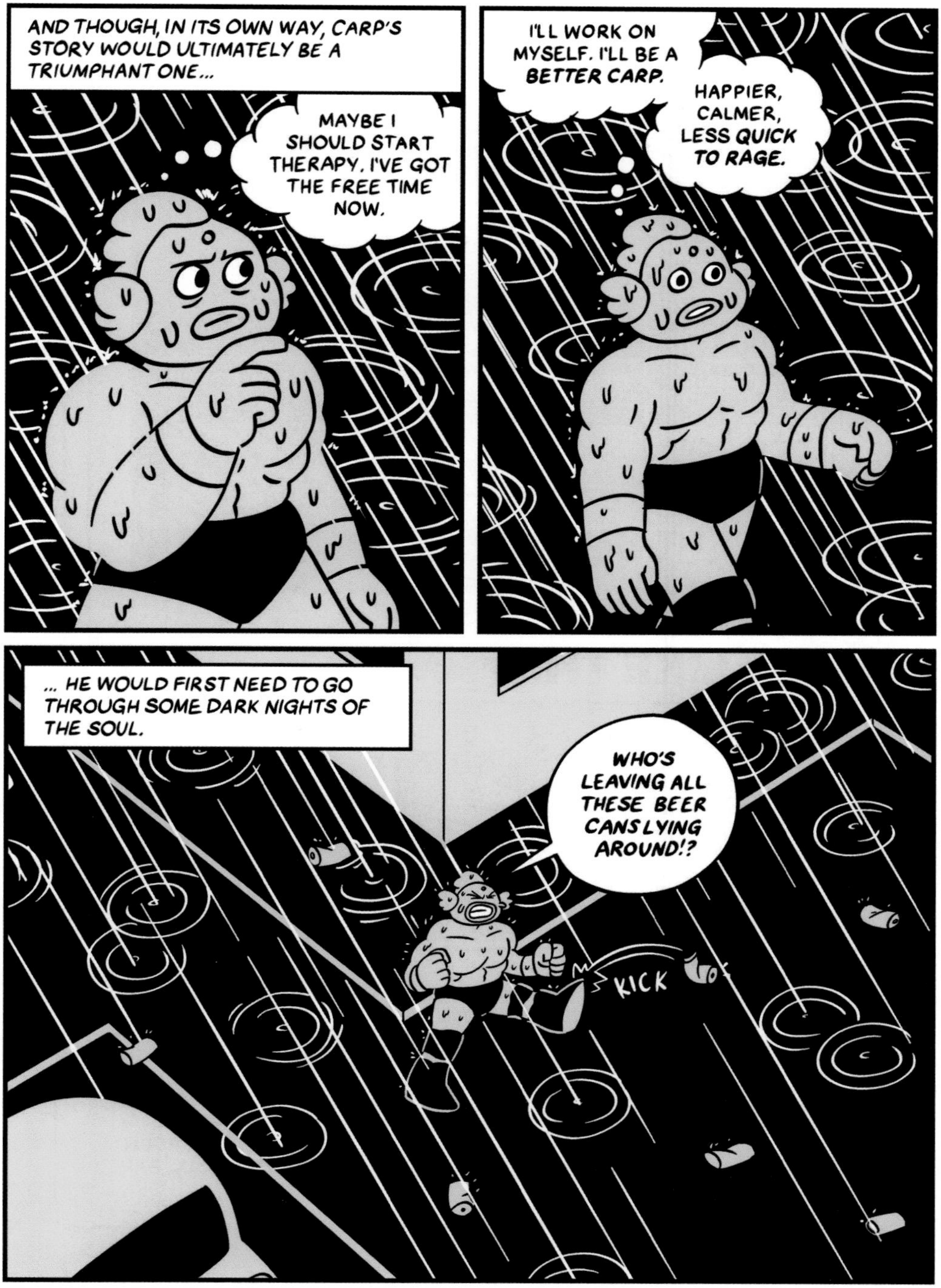
AND THOUGH, IN ITS OWN WAY, CARP'S STORY WOULD ULTIMATELY BE A TRIUMPHANT ONE...
MAYBE I SHOULD START THERAPY. I'VE GOT THE FREE TIME NOW.
I'LL WORK ON MYSELF. I'LL BE A BETTER CARP.
HAPPIER, CALMER, LESS QUICK TO RAGE.
... HE WOULD FIRST NEED TO GO THROUGH SOME DARK NIGHTS OF THE SOUL.
WHO'S LEAVING ALL THESE BEER CANS LYING AROUND!?
KICK

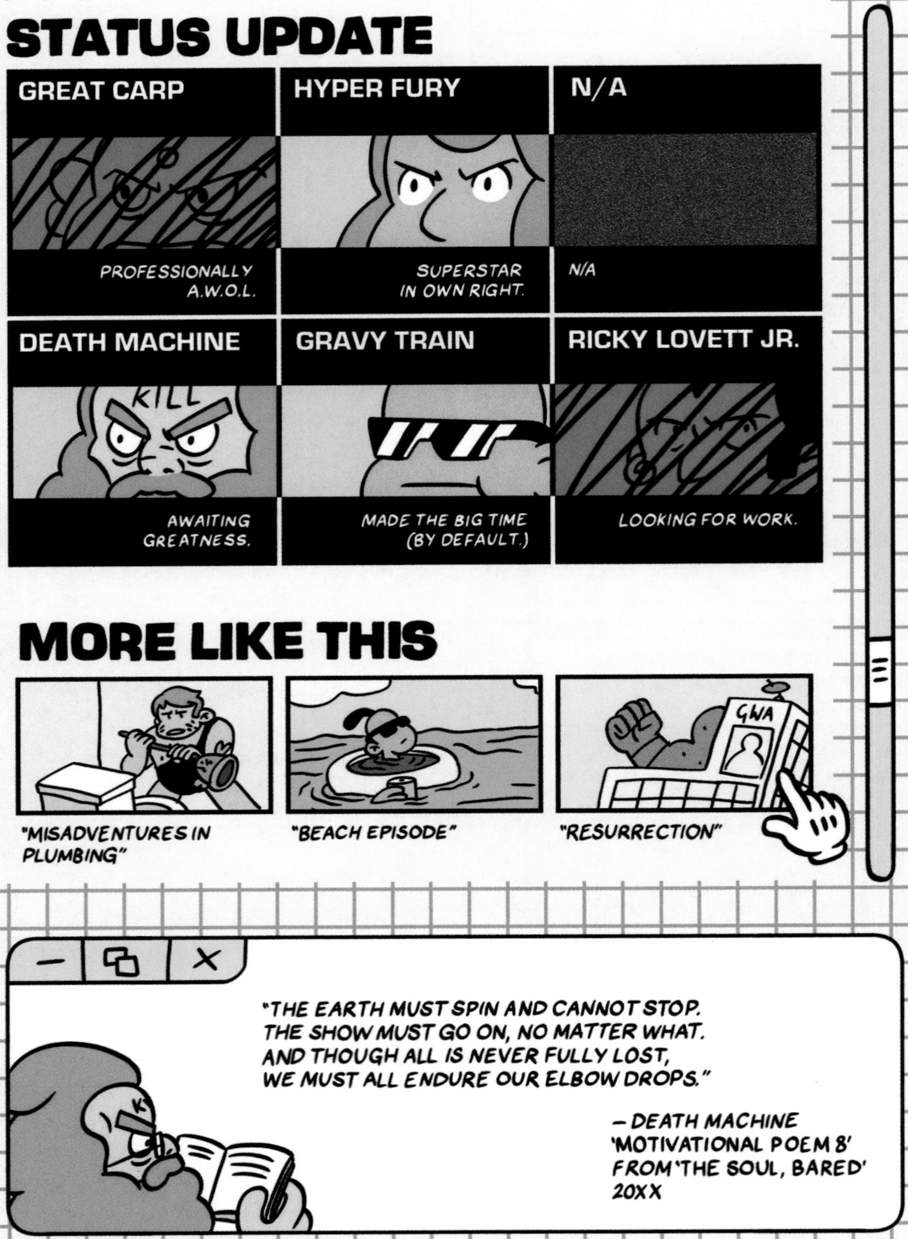
STATUS UPDATE
GREAT CARP
PROFESSIONALLY A.W.O.L.
HYPER FURY
SUPERSTAR IN OWN RIGHT.
N/A
N/A
DEATH MACHINE
KILL
AWAITING GREATNESS.
GRAVY TRAIN
MADE THE BIG TIME (BY DEFAULT.)
RICKY LOVETT JR.
LOOKING FOR WORK.
MORE LIKE THIS
"MISADVENTURES IN PLUMBING"
"BEACH EPISODE"
GWA
"RESURRECTION"
"THE EARTH MUST SPIN AND CANNOT STOP.
THE SHOW MUST GO ON, NO MATTER WHAT.
AND THOUGH ALL IS NEVER FULLY LOST,
WE MUST ALL ENDURE OUR ELBOW DROPS."
– DEATH MACHINE
'MOTIVATIONAL POEM 8'
FROM 'THE SOUL, BARED'
20XX

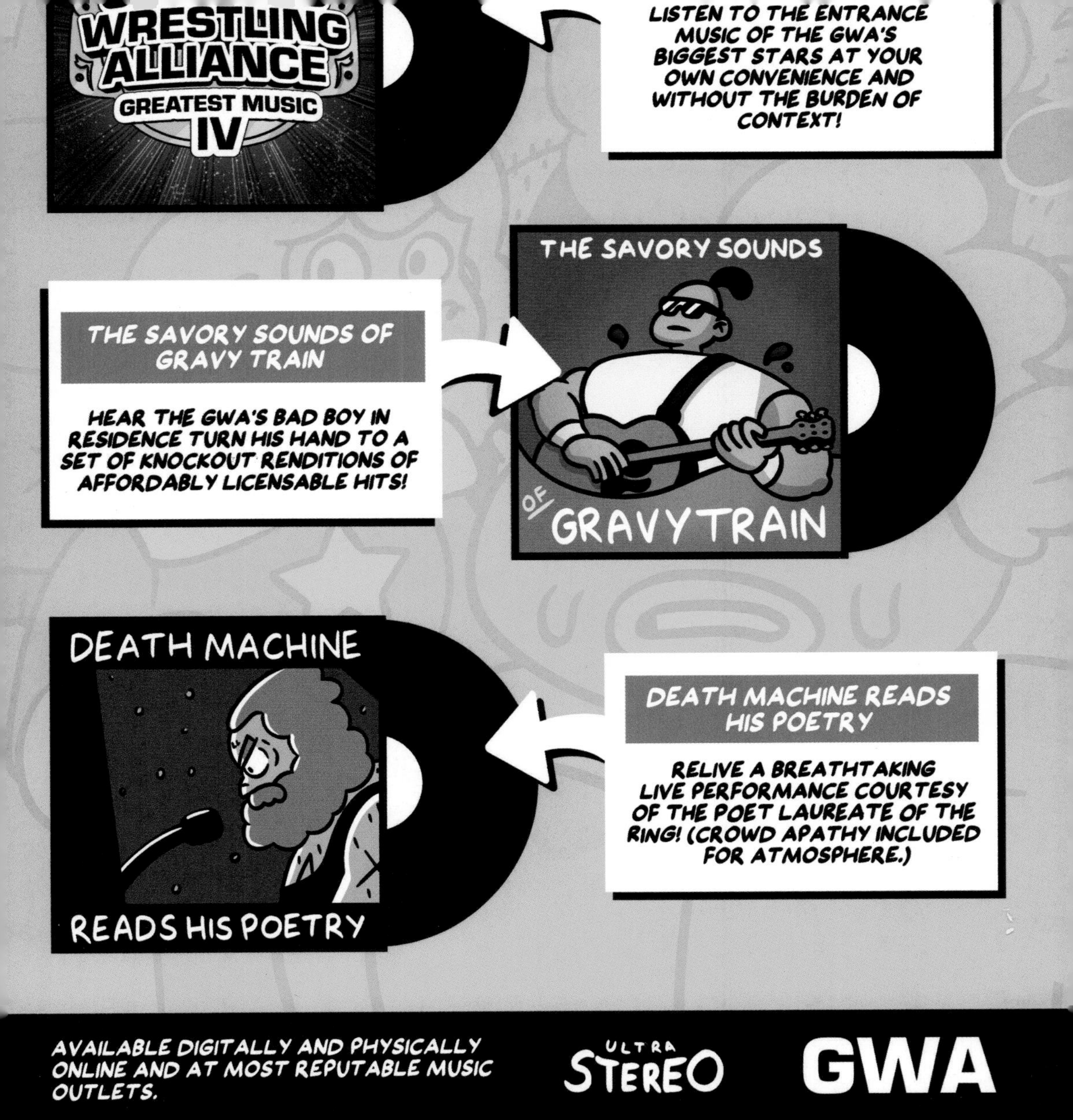
WRESTLING ALLIANCE
GREATEST MUSIC
IV
LISTEN TO THE ENTRANCE MUSIC OF THE GWA'S BIGGEST STARS AT YOUR OWN CONVENIENCE AND WITHOUT THE BURDEN OF CONTEXT!
THE SAVORY SOUNDS OF GRAVY TRAIN
HEAR THE GWA'S BAD BOY IN RESIDENCE TURN HIS HAND TO A SET OF KNOCKOUT RENDITIONS OF AFFORDABLY LICENSABLE HITS!
THE SAVORY SOUNDS
OF
GRAVY TRAIN
DEATH MACHINE
READS HIS POETRY
DEATH MACHINE READS HIS POETRY
RELIVE A BREATHTAKING LIVE PERFORMANCE COURTESY OF THE POET LAUREATE OF THE RING! (CROWD APATHY INCLUDED FOR ATMOSPHERE.)
AVAILABLE DIGITALLY AND PHYSICALLY ONLINE AND AT MOST REPUTABLE MUSIC OUTLETS.
ULTRA STEREO
GWA

CHAPTER FOUR

THE BALLAD OF GREAT CARP

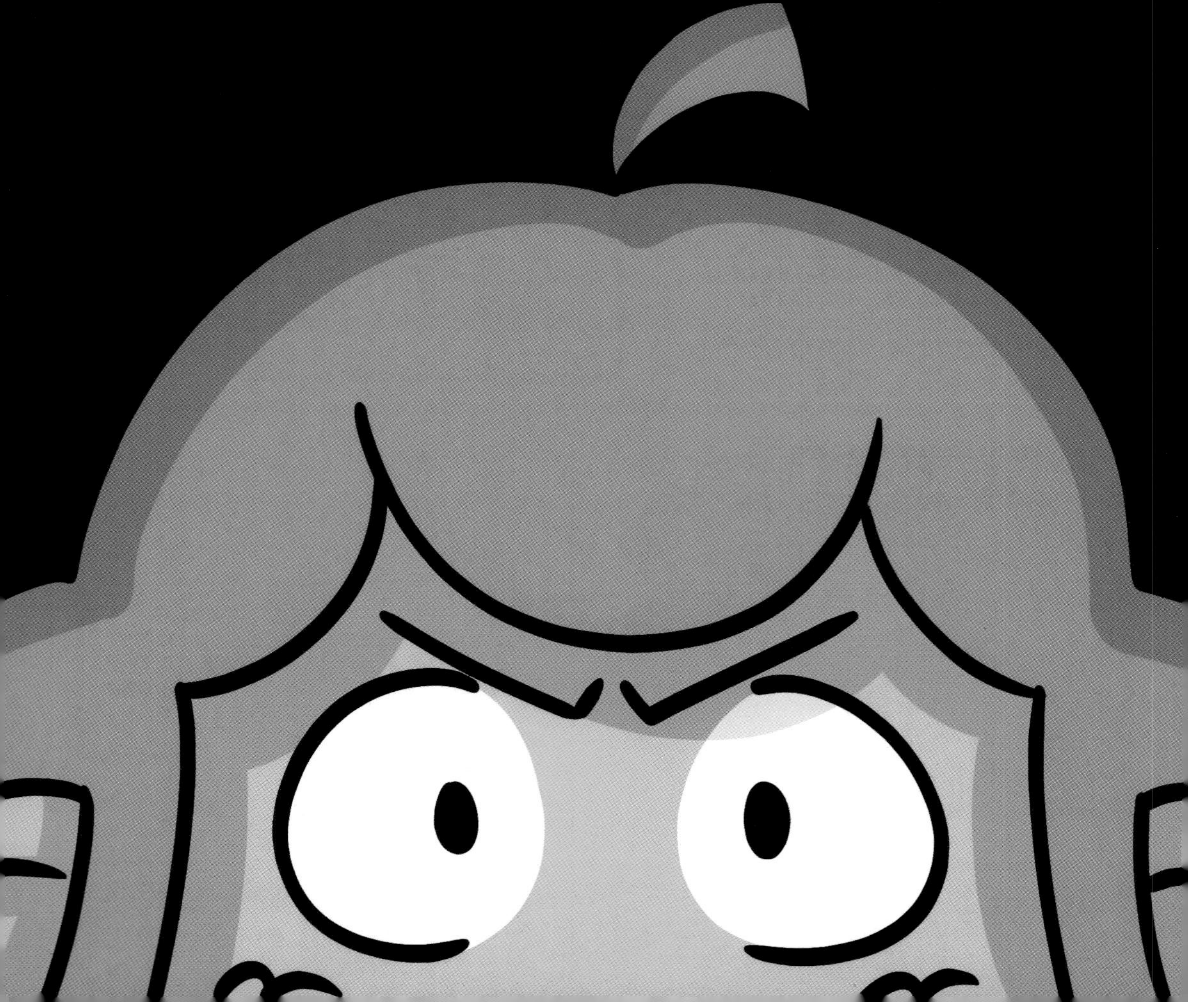

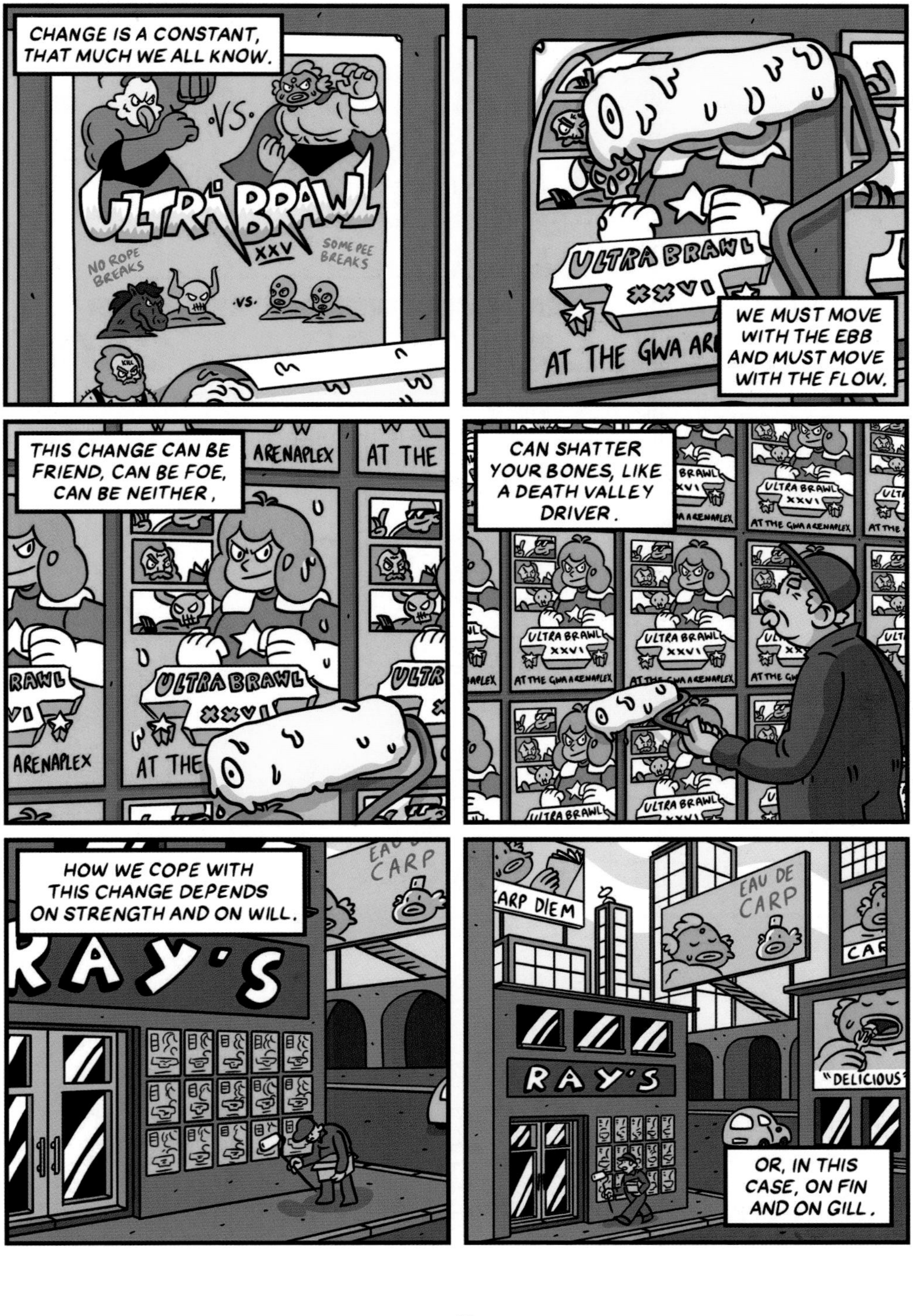
CHANGE IS A CONSTANT, THAT MUCH WE ALL KNOW.
VS
ULTRABRAWL
XXV
NO ROPE BREAKS
VS
WE MUST MOVE WITH THE EBB AND MUST MOVE WITH THE FLOW.
ULTRA BRAWL
XXVI
AT THE GWA AR
THIS CHANGE CAN BE FRIEND, CAN BE FOE, CAN BE NEITHER,
ARENAPLEX
AT THE
ULTRA BRAWL
XXVI
CAN SHATTER YOUR BONES, LIKE A DEATH VALLEY DRIVER.
AT THE GWA ARENAPLEX
HOW WE COPE WITH THIS CHANGE DEPENDS ON STRENGTH AND ON WILL.
CARP
RAY'S
CARP DIEM
EAU DE CARP
RAY'S
"DELICIOUS"
OR, IN THIS CASE, ON FIN AND ON GILL.

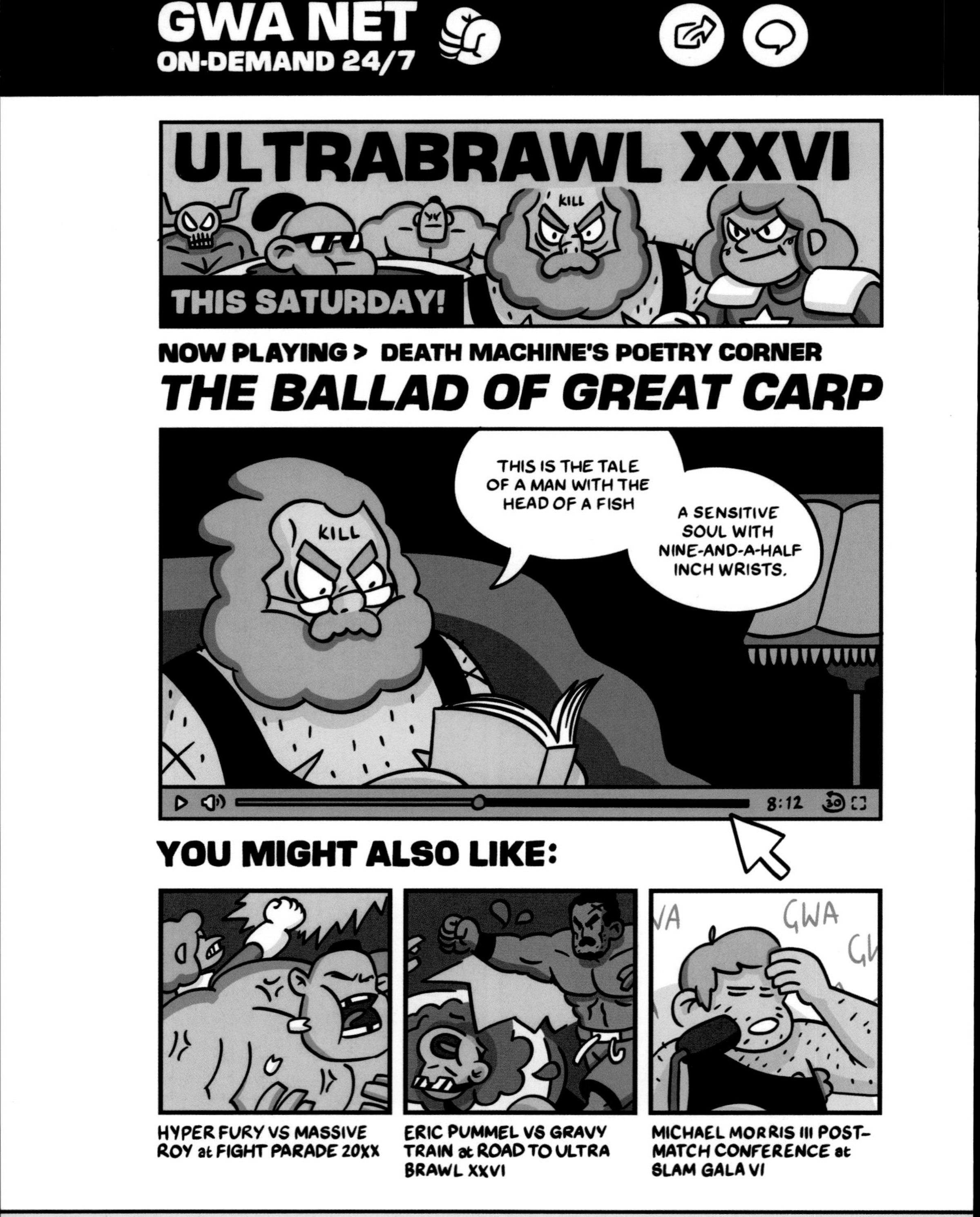
GWA NET
ON-DEMAND 24/7
ULTRABRAWL XXVI
KILL
THIS SATURDAY!
NOW PLAYING > DEATH MACHINE'S POETRY CORNER
THE BALLAD OF GREAT CARP
KILL
THIS IS THE TALE OF A MAN WITH THE HEAD OF A FISH
A SENSITIVE SOUL WITH NINE-AND-A-HALF INCH WRISTS.
8:12
30
YOU MIGHT ALSO LIKE:
GWA
HYPER FURY VS MASSIVE ROY at FIGHT PARADE 20XX
ERIC PUMMEL VS GRAVY TRAIN at ROAD TO ULTRA BRAWL XXVI
MICHAEL MORRIS III POST-MATCH CONFERENCE at SLAM GALA VI

ACTIVE ROSTER

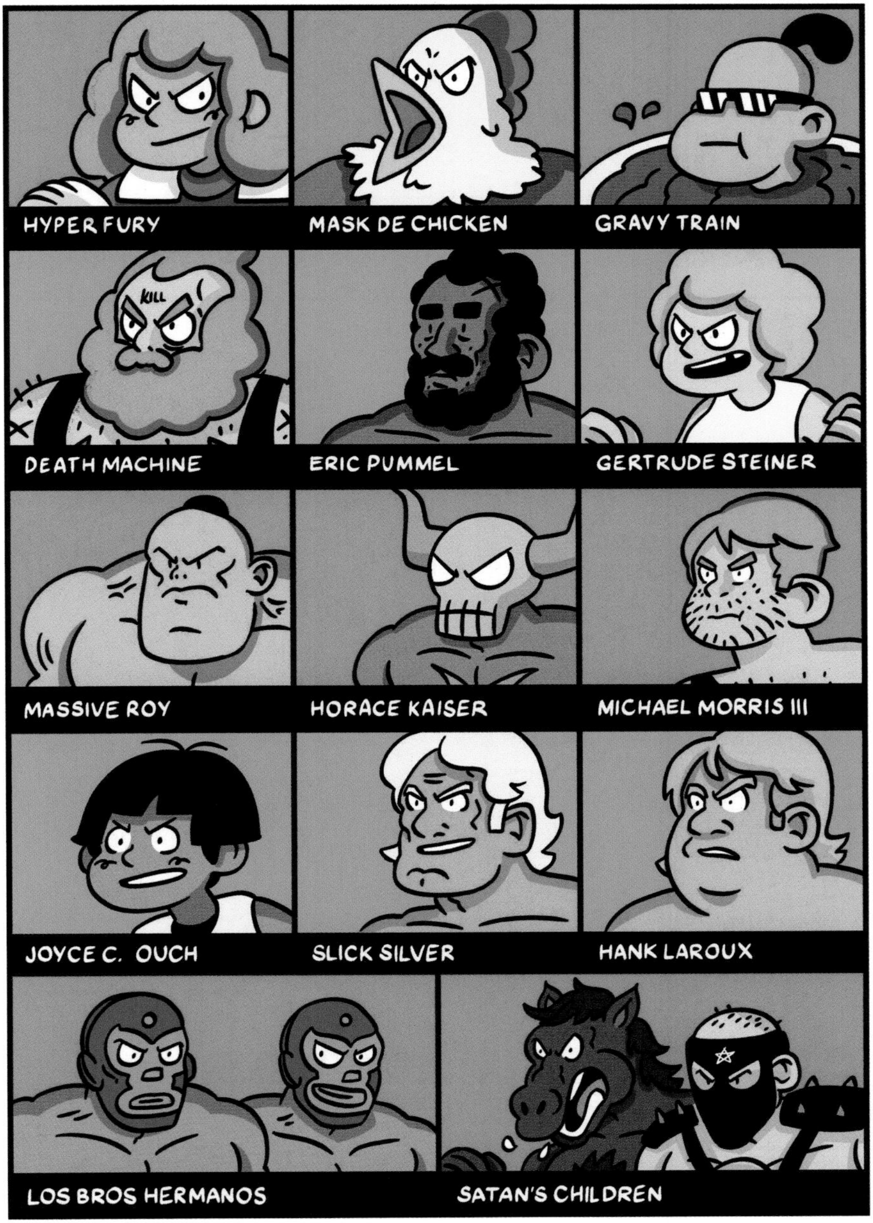
HYPER FURY
MASK DE CHICKEN
GRAVY TRAIN
KILL
DEATH MACHINE
ERIC PUMMEL
GERTRUDE STEINER
MASSIVE ROY
HORACE KAISER
MICHAEL MORRIS III
JOYCE C. OUCH
SLICK SILVER
HANK LAROUX
LOS BROS HERMANOS
SATAN'S CHILDREN

6 DAYS UNTIL ULTRABRAWL XXVI

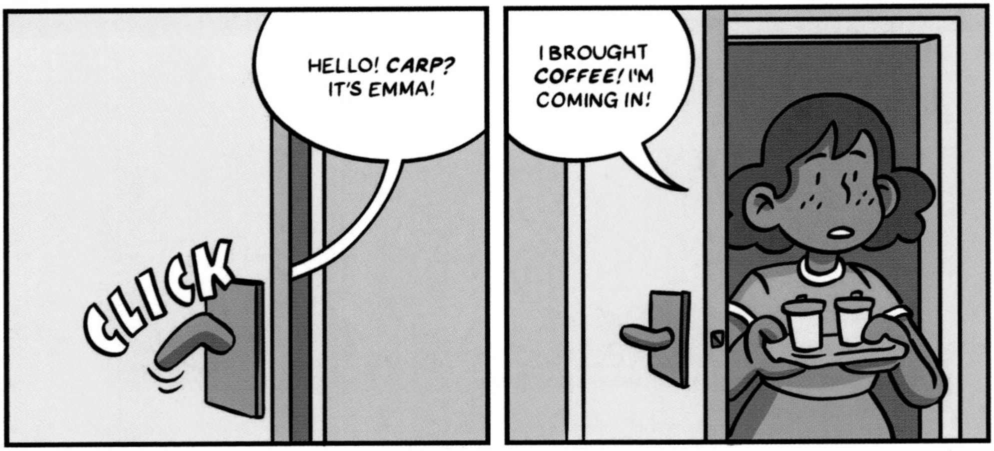

HELLO! CARP? IT'S EMMA!
CLICK
I BROUGHT COFFEE! I'M COMING IN!

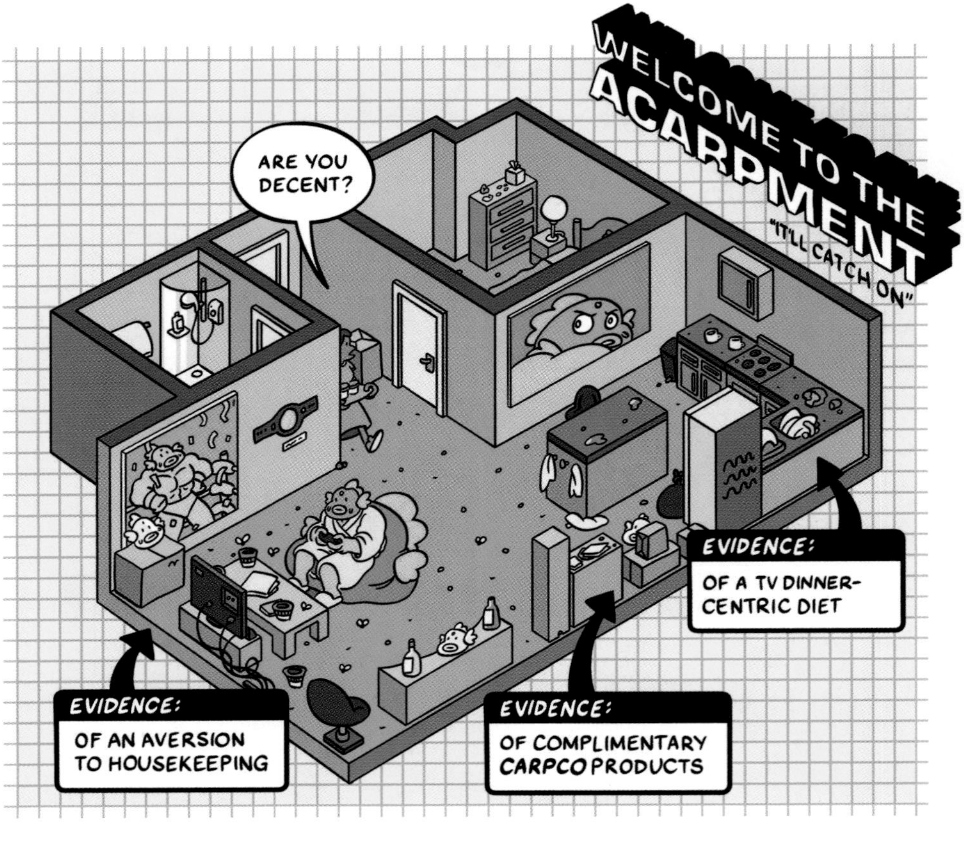

WELCOME TO THE ACARPMENT
"IT'LL CATCH ON"
ARE YOU DECENT?
EVIDENCE: OF A TV DINNER-CENTRIC DIET
EVIDENCE: OF AN AVERSION TO HOUSEKEEPING
EVIDENCE: OF COMPLIMENTARY CARPCO PRODUCTS

I'M ABOUT SIXTY PERCENT DECENT.

ARE YOU STILL PLAYING THAT GAME?

YEAH.

EVIDENCE: OF POOR PERSONAL HYGIENE

AT THE MOMENT, I'VE MADE **DEATH MACHINE** THE CHAMPION. HE BETRAYED ME IN A PIVOTAL TAG TEAM MATCH. **DICK.**

I'M CURRENTLY BUILDING UP TO BEAT HIM AND THE REST OF THE EVIL **POETRY-THEMED FACTION** THAT I MADE UP. EXCITING!!

ALSO, MY MAIN GUY IS IN THE START OF A BLOSSOMING RELATIONSHIP WITH **GRAVY TRAIN**, WHICH IS PRETTY COOL.

"HEH, THANKS. MAYBE I'LL GIVE YOU A CALL SOMETIME."

I RAN A TOURNAMENT TO SEE WHO'D BE WORTHY OF MY AFFECTIONS, AND HE WON. WE'RE TAKING IT SLOW FOR NOW!

WOW. IT'S COOL THAT THEY PUT ALL THOSE FEATURES IN THERE.

WELL, THEY PUT MOST OF THEM IN. BUT I HAVE MY OWN PAPER-BASED SYSTEM. I MADE DIAGRAMS!!

CARP WRESTLING ASSOCIATIO

THAT SEEMS... FINE? IS THIS *LITERALLY* ALL YOU'VE BEEN DOING SINCE THE LAST TIME I WAS HERE?

FIRST OF ALL, *STRUCTURED PLAY* IS AS IMPORTANT TO THE *GROWN ADULT* AS IT IS TO THE *DEVELOPING CHILD.*

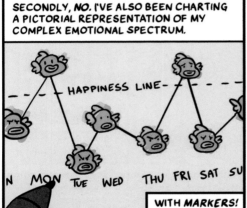

SECONDLY, *NO.* I'VE ALSO BEEN CHARTING A PICTORIAL REPRESENTATION OF MY COMPLEX EMOTIONAL SPECTRUM.

— HAPPINESS LINE —

N   MON   TUE   WED   THU   FRI   SAT   SU

WITH *MARKERS!*

WHEN DID YOU GO OUTSIDE LAST?

ABOUT FOUR *'NON-PLUSSED'* FACES AGO.

I DREW A LITTLE TREE FOR IT.

ANYWAY, THE MERCHANDISE PEOPLE DON'T LIKE ME GOING OUT IN CASE I DO SOMETHING *'DAMAGING TO THE BRAND.'*

IF I DO GO OUTSIDE, I'M MEANT TO WEAR THE BIG HEAD.

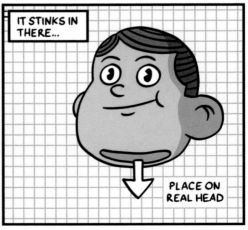

IT STINKS IN THERE...

PLACE ON REAL HEAD

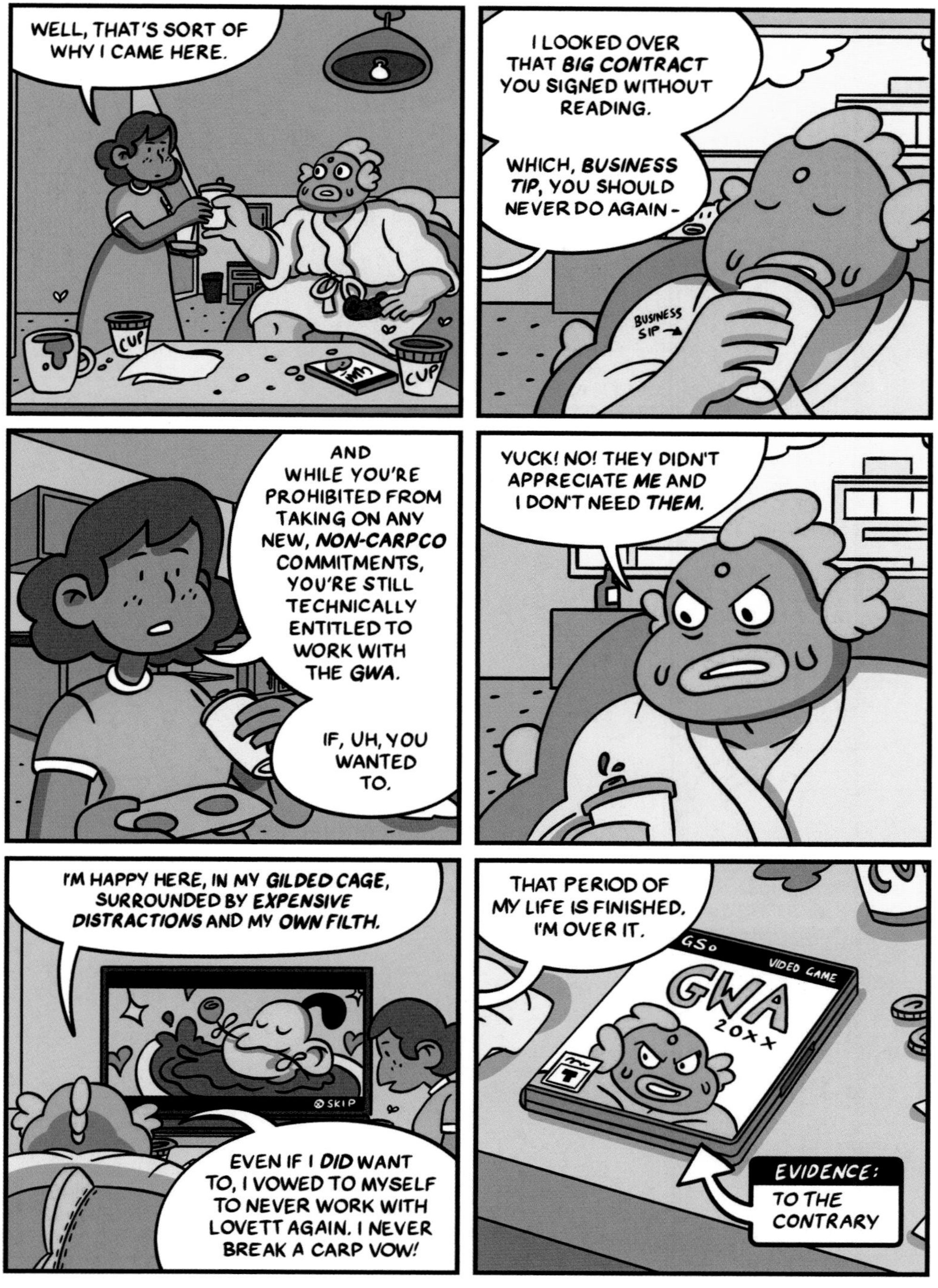
WELL, THAT'S SORT OF WHY I CAME HERE.
CUP
CUP
I LOOKED OVER THAT BIG CONTRACT YOU SIGNED WITHOUT READING.
WHICH, BUSINESS TIP, YOU SHOULD NEVER DO AGAIN -
BUSINESS SIP
AND WHILE YOU'RE PROHIBITED FROM TAKING ON ANY NEW, NON-CARPCO COMMITMENTS, YOU'RE STILL TECHNICALLY ENTITLED TO WORK WITH THE GWA.
IF, UH, YOU WANTED TO.
YUCK! NO! THEY DIDN'T APPRECIATE ME AND I DON'T NEED THEM.
I'M HAPPY HERE, IN MY GILDED CAGE, SURROUNDED BY EXPENSIVE DISTRACTIONS AND MY OWN FILTH.
SKIP
EVEN IF I DID WANT TO, I VOWED TO MYSELF TO NEVER WORK WITH LOVETT AGAIN. I NEVER BREAK A CARP VOW!
THAT PERIOD OF MY LIFE IS FINISHED. I'M OVER IT.
GS
VIDEO GAME
GWA
20XX
EVIDENCE:
TO THE CONTRARY

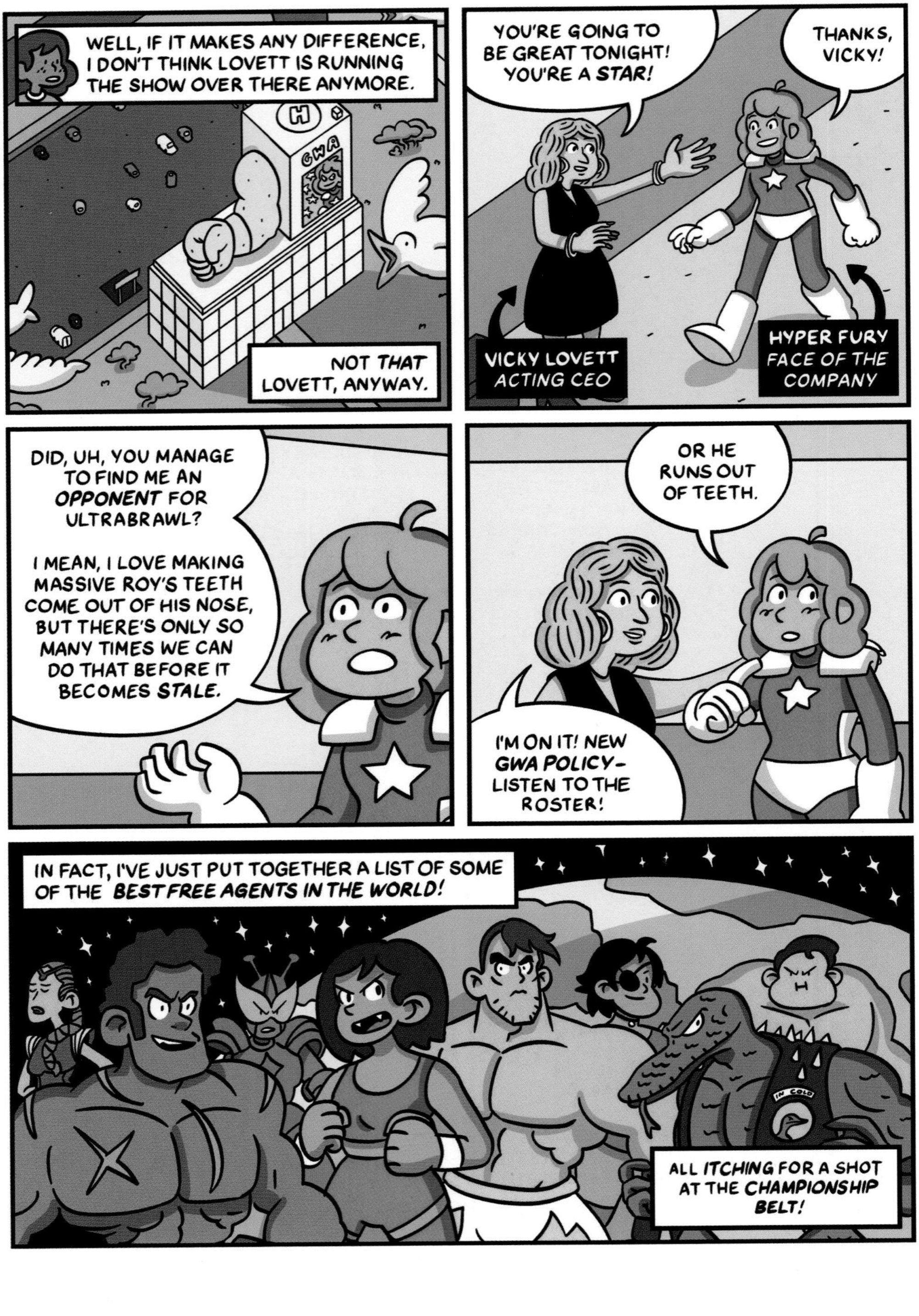
WELL, IF IT MAKES ANY DIFFERENCE, I DON'T THINK LOVETT IS RUNNING THE SHOW OVER THERE ANYMORE.
GWA
NOT THAT LOVETT, ANYWAY.
YOU'RE GOING TO BE GREAT TONIGHT! YOU'RE A STAR!
THANKS, VICKY!
VICKY LOVETT ACTING CEO
HYPER FURY FACE OF THE COMPANY
DID, UH, YOU MANAGE TO FIND ME AN OPPONENT FOR ULTRABRAWL?
I MEAN, I LOVE MAKING MASSIVE ROY'S TEETH COME OUT OF HIS NOSE, BUT THERE'S ONLY SO MANY TIMES WE CAN DO THAT BEFORE IT BECOMES STALE.
OR HE RUNS OUT OF TEETH.
I'M ON IT! NEW GWA POLICY-LISTEN TO THE ROSTER!
IN FACT, I'VE JUST PUT TOGETHER A LIST OF SOME OF THE BEST FREE AGENTS IN THE WORLD!
ALL ITCHING FOR A SHOT AT THE CHAMPIONSHIP BELT!

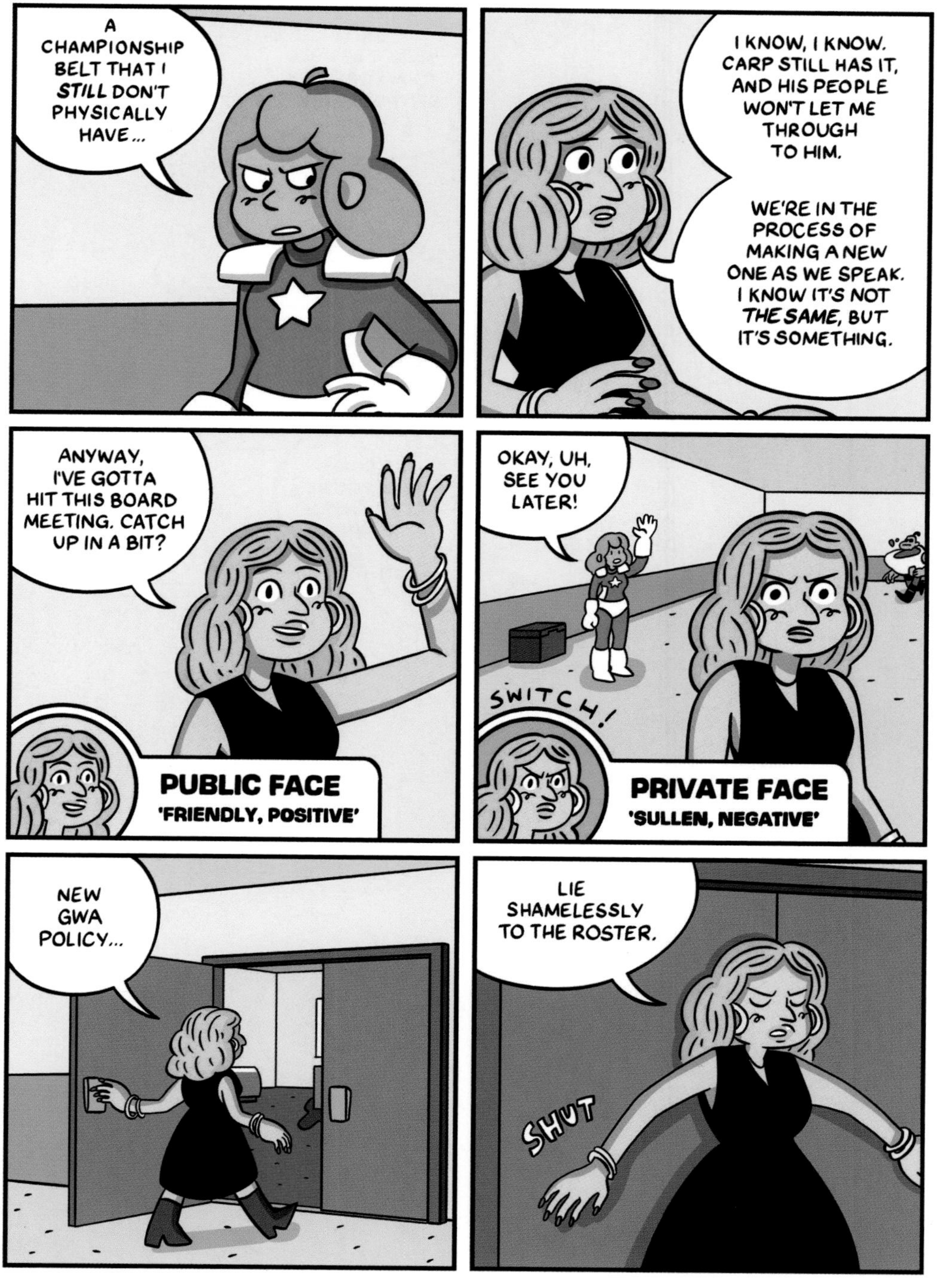
A CHAMPIONSHIP BELT THAT I STILL DON'T PHYSICALLY HAVE...
I KNOW, I KNOW. CARP STILL HAS IT, AND HIS PEOPLE WON'T LET ME THROUGH TO HIM.
WE'RE IN THE PROCESS OF MAKING A NEW ONE AS WE SPEAK. I KNOW IT'S NOT THE SAME, BUT IT'S SOMETHING.
ANYWAY, I'VE GOTTA HIT THIS BOARD MEETING. CATCH UP IN A BIT?
PUBLIC FACE
'FRIENDLY, POSITIVE'
OKAY, UH, SEE YOU LATER!
SWITCH!
PRIVATE FACE
'SULLEN, NEGATIVE'
NEW GWA POLICY...
LIE SHAMELESSLY TO THE ROSTER.
SHUT

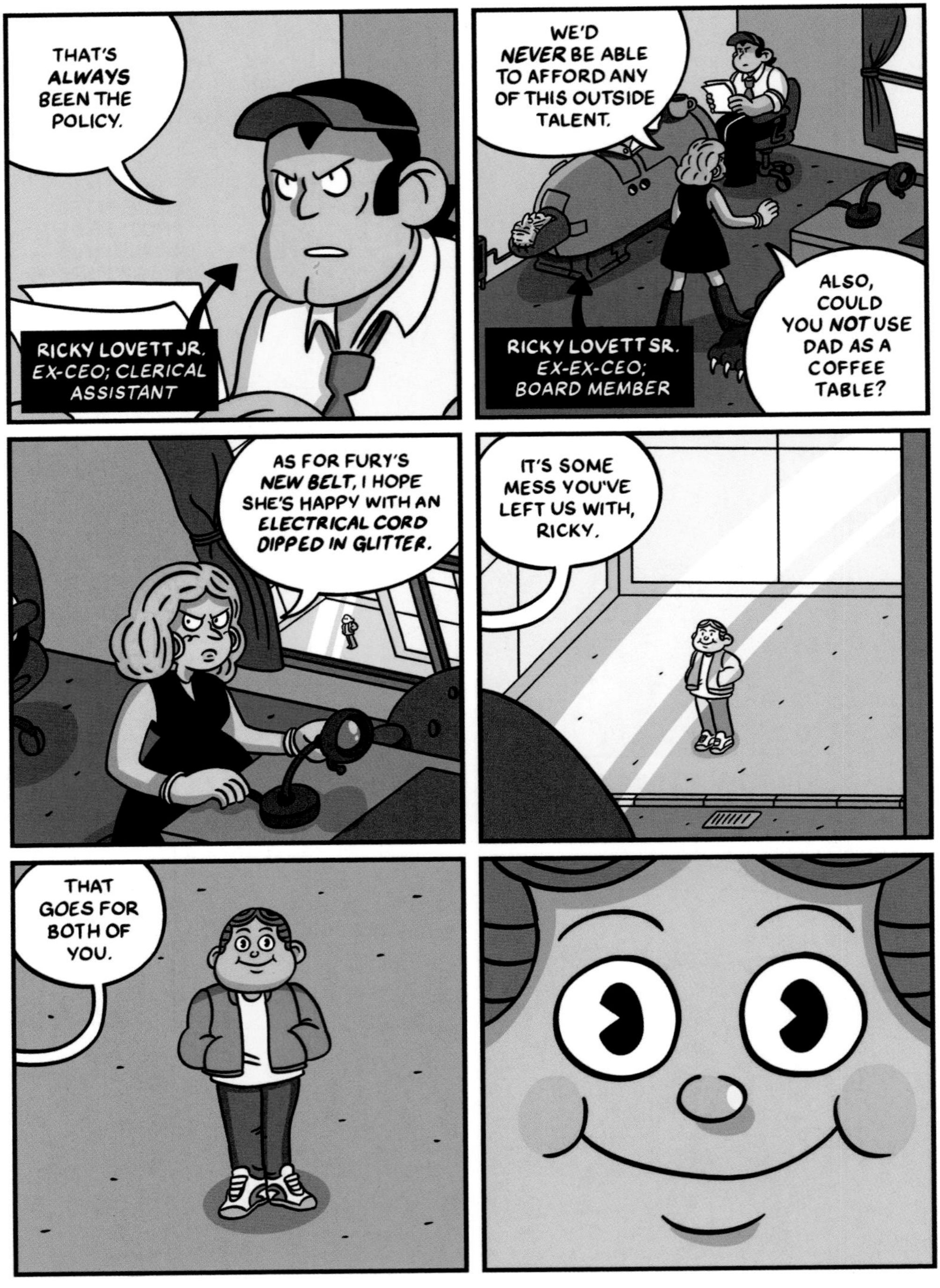
THAT'S ALWAYS BEEN THE POLICY.
RICKY LOVETT JR. EX-CEO; CLERICAL ASSISTANT
WE'D NEVER BE ABLE TO AFFORD ANY OF THIS OUTSIDE TALENT.
RICKY LOVETT SR. EX-EX-CEO; BOARD MEMBER
ALSO, COULD YOU NOT USE DAD AS A COFFEE TABLE?
AS FOR FURY'S NEW BELT, I HOPE SHE'S HAPPY WITH AN ELECTRICAL CORD DIPPED IN GLITTER.
IT'S SOME MESS YOU'VE LEFT US WITH, RICKY.
THAT GOES FOR BOTH OF YOU.

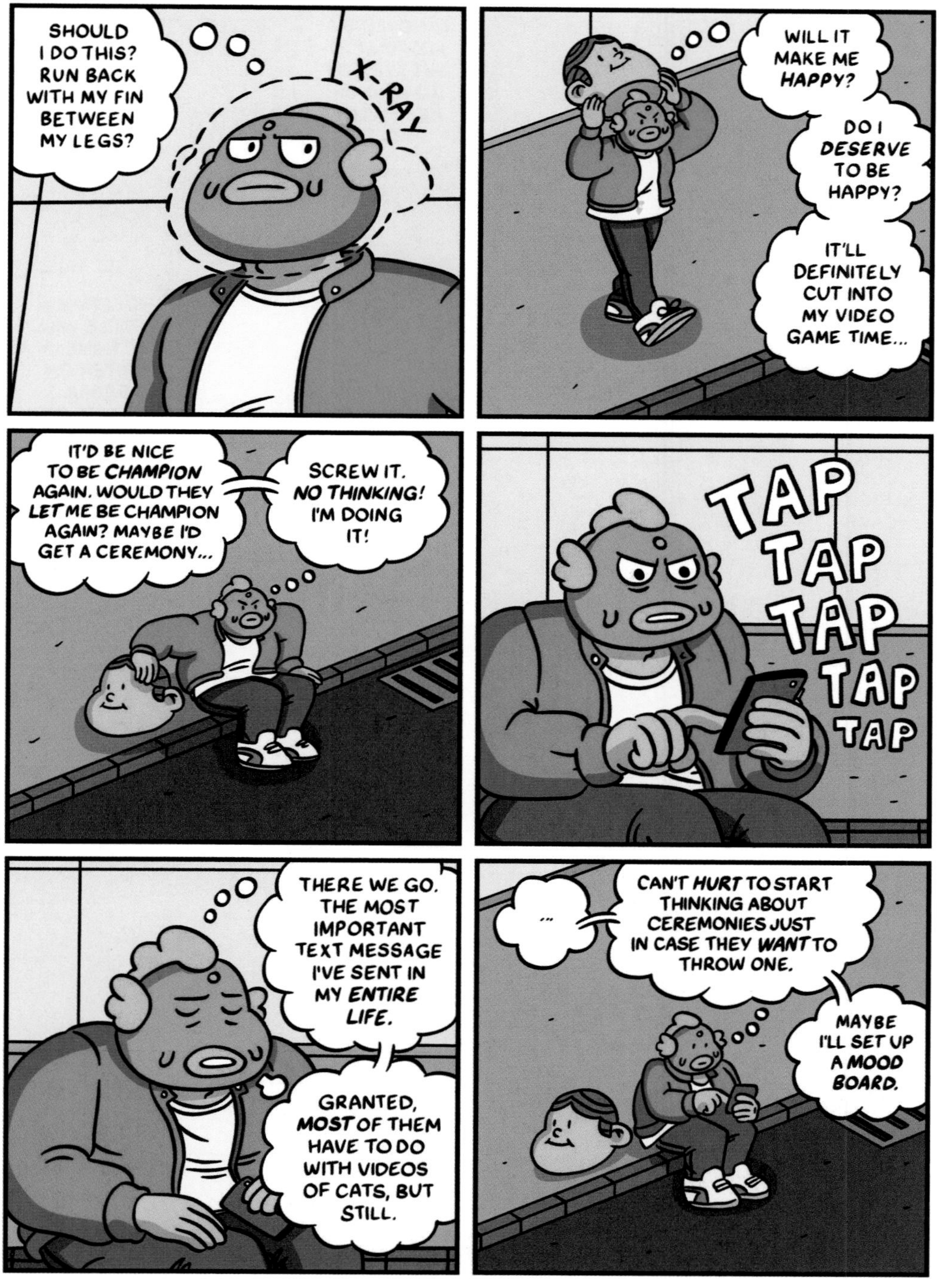
SHOULD I DO THIS? RUN BACK WITH MY FIN BETWEEN MY LEGS?
X-RAY
WILL IT MAKE ME HAPPY?
DO I DESERVE TO BE HAPPY?
IT'LL DEFINITELY CUT INTO MY VIDEO GAME TIME...
IT'D BE NICE TO BE CHAMPION AGAIN. WOULD THEY LET ME BE CHAMPION AGAIN? MAYBE I'D GET A CEREMONY...
SCREW IT. NO THINKING! I'M DOING IT!
TAP TAP TAP TAP TAP
THERE WE GO. THE MOST IMPORTANT TEXT MESSAGE I'VE SENT IN MY ENTIRE LIFE.
GRANTED, MOST OF THEM HAVE TO DO WITH VIDEOS OF CATS, BUT STILL.
...
CAN'T HURT TO START THINKING ABOUT CEREMONIES JUST IN CASE THEY WANT TO THROW ONE.
MAYBE I'LL SET UP A MOOD BOARD.

3 DAYS UNTIL ULTRABRAWL XXVI

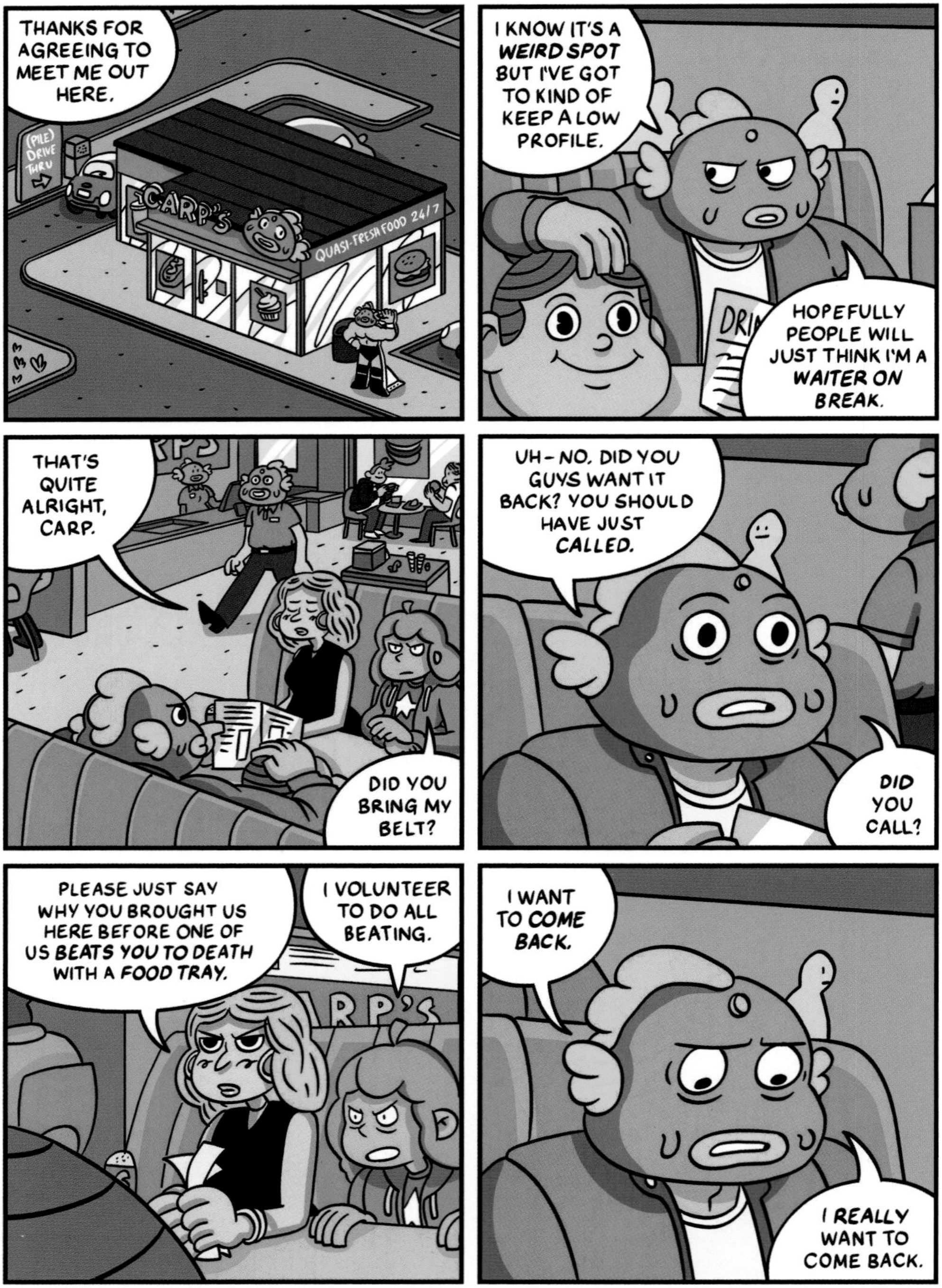
THANKS FOR AGREEING TO MEET ME OUT HERE.
(PILE) DRIVE THRU
CARP'S
QUASI-FRESH FOOD 24/7
I KNOW IT'S A *WEIRD SPOT* BUT I'VE GOT TO KIND OF KEEP A LOW PROFILE.
HOPEFULLY PEOPLE WILL JUST THINK I'M A *WAITER ON BREAK.*
THAT'S QUITE ALRIGHT, CARP.
DID YOU BRING MY BELT?
UH- NO, DID YOU GUYS WANT IT BACK? YOU SHOULD HAVE JUST *CALLED.*
DID YOU CALL?
PLEASE JUST SAY WHY YOU BROUGHT US HERE BEFORE ONE OF US *BEATS YOU TO DEATH* WITH A *FOOD TRAY.*
I VOLUNTEER TO DO ALL BEATING.
I WANT TO *COME* BACK.
I *REALLY* WANT TO COME BACK.

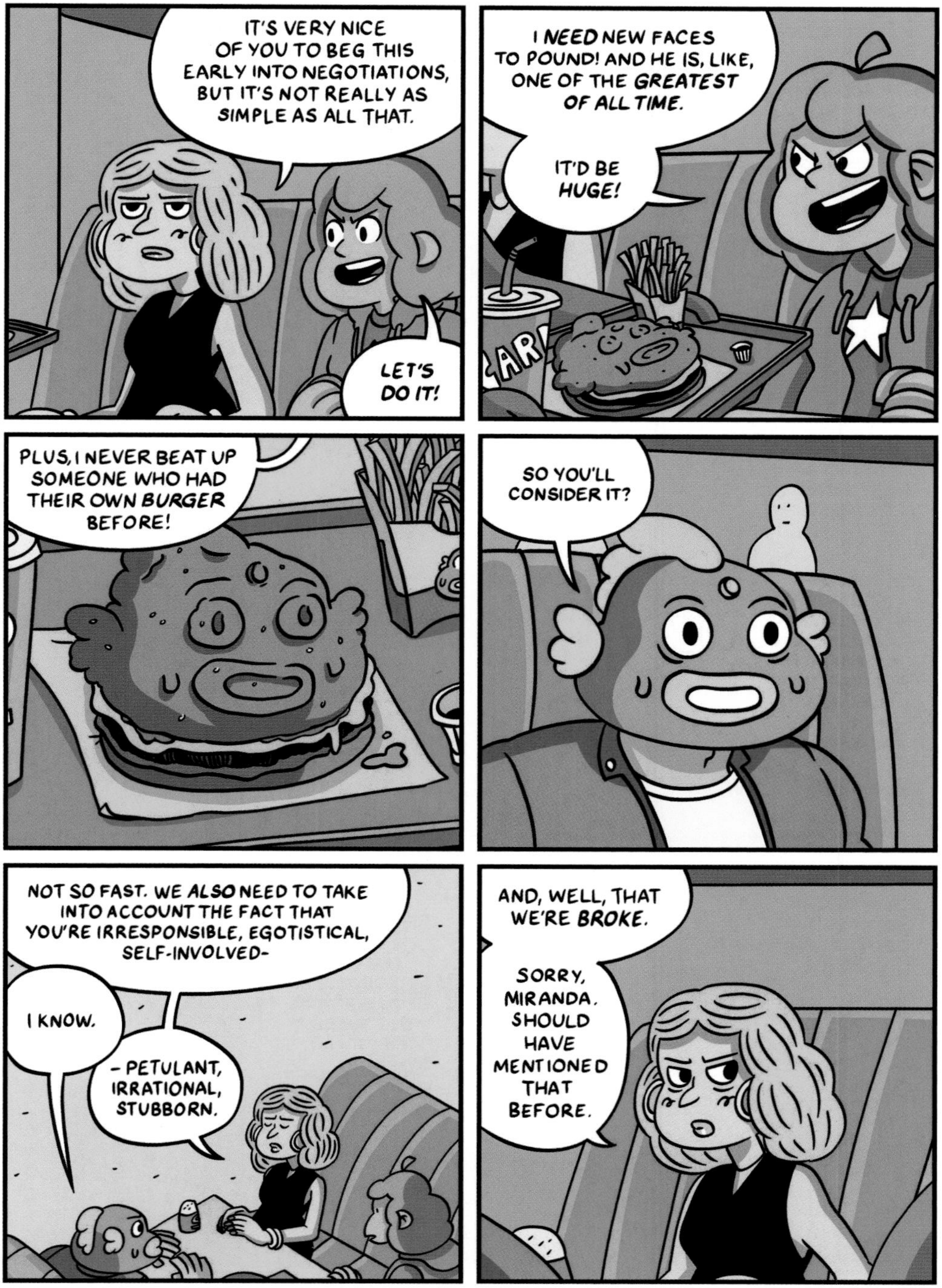
IT'S VERY NICE OF YOU TO BEG THIS EARLY INTO NEGOTIATIONS, BUT IT'S NOT REALLY AS SIMPLE AS ALL THAT.
LET'S DO IT!
I NEED NEW FACES TO POUND! AND HE IS, LIKE, ONE OF THE GREATEST OF ALL TIME.
IT'D BE HUGE!
PLUS, I NEVER BEAT UP SOMEONE WHO HAD THEIR OWN BURGER BEFORE!
SO YOU'LL CONSIDER IT?
NOT SO FAST. WE ALSO NEED TO TAKE INTO ACCOUNT THE FACT THAT YOU'RE IRRESPONSIBLE, EGOTISTICAL, SELF-INVOLVED-
I KNOW.
- PETULANT, IRRATIONAL, STUBBORN.
AND, WELL, THAT WE'RE BROKE.
SORRY, MIRANDA. SHOULD HAVE MENTIONED THAT BEFORE.

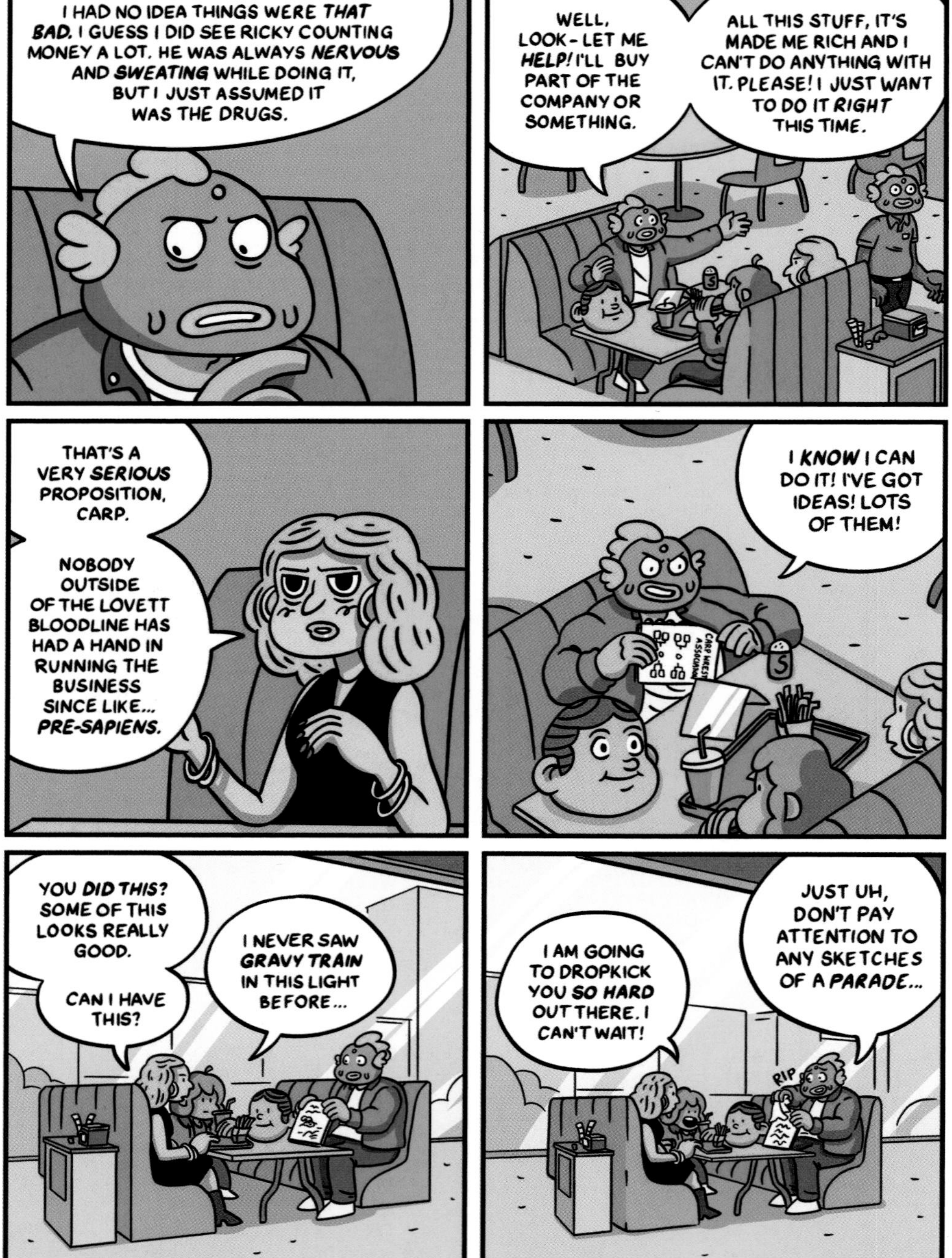
I HAD NO IDEA THINGS WERE THAT BAD. I GUESS I DID SEE RICKY COUNTING MONEY A LOT. HE WAS ALWAYS NERVOUS AND SWEATING WHILE DOING IT, BUT I JUST ASSUMED IT WAS THE DRUGS.
WELL, LOOK - LET ME HELP! I'LL BUY PART OF THE COMPANY OR SOMETHING.
ALL THIS STUFF, IT'S MADE ME RICH AND I CAN'T DO ANYTHING WITH IT. PLEASE! I JUST WANT TO DO IT RIGHT THIS TIME.
THAT'S A VERY SERIOUS PROPOSITION, CARP.
NOBODY OUTSIDE OF THE LOVETT BLOODLINE HAS HAD A HAND IN RUNNING THE BUSINESS SINCE LIKE... PRE-SAPIENS.
I KNOW I CAN DO IT! I'VE GOT IDEAS! LOTS OF THEM!
YOU DID THIS? SOME OF THIS LOOKS REALLY GOOD.
CAN I HAVE THIS?
I NEVER SAW GRAVY TRAIN IN THIS LIGHT BEFORE...
I AM GOING TO DROPKICK YOU SO HARD OUT THERE. I CAN'T WAIT!
JUST UH, DON'T PAY ATTENTION TO ANY SKETCHES OF A PARADE...
RIP

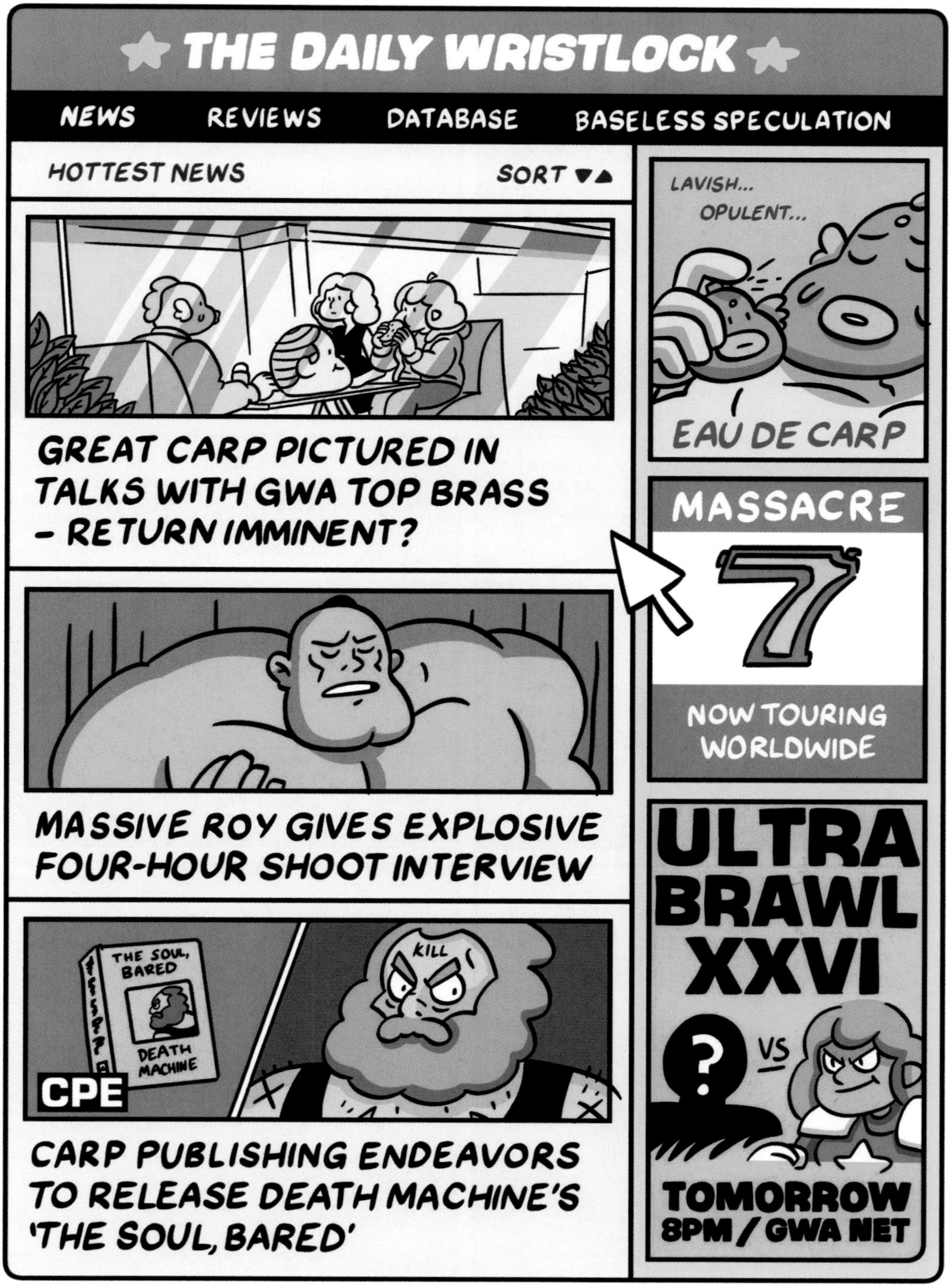
THE DAILY WRISTLOCK
NEWS
REVIEWS
DATABASE
BASELESS SPECULATION
HOTTEST NEWS
SORT
GREAT CARP PICTURED IN TALKS WITH GWA TOP BRASS - RETURN IMMINENT?
MASSIVE ROY GIVES EXPLOSIVE FOUR-HOUR SHOOT INTERVIEW
THE SOUL, BARED
DEATH MACHINE
KILL
CPE
CARP PUBLISHING ENDEAVORS TO RELEASE DEATH MACHINE'S 'THE SOUL, BARED'
LAVISH...
OPULENT...
EAU DE CARP
MASSACRE
7
NOW TOURING WORLDWIDE
ULTRA BRAWL XXVI
?
VS
TOMORROW
8PM / GWA NET

8 HOURS UNTIL ULTRABAWL XXVI

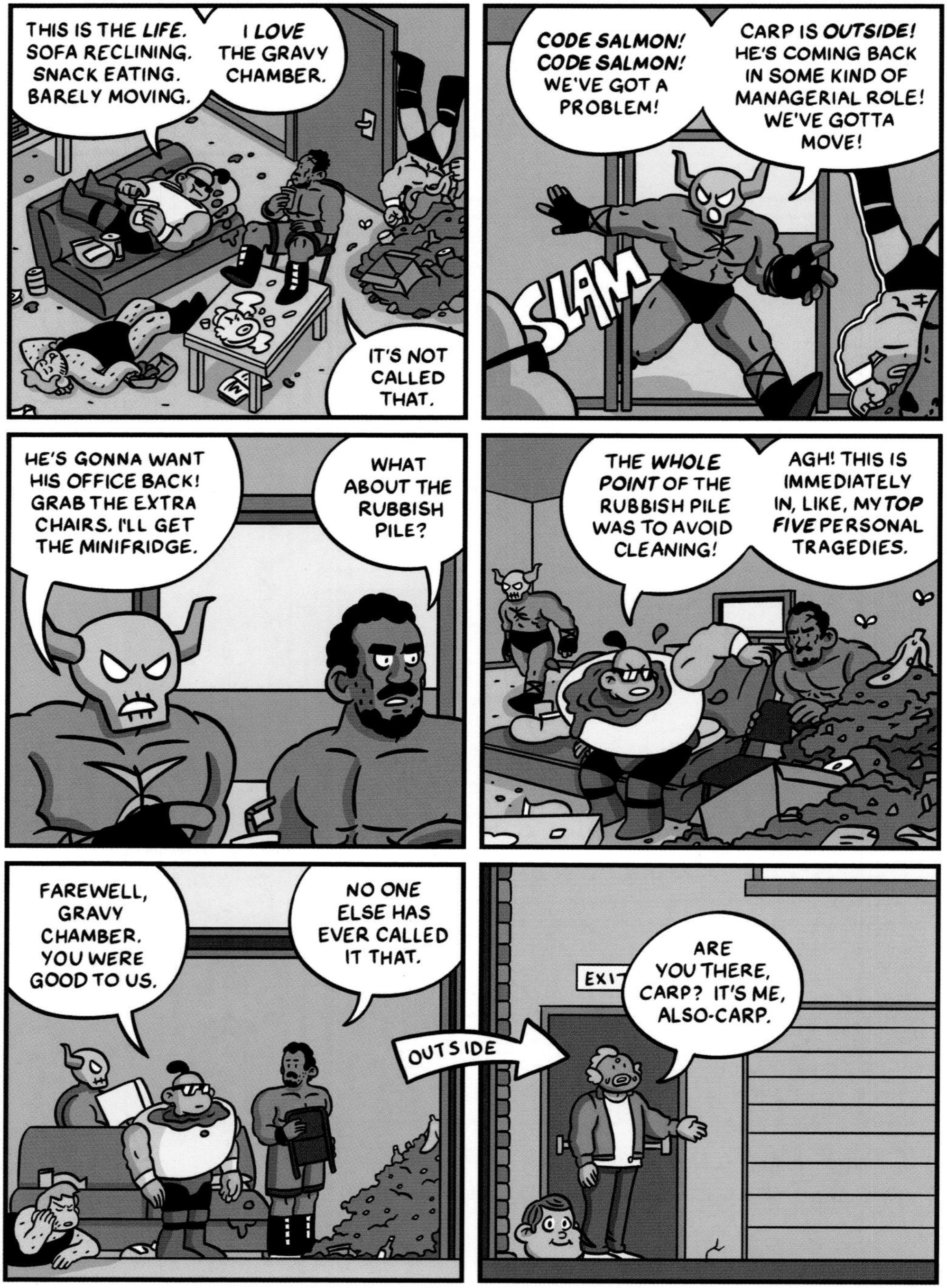
THIS IS THE *LIFE*. SOFA RECLINING. SNACK EATING. BARELY MOVING.
I *LOVE* THE GRAVY CHAMBER.
IT'S NOT CALLED THAT.
CODE SALMON! CODE SALMON! WE'VE GOT A PROBLEM!
CARP IS *OUTSIDE!* HE'S COMING BACK IN SOME KIND OF MANAGERIAL ROLE! WE'VE GOTTA MOVE!
SLAM
HE'S GONNA WANT HIS OFFICE BACK! GRAB THE EXTRA CHAIRS. I'LL GET THE MINIFRIDGE.
WHAT ABOUT THE RUBBISH PILE?
THE *WHOLE POINT* OF THE RUBBISH PILE WAS TO AVOID CLEANING!
AGH! THIS IS IMMEDIATELY IN, LIKE, MY *TOP FIVE* PERSONAL TRAGEDIES.
FAREWELL, GRAVY CHAMBER. YOU WERE GOOD TO US.
NO ONE ELSE HAS EVER CALLED IT THAT.
OUTSIDE
EXI
ARE YOU THERE, CARP? IT'S ME, ALSO-CARP.

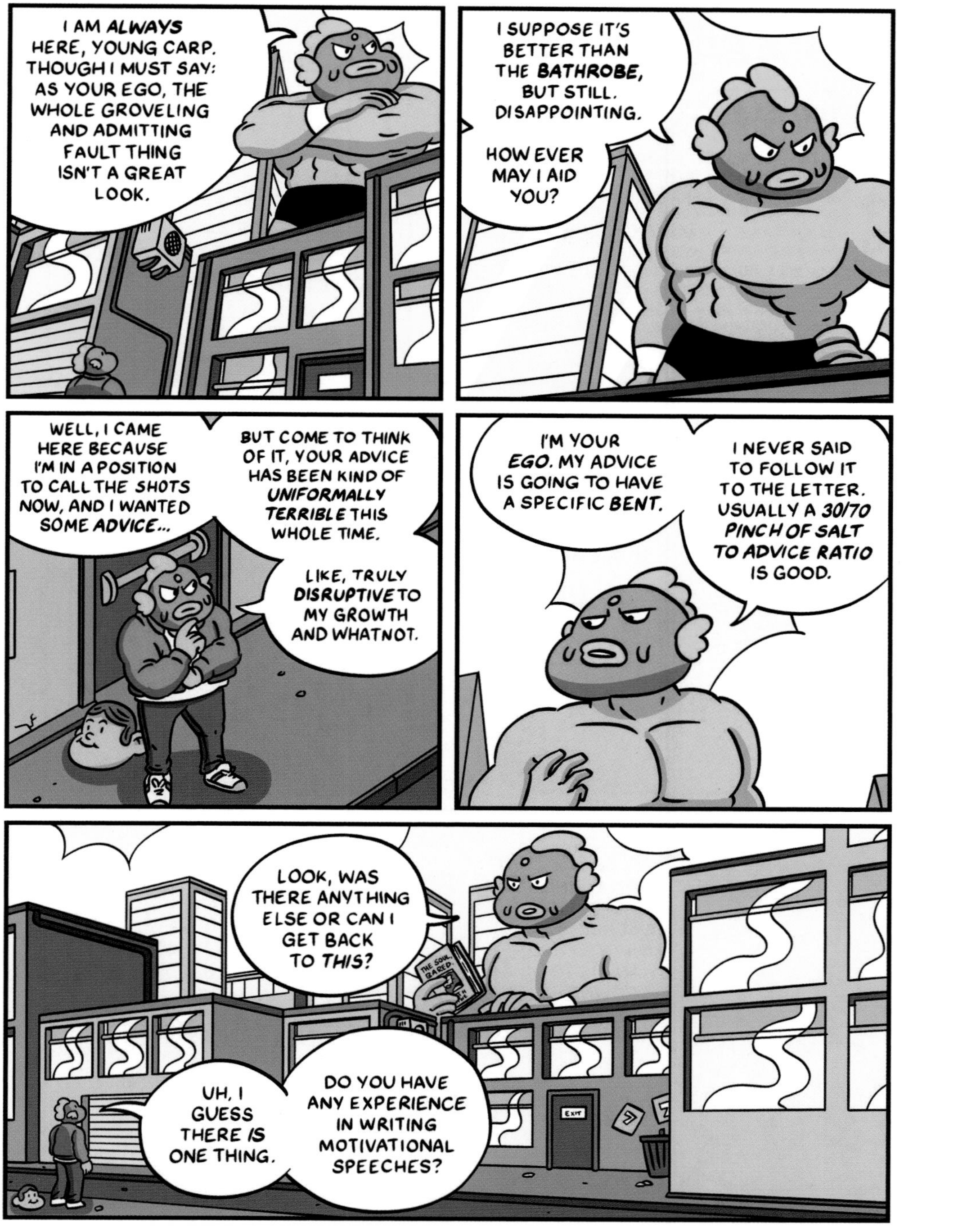
I AM ALWAYS HERE, YOUNG CARP. THOUGH I MUST SAY: AS YOUR EGO, THE WHOLE GROVELING AND ADMITTING FAULT THING ISN'T A GREAT LOOK.
I SUPPOSE IT'S BETTER THAN THE BATHROBE, BUT STILL. DISAPPOINTING.
HOW EVER MAY I AID YOU?
WELL, I CAME HERE BECAUSE I'M IN A POSITION TO CALL THE SHOTS NOW, AND I WANTED SOME ADVICE...
BUT COME TO THINK OF IT, YOUR ADVICE HAS BEEN KIND OF UNIFORMALLY TERRIBLE THIS WHOLE TIME.
LIKE, TRULY DISRUPTIVE TO MY GROWTH AND WHATNOT.
I'M YOUR EGO. MY ADVICE IS GOING TO HAVE A SPECIFIC BENT.
I NEVER SAID TO FOLLOW IT TO THE LETTER. USUALLY A 30/70 PINCH OF SALT TO ADVICE RATIO IS GOOD.
LOOK, WAS THERE ANYTHING ELSE OR CAN I GET BACK TO THIS?
THE SOUL BARED
UH, I GUESS THERE IS ONE THING.
DO YOU HAVE ANY EXPERIENCE IN WRITING MOTIVATIONAL SPEECHES?
EXIT

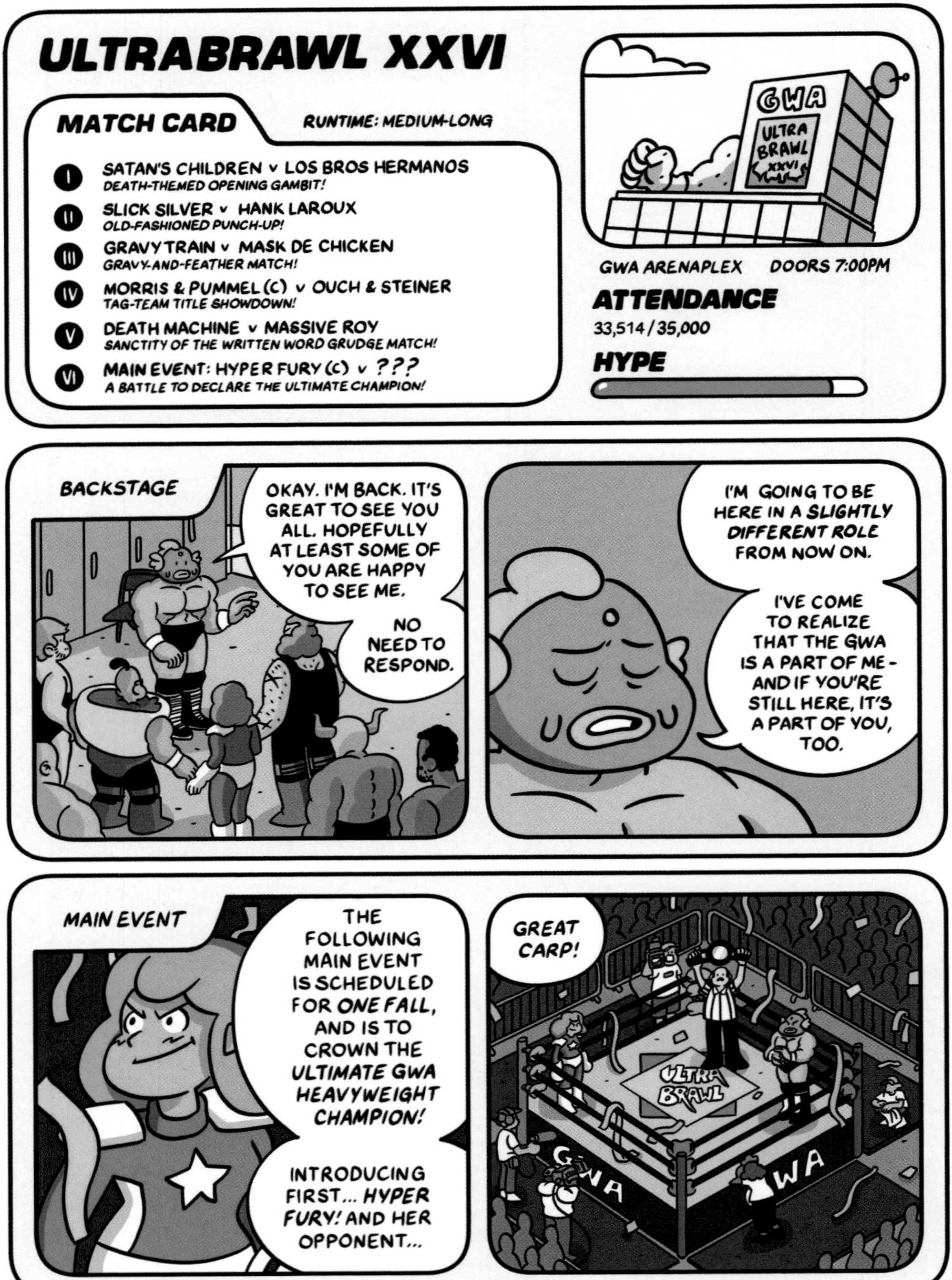
ULTRABRAWL XXVI
MATCH CARD
RUNTIME: MEDIUM-LONG
I SATAN'S CHILDREN v LOS BROS HERMANOS
DEATH-THEMED OPENING GAMBIT!
II SLICK SILVER v HANK LAROUX
OLD-FASHIONED PUNCH-UP!
III GRAVYTRAIN v MASK DE CHICKEN
GRAVY-AND-FEATHER MATCH!
IV MORRIS & PUMMEL (C) v OUCH & STEINER
TAG-TEAM TITLE SHOWDOWN!
V DEATH MACHINE v MASSIVE ROY
SANCTITY OF THE WRITTEN WORD GRUDGE MATCH!
VI MAIN EVENT: HYPER FURY (C) v ???
A BATTLE TO DECLARE THE ULTIMATE CHAMPION!
GWA
ULTRA BRAWL XXVI
GWA ARENAPLEX
DOORS 7:00PM
ATTENDANCE
33,514 / 35,000
HYPE
BACKSTAGE
OKAY. I'M BACK. IT'S GREAT TO SEE YOU ALL. HOPEFULLY AT LEAST SOME OF YOU ARE HAPPY TO SEE ME.
NO NEED TO RESPOND.
I'M GOING TO BE HERE IN A SLIGHTLY DIFFERENT ROLE FROM NOW ON.
I'VE COME TO REALIZE THAT THE GWA IS A PART OF ME - AND IF YOU'RE STILL HERE, IT'S A PART OF YOU, TOO.
MAIN EVENT
THE FOLLOWING MAIN EVENT IS SCHEDULED FOR ONE FALL, AND IS TO CROWN THE ULTIMATE GWA HEAVYWEIGHT CHAMPION!
INTRODUCING FIRST... HYPER FURY! AND HER OPPONENT...
GREAT CARP!
ULTRA BRAWL
GWA
GWA

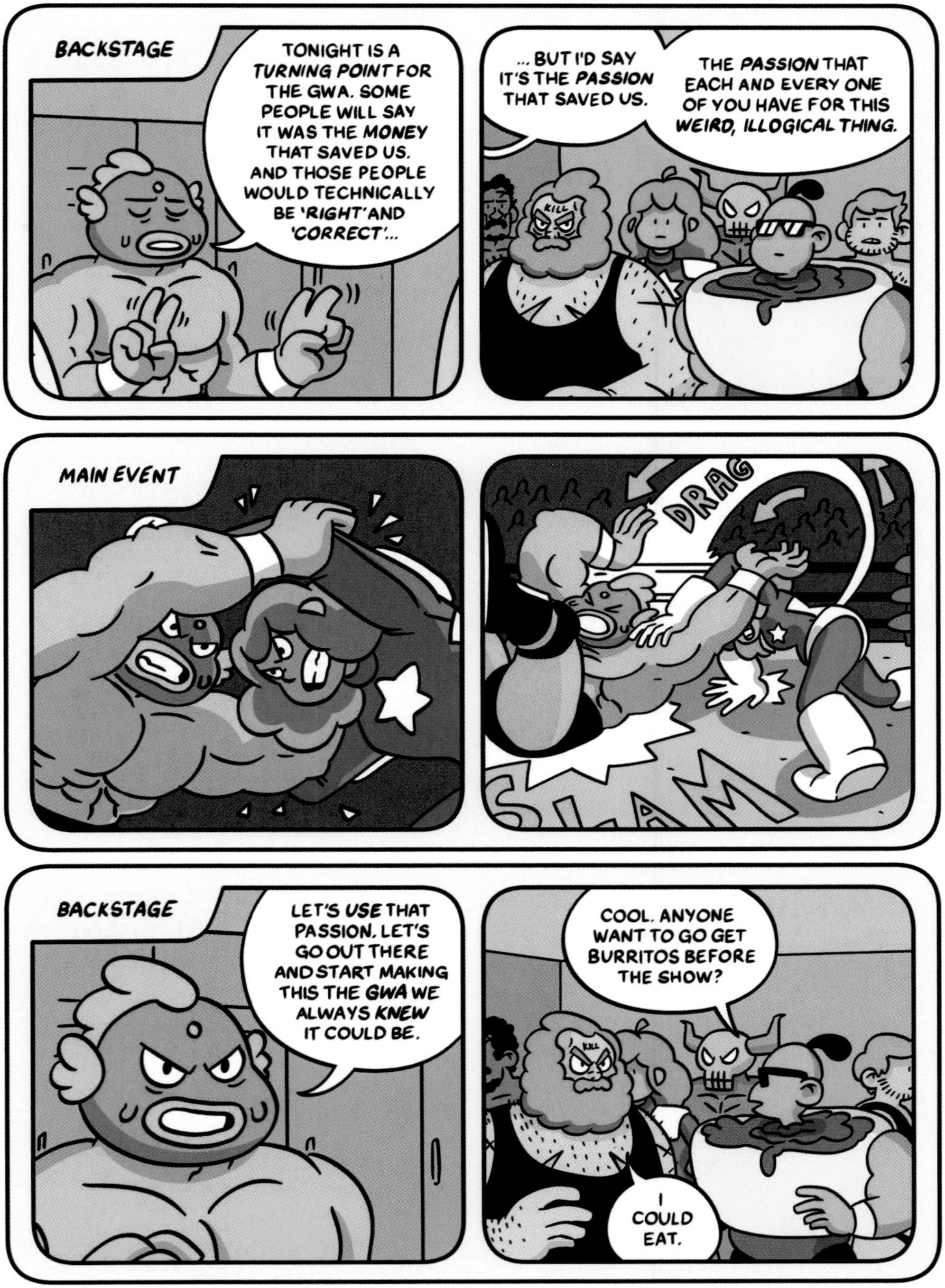
BACKSTAGE
TONIGHT IS A TURNING POINT FOR THE GWA. SOME PEOPLE WILL SAY IT WAS THE MONEY THAT SAVED US. AND THOSE PEOPLE WOULD TECHNICALLY BE 'RIGHT' AND 'CORRECT'...
... BUT I'D SAY IT'S THE PASSION THAT SAVED US.
THE PASSION THAT EACH AND EVERY ONE OF YOU HAVE FOR THIS WEIRD, ILLOGICAL THING.
KILL
MAIN EVENT
DRAG
SLAM
BACKSTAGE
LET'S USE THAT PASSION. LET'S GO OUT THERE AND START MAKING THIS THE GWA WE ALWAYS KNEW IT COULD BE.
COOL. ANYONE WANT TO GO GET BURRITOS BEFORE THE SHOW?
I COULD EAT.

MAIN EVENT

POETRY CORNER

WITH WHAT INTERNAL FIENDS YOU WRESTLE, CARP, WE MAY NEVER BE CERTAIN,

KILL

BUT A WARRIOR'S ROLE IS TO FIGHT THE FIGHT UNTIL THAT FINAL CURTAIN.

KILL

MAIN EVENT

REVERSAL

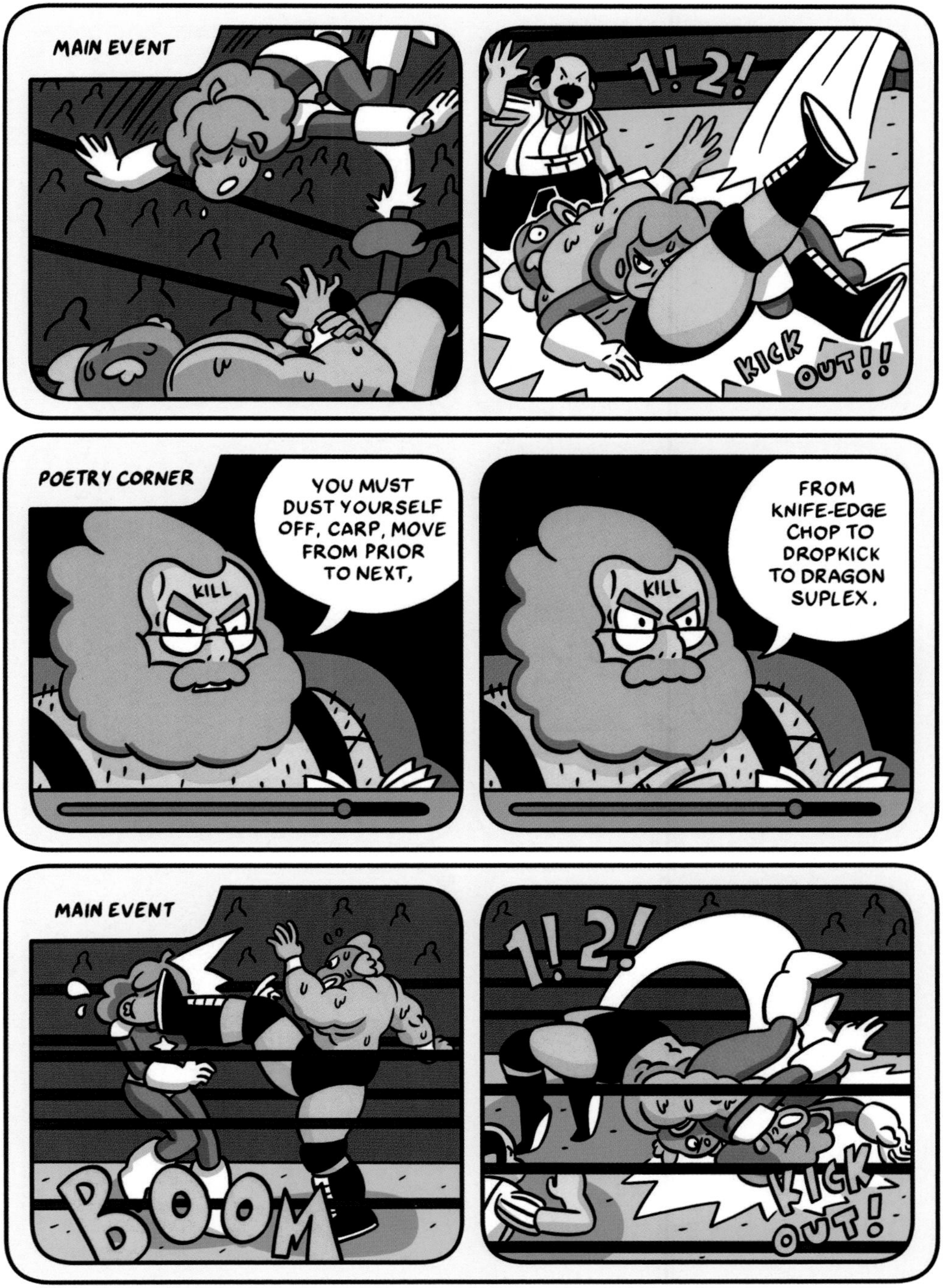
MAIN EVENT
1! 2!
KICK OUT!!
POETRY CORNER
YOU MUST DUST YOURSELF OFF, CARP, MOVE FROM PRIOR TO NEXT,
KILL
FROM KNIFE-EDGE CHOP TO DROPKICK TO DRAGON SUPLEX.
KILL
MAIN EVENT
BOOM
1! 2!
KICK OUT!

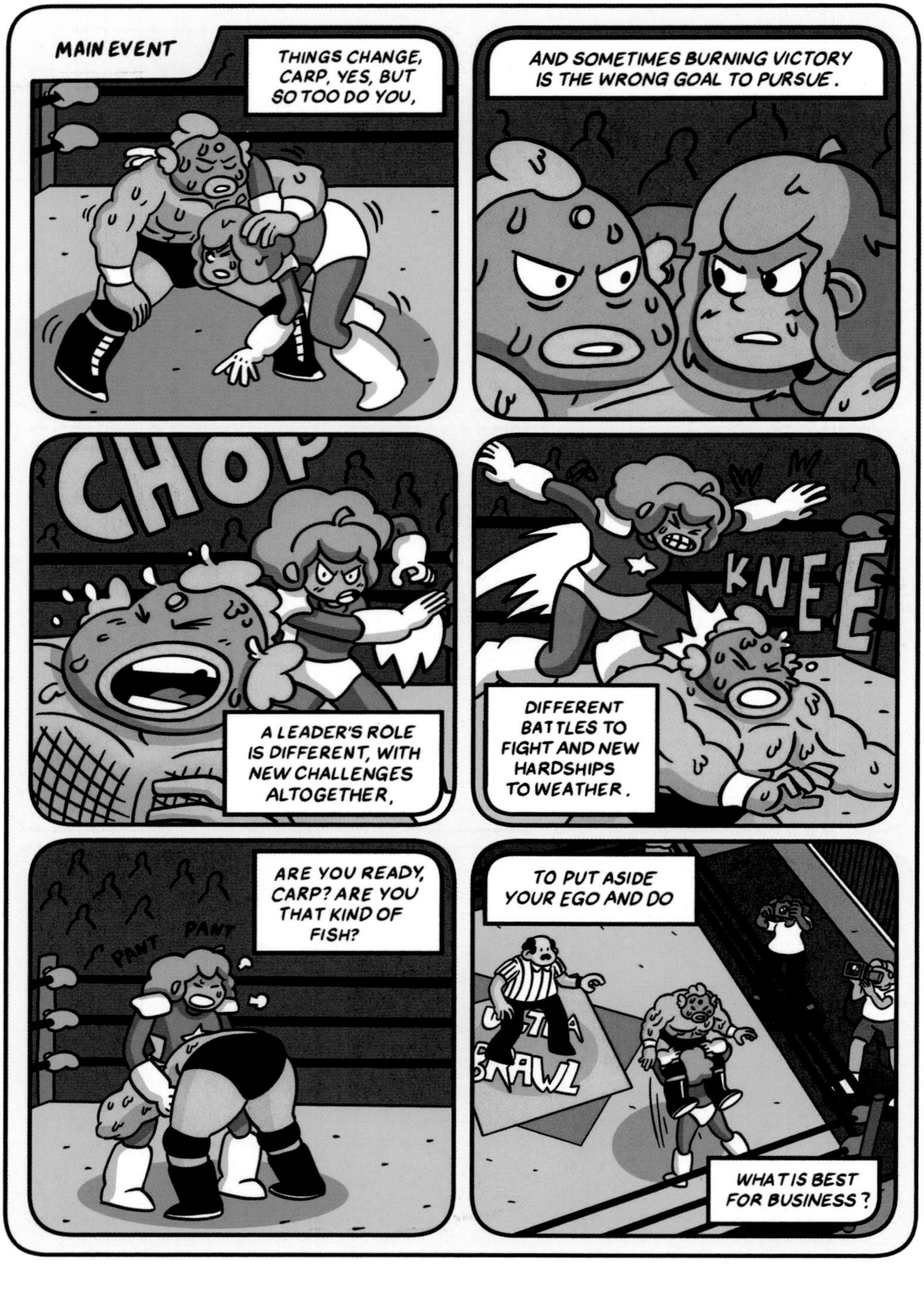
MAIN EVENT
THINGS CHANGE, CARP, YES, BUT SO TOO DO YOU,
AND SOMETIMES BURNING VICTORY IS THE WRONG GOAL TO PURSUE.
CHOP
A LEADER'S ROLE IS DIFFERENT, WITH NEW CHALLENGES ALTOGETHER,
KNEE
DIFFERENT BATTLES TO FIGHT AND NEW HARDSHIPS TO WEATHER.
ARE YOU READY, CARP? ARE YOU THAT KIND OF FISH?
PANT
PANT
TO PUT ASIDE YOUR EGO AND DO
WHAT IS BEST FOR BUSINESS?

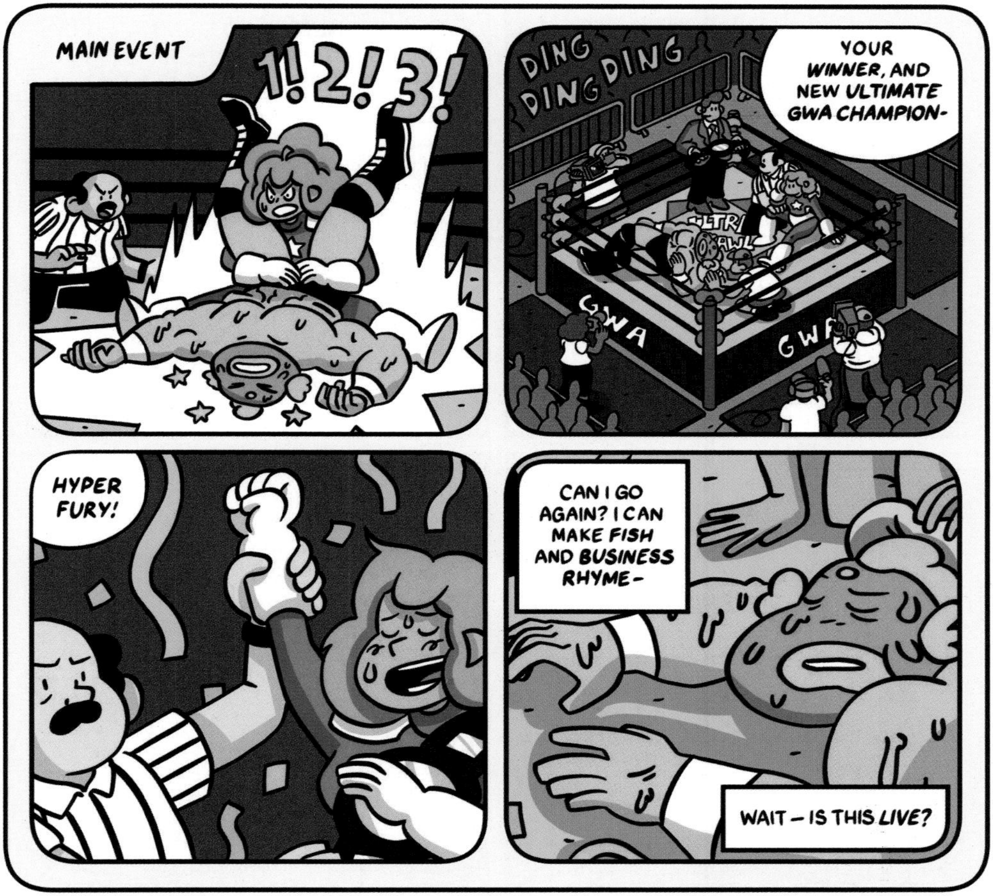
MAIN EVENT
1! 2! 3!
DING DING DING DING
YOUR WINNER, AND NEW ULTIMATE GWA CHAMPION-
ULTRABRAWL
GWA
GWA
HYPER FURY!
CAN I GO AGAIN? I CAN MAKE FISH AND BUSINESS RHYME-
WAIT – IS THIS LIVE?

ULTRABRAWL XXVI

RESULTS

I. LOS BROS HERMANOS def. SATAN'S CHILDREN
11:35, VICTORY BY PINFALL!

II. SLICK SILVER def. HANK LAROUX
12:45, VICTORY BY SUBMISSION!

III. GRAVY TRAIN def. MASK DE CHICKEN
16:12, VICTORY BY GRAVY-AND-FEATHERING!

IV. OUCH & STEINER (C) def. MORRIS & PUMMEL
18:20, TITLE CHANGE BY PINFALL!

V. DEATH MACHINE def. MASSIVE ROY
25:35, VICTORY BY SUBMISSION!

VI. MAIN EVENT: HYPER FURY (C) def. GREAT CARP (C)
37:30, ULTIMATE TITLE CROWNING BY PINFALL!

EXCITEMENT

ATHLETICISM

STORYTELLING

MERCH SALES

OVERALL RATING: A+ GOOD JOB!

351 DAYS UNTIL ULTRABAWL XXVII

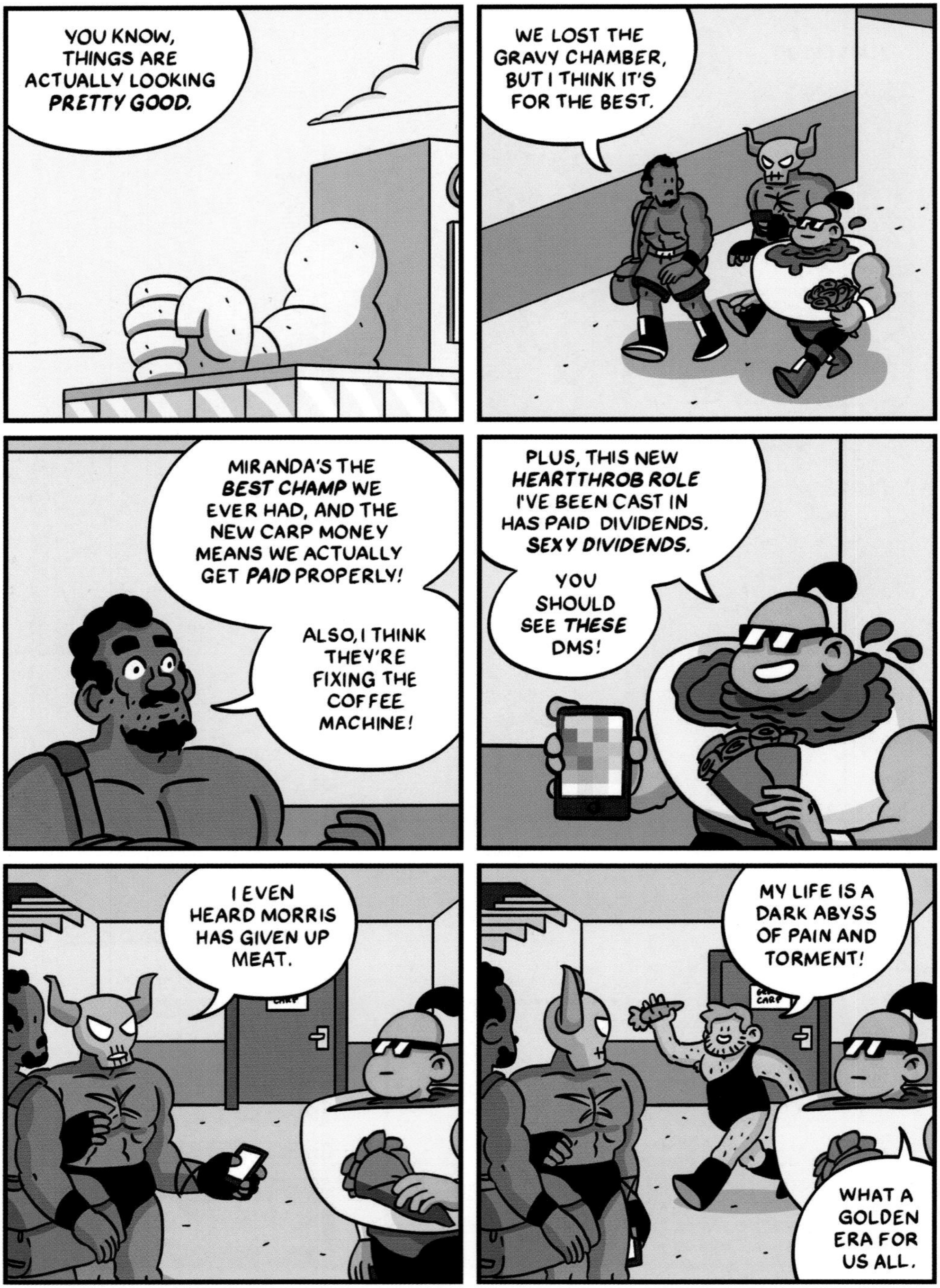

YOU KNOW, THINGS ARE ACTUALLY LOOKING *PRETTY GOOD.*
WE LOST THE GRAVY CHAMBER, BUT I THINK IT'S FOR THE BEST.
MIRANDA'S THE *BEST CHAMP* WE EVER HAD, AND THE NEW CARP MONEY MEANS WE ACTUALLY GET *PAID* PROPERLY!
ALSO, I THINK THEY'RE FIXING THE COFFEE MACHINE!
PLUS, THIS NEW *HEARTTHROB ROLE* I'VE BEEN CAST IN HAS PAID DIVIDENDS. *SEXY DIVIDENDS.*
YOU SHOULD SEE *THESE* DMS!
I EVEN HEARD MORRIS HAS GIVEN UP MEAT.
MY LIFE IS A DARK ABYSS OF PAIN AND TORMENT!
WHAT A GOLDEN ERA FOR US ALL.

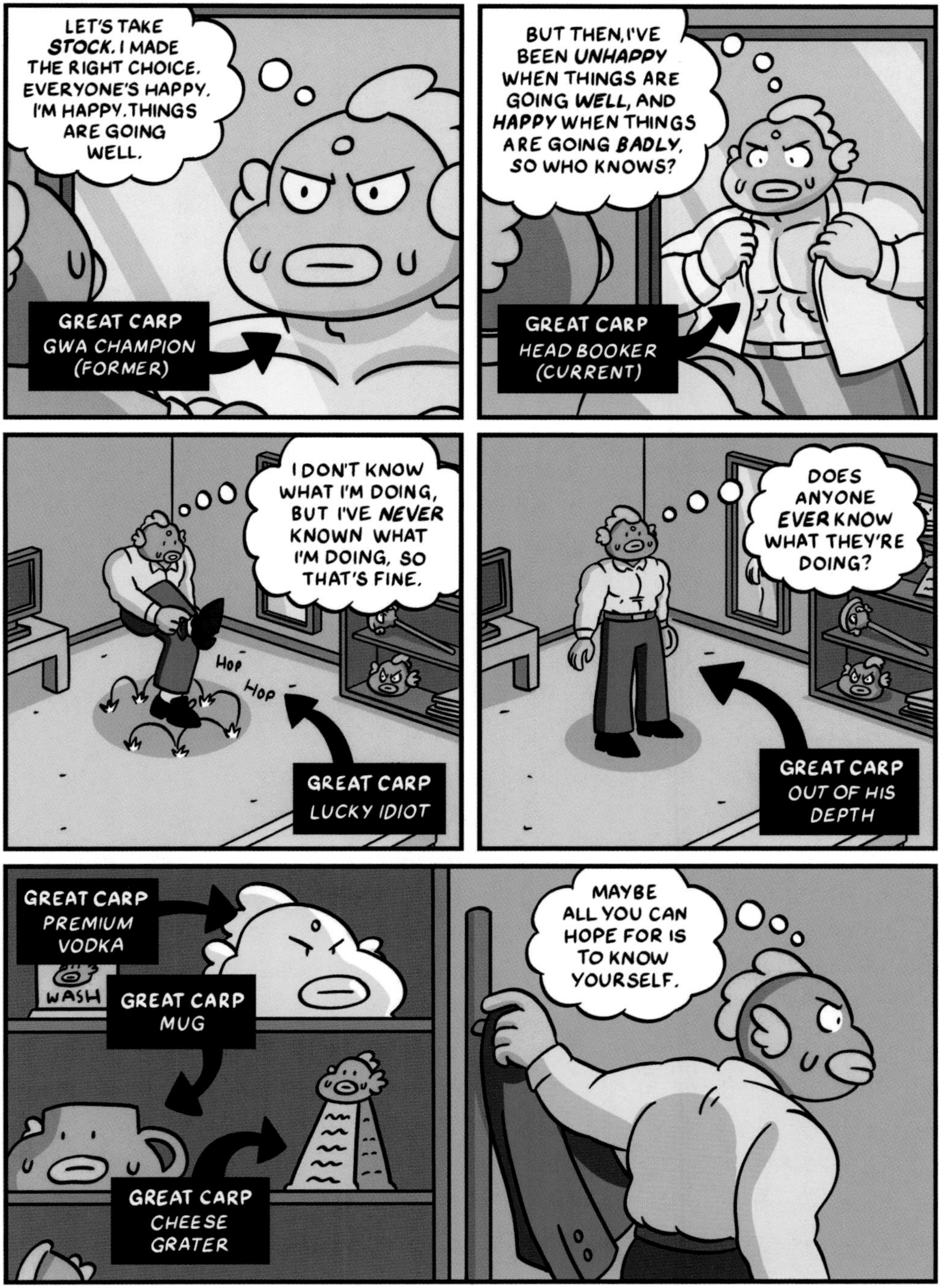
LET'S TAKE STOCK. I MADE THE RIGHT CHOICE. EVERYONE'S HAPPY. I'M HAPPY. THINGS ARE GOING WELL.
GREAT CARP GWA CHAMPION (FORMER)
BUT THEN, I'VE BEEN UNHAPPY WHEN THINGS ARE GOING WELL, AND HAPPY WHEN THINGS ARE GOING BADLY, SO WHO KNOWS?
GREAT CARP HEAD BOOKER (CURRENT)
I DON'T KNOW WHAT I'M DOING, BUT I'VE NEVER KNOWN WHAT I'M DOING, SO THAT'S FINE.
HOP HOP
GREAT CARP LUCKY IDIOT
DOES ANYONE EVER KNOW WHAT THEY'RE DOING?
GREAT CARP OUT OF HIS DEPTH
GREAT CARP PREMIUM VODKA
WASH
GREAT CARP MUG
GREAT CARP CHEESE GRATER
MAYBE ALL YOU CAN HOPE FOR IS TO KNOW YOURSELF.

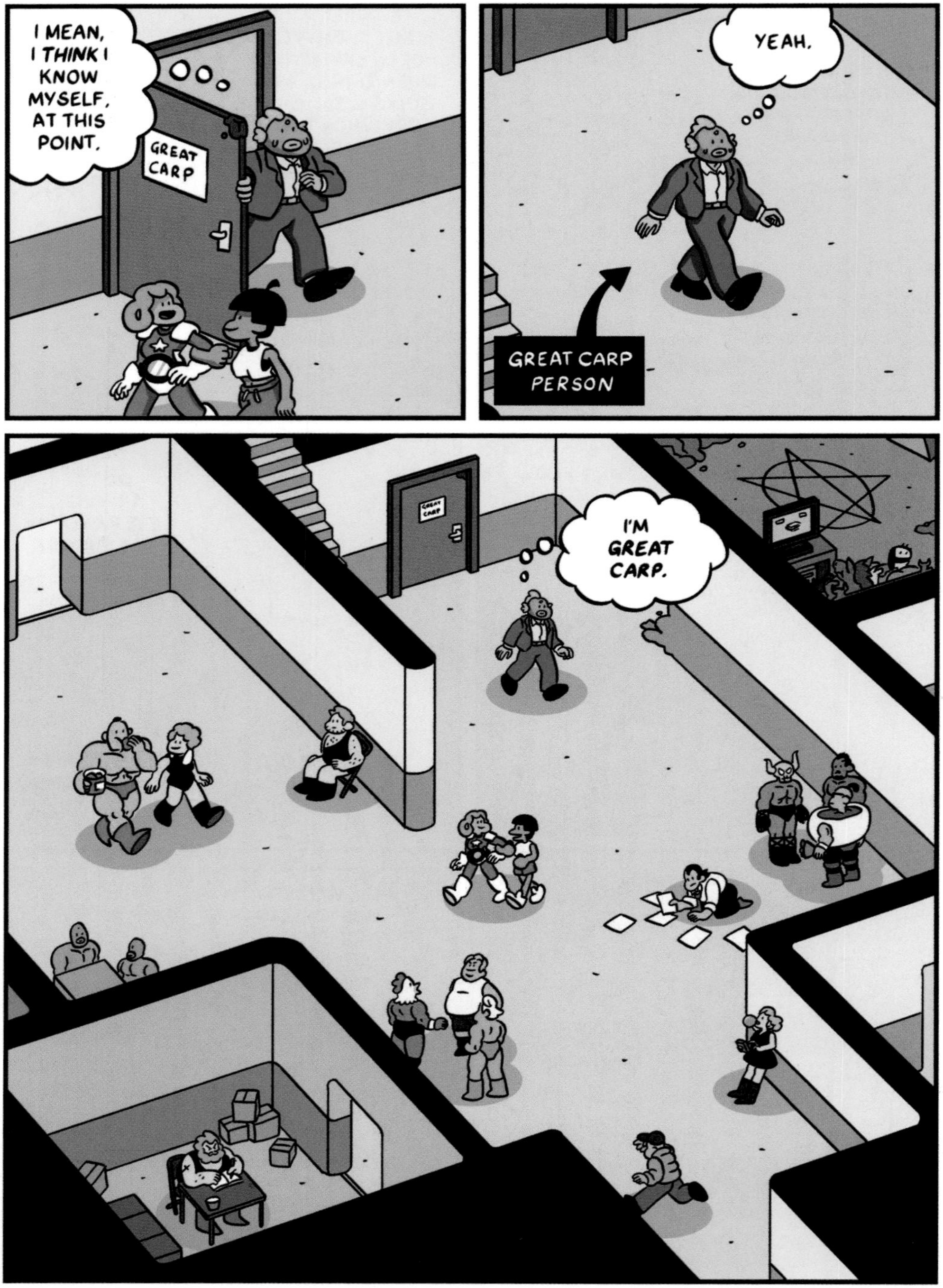
I MEAN, I THINK I KNOW MYSELF, AT THIS POINT.
GREAT CARP
YEAH.
GREAT CARP PERSON
I'M GREAT CARP.

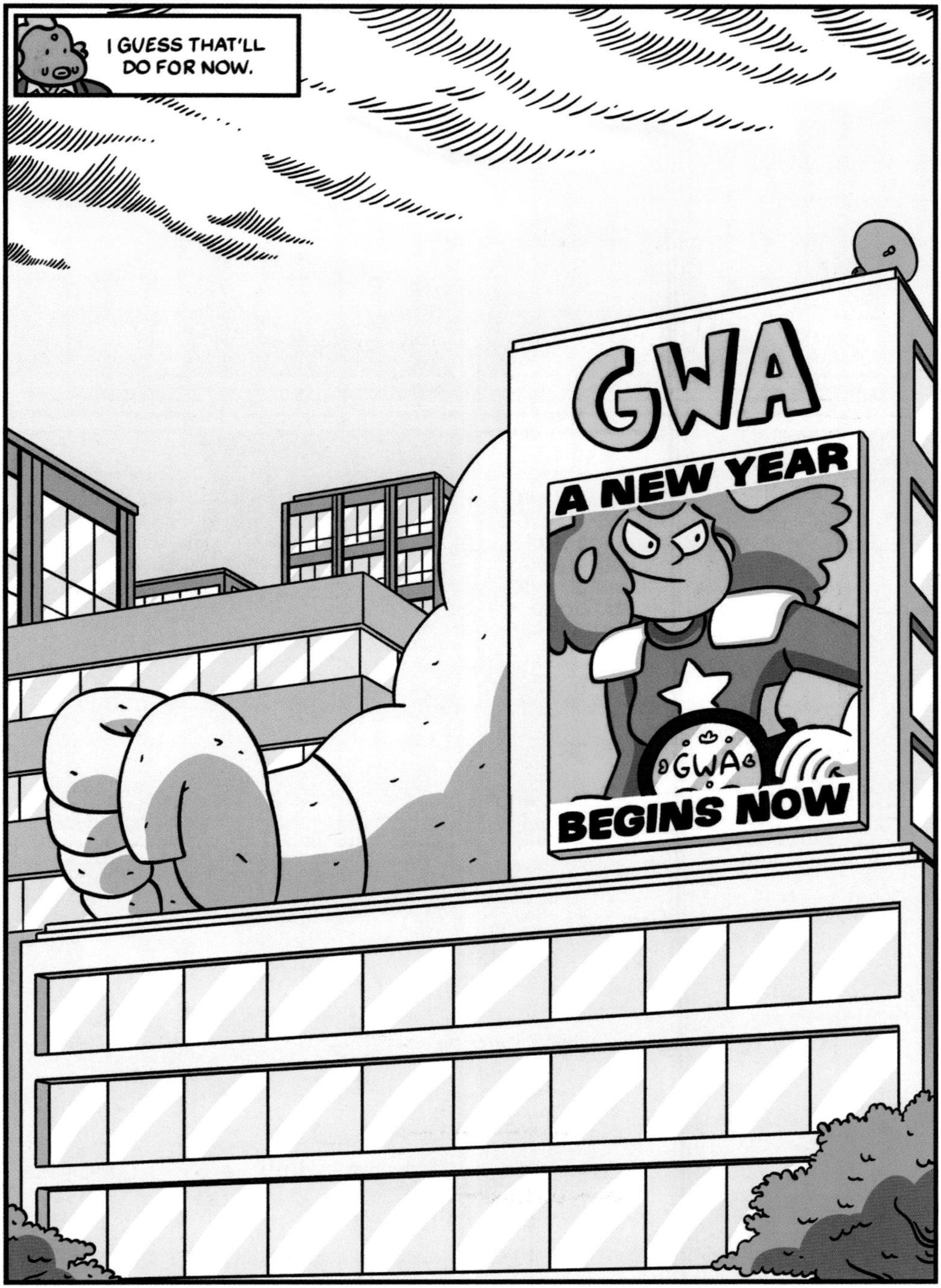
I GUESS THAT'LL DO FOR NOW.
GWA
A NEW YEAR
GWA
BEGINS NOW

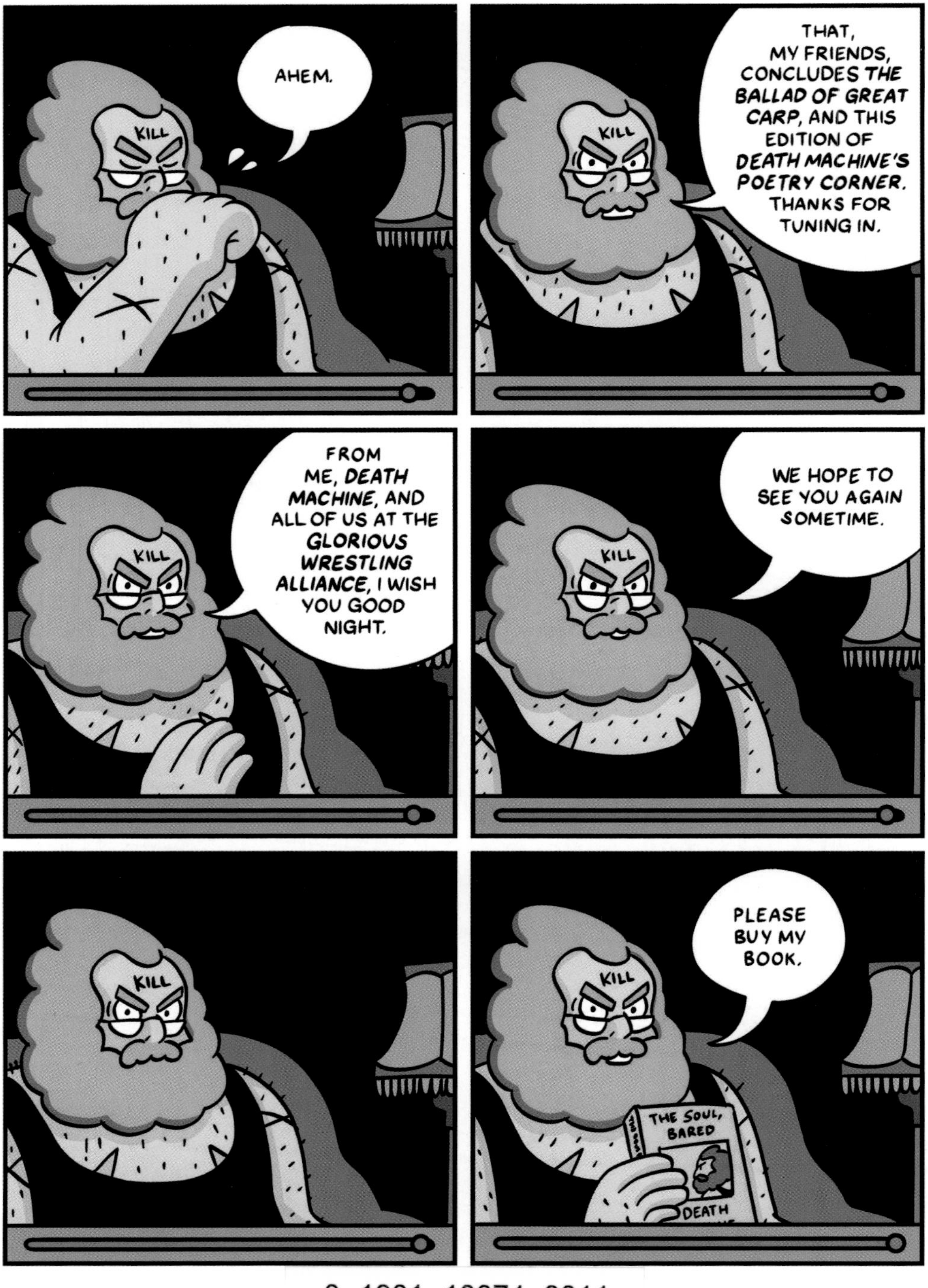
AHEM.
KILL
THAT, MY FRIENDS, CONCLUDES THE BALLAD OF GREAT CARP, AND THIS EDITION OF DEATH MACHINE'S POETRY CORNER. THANKS FOR TUNING IN.
FROM ME, DEATH MACHINE, AND ALL OF US AT THE GLORIOUS WRESTLING ALLIANCE, I WISH YOU GOOD NIGHT.
WE HOPE TO SEE YOU AGAIN SOMETIME.
PLEASE BUY MY BOOK.
THE SOUL, BARED
DEATH